this regard is particularly sharp and particularly on-point. There's a certain amount of satire going on here, but Edelman is quite serious about his world, which makes it all the easier to invest in his characters and settings."
The Agony Column

"If all novels were as chockfull of ideas as *Infoquake* is, then science fiction would never have to worry about a shortage of sense of wonder.... Edelman is like a more accessible [Charles] Stross; whereas Stross's fiction is about as dense as it can get and still be readable, Edelman's style is more inviting and, to me, more appealing. ... Few first novelists manage as assured a debut as *Infoquake*; almost all new authors stumble around a bit in their first novel, but Edelman comes off as a seasoned professional."
Orson Scott Card's Intergalactic Medicine Show

"The hyperbole surrounding this novel seems justified—drawing on cyberpunk and singularitarian themes, it boldly places a banner for what is arguably a new subgenre of science fiction.... As an engaging fictional mirror of the modern world, written from an angle rarely used, this novel definitely marks Edelman as a writer to keep an eye on."
Futurismic

"A brisk, well-told science fiction adventure set in the normally unadventurous world of business.... Edelman handles it all with considerable narrative drive.... A simple old-fashioned story, where incident crowds onto incident, where jeopardy makes us hold our breath, and rabbits are pulled from the hat only at the very last moment."
New York Review of Science Fiction

"There's always the risk that a complicated setting will overwhelm character and story, but Edelman avoids this pitfall, evoking a surprising amount of empathy for the amoral yet oddly charming Natch, and injecting a tremendous amount of suspense into what is essentially a saga of corporate politics.... The novel also addresses weighty themes: the destructive price of greed, the unchanging relentlessness of the human drive to innovate and to compete.... An entertaining and intelligent debut that should leave readers eager for more."
Fantasy Magazine

"(4½ stars) A very strong debut novel mixing a historically detailed timeline with an intriguing technological future. David Louis Edelman makes reading about corporate shenanigans fun.... *Infoquake* should appeal to just about any SF reader, but if you like [Frank] Herbert's *Dune* or any of [Charles] Stross's work, you should really enjoy this book."

SF Signal

"(Rating: 9 out of 10) This book was superb. I simply cannot believe that this is a debut novel, it reads so much more like the work of a seasoned writer.... This book however is anything but boring—it grips you from the start and leaves you at the end of the book wishing you had book two at hand."

The Eternal Night

"*Infoquake* is practically a cyberpunk novel, although unlike the works of William Gibson, author David Louis Edelman actually knows his subject and isn't prone to making errors.... Edelman has done an excellent job of bringing characters to life for a new writer. He even made business deals interesting. This is also very high-grade science fiction, using the trappings and then adding more."

SF Crowsnest

"An intense futuristic tale of business, intrigue, revenge, and technology.... This has the potential to be a terrific series filled with innovative concepts and enough double-dealing to keep the reader guessing."

Monsters and Critics

"Edelman has managed to capture the mania and obsession of Internet moguls nicely.... I found *Infoquake* interesting, and genuinely wanted to find out what happened next. The characters in the book are quite like people I've known in the world of international entrepreneurship."

SF Revu

"A study in drive and power, *Infoquake* shows the drive and need behind the rise of new corporations.... *Infoquake* remains a raw and fascinating novel, with a fast pace and nifty economic themes."

Prometheus, the newsletter of the Libertarian Futurist Society

"(5 Stars on Amazon.com) Libraries strong in speculative fiction will relish *Infoquake*.... A fast-paced, engrossing saga of social change."
   Midwest Book Review

FROM SCIENCE FICTION CRITICS

"The manner in which people who experienced *Dune* upon its publication speak about Herbert's opus is not dissimilar to the feeling *Infoquake* elicits—the genre might not be quite the same after this book.... *Infoquake* is a stunning debut novel by a lucid, precise, and talented new voice in the genre.... This may be THE science fiction book of the year."
   SFF World

"A high-speed, high-spirited tale of high-powered and low-minded capitalist skull-duggery, corporate and media warfare, and virtual reality manipulation. It's the sort of thing that would make a perfect serial for *Wired* magazine.... Edelman seems to have convincing and convincingly detailed knowledge of the physiology and bio-chemistry of the human nervous system down to the molecular level. And [he] cares about making his fictional combination of molecular biology and nanotech credible."
   Norman Spinrad, *Asimov's Science Fiction*

"*Infoquake* is a triumph of speculation. Edelman has foreseen a nanotech future of warring corporations and stock markets of personal enhancement in which both the good and the bad of the present day are reflected with an even hand and star-tling clarity.... It's *Wall Street* meets *Neuromancer*.... *Infoquake* is a tech-heavy exer-cise in scientific speculation that combines economics, high technology, and business mechanics into an all-too-human story of greed, loss, and redemption."
   Bookgasm

"Edelman has one hell of a hoot taking high-tech marketing out to draw and quarter it with style and panache. *Infoquake* is a very funny and insightful novel of modern economics through a futuristic funhouse mirror.... It's the kind of book that deserves to be passed quietly from cubicle to cubicle in tech companies around the nation and indeed around the world. And it's the kind of novel that you want to be passing, the kind of novel you want to be reading.... Edelman, [Cory] Doctorow, and [Charles] Stross are, like all great science fiction writers, not really writing about the future. They're responding to the present.... Edelman's vision in

PRAISE FOR *INFOQUAKE*:
VOLUME ɪ OF THE JUMP 225 TRILOGY

Barnes & Noble's Science Fiction Book of the Year 2006
John W. Campbell Memorial Award Nominee for Best Novel 2006
#5 on Bookgasm's 5 Best Sci-Fi Books of 2006
John W. Campbell Best New Writer Award Nominee 2008

"David Louis Edelman's debut novel—the first installment of his Jump 225 trilogy—is equal parts corporate thriller, technophilic cautionary tale, and breathtakingly visionary science fiction adventure.... Brilliantly blending the cutthroat intrigues of the high-tech business world with revolutionary world building, Edelman could quite possibly be the love child of Donald Trump and Vernor Vinge. *Infoquake* is one of the most impressive science fiction debuts to come along in years—highly recommended."
Barnes & Noble Explorations

"Slick high-finance melodrama and dizzying technical speculation lift Edelman's SF debut, the first of a trilogy.... Natch's being a borderline sociopath makes him extremely creative in business tactics and personal manipulation (and thus fascinating to read about). The world in which he operates is also fascinating, with awesome personal powers being sold on a frantic open market. Edelman, who has a background in Web programming and marketing, gives his bizarre notions a convincing gloss of detail. Bursting with invention and panache, this novel will hook readers for the story's next installment."
Publishers Weekly

"In Web designer and programmer Edelman's first novel, he moves quickly from scene to scene, building suspense with believable characters and in-the-know technical expertise. This series opener belongs in most SF collections."
Library Journal

"A thought-provoking and terribly imaginative book... *Infoquake* is one of those books that hooks you into the story and makes you never want to put the book down. But once you have decided that you must get some sleep before work the next day, you put the book down and find yourself unable to stop thinking about the questions raised by the story."
L.A. Splash

DAVID
LOUIS
EDELMAN

GEOSYNCHRON

VOLUME 3 OF THE JUMP 225 TRILOGY

an imprint of Prometheus Books
Amherst, NY

Published 2010 by Pyr®, an imprint of Prometheus Books

Inquiries should be addressed to
Pyr
59 John Glenn Drive
Amherst, New York 14228–2119
VOICE: 716–691–0133
FAX: 716–691–0137
WWW.PYRSF.COM

14 13 12 11 10   5 4 3 2 1

Library of Congress Cataloging-in-Publication Data

Edelman, David Louis.
    Geosynchron / by David Louis Edelman.
        p. cm. — (Jump 225 trilogy ; v. 3)
        ISBN 978–1–59102–792–8 (pbk. : alk. paper)
        1. Corporations—Fiction. I. Title.

PS3605.D445G46 2010
813'.6—dc22

                                    2009042451

Printed in the United States of America on acid-free paper

CONTENTS

I do not believe all men are destroyed. I can name you a dozen who were not, and they are the ones the world lives by.
—John Steinbeck, *East of Eden*

I

THE PRISONERS

$(((\mid)))$

Margaret Surina is rejuvenated.

She hovers wraithlike in the thin membrane between existence and nothingness. Skin the olive tinge of the Indian subcontinent, robe a billowing tent of blue and green, fingers long and precise as praying mantises. Hair tar black but streaked with white, manifestation of the paradox behind those sapphire eyes.

That Natch can see her at all is miracle enough. In this place he has no eyes, no face, no corporeal presence whatsoever. It is a cocoon of pure mind, where there are no points on the compass and where even time loops upon itself and disappears in a dizzying spiral of infinite improbability. Here in this place, Margaret is merely a perception of a perception, like an awareness or a manufactured memory.

Natch wants to ask her, *Don't you realize you're dead?*

He saw the empty husk of her at the top of the Revelation Spire. He stood in the courtyard at Andra Pradesh watching her corpse as the self-appointed guardians of wisdom pontificated about the passing of ages and the withering of flowers and other such nonsense. Yes, Margaret Surina is dead, there can be no doubt about it. Why then does she keep blatantly disregarding her nonexistence? Why does she keep appearing to Natch and intoning words of solemn absurdity?

MultiReal is becoming part of you, Margaret tells him. *You're not just its owner anymore, Natch—you're the guardian and the keeper.* That grating habit of enunciation to the point of ludicrousness, the way she treats each syllable like a wayward child to be nurtured. *MultiReal is* yours *now, Natch. I was foolish to have held on to it for so long. I am not my father. I'm not strong enough to make these decisions. But you . . . Natch, I picked you for a reason—because you'll resist Len Borda to your dying breath. You will resist the winter and the void. Understand this—something my father was trying to tell me. The world is new each day, every sunrise a spring and every sunset a winter. I know you'll understand this. You will stand alone in the end, and you will make the decisions the world demands. The decisions I can't make. I know this. I know it.*

Natch has heard this rant before. It's what Margaret told him just hours before her demise, sitting in the pinnacle of that cold tower with Quell the Islander at her side, her mind permanently broken. It made no sense to him then, and it makes no sense to him now.

Margaret segues into a new stanza of insanity that Natch doesn't recognize. *Onwards and upwards,* she says. *That was the dream of Sheldon Surina, my ancestor and the father of bio/logics. Towards Perfection, no matter what the cost. But it was not Sheldon Surina's fate to pay that cost, any more than it was Marcus Surina's—any more than it is mine.*

Now that fate has fallen to you and you alone, Natch. You are the geosynchron of the human race.

Natch wants to shut out the visage, to banish Margaret back to the elaborate sepulcher where the Surinas laid her, with its gold and pearl and its bas-relief carvings. But Natch has no eyelids in this place, no way of banishing the apparition floating before him. The bodhisattva keeps talking about momentous choices for him to make and earth-shaking decisions in his future. But what are they? What does she want from him? How can he decide anything when Margaret won't tell him what it is he's supposed to decide?

Go away! he tries to shout. *Leave me the fuck alone! I don't know what you're talking about, and I don't want to know.* He tries to shout, but he has no voice.

And then the nothingness enfolds Natch in its bosom and he sees no more.

(((2)))

The nothingness loosens its hold on him. The world is still black, yes, but Natch is *there*. Arms legs torso head all intact; lungs breathing oxygen; body occupying space and slogging forward through time's amber one second at a time. Alive. Alive. Alive.

He is lying on something cold and metallic. Fluid rushes through his ears, signaling steep vertical movement. Climbing. Something thunks against the platform below him three or four times. It sounds like hailstones.

A male voice, a real human voice, from somewhere nearby: "That was close."

Heavy breathing, more climbing. The thunks disappear.

"So now what?"

"I don't—I don't know." A second male voice, weary and pensive.

"After all that, you don't *know*? For process' preservation . . . I just got hit with a fucking *pipe*. In the shoulder. Do you even know how much that hurts? Thing was probably covered with rust too."

The identities of the voices elude him. Natch's brain feels like a machine jammed in low gear. He can't process the words. He can't open his eyes. He can't move or speak.

"I'm sorry about your shoulder," says the first voice in a condescending tone that indicates no sorrow whatsoever. "You didn't have to come."

"Shut up, you bloody idiot. Of course I had to come. I couldn't just let you go fetch him alone, could I? Get yourself killed. And *then* I'd have to pay for a fucking funeral." Restless shifting around. "So there he is, the bastard. Why are we even discussing this? He makes my skin crawl. Send Magan Kai Lee a message and let's get paid already."

A pause. "It's not that simple."

"Not that simple? Would you rather Len Borda get hold of him? Listen, we don't have much time. It's getting violent out there. Didn't you hear about that gun battle in Melbourne? A hundred Council officers firing on each other in the middle of the street—"

"Of course I heard about it."

"There's two sides, point I'm trying to make. Borda and Lee. We picked a side. *Getting in on the ground floor*, that's what you said. Why are you suddenly changing your mind?"

"That was before we knew the truth."

"The truth?" Coarse, mocking laughter. "Face it, what we used to think of as the truth is dead. Too much confusion. Truth doesn't *exist* anymore."

"Just give me some time to think this over. A day or two. We can fend Magan off for that long. And it's not like *he's* going anywhere." The inflection of the voice seems to indicate the prostrate body of Natch.

"Well, don't take *too* long. A day or two is all we have before Magan realizes we've got something to hide and starts asking questions."

The two men descend into troubled silence as the fluid sloshing through Natch's skull levels off. He slides back into unconsciousness.

• • •

Alive.

Natch awakens with a feeling of profound, wearying disappointment.

He is still enveloped in blackness, but this is a blackness free from magic or mystery. He is sitting in an ordinary wooden chair with his arms and legs lightly tied to it and a blindfold over his eyes. The light seeping through the blindfold and the ambient noise around him indicate that he is sitting in a large, enclosed space, perhaps a gymnasium or even a small auditorium. Natch rocks the chair side to side for a moment and feels a hard, tiled surface beneath him. Where he has ended up, he can't imagine.

Natch tries to untangle the thread of events that have led to the present moment. He fled the carnage at the Tul Jabbor Complex—Council officers firing on Council officers, Council officers firing on *him*. He leaped into a waiting hoverbird with Petrucio Patel's black code dart embedded in the back of his leg. He was taken to Old Chicago, where his old enemy Brone persuaded him to join his Revolution of Selfishness. (Multiple lives experienced simultaneously! An end to the tyranny of cause and effect!) But when Natch discovered the pattern of lies beneath Brone's stories, he ran. He ran into the wilds of Old Chicago, and then . . . and then . . .*

After that, an impenetrable void of blank memory. A big smear of nothingness. Natch can't remember if he was pursued, or how that pursuit ended. Certainly Brone would not have let him leave that old hotel without consequences. But the thread of memory simply ends on those streets. Natch's internal systems tell him that barely forty-eight hours have passed since he escaped the hotel in Chicago. That hardly seems possible. If someone were to tell him he actually spent ten years enmeshed in that web of nothingness, he would accept it as fact.

When he awoke, there was an opaque conversation between two gruff men in what Natch now realizes was the rear compartment of a hoverbird. Did these men drag him onto the hoverbird from the streets of Chicago? Did they rescue him—and if so, from whom, and why?

Natch wonders if his mental inbox might hold some clues, but the thought of checking messages makes him ill. He prived himself to the world shortly before that fatal day at the Tul Jabbor Complex; he has neither checked his messages nor read the news since. He can picture all that pent-up information as a towering heap of debris at the mouth of a river, spilling over the banks until it clogs the horizon.

And yet why should he try to relieve that pressure? Let the mail

---

*For a more detailed synopsis of the events of *Infoquake* and *MultiReal*, books 1 and 2 of the Jump 225 trilogy, see appendix A.

pile up until the calendar cycles to the end of days and the Data Sea comes stuttering to a halt. Natch has abandoned that life. He does not want to know what happened in Old Chicago, or what has become of Brone and the disciples of his creed, or who picked him up in the hoverbird, or where he has gotten off to.

He recalls a conversation with Jara, right after he achieved number one on the Primo's bio/logic investment guide. Standing in his apartment with bio/logic programming bars in hand. Flush with accomplishment, ready to challenge the world.

Do you really think number one on Primo's is the end? he told her. *Then you don't understand anything, Jara. Getting to number one on Primo's isn't an end at all—it's a means. It's part of the process . . . just a step on the ladder.*

Jara was skeptical. *So what is the end? Where do all these means lead to?*

It was once so simple, so visceral. There was a wall and a ladder and a shining, radiant *thing* on the other side for the taking. Then Natch reached the apex of that ladder in Brone's hotel in Old Chicago, and he saw what lay in wait for him. Possibilities 2.0: a world of complete, unrestricted possibilities. A world without restraints or boundaries, where multiple realities can exist and commingle freely.

A world of utter void.

He saw what was waiting for him, and he ran from it.

Natch flexes his forearms, testing the tensile strength of his bonds. He can still feel the tremors and the throbbing pains that have been plaguing him since that black code attack in Shenandoah, many weeks ago. Quiescent for the moment, but not gone. Obviously his captors noticed them too; these ropes are clearly designed to do nothing more than prevent him from tremoring right out of the chair.

Around him, Natch can hear the echo of footsteps, possibly within shouting range. The faint whir of machinery thrums in the distance, indicating the presence of civilization and all it entails. The musty smell of mold wafts through the air. There is a puzzle here to solve, but Natch resolves not to expend any mental energy in solving it. He has no doubt that he can free himself from the chair, even without the aid of MultiReal. But . . . why should he? Better to just sit and do nothing. He will eventually find out where he is and who has captured him—or he will sit here until the shaking takes control of him at last and his OCHREs give up their dance of sustenance and the Null Current pulls him under. Either result is the same.

• • •

"Hey! Wake up!"

The voice emanates from a spot perhaps five meters in front of him. It is a familiar, if not a particularly welcome, voice. The last time Natch heard that voice, it was accompanied by the pungent smell of garlic. "I'm not asleep," he tells Frederic Patel.

"Aren't you going to take off that fucking blindfold already?" says Frederic, irritated. "You're not going to just sit there in the dark forever, are you?"

"I might."

The younger Patel brother lets out a rasping sigh that makes Natch think of a serrated blade sawing through tree trunks. He decides to take off the blindfold, if only to hasten Frederic's departure. He wriggles his right arm free of the rope, reaches for the blindfold, and yanks it off his face.

Natch's initial impressions were correct. He is sitting in the middle of a large, circular chamber with a radius of perhaps thirty meters. Next to him sits a skeletal side table topped with a plate, a sandwich, and a large jug of water. A rather prosaic white ceramic tile coats the floor from wall to wall. The edges of the room are shrouded in shadow, but he can faintly make out a door on the opposite wall. The whole chamber is contained inside a dome of solid concrete that also reaches a height of about thirty meters, putting Natch in the nucleus of a perfect hemisphere.

Frederic Patel stands a short distance away, arms folded over his barrel chest. Short, stout Frederic Patel, with jowls like a bulldog's and the temperament to match. "You've been sitting there for hours," complains the engineer. "Aren't you hungry or thirsty?"

"No," replies Natch.

A minute drifts by. The impatient tapping of Frederic's right foot is causing a rather comical rippling of flesh along one fat thigh. The entrepreneur gets the feeling that Patel is expecting some kind of petulant outburst. Natch is happy to disappoint him.

"Well?" barks Frederic. "Don't you want to know where you are? How you got here?"

"No," says Natch.

Frederic's infuriated sigh fills the dome. "You are *such* a pain in the ass. Listen, do me a favor, huh? Eat that bloody sandwich so Petrucio doesn't yell at me." The tapping speeds up until the younger Patel brother's foot is a blur of angry motion. After another twenty seconds of silence, a florid Frederic throws his hands up in the air and stomps off. "Suit yourself." Natch can hear the sound of angry footsteps as Patel retreats through some second doorway behind him, beyond his peripheral vision.

The entrepreneur stares at the sandwich for a good ten minutes, then frees his trembling left hand and takes a hold of it. Crusty sourdough bread, seasoned faux pork, an assortment of peppers, lettuce so crisp it crinkles under his fingers. Natch takes a single bite and lets the flavors mix on his tongue, then swallows. The sandwich is more tantalizing than anything he has eaten in weeks, but he wasn't lying to Frederic. He's not hungry.

Instead he gazes up at the pockmarked concrete of the dome, trying to pick out clues to his location. The Patels' business is based out of São Paulo, if Natch remembers correctly. A bustling yet ancient city, full of ghosts. He has no reason to think that Frederic and Petrucio would take him anywhere else. Then again . . . he has no reason to think they would put him in a hoverbird, drag him to some empty chamber, and tie him to a chair in the first place. He remembers the black code dart in his leg that Petrucio put there after a long and wearying battle of MultiReal choice cycles. Clearly there is some connection between that dart and Natch's winding up here. But . . . what?

Don't think, he tells himself. *You'll know soon enough. Or you won't.*

Petrucio Patel walks into the room several hours later, as thin and dapper as his brother is squat and slovenly. Petrucio is dressed, as always, in a slick brown suit that would look perfectly at home in a corporate board meeting or the sales office of a luxury hoverbird manufacturer. He stops in approximately the same spot as Frederic and regards Natch with a suspicious gaze, noting that the entrepreneur has made no move to untie his legs from the chair. "What are we going to do with you?" he says, giving an almost playful tug at his mustache.

Natch shrugs. "I don't know."

"You don't know, huh? You wouldn't say that if you knew some of the things Frederic's been suggesting. He wants to start testing weapons on you." The dry humor never sits far beneath the surface of Petrucio's voice, and today is no exception.

"Frederic doesn't scare me," says Natch.

"No, I suppose not. You've got MultiReal! Why would you be afraid of anyone?" Petrucio takes a step closer and crouches down on his haunches. Natch expects the mocking stare of the hyena in Petrucio's eyes, but he doesn't expect to see another emotion that is almost . . . pitying. "All right, Natch. You don't really want to sit in this chair all day, do you? Go ahead, then. Activate MultiReal. Catch me in a choice cycle loop and make me untie you."

Natch's thoughts drift back to that MultiReal conflict in the Tul Jabbor Complex. Petrucio firing a dart at him, Natch dodging, over and over again. Possibility stacked on top of possibility, will versus will, until Natch abruptly found himself out of choice cycles. He remembers the bite of the black code dart in the back of his leg as he jumped onto Brone's waiting hoverbird.

"This isn't like the Tul Jabbor Complex," growls Natch, suddenly irritated at Petrucio's mockery. "The only reason you were able to hit me with that dart was because Jara fucked with the program behind my back. It's not like that anymore. I've moved the databases."

"*Yes*, you sure have." Petrucio drawls the words in childish singsong. His face remains cool and collected. "I don't have access to MultiReal at all. Frederic and I haven't been able to open the program in MindSpace for a week. So go ahead. I'm defenseless. Find that possibility where you humiliate me, where you make me fall on my face right here in front of you. Come on, I'm waiting." He points to his nose, and then to the floor.

Bait, thinks Natch. *I'm being thrown bait.* Obviously Petrucio is doing his best to provoke him, to goad him into a rash decision— something to which Natch is admittedly all too vulnerable. Yet what does he possibly have to fear from the Patel Brothers? He has faced down ten thousand Defense and Wellness Council black code darts and emerged without a scratch. He has used the power of MultiReal to bend the will of Speaker Khann Frejohr. Why should he be intimidated by a chair, a rope, and a smirk? Why *not* take the bait and find out what's behind Petrucio's smugness?

Natch gives his internal system a silent command to activate MultiReal.

Within the flicker of an instant, Natch can feel his previous ennui retreating before the dazzle of MultiReal. He can sense the infinite probability of the multiverse unfolding before him. Anything he can imagine, any combination of event and happenstance—it all lies sprawled before him, no more than a mathematical progression of muscle movements away. He can sense potential realities ranging from the vindictive to the comical to the absurd—realities where Natch hurls insults or oozes flatteries or utters nonsense syllables. All he needs now is to use the power of MultiReal to latch on to Petrucio's neural interfaces. And then the pas de deux will begin: Natch's mind leaping with possibilities, Petrucio's mind twirling in unwitting response, over and over again in the space between frozen seconds. At the Tul Jabbor Complex, when Petrucio had his own version of Multi-Real, he could choose realities of his own; here he will be helpless as a marionette, victim to Natch's manipulation of his own subconscious. When Natch finds the one potential reality that suits his purposes, he will close the choice cycle, and for that instant the world will conform to his desires. Petrucio will follow through with the possibility Natch has selected for him, powerless to do otherwise.

Natch lunges for Petrucio's neural interfaces with a mental reflex that feels like throwing a lasso.

And finds nothing.

It is as if Natch has attempted to engage in a tête-à-tête with the slab of domed concrete above him. MultiReal has called out, but Petrucio's mental facilities are not responding.

The panic must be visible in his eyes, because after a few seconds a wry smile creeps up one side of Petrucio's face. It is not a cruel smile or a malicious smile so much as an amused one. He straightens up and smoothes the wrinkles from his designer slacks with a brisk flick of the wrist.

"I thought so," says Petrucio. "Frederic and I aren't afraid of your MultiReal tricks. They won't work in *this* place." He gestures at the shadowy apex of the dome above him. "You might as well conserve your energy, Natch. You're not going anywhere."

And within a few seconds, he is gone, leaving Natch alone with the gloom and the darkness.

$(((3)))$

At first it was nothing more than an occlusion of the stars, one of the million bits of detritus covering the Earth like an aura. Satellites functioning and not, metal garbage from ancient construction, dead space elevators. But unlike the rest of the rubbish, this occlusion was expanding in that telltale pattern that indicated an approaching vector. A ship. It was an ugly bastard, too, mottled gray and brown, with guns protruding on all sides. Big enough to transport half a dozen hoverbirds, agile enough to conduct military exercises—but not quite fast enough to avoid detection. By the time the ship extended its grappling gear to make the hookup with the Orbital Detention and Rehabilitation Facility, Twelfth Meridian, the unconnectibles were ready for it.

Quell had been kneeling behind an unlabeled crate on the dock with dartrifle in hand for over ten minutes. Something must have staggered into that crate and died months ago, by the smell of it. He was just about to make for another spot when a finger tapped him on the shoulder. "What now?" he grunted.

"You're sure it's Islanders on this one?" said Plithy, his voice squeaky with nerves. Quell turned to face the boy and noticed that the cartridge of black code darts on his gun was loaded crookedly and primed for a misfire.

"*Course* I'm not sure," said Quell. "You got the same information I did."

"And what if the information's wrong? What if *they* get the jump on us, like last time?" Plithy craned his scrawny neck towards the opposite side of the dock, where the connectibles were hunkered down awaiting the same ship. Every once in a while, Quell caught the glint of an overhead light bouncing off the barrel of one of their dartguns. There were only about twenty meters separating the two teams; it would be difficult to miss at such close range.

Quell shrugged. "Stick to the plan, and you'll be fine. *I'm* the one who should be worrying."

"But—"

The Islander made a strangled noise of frustration. "Just be quiet and get back in position. And for the *last* time—" He grabbed Plithy's dartgun and snapped the misloaded cartridge into place with a single aggravated motion. The boy shut up and retreated to some crack or crevice outside Quell's view. *Wisest thing he's done all day.*

He could hardly blame Plithy for his jangly nerves. The boy was only sixteen, much too young to be worrying about black code darts. Even for someone of Quell's age and experience, it wasn't easy, racing to the dock at a moment's notice with weapon in hand, never sure who would emerge from the airlock. Sometimes the ships carried connectible prisoners; sometimes they carried unconnectible prisoners. The information was sketchy and of unknown provenance. Your job was twofold: shepherd the unconnectibles to the unconnectible level of the prison before the enemy captured them, and capture as many connectibles as possible before they escaped to the connectible level of the prison. If you had accurate information and brought the right number of troops, the job was pretty straightforward. Otherwise you had a long and messy dartgun battle on your hands.

And if you failed? If the connectibles managed to drag the newcomers away first? The Defense and Wellness Council wouldn't tolerate out-and-out murder in their prisons. But anything short of that could be winkingly ignored.

Quell glanced over at poor Rick Willets, huddled behind a metal post, trying to cradle a rifle in his mangled hands. The connectibles had caught him two weeks ago nosing around the dock for food. He was found three days later. The microscopic OCHREs in his blood and tissue would eventually return his thumbs to their opposable positions; until then Willets would be down a few chits in the evolutionary game. If he had neural bio/logic machinery, he could heal even faster, but Willets was an Islander, an unconnectible, a technological skeptic. He would just have to wait.

The Islander turned and spat on the floor. The whole business reminded him of the shoot-'em-up holo games he had played as a kid, all monotony and repetition and mindless adrenaline. *Except this is only half as exciting*, he thought, *and twice as pointless.*

Still, he didn't expect any casualties like Rick Willets today. The manifest indicated a batch of Islanders along with a few Pharisees and one prisoner with no stated place of origin, usually shorthand for the diss. Quell had brought fifteen men to the dock. The connectibles only had a token force of twelve, and were not expected to put up much of a fight. Not worth risking too many men unless reinforcements were at stake.

A few meters down, Plithy settled in behind a drum of industrial lubricant and aimed his pistol at the hangar doors. The others were safely out of sight, as the plan dictated. Twenty minutes passed. Uncertainty stretched the nerves, but it was the long waits that snapped them. Quell watched the gun slowly droop out of the boy's quivering hands until the barrel was lying on top of the drum along with the grip.

"Crazy crazy crazy," muttered Willets to himself, a mantra to ward off harm. "Crazy crazy crazy."

Quell nodded. Yes. Crazy way to run a prison indeed.

● ● ●

This was decidedly not what Quell had expected from prison.

The Islander had known the Defense and Wellness Council would not treat him lightly. In their eyes, he was a dissident, an agitator, member of the only group to cast off central government rule and form a functioning opposition. Not only that, but Quell had defied the Council's direct orders during the chaos at Andra Pradesh—and lobbed a pulse grenade at a dozen Council officers—*and* taken a shock baton to Lieutenant Executive Magan Kai Lee himself. With the help of MultiReal and the crackling energy of the baton, he had given Lee a blow that might have split another man in two. But at the last possible instant, *her* words had come bubbling to the front of Quell's mind: *All of us are looking for a way to deflect our own suffering.* Words she had spoken to him decades ago when he was a stubborn student and she was merely a sheltered rich girl.

He had wondered if killing Magan Kai Lee would be the deliberate act of a rational mind, or a decision made cowering under the aegis of searing pain. Did he really want Magan dead—or was he just deflecting his own suffering?

No. Quell would prove her wrong. He would not deflect; he would absorb.

So Quell had pulled the blow at the last instant, and Magan had lived. He had let the officers of the Defense and Wellness Council take his weapon away and yank the thin copper collar off his neck, severing his Islander lifeline to the multi network. He hadn't protested the kicks to the stomach and groin that had followed in the elevator, or the blow with the gun butt that had broken his knee in the courtyard. He had known that he could use the quantum prestidigitation of Multi-Real to escape the Council's clutches at any minute. He had known that he could kill every single one of those motherfuckers if he wanted to, dartguns or no dartguns. But he would not. He *would not.*

The Council officers had shoved the Islander into a waiting hover-bird and lined up for one last beating. It had suddenly occurred to Quell that this might be his last opportunity for escape. Rumor had it that the hulls of these government 'birds could even block subaether transmissions, a feat that seemingly violated the universal law of physics. No subaether meant no access to the Data Sea meant no access to MultiReal—possibly forever.

All of us are looking for a way to deflect our own suffering.

He had let it happen. The door had slammed shut.

There had been a long interregnum of blackness, pain, and silence. Three hoverbird transfers with no food or water. More beatings.

So much for a trial by jury, Quell had thought.

When he had come to, Quell was kneeling on the icy floor of an airlock with his wrists shackled, surrounded by dispassionate guards wearing the white robe and the yellow star. Outside the airlock, he had heard the metal din of ships coupling. He had waited for the taunts and excoriations to resume, but instead the guards had simply stood there, for two hours. Quell had been torn. On the one hand, he had wanted to give his OCHREs time to prepare for another battering. On the other, he had just wanted to fucking *arrive* wherever he was going to arrive already.

And then, in quick succession, as if they'd been rehearsing for days, the door had opened, the guards had lifted Quell by his elbows and knees, they had flung him out onto his face, and the door had whooshed shut behind him.

At which point the chaos had begun.

A black code dart had zipped by Quell's ear, missing by centimeters. Someone had kicked him in the stomach, then someone else had smashed the kicker in the back with a metal pipe. The Islander had soon found himself ducking and bobbing through the middle of an epic melee, goal unknown, strategy uncertain, clutching onto that primal instinct to just stay alive for another few seconds. There had been three dozen people in the corridor hell-bent on pummeling each other to pieces. A man had stepped in front of him swinging some crude variety of welding tool. Quell had formed a cudgel with his cuffed fists and delivered an uppercut to the man's chin, lifting him a few centimeters off the ground before relieving him of consciousness.

The Islander had been trying to pick up the man's dropped weapon when a voice had come streaking through the maelstrom: "Remember the Band of Twelve!"

Quell had looked up, startled. The Band of Twelve. The original

unconnectible dissidents, the legendary founders of the Islander movement. As a child in Manila, Quell had memorized their names before
he had learned long division. Years later, his proctors would peel back
the onionskin and reveal a number of unpleasant truths about the Band
of Twelve—three were convicted thieves, one was a rapist, and five of
them were tax evaders. But none of that had mattered to Quell in the
middle of the prison tumult. *Remember the Band of Twelve!* That familiar
morsel of propaganda had been like a taste of home. He had lunged in
that direction.

The voice had belonged to a young Islander named Plithy who had
been cringing behind a structural support pillar. He had greasy brown
hair and the posture you might expect from a zombie. Quell had followed him out of the battle towards the unconnectible level of the
prison, head-butting a charging connectible in the process.

The prison itself was your basic nightmare of design by committee:
lots of long corridors and useless alcoves. But strangely, there were no
doors or locks anywhere to be found, and no sign of the Defense and Wellness Council either. Quell had followed the boy through the labyrinth,
weaving around glazed-over and disaffected Islanders by the score. Finally
they had arrived at a room with a bunk waiting, newly made, along with
a bowl of greasy stew left like a burnt offering. Quell had wanted nothing
less than to be in a stranger's debt, but hunger had trumped any other
considerations. He had sat on the bed and tucked into the bowl.

"What're you in for?" Quell had muttered between spoonfuls of
stew to the boy, who, disconcertingly, did not leave. It had seemed like
a question prisoners were supposed to ask one another.

Plithy had plunked his hands into his pockets and looked down at
the floor. "Throwing stones at Council officers," he had said.

Quell had nearly dropped his spoon. "They put you in *here* for
that?" Harassing Council officers with stones and bottles was practically a team sport for young men in Manila. Quell had gotten quite
proficient at it himself as a boy.

"One of the stones hit a commander," Plithy had explained.

"But—"

"In the eye."

The Islander had begun to get the feeling that Plithy was an albatross in search of a neck to latch on to. Evidently the old proverb about rumor traveling faster than the speed of light was true, because Quell had soon discovered that the boy had already heard about the altercation with Magan Kai Lee. He had apparently then magnified the story to mythical proportions and used it as an excuse to dedicate his life to Quell's service. Quell had wanted no part of it, but he couldn't afford to be so selective in his friends right then. He had scraped the bowl clean of gravy, laid back on the bunk, and asked Plithy for the lowdown on the prison. The boy had obliged.

The Orbital Detention and Rehabilitation Facility that hovered over Earth's Twelfth Meridian was a simple structure: two wheelshaped platforms connected by a thick axle. The unconnectibles inhabited the "lower" wheel and the connectibles inhabited the "upper," the terms being more or less arbitrary in space. The axle contained the dock, where Council ships arrived to deliver the prisoners, the food—and the weapons.

The whole setup beggared belief. And in fact, Quell had refused to accept it until he had seen the stockpiles for himself. What kind of prison gave its prisoners *weapons*? But there they had sat, still crated and fresh from the factory. Dartguns, dartrifles, magazine after magazine of black code darts loaded with nonlethal stun programs. Quell had picked one of the rifles up, polished the barrel on his sleeve, and aimed it at an imaginary Council officer bursting through the airlock. "Aren't they afraid we're going to break *out* of here?" he had asked Plithy.

The boy had chuckled. "How?"

It was a good point. The Defense and Wellness Council controlled everything in their orbital prisons, from the air to the food supply to the gravity itself. The only transmissions allowed in or out were those that pinged Dr. Plugenpatch databases to pull down healing bio/logic software. The officers who did the unloading in the dock were well armed, and inoculated against the black code in the prisoners' dartguns to boot. Suppose a group of prisoners *did* manage to overpower those guards and take control of their ship, against all improbability. What then? How could they fly a ship without proper authorization codes? How would they deal with the battery of Council hoverbirds patrolling the area? And where would they escape to anyway?

Quell had soon realized that not only was escape impossible, but for the unconnectible prisoners even *planning* to escape was fiendishly difficult. They belonged to a society that deactivated neural OCHRE bots at birth. They depended on the accursed connectible collars to sense projections on the multi network, and the Council had taken their connectible collars away. Who could say that the Council didn't have spies in multi roaming the hallways and listening to their conversations? Who among the unconnectibles was capable of detecting them?

So they played this juvenile game the Council had set up. Studying schematics of the prison, conducting raids on the enemy, shoring up defenses, risking bio/logically enhanced torture to protect a square kilometer of empty metal. Breaking the thumbs of their connectible captives, because that was what the connectibles did to them. It really *was* quite similar to those shoot-'em-ups from Quell's childhood. You had two factions, limited resources, and violence waiting around every corner, with an unseen CPU mindlessly hurling obstacle after obstacle in your path until you died or time ended.

In one of his more philosophical moments, lying in his bunk and listening to Plithy prattle on about the Islander resistance, Quell had decided that the game they played here was not unique. Wasn't it, in fact, the same game the centralized government had been running Earthside for generations? Connectibles versus unconnectibles; rebels versus the establishment; the powerful versus the powerless. Artificial distinctions all. He had pictured the man responsible for this state of affairs. Not a mindless CPU, but a perilously old man, bald as stone and despised by about seventy-eight percent of the population, according to the last polls Quell had seen.

How could this grotesque game possibly benefit High Executive Len Borda?

Quell shook his head. He checked the action on his own dartrifle now as he waited for the airlock to open and disgorge the new batch of prisoners. It was pointless to speculate about the mind of Len Borda. Pointless to anthropomorphize human reason and logic when the situation clearly lacked both.

"I think the airlock's about to open," said Plithy in stage whisper from his crevice, snapping Quell back to the present.

Quell let out a scowl. *"Quiet."*

"Crazy crazy crazy," muttered Rick Willets.

A thought suddenly occurred to the Islander. Why had he never heard about this place before? Borda couldn't keep the goings-on in these orbital prisons shrouded in mystery forever. In a world where thousands of drudges clambered over each other to report on Jeannie Q. Christina's hairdo every day, there had to be at least a few people drudging up the truth on the Defense and Wellness Council prison system. Certainly one of them would have thought to interview a paroled prisoner from one of these places by now . . . unless there *were* no paroled prisoners.

Quell looked with sadness on the boy Plithy. The commander whose eye he had bloodied must have had a lot of stripes on his uniform. Plithy must have seriously pissed *someone* off for the Council to relegate him to this state of limbo, without trial, without purpose, without end.

How the fuck was Quell going to get out of here?

He supposed that if he were a brilliant schemer like Natch, he would have already deduced an escape. Or if he were a charismatic statesman like his son Josiah, he would have managed to forge a truce with the connectibles by now. He would have shown them all the futility of playing silly war games and breaking thumbs to suit the whims of a madman.

But Quell was neither schemer nor statesman. He was a bio/logic engineer and a stubborn old fool, and he could think of nothing to do but lie in the rut the Defense and Wellness Council had thrown him in.

• • •

The door to the airlock opened and eight prisoners came stumbling out. All Islanders but one, by the rustic look of their wardrobe.

Quell felt the battle frenzy take hold of him. He vaulted over the crate and let out a cry of anger that reverberated throughout the dock. The prisoners froze in place, panicked; one of them collapsed quivering to the ground. And then Quell was pounding across the floor, a bellowing behemoth with rifle held aloft in both hands. Three black code darts went flying past Quell's right shoulder as three different connectible gunmen underestimated how fast a big man could run. In seven long strides he made it to the row of crates the enemy had staked out. He hoped that Plithy and the others were following the plan, but he was quite past the point of return by now.

The Islander made a flying leap over some big steel drum and began wildly spraying the gathered connectibles with dartfire in midair. There were twelve of them and only one of him, yet clearly Quell had put them on the defensive. Two of his darts even found targets before he felt half a dozen pinpricks line up along his torso. Icy paralysis grabbed hold of him.

Shit, thought Quell as he caught a glimpse of the hard concrete block that he would be crashing against any second now. *Why do I always forget to watch out for the landing?*

He crashed, hard.

But not before seeing the connectibles all collapse to the ground themselves, victim to the Islanders who had snuck up behind them. Even Plithy had managed to plug one of the bastards.

Quell smiled to himself in spite of the agony. Misdirection: it was the oldest and simplest of combat tactics, one that even a bio/logic engineer with no military training could figure out. Draw the enemy's attention and their fire with the largest, loudest distraction you could find, then launch the *real* assault where they least expected. Sometimes the simplest tactics were the most effective.

The Islander clawed his way back to consciousness ten minutes later. He felt as if someone had doused his chest with flaming tar, and he could scarcely move his arms or legs. But he knew from experience that these black code pain routines only lasted so long. Blistering agony for half an hour was better than weeks of grinding pain from broken thumbs.

"Fucking incredible," said a grinning Plithy as he and Rick Willets draped Quell's arms over their shoulders and helped him to his feet.

"Crazy," agreed Willets.

All of the connectibles had been corralled into the center of the dock and roped tightly together. Most of them would be left in the dock for the next connectible patrol that passed through. A few would be singled out for the thumb treatment, or worse.

Meanwhile, most of the new prisoners had already vanished down into the unconnectible level of the prison, where doubtless some young punk like Plithy was giving them an initiation into the ways of the Orbital Detention and Rehabilitation Facility, Twelfth Meridian. All except for one, the tall, gangly fellow who had slipped to the floor in shock when Quell had let out his war cry. Seemed like the man had managed to smack his forehead against the floor when he fell. He was sitting up, dazed but being tended to by two of the unconnectible team.

Quell took a closer look and strangled back a gasp. He knew this man. This man had been at the top of the Revelation Spire on that hor-

rible day a few weeks ago, the day that Quell had scuffled with Lieutenant Executive Magan Kai Lee. He was a man of thin limbs and sharp
angles, with a bulging Adam's apple and eyelids so prominent they were
practically reptilian. Today he was dressed in the standard streetwear of
breeches and a brown shirt, but on that day he had been wearing the
white robe and yellow star of the Defense and Wellness Council.

Papizon, that was his name. One of Magan's flunkies.

Plithy and Willets were dragging Quell away from the dock now
and into the long, wide hallway that led to the unconnectible level of
the prison. Soon they were back in friendly territory, and Quell was
able to muster a half-walk, half-shamble with the support of his two
comrades. But his mind remained on the dock and that odd flamingo
of a Council officer. Quell had no idea how many of these orbital
prisons Len Borda maintained, but Papizon's arrival at this one was
certainly no coincidence.

He tried to sort through all the rumors he had heard about the
Defense and Wellness Council from later arrivals at the prison. Magan
Kai Lee was in open rebellion against Len Borda, they said; the Council
had fragmented between the two groups; Magan's officers and Borda's
officers were openly skirmishing in the streets. Were the prisons still
under Borda's control? If so, did that mean that Papizon was here on
some kind of clandestine mission? And what kind of mission could
that be, except to take revenge on Quell?

The three of them arrived at Quell's cramped prison cell. Four
walls, a nonfunctioning viewscreen, a metal chair, a few changes of
clothes he had scrounged from the supply depots, a poor excuse for a
bunk. Plithy dragged the older man to his bunk and deposited him
there as gently as he could. Quell flopped onto his back and groaned.

"Quell," said Plithy. "Can I ask you something?"

The Islander gave a snort of assent.

"What was . . . *she* like?"

"Who?"

A nervous pause. "Margaret Surina."

"Beautiful," said Quell, then rolled over to face the wall, signaling that the conversation was over.

(((4)))

Silence. Gloom. Darkness.

Don't think.

Jittering in his arms and legs and teeth. Patches of consciousness stitched together with long threads of void.

Natch keeps consulting his internal systems, looking for some kind of baseline, a pulse for the universe; but time has become unpredictable. There is no consistency to those numbers. The only constant is steadily mounting hunger, the kind of hunger that spurs the heartbeat to race, the kind that stabs rational thought in the back.

Don't think.

Too much. The hunger is too much. He has vowed to let the world do to him what it will. But does that include just sitting here in this dungeon and letting himself starve to death? That's not surrender to the lofty Fates, that's submission to the timetable of a more mundane authority, namely, the Patel Brothers. And even in his current state of inaction, that's a repugnant thought.

Natch pushes himself up weakly from the chair. The ropes puddle at his feet. He steps outside of them and makes for the doorway at the other end of the chamber, steadfast in his refusal to make any plans after he leaves this infernal place. Perhaps he'll find Petrucio. Perhaps there will be something to eat.

Six paces. Nine paces.

A high-pitched whistle, a drift of wind brushing across his cheek. Natch looks up and sees—

Silence. Gloom. Darkness.

It's not the darkness of the Patels' domed cavern, however, but the darkness of a five-year-old's room. It's still two hours before dawn, and in the hive all is quiet except for the light patter of spring rain and the soft creaks of slowly weathering wood. Children don't stir at this hour, and even the proctors have abandoned their restless wandering of the halls.

Natch is lying on the floor. Above him, he can see nothing but the dark wood of the bureau he has scooted himself under. It's a massive piece, hand-carved and probably donated from some moldering estate. The weight would be crushing enough were the bureau completely empty. But Natch has loaded its drawers with rocks specially gathered for this purpose until the burden is heavier than anything he has ever tried to lift; anything less would make the plan an obvious setup. And Natch can't afford to fail. There are older boys out there who have been thrashing him in the hallway and teaching his OCHREs new injuries. These bullies must be dealt with.

Natch takes a deep breath, counts to three, and kicks out the block of wood that's been propping the end of the bureau up, hard. The block goes skittering under his bed.

He feels unbearable pain as the full weight of the piece comes down on him. There's a screaming in his left forearm that he hasn't anticipated as something sharp on the bureau's surface bites into his skin. It's sharp enough to draw blood. OCHREs start to kick in and dull the ache, but Natch forces himself to relax, to take in the pain. He's not out on the street or in Serr Vigal's apartment now; he's in the care of the hive, and a huge burst of OCHRE activity will only summon suspicious proctors. It takes a tremendous amount of effort, but Natch soon manages to set aside the pain. He looks on the bureau's opposite side and sees a maker's mark carved into the wood: a flowery flourish of the letters S and N, the carving jagged and splintery from years of neglect. It must be the complement to this maker's mark that's digging into his pinioned left arm, but there's nothing he can do about it now.

When the proctors finally arrive and raise the alarm, when three of them heave the bureau off and drag him to the infirmary, when he is lying in bed quietly telling the head proctor a false story about how the bullies had thrown that bureau on top of him, Natch can feel the bloody imprint of the maker's mark in his left forearm. S and N. His OCHREs will eventually close up the gash and erase the scar, but for several nights Natch will sit in the darkness staring at the wound and wonder what S and N stand for. A carpenter long dead? A company long defunct? A city, a country?

S and N. S and N.

He is still watching the brand on his arm as he sits with Serr Vigal in one of the hive's wood-paneled dens twenty-four hours later. His guardian is complaining about the quality of the tea. Natch can see that there's something troubling the neural programmer, that Vigal can't quite slip the story of the bureau into that mental file of verified fact. He suspects something. *Why should I care?* Natch tells himself. *I'm not a truthteller. I don't always have to tell the truth, do I?*

Don't think.

He opens his eyes. Enough of this. Sitting here in this chair, staring at the pockmarks on the dome, waiting for Petrucio and Frederic to torture or dispose of him—enough of it. To die of his own volition? Maybe. To die on a twisted whim of the Patels? Something bilious rises up in his stomach at the thought.

Natch stands. He looks down and wonders why the ropes that were binding his legs are now gathered at his feet. Did one of the Patels do this? And if so, how?

But there will be time for questions later. Right now, Natch is starving. He takes a wobbly step forward, then another. Decides to head for the door at the far end of the dome. Natch takes six more steps. He hears the whistle of the wind from somewhere above, looks up, and sees—

Silence. Gloom. Darkness.

But this is a darkness of Natch's own making. He's purposefully dialed the lights down, preferring to see his office as it would appear were there no human eyes to see it. Of course, without a human presence, the entire room would be neatly compressed into a few cubic meters of collapsed wall with the furniture clamped down in place. A petty distinction, but an irritating impediment in Natch's mind.

Stop wasting time. Do what you came here to do.

He walks up to his workbench and waves his hand. Before he's even finished the gesture, the space above the workbench's surface is no longer empty. Now there's a transparent bubble, barely visible in the darkness, and inside that bubble hovers a holographic pyramid. The pyramid is colored a sickly green, the color of mucous, and looks like it's been pierced dozens of times with long needles that stick out of the sides.

The bio/logic program has no identifying label, but Natch's contact has told him exactly what it is. He has spent countless days swimming through dark and dangerous trenches in the Data Sea looking for this code, and now that he's found it he's spent countless nights hammering away at the spikes on his workbench. It must be the perfect, untraceable, anonymous communication machine. The ability to spray the whole world with convincing forgeries at stunning speed. Yes, his plan relies more on social engineering than on bio/logic engineering, but a few slack connections could expose him to ruin and put number one on Primo's forever out of his reach.

Yes, number one on Primo's. That is what this code will accomplish for him. It's the token that will gain him admittance to a larger realm. It's the talisman that will place him above the Patel Brothers and Lucas Sentinel and Bolliwar Tuban and Pierre Loget and all the rest of the imbeciles he's been jousting with for a few years now.

He looks at the spiked green pyramid and hears Horvil's meek protestations from the previous day. *What if we spark too much panic? I mean, we're all connected, and so we're all vulnerable. There could be another black code attack on the Vault any day now. Everyone knows that. The Council might really be gearing up for another assault. What if we cause too much panic? There might be a rush on the Vault. People might stop trading. The whole financial system could collapse.*

Natch had laughed at the engineer in response, but he knows that it's a serious possibility. What are markets but contained panic and quantified disaster? What keeps the whole thing functioning but confidence?

He thinks of Captain Bolbund deluging him with his rancid poetry. Of Brone taunting him with defeat. Of the bullies in the hive pouncing on him and beating him close to unconsciousness. Of all the stings and jabs he's felt over the past few years during his ascent up the Primo's charts.

Too late.

Natch closes his eyes and launches the program.

He opens his eyes to find himself lying facedown on the floor of the Patels' dungeon. One arm and one leg are throbbing crazily, out of control. He's ready to be anywhere else but here. Something about this place unsteadies his nerve.

Natch takes a deep breath, pushes himself up to his knees, then clambers to his feet. He takes one step, then another, then another, then—

Don't think.

Silence. Gloom. Darkness.

Walking in circles around the chair, staring at the spindly table, now occupied by an empty plate and an empty glass.

Silence. Gloom. Darkness.

Natch tries to open his eyes, but they sting with smoke. The smell of creosote fills his nostrils. He reaches up, rubs his eyelids brusquely with his forearm, waves the smoke away. His fingertips touch flame and he yanks them back. He looks down at his fingers and is surprised to see a spreading smudge of blackness where the fire has burned him. *Remember what the proctor said,* he tells himself. *No OCHREs out here in the wilderness.*

The boy holding the torch looks astonished to see him. It's one of Brone's friends, a stick-thin boy who spent much of the previous night making obsequious comments to support Brone's plan for getting the camp through the winter. And now all he can do is stare dumbly in terror at the bear rampaging through the trees a few meters away, blood on its claws.

Natch yanks the torch from the astonished boy's hand and runs.

Runs not away from the bear but towards it. Fear must be confronted. Adversity must be tackled, not fled from. But you must have a plan, and Natch has one.

Don't think.

Silence. Gloom. Darkness.

He is tearing through the woods with the bear in pursuit, ignoring the branches slashing at his face. He must reach the clearing he knows. A place he has spent many hours in quiet introspection, trying to pinpoint his future. If he can only reach that spot, he will be safe, and so will the camp. Behind him, the savage roar. The smoke of the torch still seeping into his eyes. Claws grappling at his back, nearly catching on the stray threads of his shirt.

He reaches the slight hill leading to the clearing. Footsteps in the snow leading up in that direction. Natch catches a glimpse of a distinctive green shirt he has seen many times over the past few months. Brone.

The bottom of the hill. Two paths. The path up leads to the clearing he knows so well, leads to his own safety, leads to Brone. The other path leads farther off into the woods, leads to his plan dashed, leads to risk and an uncertain outcome.

Natch pauses. Looks both directions. Throws a foot towards the lower path.

Silence. Gloom. Darkness.

Brone is explaining to him the power of Possibilities 2.0. The ability to be in two places at once and to live two lives at once. No more regretted choices!

With infinite possibilities at your disposal—with all those realities ripe for the plucking—why stop at just outputting one? . . . Our minds have more than enough processing power to run several tracks of consciousness at the same time. Consciousness is itself little more than a parlor trick, a low-bandwidth illusion. We've known this since ancient times. Yet we've never been able to duplicate it, until now. . . .

Just imagine it! Two roads diverge in a wood. Why choose between them when you can take both? You can spawn separate multi projections to travel them and give each one a separate consciousness to experience them. Who's to say you can't choose two different jobs, two different companions, two different Vault accounts? And if one of these lives leads to bad consequences—well, then wipe it out! MultiReal can erase your memories, Natch, and the memories of those around you!

Brone throws two coins in the air in different directions. Natch activates Possibilities 2.0 and leaps after both coins at once.

Darkness.

His foot strikes white tile and his knee twists. Where are Petrucio and Frederic? How much time has elapsed? Why has he not left this place?

Natch gazes all around, sees the door on the wall of the dome that the Patels both disappeared into. That is where he must go. He can't say what will happen after that, or if there will *be* anything after that. But he cannot sit here in the darkness any longer.

Don't think.

There is a high-pitched whistling sound. Startled, Natch looks up.

A murderous metal blade like the business end of a guillotine. Lowered lightning-quick on an extended metal rod and aimed directly for his neck. Swinging towards him too fast for the dodging instinct.

Silence.

He ducks, and the bear's claws go swishing over his head. Death forestalled by another few seconds.

Natch vaults to his feet once again. He is pointed deeper into the woods, towards a life where the bear disappears into the wilderness, a life where Brone carries his eye and arm intact with him back to camp, where he puts that arm over Natch's shoulders and says *Thanks, man, you saved my ass*, where Natch's quick thinking is commended and his respect among the boys regained. Or maybe a life where the bear catches up to Natch and mauls *him* instead, a life where he becomes a martyr for the camp, his sins forgotten, nobody honoring him more than Brone, who vows to live up to the selfless example Natch has set for him, who turns down the apprenticeship offer of Figaro Fi and founds a charitable institution aimed at helping those less fortunate than himself. Or maybe a life where Natch carries the scars that were destined to be Brone's, the lost eye and the lost arm, a life where he broods over the futility of his feud with the other boy, of his relentless and aimless ambition, a life where he retreats into the memecorp sector under his mentor Serr Vigal's tutelage and becomes an expert on the capillaries that run into the brain—

Each future a single footstep away.

He shifts and heads up the hill.

Don't think.

There is no explanation that can encompass it. One instant there are two paths. The next there is a path taken and a path abandoned, and as for that split-second of decision, no amount of science can penetrate it. The choice has not been made, then the choice has been made. The world proceeds on its track through time leaving only inadequate explication in its wake.

Brone, huddled at the top of the hill, looks up in shock as Natch and then the bear come streaking in his direction.

Natch stumbles and falls on the white tile.

Silence. Gloom. Darkness.

He knows these are no ordinary bonds that keep him ensnared in this chamber. Only the neural legerdemain of Margaret Surina's Multi-Real program can effect such conditions. How and why he cannot say. All he knows is that MultiReal is no longer responding to his commands, and despite the fact that the Patels no longer have access to it, the program seems to be at their disposal.

He can go nowhere. He can do nothing.

Once the world was laid out before Natch like glittering jewels in a display case, there for the plucking. Now his universe has been reduced to a circle about ten meters in diameter beyond which he cannot cross. Outside that circle there is nothing. Friends who have scorned him, a guardian who has abandoned him, enemies who have entrapped him, a government and a public that despise him. The programs he has created will dissipate into the endless currents of the Data Sea until his name only exists in the deep strata of the changelogs. The history of his accomplishments will wither. His name will be forgotten.

But there is no outside agency he can blame. The path to this impotent circle is one he has charted himself, second by second, day by day, decision by decision.

No way forward.

No way forward.

(((5)))

No way forward.

"You wanted a day or two to think things over. Fucking fabulous." Feet shuffle against the floor, a foot idly kicks at the wall. "If we'd got in touch with Magan Kai Lee when we said we would, everything would be fine right now. We'd be up to our asses in Vault credits. Well! Look what's happened *now*." Another kick.

"So . . . *two* squadrons? Are you sure about that, Frederic?"

"Am I sure? Of course not. This is the Defense and Wellness Council. They don't go broadcasting their plans all over the Data Sea. But why else would they be doing reconnaissance missions way the fuck out here?"

The sound of nervous foot tapping. "I suppose the real question is whether those squadrons belong to Borda, or whether they belong to Lee."

"Guess again."

Silence.

"One of each?"

More silence.

"Shit. What do we do?"

"You know exactly what I want to do, 'Trucio."

An exasperated sigh. "You're not going to bring that up again, are you?"

"Why not? There's still time to pull this thing out of the fire. If we can hand MultiReal-D over to Magan before Borda's thugs get here, we can still fulfill the contract."

"So then let's do that."

"Don't be naïve, 'Trucio. Nobody's going to give us shit unless we can prove it works. The contract specifically says *working prototype*, remember?"

"Of course it works. Natch is still sitting in the chair, isn't he?"

"I'm talking about in the *real* world. Solid weapons. Real steel."

"It worked in Old Chicago. That was real."

"How do you know? Come on, 'Trucio, we have no idea what happened out there in Old Chicago. What the fuck was he doing wandering those streets in the first place? Who was it tried to murder him? Some diss throwing stones? Bullshit."

Pacing. Tense, thoughtful silence. "There's too much at stake. What if the program breaks down and he winds up dead? *Then* what do we do?"

"Don't tell me anybody's going to mourn for that motherfucker."

"That's not the point. I'm not going to risk killing him just to fulfill a contract. I don't care how much we're getting paid, Frederic, even in *your* L-PRACG murder is illegal."

An angry snort. Something thrown against a wall. "It'd make our lives much easier if he was dead. It would get the Council off our backs."

"Oh, really, would it now?" A derisive snort. "Are *you* about to go in there and cut his throat?"

"What makes you think I wouldn't?"

"Use your head, idiot. You can't kill him. Didn't it ever occur to you that if he dies, the MultiReal databases disappear for good and there's no getting them back? *Then* who's going to pay us, Frederic?"

A wet razzing sound. "You're being ridiculous. We know this works. I just spent nine months of my life working on this stupid MultiReal-D program. I'm not gonna let it all go down the drain without a fight. *Somebody's* gonna have to put his neck on the line to test this thing. Why not him?"

"Forget it. The answer's *no*, and that's final."

Furious stomping around, the sound of things smashing. "In two hours, we're going to have the fucking *Autonomous Revolt* happening right outside our door. Borda and Lee are going to blow this place to pieces trying to find Natch. All because you're afraid of getting your hands dirty."

"Just give me twenty minutes, Frederic. I'll think of something."

• • •

The chamber is dark. Natch is tied to the chair once again, and this time he's bound tight enough that he can't even wiggle an arm free. Any attempt at escape from this accursed chamber would be futile anyway. Spider, web, helpless fly.

Natch thinks: if he died here today, if he were never found or heard from again, what would he leave behind?

The list is not an encouraging one. The MultiReal databases—to which he has only had time to contribute the merest fraction of code. His fiefcorp—which has been handed to Jara and will likely be dismantled by the end of the year. His bio/logic programs and RODs—scattered now among a dozen different fiefcorps and diluted beyond recognition. His modest possessions—which will remain sequestered in the dark crevices of his compressed apartment until the building management finally liquidates them. His record of defiance against the Defense and Wellness Council these past few months—soon to be engulfed by the vast bureaucratic ocean of official government business where it will be forgotten. The few personal relationships he has maintained over his lifetime—each sullied and denigrated by his own hand.

Brone told him some of the same things back in Old Chicago. *Don't try to blame me for this state of affairs. If you want to blame someone, blame yourself. You've done a much better job isolating yourself than I could have ever done. I daresay even those few you label your friends will give up on you soon enough.* He remembers the words, but not the conversation they came from. When did Brone confront him in such pointed terms?

He tries to summon in his mind the evening before the Shortest

Initiation, the last evening in the hive. The night where he discovered that Brone had bested him. He had a meeting, he thinks. But with whom? And for what purpose? He probes that alcove of his memory, but the shelves are empty. Somehow he knows that this is not a moment of stress-induced amnesia, not a mere temporary misconnection in the neural circuitry. That night is gone. Scoured clean.

Natch feels a brief moment of panic. The night before the Shortest Initiation, gone. Whatever happened in Old Chicago, gone.

He knows he was ambushed on the streets of Shenandoah, a few months ago. He remembers talking about it. He can still feel the black code worming its way inside him. But when he tries to summon an image of his attackers—shadowy figures in black robes, Thasselians, disciples of Brone—there is nothing.

Gone.

Something has been happening to his memory ever since he arrived in this place. It's not only the chronology of the present that's blurred and confused, it's the past as well. Long-settled events in Natch's mind, bedrock memories, are disappearing. He feels like he is sliding down a tightly coiling spiral into nothingness. His accomplishments, such as they were, have all been stripped away. His willpower has been effectively nullified within this nine-pace radius. And now, even his memories are slipping down into the void as well.

A slice of light appears on the far wall, with Natch's bound silhouette framed in the middle. The door behind him is opening.

Frederic Patel doesn't so much walk in front of Natch as he slinks, with hunched shoulders and a furtive expression of hatred on his face. He's clutching one or more objects to his chest, but Natch can't see what because they're hidden in shadow. He comes closer and cocks an ear to the domed ceiling as if listening for a pursuer. Natch can see one of the objects Frederic's holding: it's a sword.

A *sword*? Natch's mind reels. Yes, an actual Japanese katana, smooth and sheathed and yet still deadly.

"Awake?" says the boorish younger Patel brother in a hoarse whisper.

Natch says nothing, but he knows that Frederic can see his unblinking eyes just fine.

"Good." Frederic nods, kneeling in front of Natch and dropping the sword onto the tile from a distance of a dozen centimeters at most. The katana hits the tile with a soft, reverberant clang. "Would hate for you to die in your sleep."

And then, before Natch has time to even contemplate a response, Frederic makes a stabbing motion with his left hand. The entrepreneur feels a slight sting on his left forearm and catches a glimpse of a syringe, its plunger now deployed.

Natch glances over at the pinprick in his arm with its infinitesimal drop of already-scabbed-over blood. He should be inured to the idea of invasive black code flowing into his bio/logic systems by now—he is, after all, still playing host to Thasselian black code from his attack in Shenandoah, not to mention the mysterious program from Petrucio's dartrifle in the Tul Jabbor Complex and Margaret Surina's MultiReal back door. But he feels that frisson of impurity, that shiver of uncleanliness anyway. Foreign code. Unknown.

Frederic stands, then leans down to grab the sword. He unsheathes it and grins the grin that only sadists know.

Natch stares at the katana, wondering where Frederic could possibly have gotten hold of such a thing. Neither Patel brother is a collector of Japanese relics, as far as he knows. The jade green pattern running around the pommel of the sword looks much too ornate for a weapon of everyday use; not like there are samurai running around using edged weapons anyway. But this katana is clearly a museum piece, an expensive gift from some gracious capitalman.

He looks at the blade and thinks, *He's really going to kill me.*

It's a wholly unique sensation. For months, he's felt the undertow of the Null Current dragging at him at every turn: a relentless force that flows beneath everything human, like groundwater, a subterranean tide that tugs and pulls at all thought and emotion, that seeps through all the petty barricades of society without pause or consideration. It was there when Brone's minions shot him full of black code in that alleyway in Shenandoah. It was pulling at him when he escaped ten thousand deaths by Council dartgun at the Tul Jabbor Complex.

But now Natch knows that his death is here, standing right in front of him. It's an absurd death, one he could never have foreseen—slain by a sword, in an anonymous dungeon, by Frederic Patel, of all people? He knows that Frederic despises him (and the feeling is mutual), but why the engineer should choose to decapitate him he doesn't know. And he will likely never know the reason. There will be no escape with the help of MultiReal miracles; Petrucio has ably demonstrated the Patels' baffling ability to nullify the program.

He thinks, *I have thirty seconds left before I die.*

No way forward.

Don't think. Don't struggle.

Patel hefts the sword in two heavily calloused hands and tries to get a proper grip. Natch knows virtually nothing about samurais or katanas beyond what he's seen in the dramas, and he's fairly certain that Frederic knows little more. He half expects that the edge of this gilded weapon will be too dull to actually cut through flesh. But as the engineer gingerly touches the blade to Natch's neck and makes the most delicate of testing cuts, Natch realizes that this is not the case. The sword is sharp enough to make expertise a luxury.

Frederic leans back for a swing. He bares his teeth and snarls.

Natch waits for the long-anticipated feeling of relief, of ending. The dead have no responsibilities, no anguish, no *wanting*. No confusion or uncertainty, because to die is to be utterly certain and unambiguous, for the first time, for the rest of eternity. Is this what he has been striving for? Simplicity, absolutism, peace?

Is it, or isn't it?

He hears the door open, followed by the sound of madly scrambling feet. *"Frederic!"* cries Petrucio Patel.

But it's too late. Frederic's muscles tense and the sword begins its death arc. His aim is true. Death is a second away. Unavoidable, beyond the reach of any wild probability. And as Natch sits here, trussed and helpless—as he watches the edge of the blade approach—the realization explodes from the depths of his consciousness.

He doesn't want to die.

He wants to live.

Natch screams. Petrucio bounds across the room, hand extended. But it's too late. The katana flies through the air in its killing stroke. The glint of reflected light strikes Natch in the eye. The icy blade touches flesh—

• • •

Frederic Patel is kneeling in front of the entrepreneur, syringe in hand, expression unnaturally gleeful. The sword lies on the floor, still sheathed. Natch's head is definitely still attached to his shoulders.

Petrucio bursts through the doorway, bounds across the room, and extends his hand. Natch sees the black gleam of a dartgun. Petrucio fires.

At Frederic.

The dart strikes Frederic right between the shoulder blades. There isn't even time for the younger Patel to display a look of shock on his face before he slumps to the floor.

(((6)))

Natch's feeling of cognitive dissonance only multiplies when Petrucio Patel snaps the fingers on his right hand and makes the entire dungeon vanish. One instant they're in an oppressive, dome-shaped chamber with a radius of thirty meters; the next they occupy a ten-meter-square storage room lined with shelving and assorted household objects. Dusty furniture, gardening tools. Only the chair and side table remain. *SeeNaRee*, thinks Natch, stunned from his near decapitation and embarrassed it hasn't occurred to him he might be a captive in a virtual environment rather than a literal one.

He watches the sprawled figure of Frederic twitch and moan in unconscious discomfort as Petrucio unties the ropes binding Natch to the chair. Petrucio keeps the dartgun leveled at Natch's chest as he motions for the entrepreneur to stand and move towards the door. Patel clicks his tongue reproachfully at his insensible brother and retrieves the katana before they leave. His expression is serene, but not untroubled.

They climb a flight of stairs and emerge in the first floor of a house whose construction dates back hundreds of years, or at least it's been built to look that way. They pass through a room full of kitschy memorabilia from ancient Japan, including a print of Hokusai's *Great Wave*, porcelain geisha dolls, and a pair of katanas much like the one Petrucio has under his armpit. The programmer deposits the sword on a table and then gestures Natch out the back door.

They emerge in a drizzly countryside with no sign of other human habitation for a kilometer or more. A dark green Falcon hoverbird sits parked next to the building. Natch offers no resistance as Petrucio eggs him through the hatch and then climbs aboard after him.

"Frederic not coming?" yawns a bored pilot almost thin enough to get lost between the seats.

"He'll catch up with us later," replies Petrucio drily.

The pilot doesn't seem to care. "Ready?"

"Ready. And thanks again for letting us use the basement, Hiro. We owe you one."

The pilot nods, yawns again, initiates the hoverbird's launch sequence. Seconds later, they are off. Once they've climbed high enough to see the surrounding territory, Natch starts scanning the horizon for landmarks. He zooms in on the corroded husk of a building far off in the distance, pointing to the heavens like a finger. Pinging the Data Sea with the image, Natch confirms that this is the Banespa Building of São Paulo, one of the tallest ancient skyscrapers still standing. Petrucio, meanwhile, gazes nervously to both starboard and port as the vehicle rises; he visibly relaxes when he determines there's no one else around.

Natch is strapped into a chair opposite Petrucio, watching the retreating fog-shrouded lights of the city. He can't say why he doesn't fear the dartgun in Petrucio's hand, even though it remains aimed at his head for the entire ascent. Nor does he understand why that head is still seated firmly on his shoulders and not rolling on a cold tile floor at Frederic Patel's feet. He reaches up and rubs the spot on his neck where the cold steel of the blade touched his flesh. All he can think is that he is glad to be alive.

Glad? Yes, definitely glad to be alive.

As soon as the 'bird levels off, Natch is astounded to see Petrucio flipping his dartgun around and offering it to the entrepreneur grip first. Natch reaches out hesitantly and lets Petrucio push it into his hands.

He feels a mental ping. "We'll talk over ConfidentialWhisper, if you don't mind," says Patel, arching his eyebrows in the direction of the pilot. Probably a needless precaution; the rhythmic bobbing of the thin man's neck hints that he is absorbed in some slow, sensuous groove on the Jamm. Natch shrugs.

Petrucio leans back and stretches one arm over the seat next to him. "There's three darts left in the gun," he says. "When we land on the outskirts of Angelos, you're going to plug Hiro in the back once, and then use the last two darts on me." His voice is disarmingly calm. Up front, Hiro blithely runs a hand over the instrument panel, still lost in his musical reverie. "Don't worry, it's nothing dangerous," continues Patel. "Temporary blackout. Same thing I used on Frederic."

The entrepreneur stares at the dartgun in his hand. Natch's memory has sprouted a disconcerting number of leaks lately, but to the best of his recollection he has never actually held a black code weapon before. It's significantly lighter than he expected. "What makes you think I'm going to do any of that?" he says.

"Because it'll give you a two-hour head start."

Natch frowns. "You're going to chase *after* me?"

"*I* won't. But Magan Kai Lee will. He's on his way to São Paulo now, with Borda on his tail."

Natch leans forward in the seat and ducks his head under the canopy of his clasped hands. He closes his eyes to block out the dartgun in his lap and pictures the diminutive Council lieutenant. Natch has always believed that human beings are constructed on scaffolds of emotion and irrationality, scaffolds that invariably have their weak struts. He has built his career on this belief. But Magan Kai Lee does not seem to have such an architecture; he's a man of rigid calculation all the way through. Natch tries to recall the first time he ever saw the lieutenant, back when he was just another faceless minion of Len Borda's ubiquitous military and intelligence force. He has a fleeting memory of Magan standing on the stage of a Council auditorium, pointing out into the audience . . . but no, the memory is gone now.

"What is he up to?" says Natch over ConfidentialWhisper. "What does he want?"

Petrucio leans his head back to face the roof of the hoverbird and closes his eyes, mimicking sleep. "He wants MultiReal."

"For his rebellion."

"I don't know for sure. But that's my worry, yes."

At first it seems ludicrous: why *worry* that someone might overthrow Len Borda? But then Natch thinks about the Council lieutenant standing in the midst of the Prime Committee's auditorium, with the power of MultiReal at his command. Unassailable, unconquerable. And suddenly he can understand Petrucio's hesitation.

What does Magan Kai Lee represent? What are his aims and goals? The man is accumulating a rebellion almost solely from the public's hatred of Len Borda. His own beliefs remain an enigma. Does he support Islander sovereignty? What is his position on public funding of TubeCo? Is he capable of balancing a budget? What will Magan Kai Lee do with MultiReal, if he gets ahold of it? Would that be better or worse than if Len Borda should get MultiReal in his possession? Natch recalls the aphorism he has heard many times recently about the wisdom of preferring the known enemy to the unknown enemy. The world has suffered much under the stern rigidity of Len Borda—but is replacing that rigidity with a blank cipher any less frightening?

And are either of these alternatives better than putting MultiReal in the hands of Brone and his Thasselian disciples?

It's all too confusing, and not for the first time Natch wishes he could return to that time of simpler loyalties. When he was merely an entrepreneur looking out for his own ass, when his enemies announced their intentions with press releases, when a single incontrovertible authority filed winners and losers into slots of descending order every hour.

"I don't understand why you're not handing me over to the Council," says Natch over the silent channel. "I assumed you and Frederic were working for them."

"Honestly, so did we." Petrucio chuckles softly. "Shortly after Margaret recruited us to help her finish MultiReal, we signed another deal with a faceless shell company. We were to continue our work with

Margaret as agreed. But on the side, we were to construct MultiReal prototype programs. Defensive programs, code named MultiReal-D. The deal was negotiated, signed, and paid for by Magan Kai Lee from an untraceable Vault account. We figured he was acting on behalf of the Council."

"And it didn't bother you to go behind Margaret's back like that?" says Natch, surprised at his accusatory tone.

Petrucio's lips curl into a half-smile. "It was a different world then. A plum military contract with a big paycheck, no oversight, nobody looking over our shoulders? Why not? I didn't really understand what Margaret was building out there in Andra Pradesh, and neither did Frederic. It didn't occur to us that Magan might be doing this behind Borda's back. But now . . ."

He pauses, but Natch does not need him to fill the gap. He knows what MultiReal can do. Sometime in the past three months, the world has been remolded.

Petrucio sits up and looks Natch straight in the eye with an earnestness that's atypical for a Patel. "You and I are businesspeople, Natch," he continues over the 'Whisper connection. "We're not king-makers. Politics . . . war . . . madness and freedom . . . it's not our domain. And it *certainly* isn't Frederic's.

"Magan Kai Lee knew you'd turn up in São Paulo eventually. He figured we'd have no problem handing you over to him. But that puts me and Frederic in a very difficult position. If we hand you over to Magan, his rebellion will be a fait accompli. If we allow you to fall into Len Borda's hands, the rebellion will be crushed." Petrucio weighs these two options with his hands on an imaginary balance scale. "We can't keep you here forever; sooner or later Magan will come around asking questions. But if you manage to escape . . ."

Natch does not hesitate. "I'll disappear."

"Exactly. We tell Magan that you overpowered Frederic and took his dartgun. That's not hard to believe. Then you kidnapped me and had me charter you a flight to Angelos. You completely vanish, and we don't have to be responsible for what happens."

"And is Frederic on board with all this?"

"Frederic." Petrucio sighs dramatically and then rolls his eyes. "Don't worry about Frederic—he'll see things my way, eventually."

"Assuming the Council doesn't kill him when they reach your pilot's house."

"No, Borda and Lee will leave him alone. He's got nothing they want." Patel stares at his hands, and Natch wonders if he's having second thoughts about shooting his own brother in the back with black code. "Frederic needs to realize that things have changed. The world can sort out its own messes without us. And without Multi-Real." He lapses into a moody silence as the South American continent below disappears underneath a gray gauze of cloud.

● ● ●

Half an hour passes. Inside the hovercraft, there is no sound except for the almost-undetectable tapping of Hiro's foot in time to the Jamm channel that has enveloped his senses. Either the tempo has picked up considerably, or he has switched channels to something more upbeat. Natch wonders exactly how complicit this pilot is with Petrucio's schemes. Complicit enough to let the Patels use his basement as a makeshift prison, and then to fly their prisoner hundreds of kilometers out of his way at a moment's notice. But does he know he's going to get shot with black code when they arrive? Does he know the Defense and Wellness Council could be at their heels? Natch supposes it's none of his business; Petrucio is capable of sorting out his own personal affairs.

Natch opens another ConfidentialWhisper channel with his erst-while enemy. "If you expect me to go along with all of this, then I'm going to need some answers."

Petrucio's been gazing out the window for the last half hour, lost in reflection. "Would you prefer to stay in São Paulo and wait for the Council to show up?" he replies, deadpan.

"No. But maybe I'd rather not wait until we land to use this dartgun." He holds up the weapon and points it at Petrucio's forehead. A can't-miss shot at this range. "Maybe I'd rather shoot you right now and dump you in the middle of the ocean. For fuck's sake—you *imprisoned* me, Petrucio. Just because you decided to let me go doesn't mean I'm going to forget this."

Petrucio's face sparks into a grin. For some reason, extreme adversity always seems to bring out the jester in him. "All right, what do you want to know?"

"These defensive programs you've been building. MultiReal-D. If I'm going to stay a step ahead of Magan Kai Lee and Len Borda, I need to know what they are."

"Fair enough." Petrucio stretches, sits up, and gives his most serious stare while Natch lowers the gun back to his lap. Natch is under no illusion that his threats have convinced Petrucio of anything. It's obvious that the programmer resolved to impart this information to Natch as soon as he burst into that SeeNaRee room and shot his brother in the back.

Petrucio narrows his eyes for a few seconds, trying to decide where to begin. "Tell me how you can use MultiReal," he says, "to reverse death."

Natch again resists the urge to rub the spot on his neck where he should have met his mortality. "I don't know," he replies.

"Now you're just being lazy," chides Petrucio. "You've had Margaret's program for months. You haven't spent the *entire* time dodging black code darts, have you? You must have thought some of these things through. Suppose the lieutenant executive of the Defense and Wellness Council gives you unlimited funding to build a MultiReal program that reverses death. How do you do it?"

Natch drops a token thought or two on the problem. "Impossible," he shrugs. "Or at least, that's what you want me to say."

Again, the wry smile. "Frederic and I thought it was impossible too, at first. Time only moves in one direction, right? Prengal Surina proved that. But then I had an inspiration. If you send a multi projection into a real building, and that real building collapses on top of you, do you die? No, of course not—because you're not actually *in* the building in the first place. It's just an illusion. Neurons firing." Petrucio taps the side of his head with one finger. "When the building collapses, the multi network can sense trauma coming an instant before it happens. It cuts off your projection and you wind up standing on your red tile again. So I thought: if you can project a virtual body into space . . . why not project a virtual body into *time?*"

"That doesn't make any sense," says Natch, shaking his head. "Virtual time? What would that even look like?"

"Tell me what time it is."

"What—"

Petrucio cuts him off. "You'll find out. Just tell me what time it is."

The entrepreneur turns his attention to the internal clock that has been acting as metronome for the bio/logic symphony in constant performance since the hour of his birth. "It's 10:04 a.m. São Paulo time."

Petrucio puts the palms of his hands together and touches his fingertips to his nose. "You're sure about that."

Natch makes no response. Ever since he hit number one on Primo's, ever since he got enmeshed in Margaret Surina's tangled skein of MultiReal programming, all of the sureties in his life have been vanishing one by one. Career, friends, ideals. Why should time be the exception?

"In actuality," continues Patel, his demeanor maddeningly placid, "it's 10:03. You want to know what virtual time looks like? You, my friend, are living in it."

Natch grips the armrest of his seat as his stomach does backflips. He remembers the feeling of queasy vertigo that wormed through his extremities when Brone and Pierre Loget demonstrated how he could stand in two places at once. He's suffered this primordial shock so often these past few months it should almost feel commonplace by now. But no matter how hard he tries, Natch simply can't adjust to this new world of constant gut-wrenching change. "*You* did this to me," he mutters over ConfidentialWhisper. "At the Tul Jabbor Complex. The black code you hit me with when I jumped on the hoverbird."

Petrucio gives the slightest nod of affirmation. "Magan's idea," he says.

"This doesn't help me at all. So my clock's out of sync. I still have no idea why that matters."

"Let's take a step back." The programmer settles deeper into his seat and waves one hand in the air like a professor diving into a didactic lecture. "What does MultiReal do? It lets you explore alternate realities in your mind, before they happen. Glorified probability calculation, right? Run the program with someone else present, and it becomes a collaborative process. You still see the potential realities, but now the other person is effectively telling you what they're going to do, before they do it. MultiReal can project all this much, much faster than real time, because it's all just mathematical calculations in your head." Petrucio points again to his own head, with its neatly combed slick of hair. "Once you've chosen the reality you want, you still need to make it actual. It hasn't happened yet; it's just potential. So you close the choice cycle and turn that possibility into a reality. If we're using the baseball analogy . . . you choose where you want the ball to go. You close the choice cycle. MultiReal tells your body to hit the baseball just like *so*, and tells the other person's body to catch it, or not catch it. You with me so far?"

"Yes."

"It only takes a fraction of a second for your brain to project all those realities and for you to make a choice. But the actual hitting and catching of the baseball takes several seconds. So what are you doing during those several seconds?"

Natch frowns. "I don't know. You're acting out the choice, I suppose."

"Sure. But who says your mind can't *continue onward*? While your body is hitting the ball and running for first base, why can't MultiReal just keep calculating further into the future? Why not keep going for a whole sixty seconds—and why not *stay* sixty seconds ahead of everyone else?"

The entrepreneur has no answer.

"If you did this continuously, without stopping, then you'd effectively be living in the future, wouldn't you? One minute in the future. As long as life conforms to the probability calculations in your head, the outside world would unspool in 'real time' behind you. All of your interactions with the people around you would happen ahead of time in that collaborative virtual space. Even when unpredictable things do happen, the program can usually just back up and weave those things into the virtual fabric. MultiReal can erase those nascent memories, so nobody would be the wiser—including you."

"It's a neat trick," says Natch, "but I still don't see how that's going to reverse—" He stops short.

Petrucio's face blooms into a massive smile. "You're starting to see it, aren't you? Anything that happens during that sixty seconds—someone shooting you with a dartgun, someone pushing you off a ledge—"

"Frederic cutting off my head with a samurai sword," grumbles Natch.

"—it hasn't really *happened* yet, right? It's just a possibility you're exploring in your head. A collaborative fantasy. You've still got time to alter your path and avoid that future. So back to our original analogy. If you're a multi projection standing in a building when it collapses, the system cuts you off and brings you back to reality. Same thing here. If someone decapitates you with a sword . . ."

"You get snapped back to 'real' time, one minute in the past."

"Exactly."

Natch stands up abruptly, tries to pace in the cramped hoverbird cabin. Now that he's caught the scent, his mind is charging ahead, galloping through the possibilities with furious speed. From the pilot's chair, Hiro starts to turn around to see what's going on, then thinks better of it and disappears back into his mocha grind haze.

"You told me MultiReal-D erases nascent memories," says Natch. "Then why do I still remember Frederic swinging that sword at my neck?"

"Did you see the syringe he injected you with?"

"Yes."

"Modified OCHREs, for testing. So you'd remember the whole thing."

Natch's mind is reeling. It's insane, ludicrous, borderline nonsensical—but if he accepts the original premise of MultiReal, where's the logical break? There is none. It follows. And furthermore . . .

"A bio/logic program can't really *know* when you're about to die," he says over ConfidentialWhisper, more to himself than to Petrucio. "All MultiReal-D can do is guess. All it can do is take your sensory input and calculate the probability of death, based on the factors it's given."

"Correct."

"So if someone shoots you in the back, or poisons your food, or pushes you over a cliff when you're not looking . . . If you can't see the assassin coming, and he's not looped in to your collaborative process, then MultiReal-D provides no defense."

Petrucio purses his lips thoughtfully. "True."

"Yet if you *can* see death coming . . . somebody could take advantage of that. That person could set up a SeeNaRee environment where you're completely surrounded by certain death. Every time you get close to the edge of the room, a guillotine comes down from the ceiling and cuts you in half. It's not a real guillotine, but you don't know that. As long as your brain *thinks* you're going to die, MultiReal-D will keep yanking you back a minute into the past—into the *present*—every time. The potential memories would get erased. You'd be trapped."

Petrucio extends his hands behind his head and puts his heels up on the seat that Natch has just vacated. He seems extraordinarily pleased with himself. "Clever, isn't it?" he says. "But don't give me the credit for *that* idea—that was all Frederic's doing."

• • •

Natch's mind won't stop its mad charge through the possibilities, as if trying to make up for lost time. He's been in the dark for so long—both literally and figuratively—he feels like he must continue pressing on until all the questions are answered.

He wheels on Petrucio and extends an accusatory finger. "You're still not telling me everything. Someone tried to kill me in Old Chicago."

The programmer has quickly moved from satisfied to pleasantly exhausted, and seems on the verge of slipping into a nap. "We think so, yes. That's why Magan had me put the code in you to begin with. To protect you, and to track you."

"I don't understand this. I'm standing on the street in Chicago when someone tries to kill me. The program stops calculating my future and snaps me back a minute in the past, to 'real time.' But what if in real time, I'm *still standing on the same street with the person who's trying to kill me?* Neither of us would know any better, because our memories have been erased. So why wouldn't we do the same thing over and over again until our OCHREs wore out? Why wouldn't he just try to kill me *again?*"

"Ah," says Petrucio playfully. "Here's where things get fun. We think he *did*."

"So then what happened?"

"Nothing happened. Things *un*happened."

Natch simply gapes at the programmer.

Petrucio, though caught in a sleep spiral, is clearly happy at the entrepreneur's befuddlement. He has the same kind of brain as Horvil, one that derives pleasure from tough logical conundrums and mathematical challenges. "You're right," says Petrucio, letting out an enormous yawn. "The program's not all that useful unless you can solve that problem. But it's not as difficult as it sounds. During the whole time that MultiReal-D is active and calculating the future . . . why not keep a record of everything that's happening? Keep the whole memory trail stored in case you get caught in an endless loop of attack and reprisal. If that happens, start backtracking."

"How?"

"By *un*doing everything you've done." Petrucio interrupts Natch's budding protest with another yawn. "Impossible? Hardly. We live in a virtual world, Natch. Memories can be erased. Vault transactions can be reversed. Posts on the Data Sea can be taken down. You can rearrange the furniture in your apartment by editing a database entry. You can move your multi projection back to the same place you were standing yesterday with the blink of an eye. You'd be surprised how many of your actions can easily be reversed."

"Until?"

"Until the program finds a point in the past when you're no longer in imminent danger."

Natch catches himself on the ceiling of the hoverbird, feeling as if he's about to faint. Margaret Surina promised in her big speech before the world to eliminate the *tyranny of cause and effect*—and from all appearances, her program has done just that.

He tries to reconstruct that day in Old Chicago with his newfound knowledge. Natch discovered that Brone was not telling the truth about the black code, and so he fled from the hotel. He was pursued by Brone and his minions. But this time, Brone was not satisfied with threats; he actually *killed* Natch. Or at least, death was so imminent and irrefutable that MultiReal-D concluded Natch's only recourse was to wade into the morass of unhappening. The program began erasing memories, both his and Brone's, until it found a point where Natch could escape the Null Current one more time.

"How . . . how much time did I lose?" says Natch.

Petrucio's eyes are closed now, and he's clearly only keeping himself awake with great effort. "You couldn't have lost too much, or you would have noticed. I imagine only an hour or so. Don't forget that this is all still experimental, Natch. There are plenty of things the program can't reverse. It can't actually move objects. It can't reprogram bio/logic code. If you burn down a building, MultiReal-D isn't going to bring the building back. There are a number of Vault transactions that we can't figure out how to reverse."

"Don't you think it would be easier if the user didn't lose his memory?"

Patel shrugs. "Perhaps. But that brings its own problems. You can imagine how that could be quite disorienting in a combat situation, which is what the program was commissioned for. . . . Listen, we're a long, long way away from this being ready to deploy. A lot could change between now and then."

Natch nods. He's still trying to make that last mental leap, from him lying in the street in Old Chicago to the Patels heaving him onto a hoverbird bound for São Paulo. "How did you find me?"

"I told you, Natch—this is just a prototype. When we're testing the program, we can't risk someone's memories getting erased to the point where they're lost with no idea how to get home. It's almost happened too many times to count. So whenever the rollback kicks in, Frederic and I get notified exactly where and when it happened." He shifts in his seat and crosses one leg over the other. "We got a ping from Old Chicago. You were the only one running the program."

Natch staggers back into the seat next to the one where Petrucio's feet are now resting. There seems to be no end to the vertiginous implications of this infernal program. It can enable impossible feats of physical skill, it can control minds, it can enable you to be in two places at once . . . and now it can even reverse death? All by opening up a vista of possibilities and allowing you to cherry-pick between them. "If only Margaret had known about this," he says quietly over the 'Whisper channel. "She wouldn't have ended up how she did."

"If only she had known?" Petrucio opens his eyes and fixes them on Natch. The levity has completely drained from his face. "Who do you think built all this in the first place? You don't think Frederic and I wrote that whole program in nine months, do you? Everything we needed to make MultiReal-D work was already inside those databases. All we had to do was find it."

And then Petrucio cuts off the ConfidentialWhisper program and falls asleep.

(((7)))

It was three a.m. Which meant little to those like Rick Willets who had been in orbit long enough to have discarded any hope of trial or release. Why bother synchronizing to the Earth's circadian rhythms when you would likely spend the rest of your life under artificial light? But that was not Quell. Quell intended to get out of there, he intended to reintegrate himself with the planet, and so, for fuck's sake, three a.m. meant *sleep*.

"What?" he growled to the hand shaking his shoulder.

"Get up," said a voice. Quell rolled over on his bunk to face his tormentor, and found himself staring deep into the eyes of Papizon. The man was much closer than anyone who wasn't a lover or a parent ought to be.

The Islander shoved him brusquely across the room. Papizon wobbled like a scarecrow to regain his balance, but didn't seem to take offense. In fact, his face morphed into some rough approximation of a smile. "What do you want?" said Quell. He yawned, stretched, struggled to prop himself on his left elbow—all the while, discreetly reaching with his other hand for the dartgun he kept wedged between the mattress and the wall.

"Looking for . . . this?" grinned Papizon, brandishing Quell's pistol with the barrel in his fist as if he intended to stir soup with it.

Quell gaped at him, trying to summon a contingency plan from beneath the fog of his sleep-addled brain. He glanced in his peripheral vision for Plithy, but the boy was nowhere to be found. Had Quell's doom finally caught up to him? And despite all his stubborn survivalist instincts, did he really care?

Then Papizon tossed the pistol into Quell's lap. He followed this with an assortment of dart canisters that he produced from inside his jacket. "Might need these—paralysis, blindness, infusion of fear. . . ."

Not knowing what else to do, Quell pocketed them. "You mind telling me what's going on?"

"Shhh," said Papizon. "In a bit. First we've got to—wait, hold on . . . ten seconds . . ."

"Ten seconds to what?"

"Four, three, two, one . . ."

An explosion.

The prison shuddered beneath them as if the whole bloody thing had just slammed aground. Something not too far away had combusted like nothing on an orbital station should combust. Before Quell knew what was happening, he was hauling ass down the corridor in pursuit of Papizon, loading his gun with one of the canisters of darts from his pocket. Magan Kai Lee's subordinate seemed to know exactly where he was headed. In fact, he seemed to be timing his steps to some internal metronome, speeding up at certain intersections and slowing down at others. They had been sprinting for a good two minutes before Quell realized that he had forgotten to throw on a pair of shoes.

Four unconnectibles came barreling around a corner. Quell plugged the first one in the chest with a black code dart before realizing it was Plithy. He dimly remembered that the boy was scheduled to be on the team meeting the next shipment of prisoners. *Always in the wrong fucking place at the wrong fucking time.* Plithy clawed at his face and tumbled screaming to the floor. Papizon stepped neatly over the boy without even breaking stride, as if his plan had called for a body to be twitching in that spot all along.

Quell clapped one of the other stunned unconnectibles on the shoulder, yelled in his ear. "Just blindness, I think! Wear off in ten minutes!" He wanted to stay and help pick Plithy off the floor. Though the boy might not have saved his life, he had certainly saved Quell from a pair of broken thumbs. But Papizon was already disappearing out of sight, and the Islander knew that whatever opportunity the lanky Councilman was offering—freedom, revenge, a quick death—it was an opportunity he couldn't pass up. "Sorry!" bellowed Quell to the boy, hoping it would be some consolation. Plithy mewled something unintelligible, and then Quell was off.

Another explosion, this one deeper, louder.

The Islander caught up to Papizon and grabbed hold of his bony right forearm. "*Where* are we *going?*" he yelled.

"To the dock," replied the Council officer, stupid grin still pegged to his face.

"Dock's *that* way," said Quell, pointing back in the direction they had just come. The direction Plithy's team had been headed.

Papizon pursed his lips like an eight-year-old boy playing a practical joke. "Not that dock. *Our* dock."

"Our . . . ?" But before Quell could complete his question, the scarecrow had wriggled free and was tearing off down the corridor again.

The Islander looked down at the dartgun in his hand, then looked at Magan Kai Lee's rapidly fleeing minion. Did he have any reason to trust Papizon? It was entirely possible that the Council officer was setting up some kind of deadly retribution for what had happened at the top of the Revelation Spire. Quell remembered the thunk of his shock baton striking Magan's chest, the sound like a chef tenderizing meat. *Just shoot this idiot in the back and run for safety*, the Islander told himself. He centered the pistol on a spot between Papizon's shoulder blades. An easy shot . . .

But of course, it wasn't that simple. With Magan Kai Lee, it never was. The ammunition in Quell's dartgun had come from Papizon's own hands, hadn't it? Not likely Papizon would be stupid enough to hand out black code darts that he himself hadn't been inoculated against.

Sounds of running, shouting, shooting unconnectibles came wafting down the corridor.

Quell didn't think he had it in him to shoot Papizon in the back. But that didn't mean he couldn't be prepared for whatever lay in wait. The Islander slid a hand into his pocket, wriggled around until he found another hidden inner pocket, and retrieved a carefully wrapped tube of black code needles. *Guaranteed he's not inoculated against* this *shit*, thought the Islander, quietly replacing the ammunition in the pistol. "Trust in your fellows, but depend on yourself," he muttered, quoting one of the aphorisms of Creed Thassel.

Papizon had disappeared somewhere around the next corner. There were only three doors he could have entered, and the first two contained only shelving units stocked with standard industrial supplies. The Islander opened the third door and was greeted by the odd sight of Papizon hopping on one leg, fumbling his way into a black evac suit. Hanging on a wall hook was another black evac suit, size extra large, built to contain Quell's massive frame.

"Well?" said Papizon, as if his plan were self-evident.

The Islander looked back and forth from the Council officer to the shelving units to his gun. If there was an airlock anywhere in sight, Quell certainly couldn't see it. Then something else exploded far off in another part of the prison. Quell hastily donned the extra suit, grumbling to himself about the coldness of the material. Shoes would have been a big help here.

He doubted many Islanders had worn anything like this before, and he was sure his father would have had something disdainful to say about it. The suit had row upon row of gleaming yellow buttons lining the arms and nothing but a slick transparent film to protect his face. Quell had seen any number of videos of OrbiCo workers bouncing around EVA in these skintight contraptions, limber and carefree as chimpanzees. But now that he was actually wearing one, it seemed much too brittle to withstand the coldness of space. Quell poked at the bubble covering his nose and mouth. Could this thing *really* generate enough oxygen to keep a man of his size alive for more than a few seconds?

"Ready?" said Papizon, now fully suited and looking like some mutated crossbreed of seal and stickman. "Then hang on to your knickers—"

Before Quell even had a chance to ask what *knickers* were, the door shut behind him and the room echoed with a deafening bang, like the blast of an ancient shotgun. The Islander flinched. He could hear the clatter of metal bolts bouncing off something solid.

Suddenly, the shelving unit and the wall opposite him collapsed outward. Not into the blackness of space, as Quell had feared, but into the mustiness of a docking tube. The corrugated metal cylinder extended perhaps ten meters to the door of a hoverbird, painted white with a yellow star on its handle.

Papizon tapped the chest of his evac suit. "Just a precaution," he said, then scrambled for the hoverbird door.

Quell let out a sigh, both relieved and disappointed that he wouldn't get a chance to play around with the suit. He looked back at the room they had entered, thinking that the next man to open that door would be in for a big surprise. But surely Magan would have planned for that too? Quell realized that at some point he was going to have to lay his humanitarian impulses aside if he wanted to get out of here. He grabbed the dartgun off the shelf where he had left it and followed the Council engineer to the door, which was already opening for them.

The hoverbird was a standard Vulture model used by business executives the world over. There were two facing rows of plush passenger seating, multiple viewscreens, and a foldable conference table. Quell half expected to see a couple of stiff executives sipping Turkish coffee and discussing Primo's ratings. Papizon was already halfway out of his evac suit and halfway into the copilot's seat, next to a jovial woman with short red hair. Sitting in the row of passenger seats facing the door was a lithe woman with long, braided hair and skin of dark mocha—the Defense and Wellness Council's chief solicitor, Rey Gonerev, whom some called the Blade.

Gonerev gestured at Quell's dartgun, which he had unconsciously aimed in her direction. "So are you going to shoot me, or are you going to come in and sit down? We don't have all day."

"What—"

"We're breaking you out." A pause, which nobody filled. "Of *prison*. Now sit the fuck down."

Quell did. He pulled the mask of the evac suit up over his head and let it hang off the back of his neck, then laid his gun on the table.

"All right, Panja," said the Blade. "Let's go."

Within seconds, the door behind Quell shut and sealed itself, there was the sound of disconnecting clamps, and the hoverbird streaked away. Normally the prison was ringed with a cordon of patrolling Council hoverbirds. But for whatever reason, today the skies were clear, except for their ship and an escort of half a dozen Vulture 'birds. Quell caught one last glimpse of the Orbital Detention and Rehabilitation Facility, with the corrugated docking passageway dangling off the bottom like a hangnail. There were little flares of light coming from windows all over the unconnectible wheel of the prison, but the structure looked perfectly intact. He hoped Plithy was okay.

No more dock runs, thought the Islander, flushing with relief. *No more inedible stew. No more broken thumbs . . .*

"Here," snapped Gonerev. "Take this." The flick of her wrist was so abrupt that Quell almost missed the small copper disc she tossed in his direction. He caught it and recognized a connectible coin, one of the devices he had put together from Margaret's specs to mimic the bulkier connectible collars mandated by the Defense and Wellness Council. The Islander experienced a mental flutter. How did the Blade get ahold of one of *these*?

Gonerev stared at him with a look of scarcely concealed impatience. "Would you rather wear a collar?" she said. "I'm sure Papizon can dig one up somewhere if you want."

Papizon poked his head over his seatback. "*I don't care*," he said, his voice a clear parody of Quell's own. "*I'm never wearing one of those fucking things again. Do you hear me? Do you hear me?*"

Quell shook his head, recognizing his own words after Magan's officers had yanked his collar off at the top of the Revelation Spire. He suspected that Papizon was trying to exhibit a sense of humor, but the concept was clearly beyond the Councilman. The Islander took a deep breath and clamped the coin to the neckband of the evac suit.

It took a few seconds for the coin's subaether signals to lock on to the OCHREs floating in Quell's bloodstream. He heard a sudden mellifluous tone as the coin tested a number of different audio frequencies; the world was briefly covered with a thin gauze of red, then green, then blue. Finally the coin had fully hooked up to Quell's personal bio/logic systems. He could sense the vastness of the multi network surrounding him, penetrating the hull of the hoverbird, binding him to the connectibles' virtual expressway.

Quell blinked. The seat next to Rey Gonerev was no longer empty. Now it contained the calm figure of Magan Kai Lee.

There was no point in reaching for his pistol; black code darts would zip right through the man's virtual presence without effect. But Quell had to restrain himself from reaching for it anyway. He had already seen the lieutenant executive of the Defense and Wellness Council thrown off his game once; he wasn't likely to see it twice in his lifetime. Quell decided his best move at this point was to project an aura of serene confidence. He leaned back in his chair. "Whatever torture you've got in store for me, I can handle it."

The lieutenant executive displayed the trace of a smile. He looked almost childlike, seated in a chair designed for someone twice his size. "Oh, I'm certain of that," he said. "In fact, we're counting on it."

(((8)))

The delineation is as clear as anything in the world. Below, the ocean. Above, the sky. Dividing the two, the ever-so-slight parabola of the Earth's horizon.

Natch stands at the window of an observation tower in the suburbs of Angelos and watches that dividing line slowly devour the setting sun. It's a short tower, only three stories, and it's painted light peach like so much of the architecture out here. But the builders placed it at the end of a man-made promontory out into the ocean, so the view is impeccable. A smattering of lovers and tourists share the view with him from a distance just large enough that nobody can quite make out his face.

The gun Natch used to shoot Petrucio and Hiro is now floating out with the tide, where it will likely be netted by the local L-PRACG trashsweepers and then analyzed by the Defense and Wellness Council. Natch is unclear how long information about the gun's recent firing will survive in its memory banks, and whether that will be enough to trace it back to him. If the Council can indeed deduce that Natch used the weapon to make his escape, then Petrucio will be off the hook. Regardless, any such deduction is days away at the earliest.

The entrepreneur hadn't expected much in the way of gratitude, but Patel was still capable of surprising him. Not only had he given Natch a comradely pat on the shoulder as they left the hoverbird, but he had offered something much more valuable: a process for disabling his tremors and blackouts. Which, Petrucio had assured him, are caused by the code that provides backdoor access to MultiReal, and not by any Thasselian programming.

"This isn't a permanent cure, you understand," Patel had said. "There isn't one. You'll probably have to keep tweaking the code a few times a year for as long as you own the program. But if you follow these instructions, it should buy you two or three months."

Natch had stared at his throbbing left hand with a peculiar mixture of relief and apprehension. "But . . . how do you know about this?"

"Because Frederic and I had the tremors too, back when we had access to that security back door. So did Margaret. Manifests differently in everyone, of course. Frederic had a stutter, and I had a twitching eyelid. Margaret said it was one of the consequences of letting three-hundred-year-old code roam free in a modern OCHRE system."

The entrepreneur's jaw had dropped. "Three *hundred* years old?"

"That's what she said," Petrucio had continued with a dismissive hand gesture. "Who knows whether she was telling the truth. Who knows if she even *knew* the truth."

Natch recalls the specter of Margaret Surina he saw atop the Revelation Spire a few weeks ago. Only hours before her sudden and inexplicable suicide, if Brone's story could be believed. Her eyes were probing the walls for imaginary enemies, and her mind was a tattered remnant of what it used to be, barely cognizant of anyone or anything but Quell the Islander. The ultimate *consequence* of sixteen years of cohabitation with that MultiReal back door? He looks down at his own trembling hand again, product of a mere few months of exposure. It's plausible.

All he knows is that he does not want to end up like Margaret.

He wants to live.

The realization, only hours old, shows no signs of subsiding. It's a peculiar feeling. A feeling that makes his extremities quiver and his stomach hollow—not totally unlike the *want* that has powered him as long as he can remember—but this is a sensation that points outward to the world rather than curling in on itself.

Natch wants to live, but what irony that the world he wants to live in no longer exists.

Margaret had warned him of this. She had stood in front of a billion people and prophesied a world free from the tyranny of cause and effect.

What would our lives be like if we had made different choices? she had said. *In the Age of MultiReal, we will wonder no more—because we will be able to make* many *choices. We will be able to look back at checkpoints in our lives and take alternate paths. We will wander between alternate realities as our desires lead us. The ever-changing flux of MultiReal will become reality.*

But what are the terms and boundaries of this new reality that Natch has wandered into? Suddenly Frederic Patel can decapitate him with a samurai sword and he cannot, both at the same time. Brone can chase him through the ruins of Old Chicago and then forget. Memories can blur and devolve. Things can happen and then unhappen. In such a world, how can Natch trust that he is really standing here in an observation tower staring at the setting sun? Will that too be yanked away from him? Does anything in the universe in fact exist—or is existence itself only a temporary delusion, a momentary wave that can suddenly recede back into the nothingness without warning?

Natch shakes his head. Sophomoric speculation that belongs in the realm of the adolescent.

But. He has seen it. He has *lived* it.

If Natch can't trust the basest proposition that what happens, *happens* . . . what can he trust? Is there anything solid enough in this world for him to plant his feet on?

• • •

Petrucio had been kind enough to clear up one more discrepancy that had been troubling Natch since the dungeon in São Paulo. Namely, how the Patels had found a way to immunize themselves from the effects of MultiReal.

"A *trick?*" Natch had yelped in red-faced disbelief.

Petrucio had put an avuncular hand on the entrepreneur's

shoulder. "You think you're the only one who knows how to use social engineering to his advantage? Don't feel bad. There's no way you could have known that you weren't really interacting with me or Frederic in there. They were digitized projections. Remote-controlled puppets, more or less. We couldn't have actually walked into that room, or you would have used MultiReal to find the possibility where we freed you. We had to wait until you were convinced the program was useless."

In exchange for all of Petrucio's unexpected generosity, Natch had decided to reveal something of his own. "The MultiReal-D unhappening," he had said. "The rollback of memories. It's dangerous."

Petrucio had stroked his mustache in consternation. "How so?"

"Something's been happening to me ever since I left Old Chicago. I didn't have any explanation for it until you told me about MultiReal-D. I've got these . . . *blank* patches in my memory. Random things, just gone. Things that happened to me a long time ago, unrelated things. They just seem to have disappeared."

Patel had moved his hands from his mustache to his forehead, where he had begun rubbing firmly at his temple, as if trying to soothe away pain. "It's not an exact science, you know—erasing memories. I don't know how much you learned in the hive about how the brain stores memory. . . ."

"Not much. That was always Serr Vigal's line of study, not mine."

"It's incredibly complex. It's not like a recording that you can just rewind and erase. The brain stores bits and pieces all over the cerebral cortex, and it's not organized in any way that makes sense to you and me. So if you try to erase a memory of running through Old Chicago, and there's a calculation error—even a minuscule one—well, you might end up erasing a memory of running through the playground when you were a boy. Or you might forget the word *Chicago*. Crude examples, but you get the point. There's no way to know for sure." Petrucio had tossed one hand up in the air as if trying to discard the whole thing. "Guess that's why you build prototypes before you put code into production."

Natch had not been satisfied with this response. "But was this a problem with Margaret Surina's original code—or your implementation of it?"

"I don't know. Frederic and I only tested the 'unhappening' on very short spans of time. Seconds. A few minutes."

Natch had taken this information in with a solemn countenance. "I need one more thing from you, 'Trucio."

Patel had looked at him wordlessly.

"You need to tell me how to turn off this fucking MultiReal-D." And then, in answer to the question Petrucio had been about to ask: "Because it frightens me. I don't need it, I can take care of myself. What I need right now is solid ground underneath my feet. What I need is to know that what happens, happens."

He could tell that Petrucio did not understand, but Petrucio nodded in acquiescence anyway.

Brone would understand, Natch tells himself.

The notion startles him, but Natch instinctively recognizes it as truth. This is one situation where his friends would be of little help. Horvil would regard his predicament as an intricate maze to be woven through; Serr Vigal would float off into even further abstraction; Jara would chide him for engaging in useless mental masturbation. No, the only one who can really appreciate the paradoxes at play here is his old enemy, the man whom he maimed during the Shortest Initiation. Brone.

He wonders what Brone is doing right now. If Petrucio's theory is correct, and Brone did indeed try to kill Natch in Old Chicago, then MultiReal-D must have left him in an impotent rage. He would have discovered that Natch had somehow eluded him, despite all his precautions, but he would not remember any more of the details than Natch. Certainly he must have taken stock of the entrepreneur's disappearance and concluded that MultiReal had something to do with it. Perhaps he might have even connected it with Petrucio's black code dart at the Tul Jabbor Complex. What will he do now?

And what, for that matter, will Natch do?

Natch wants to live. He has the power of MultiReal at his command, the power that gives him mastery over cause and effect itself. He has no connections, no belongings, no ties, and no responsibilities. Yet the whole world is after him—businesses, governments, creeds, drudges, and practically everyone else. He has the power to go anywhere and the opportunity to go nowhere. Only twenty-four hours ago, such unencumbrance felt like the nothingness at the center of the universe. But now? What can he do in such a situation? What does he want to do with this new life in this new reality . . . ?

The honk of a seagull brings Natch's mind back down from the aether. The bird has perched on the windowsill right on the other side of the glass where it regards the entrepreneur curiously. Then it whizzes off, snatches a fish, and makes for the deeper water.

He turns back to contemplate the sunset. What was previously two isolated containers of clear blue and sea green has now become a jumble of improbable colors as the pigments of the sun dissolve in the deep. Delicate pinks and sturdy blues, concentrated yellows and bashful reds.

Natch stretches his arms, looks up to the stars that are just beginning to peek through the curtain of the day. Frederic's MultiReal-D demonstration triggered something inside of him. Natch has faced death. He has been through it and come out the other side.

Petrucio said he would have two to three months of clear, tremor-free existence once Natch follows his instructions. What can happen in two to three months? Anything can happen.

Anything.

2

A GAME OF CHESS

(((9)))

Jara's grandfather Herschel had been a small man. He had only stood a hundred and sixty centimeters tall, even if you measured from the soles of his feet to the peak of his mountainous hair. But he had died when Jara was still a year shy of puberty, so he had always seemed like a giant to her.

Few of his business colleagues had shared that estimation. Long-suffering Herschel had made a hardscrabble living as a freelance accountant, balancing (and occasionally cooking) books for the unscrupulous, for companies who wobbled on the brink for the entirety of their brief and miserable existences. The little man had done his job uncomplainingly if unenthusiastically.

But when he sat in front of a chessboard, the giant would emerge.

Jara had gotten her parents' permission to accompany Herschel to one of the grand tourneys on 49th Heaven when she was eight years old. Or, more accurately, she had stowed away on his hoverbird and Herschel had pretended not to discover her presence until it was too late to turn back. Watching her grandfather demolish players twice his size in match after match was one of the great memories of her childhood. He had never seemed to waver or lose his temper, no matter how far he had been pushed into a corner. More often than not, the retreat to the corner had been nothing more than a feint, a multidimensional strategy, and Jara would experience the extreme pleasure of seeing Herschel swoop out of nowhere and checkmate an opponent with a few deft moves. Witnessing the sudden transformation of smug and overconfident players into sweating nail-biters had been more of an education than anything in her hive curriculum. Jara's grandfather had emerged from that tournament among the top hundred players in the world, with a nice pot of winnings that he had quickly blown on gifts for friends and family.

Jara had asked what his secret was over breakfast one morning.

It's all a question of knowing what to sacrifice, Herschel had told her. *You know what I'm talking about?*

Jara had built up a reservoir of jam on one side of her plate, then carefully dunked a crepe into the deep end. *I guess. Is it like that saying where you lose the battle but win the war?*

Sure, her grandfather had replied. *Sometimes you've got to let the enemy take your knight in order to save your queen. But it's bigger than that. Sometimes you don't just have to lose the battle—sometimes you have to lose the whole war in order to get across the point you were trying to make in the first place. Y'know, Jar, sometimes you even have to give up the point you were trying to make if you want to win the biggest game of all.*

What's that?

Life. Herschel had stabbed his fork across the table and speared a chunk of jam-drenched crepe from Jara's plate, then popped it into his mouth with a wink and a smile.

The girl had solemnly chewed upon her grandfather's words for a while. *So how do you know when to win and when to lose?*

You just have to figure out what's important to you, Herschel had said. *Do that, and you're golden. Win, lose, it's all the same.*

Jara felt like this was a particularly apropos lesson for her to remember today, as she sat in the den of the official West London Grandmasters' League and watched some teenage girl parcel out her ass and hand it to her, move by move, piece by piece. Jara's bishops were the first to go, followed by both knights and then—agonizingly—her queen. Meanwhile, all she had managed to capture was a rook, a bishop, and a handful of pawns.

The fiefcorp master wasn't entirely sure why she had decided to join the Grandmasters' League in the first place. Like so many of the bizarre things she had tried lately—the visits to esoteric creeds, the sexual exploration on the Sigh, the excruciating sessions of "gong therapy"—this suggestion had come from her fellow fiefcorper Merri. The weeks on the Sigh hadn't turned out too well; Jara had almost succeeded in forgetting the name of the sandy-haired dimwit who had served as a Natch surrogate in her bed for a few weeks. She had decided that an intellectual challenge was more her speed, something that would keep her mind racing while at the same time distract her from the frustrations of the Surina/Natch MultiReal Fiefcorp.

So, chess.

Jara had begun two weeks ago a surprisingly lousy player. Apparently, skill in chess was neither genetic nor did it transfer by osmosis. She had endured humiliating defeat after humiliating defeat, trying to keep her grandfather Herschel's words close at hand.

You just have to figure out what's important to you. Do that, and you're golden. Win, lose, it's all the same.

Only now, two weeks into her chess odyssey, was Jara beginning to see the truth to that advice. The stringy-haired girl across the table was busy eliminating the last defenses around Jara's king. But suddenly the fiefcorp master noticed that her opponent was still zealously guarding her queen, beyond the point of good strategy or even rationality. This was something she could use in the future, and she would not have discovered it if she had managed to eke out a victory. This was her key to winning the next match with this young upstart, and the next one, and maybe the next one after that.

Jara handed over her king with a nod and a smile.

•   •   •

She left the clubhouse of the West London Grandmasters' League and quickly found herself surrounded by drudges, in much the same way her king had been surrounded on the chessboard by pawns.

"Towards Perfection!" said John Ridglee, merging smoothly into step beside the fiefcorp master. His fingers danced across a crisp black van dyke that might have taken him two hours to groom. "Nice day for a stroll, isn't it?"

"It was," replied Jara, eyeing Ridglee's competitor Sen Sivv Sor, who was flanking her other side. With his shock of white hair and angry red birthmark on his forehead, he might have been the yin to Ridglee's yang. *Or the Tweedledee to his Tweedledum*, thought Jara sourly.

"Interest you in a cup of chai?" said Sor.

"You're buying?" said Jara.

"Of course."

The fiefcorp master shrugged. "All right then."

There had to be some urgency to Ridglee and Sor's mission if it had inspired the hated rivals to join forces. A few scant weeks ago, she would have bolted at the sight of either one, possibly stopping to deliver a kick to the crotch first. There had been so many inquisitive media types hounding the fiefcorp then that Jara had been able to use them as a shield from the Defense and Wellness Council. But that was eons ago, back when the Surina/Natch MultiReal Fiefcorp was a real, functioning company. The drudge attention had all dissipated when Natch disappeared. Now she could stroll around London at her leisure without being accosted by a single frenzied drudge or menacing figure dressed in the white robe and yellow star.

Meanwhile, the company name had become something of a joke: Margaret Surina was dead, Natch had turned phantom, and MultiReal had evaporated with him. All the fiefcorp had left was a handful of bad bio/logic products they had purchased from Lucas Sentinel, and a lawsuit against them by the Surina family that was already growing so tangled and pointless it verged on the Kafkaesque.

Perhaps if both John Ridglee and Sen Sivv Sor were seeking her attention, there might be some news worth hearing. Maybe even some news about—

"Natch," said Ridglee five minutes later, sliding a steaming mug of chai across the table at the local pub.

Jara wafted the cinnamon towards her face and inhaled deeply. "What about him?"

"Have you seen him?"

"No. You?" The fiefcorp master lifted the mug with two hands and sipped delicately. "John, you asked me the same thing last week *and* the week before. What makes you think anything's changed?"

"Come on, Jara," said Sor, "we all know that Natch hasn't had an unchoreographed moment his whole life. You expect us to believe he *didn't* plan that circus at the Tul Jabbor Complex?"

Jara frowned. It was truly bizarre how much cachet Natch's name had acquired during his absence. It was only a month ago that drudges like Sor and Ridglee were ranting about Natch's shady business tactics and accusing him of murdering Margaret Surina. Now, it seemed, Natch had become some sort of demigod. Suddenly he was the man who had topped the Primo's bio/logic investment guide faster than anyone in history, the man who had taken on the Patel Brothers and the Defense and Wellness Council, the man who had shrugged off an assassination attempt by Len Borda and disappeared right under the noses of a billion spectators. The drudges were starting to spout phrases like *as cunning as Natch* and *a problem only Natch could solve*, which made Jara want to retch.

"Sen," said Jara, "you really think Natch planned that attack at the Tul Jabbor Complex? Boy, he must really be a masochist. Go ahead, tell me why he would *possibly* goad the Council into trying to murder him."

"*You* know why," said Ridglee, his voice hinting at a friendly familiarity that he and Jara didn't share.

The fiefcorp master caught the attention of the woman behind the counter, mouthed the word *scone*, and pointed to the tabletop. "No. In fact, I don't know why at all."

Sen Sivv Sor gave a furtive look around at the bar patrons who couldn't have been paying less attention. He opened a Confidential-Whisper channel. "*The lawsuit*," he said, using a melodramatic stage whisper even over silent mental chat.

Jara laughed, barely refraining herself from spraying the drudge with a mouthful of chai. "Suheil and Jayze Surina's lawsuit?" she said aloud, making no effort to modulate her voice. "Are you serious?"

"Absolutely," replied the drudge, unfazed by her ridicule.

"Sen, they just want *money*. You've met those two, haven't you? The only reason Jayze is trying to recover the funds that Margaret poured into the company is because she's vindictive. And Suheil is just playing along because he has no spine." The scone arrived. Jara smiled at the waitress and pointed in Sen Sivv Sor's direction to indicate that he'd be handling the bill. "Natch doesn't care about money. He wouldn't pay any attention to this dumb lawsuit, even if he was still running the company."

"Ah, but this lawsuit isn't really about money, is it?" interjected Ridglee, leaning forward over the table for emphasis. "It's about"—he repeated Sor's conspiratorial glance at the surrounds, and tried to switch the conversation back to ConfidentialWhisper—"*MultiReal*."

"We don't have access to MultiReal anymore," replied Jara in her natural voice, refusing to follow the drudge's lead. "Natch ran off with the databases. The Surinas know that, and so do you. Even if we *did* know where to find MultiReal, it's been seized by the Prime Committee." She dug into the pastry on the plate in front of her. Dry. Flaky. Good.

Ridglee and Sor shared a look that hinted at a list of confidential sources being exchanged and compared. As Jara polished off her scone, the knowing glimmer in their eyes only seemed to increase. The fief-corp master felt the first twitches of doubt.

"Try this on for size," said Ridglee over the silent channel, sitting back in his seat and folding his arms brashly across his chest. "Natch stages a disappearance at the Tul Jabbor Complex to draw Len Borda off his scent."

"To draw *everybody* off his scent," put in Sor.

"He lets the Surinas proceed with their trial and build up a big head of steam. He waits until they're at the very edge of victory. Then he shows up as a surprise witness after the Surinas have rested their case with a ton of exculpatory evidence. The court rules in the fiefcorp's favor, establishing a legal precedent. So when Magan Kai Lee finally overthrows Len Borda—"

Jara made a dismissive noise under her breath. "That's a big leap."

"—Natch is in a good position to appeal the Prime Committee's ruling. Once Borda's gone, the Committee won't be under the high executive's thumb anymore. They might reverse their decision to seize MultiReal. That leaves Natch as the sole supplier in the marketplace of MultiReal products." John Ridglee gave a self-satisfied nod in Sor's direction, which Sor echoed right back. "So what do you think?"

The fiefcorp master lifted her cup of chai and slurped the last few centimeters down. Then she placed the cup firmly on the table and stood. "I think you owe the pub twenty-five Vault credits," she said. "Towards Perfection, gentlemen."

●　●　●

"Do you want to know the most annoying part?" said Jara.

Horvil chose to ignore her and concentrate on his dive instead. He stood at the edge of the platform in a plaid robe, loosely sashed, with his hands over his head and fingertips pressed together. He counted to three and made a surprisingly graceful leap off the side. Jara propped herself up on one elbow and watched as Horvil did a pair of loop-de-loops through the air beneath the transparent platform. He landed on the opposite edge, did a tuck-and-roll, and flopped down beside her on the pile of cushions. "No," he said. "*What* is the most annoying part?"

Jara knew that the engineer was angling for a laugh, or at the very least, a playful look of exasperation. She gave him a half-smile instead and pressed on with the conversation. "It's the way the drudges treat Natch like some kind of miracle worker. When Natch was around, they couldn't stop pointing out what a monster he was. Now that he's gone, they fawn over him like he's Sheldon Surina."

Horvil grinned and lay back with his hands behind his head. "Natch *did* do a good job of manipulating everyone for a few months," he said.

"Of course. But the drudges can't even conceive of the idea that someone might have finally gotten the better of him. You should have heard Ridglee. *Natch stages a disappearance at the Tul Jabbor Complex to draw Len Borda off his scent.*" She puffed herself up and stroked an imaginary goatee in caricature. "Like Natch is capable of just snapping his fingers and rearranging the world."

The engineer shrugged and put one arm over her shoulder. Jara wondered fleetingly if she had offended him. Horvil wasn't the type to take offense easily—but then again, they were talking about Natch, his oldest and best friend. Even when Natch had threatened Horvil's career a month ago, Horvil had had nothing but excuses for the entrepreneur's behavior.

"Do you think that Ridglee and Sor might be on to something?" asked Horvil.

"Come *on*. Natch can't just stage manage Len Borda like—"

"No, no, forget about Natch for a second. I'm talking about the lawsuit. This isn't the first strange thing we've seen with this case."

"You mean the Pharisee?"

Horvil made a noncommittal sound, but Jara could tell she had struck home. She had only met two or three Pharisees her entire life, even through the whole MultiReal experience. But now some representative of the Pharisee tribes had evidently taken an interest in the case. He had attended every day of the preliminaries so far, sitting in the back of the chamber like a shaggy harbinger of doom. He was a bulky man, almost Horvilesque, this representative of the unconnectible tribes living beyond the edges of civilization. But unlike Horvil, who bore such an air of humor and civility that he threatened no one, this

Pharisee was a cipher. His body language betrayed nothing. He simply sat in his seat and stared for hours from beneath his tremendous curly hair and beard, tugging irritably at the connectible collar that the Prime Committee mandated he wear in public. It was unnerving.

"Yeah, there's the Pharisee," said Horvil. "But that's not the only odd thing about this lawsuit. Jayze and Suheil have been acting strange too. Did you see the way that their legal team suddenly doubled in size overnight?"

Jara nodded. "Then there are all those Council officers marching in front of the building day and night."

"Listen, Jara. Ridglee and Sor might be idiots—but you can't deny they've got sources. Lots of sources. They didn't come up with this idea on their own. *Somebody* put this bug in their ears."

"So what do you think is going on?"

Horvil had no answer.

The fiefcorp master lay back against Horvil's collarbone and tried to fit the pieces together in her head. Some of the oddity could be attributed to the aura of chaos that surrounded everything the Surina clan touched. Undoubtedly people were curious how Jayze and Suheil were going to run the family's affairs now that Margaret had passed on. People were curious how long their uneasy truce would hold. Yet that didn't explain the presence of factors beyond the Surinas' sphere of influence: the Council, the Pharisee, the drudges.

"It feels like I've stumbled into one of my grandfather's chess games," said Jara. "I'm standing there on the board watching the players execute all these complicated strategies. But I can't even figure out who's playing. There are higher powers out there trying to change the outcome of this stupid lawsuit. Why? For a pile of money and the title to a program that's technically already been seized by the government. So who are these higher powers? And should I be fighting them, or helping them?"

"There's only one thing to do," announced Horvil somberly.

"What's that?"

The engineer burst into a goofy grin. "Forget about it for another half hour, and spend more money on the Sigh." He flicked his fingers into the air, causing an enormous text box to appear before them. CHOOSE AN ENVIRONMENT, said the box. Horvil tapped the drop-down arrow, causing the list to scroll through thousands of absurdly named Sigh environments at ludicrous speed.

Jara suppressed a giggle. Only Horvil could find his libido roused by a discussion about chess. But maybe he was right; angsting about the problem without any data was only likely to produce more angst.

She turned her attention to the list of virtual environments. Remarkable how much fun the Sigh could be if you had a tender and creative partner. For Horvil and Jara, sex could be awkward in the world of flesh and bone. Even though the engineer had taken off almost ten kilograms in the past two months, he was still twice her size. But here on the Sigh, Jara could be a hundred meters tall if she wanted. She could be the pop star Jeannie Q. Christina or a porpoise or a swarm of bees, for that matter.

"How about this one?" said Jara, holding her finger over the list. "'Floating Tapestry of Love.'" The listing burst into mock Arabic script as she pointed to it.

"Hmm," replied Horvil. "I had my eye on 'A Rut in the Mud.'"

"Or maybe 'Romance in Durango.'"

"What about 'Fawning Slave Girls of the Sultan'?"

"'The Princess and Her Squire.'"

"'Contortionist Whores of 49th Heaven.'"

"'Aquatic Erotic Adventure.'"

"'Vat of Baked Beans.'"

"Horvil, we are *not* going to have sex in a virtual environment called 'Vat of Baked Beans.' It's just not going to happen."

"Okay, then what about 'Chocolate Waterfall' . . . ?"

In the end, they decided to do what they always did: let the shifting currents of the Data Sea choose an environment at random. They ended up floating on a cloud of metallic pixie dust while Valkyries did battle with tridents and spears all around them. No matter. Within seconds, their eyes were focused squarely on each other, and the outside world was safely forgotten.

(((10)))

At its essence, Jayze and Suheil Surina's complaint was an old and familiar one. Margaret Surina had given fifty percent of one of the family's greatest assets—MultiReal—to an outsider. But this outsider wasn't just anyone; he was Natch, one of the world's most notoriously Shylockian businessmen. Margaret had spent the next few weeks shedding her sanity like clothing on a hot day and then died under suspicious circumstances, leaving MultiReal in Natch's hands. Obviously, claimed the Surina family's lawyers, her agreement with Natch should be rendered null and void.

"Face it," Horvil had sulked after his first read-through of the complaint. "They've got a solid case."

"But not airtight," Jara had replied.

The complaint had been filed with Natch's freewheeling libertarian government in Shenandoah, where the judges were quite lax on matters of ceremony. It almost felt like you could stand up in court there and hash through disagreements in plain speech like civilized human beings. The judges felt more like friendly arbitrators than grim custodians of the distant and impersonal Law.

But the fiefcorp quickly lost the battle for jurisdiction soon after Jara's run-in with the drudges. "Why try the case here in Shenandoah when Natch is nowhere to be found?" Suheil and Jayze's attorneys argued. "Nobody else in the courtroom has any connection to this city." Jara grudgingly admitted they were right, and unfortunately, Natch's L-PRACG agreed too. So the case migrated from Shenandoah to the Surina family's pet government in Andra Pradesh. Jara and Horvil temporarily put all other fiefcorp business on hold so they could travel to Andra Pradesh and get this lawsuit out of the way.

It soon became apparent that the courts in Andra Pradesh were not like those in Shenandoah. Horvil and Jara had to endure endless debate about trifling matters of ritual, like whether the plaintiffs should sit on the left side as customary in Western courtrooms or on the right as customary in modern Indian courtrooms; like whether they should impose a cutoff on the number of drudges allowed to view the proceedings; like whether the court should follow the Pevertz-Laubumi Disambiguation Procedure, which required witnesses to parse their sentences in three different ways to avoid any possibility of misunderstanding. It all felt like a transparent ploy by the Surinas to keep the lawyers jawing as long as possible and exhaust the fiefcorp's legal defense fund.

Jara felt like she should bring this up with Martika Korella, their attorney. But she soon decided that she trusted the woman about as much as she trusted an Autonomous Mind. In short, not at all.

It wasn't that Korella was incompetent. On the contrary, multiple sources had recommended her as a woman of principle, fierce intelligence, and thorough familiarity with the idiosyncrasies of the Indian legal system. In the days leading up to the trial, Korella had assured them this was a winnable case and seemed to be preparing a cogent defense. Then one morning she had appeared in court with the look of a woman who had not only seen a ghost but had invited that ghost for tea and chatted with it about the weather. Korella's enthusiasm for the case had simply dried up overnight.

"I don't know how to explain it," Jara told Horvil. "It's like she knows she's in a fixed fight."

"So shouldn't we fire her?" the engineer replied.

"Well, the thing is . . . I think the fight might be fixed *in our favor*. I can't tell. Besides, if someone can get to *her*, they'll get to anyone we hire to replace her."

Fixed or not, Suheil and Jayze Surina didn't look too happy with the state of things in the courtroom either, but those might simply have been their natural dispositions.

Suheil, dour and dim-witted in the best of circumstances, had been

advised by his handlers to avoid the courtroom. His temper was legendary throughout the Indian subcontinent, and he appeared to be
congenitally unable to talk in a low tone of voice. He followed his handlers' advice most of the time and kept to the hallways, glowering at
passersby and kicking things. Jara thought he looked like a troll.

But Jayze had been given no such counsel. She lorded over the
plaintiffs' wing of the courtroom like a petty despot, making imperious
gestures to her aides for glasses of water throughout the day. Her retinue seemed only too eager to appease her. She bore an uncanny resemblance to her second cousin Margaret, which made it difficult for Jara
to watch her. With her precise mannerisms, her wide blue eyes, and her
limp black hair, Jayze Surina might have been Margaret's evil twin.

Things only deteriorated once the testimony began. Jara found
herself stewing for hours in her seat at the unfairness of it all.

The core of Jayze and Suheil Surina's argument was that Margaret
had shown signs of mental instability long before she had signed a deal
to hand day-to-day operations of the company over to Natch. Therefore, the bodhisattva had clearly not been of sound mind when she
made the agreement.

The prime piece of evidence? The agreement itself.

"It's absolutely not legitimate business practice," scoffed a leading
economic scholar on the stand to the plaintiffs' attorney. "Just handing
over fifty percent of a company with four hundred years of name recognition to a complete stranger? I can't think of a single precedent for
that kind of behavior."

"Not one," parroted the attorney.

"It doesn't sound like an agreement that anybody would sign if
they were in their right mind, does it?"

"No, it doesn't to me either."

Jayze and Suheil's attorneys did not stop at impugning Margaret's
business sense. A parade of Surina family retainers made their way to
the stand to testify about her bizarre behavior for the whole of the last

decade. One of the minor bodhisattvas at Creed Surina complained about how Margaret had paused during a major speech to the devotees and simply walked offstage without explanation, midsentence. Aides detailed how she would send them on inexplicable and sometimes contradictory errands at all hours of the night. Professors divulged how she had gone from being a merely odd steward of the Gandhi University to a strangely self-destructive one.

On and on the testimony went. Jara could sense the scales of justice tilting in Suheil and Jayze's favor with every nugget of irresponsibility and irrationality the witnesses piled on. "Do you think Jayze and Suheil are paying these people to perjure themselves?" she asked Horvil.

"You mean, have they been bribed?"

"Yeah."

The engineer scowled and shook his head. "Why would you *need* to bribe them? Margaret never explained herself to anybody. She must have made a million enemies."

Jara recalled her own interactions with the bodhisattva. As far as she could remember, she had only met the woman twice. She had sat in a conference room and watched Margaret trade bon mots with Natch as if they were reciting lines from Oscar Wilde. And a few days later, she had argued with Margaret about Natch's disappearance, causing Margaret to pull out a dartgun and retreat to the top of her skyscraper. Ten, fifteen minutes of interaction at most. Could Jara herself vouch that the last heir of Sheldon, Prengal, and Marcus Surina had been of compos mentis when she signed that deal with Natch?

As the crazy proceedings went on and the case tilted farther and farther in the Surinas' direction, the unnamed Pharisee sat in the back row, day after day, watching the proceedings with grave interest. He spoke to no one that Jara could see. Whether he even comprehended what was going on was unclear.

Meanwhile, in the outside world, tensions between Len Borda and

Magan Kai Lee were mounting by the day. For the most part, the two factions of Council officers tried to show a unified face to the public during routine security operations. But once a week, it seemed, some turf battle would spontaneously erupt, leaving handfuls of dead or incapacitated Council officers to litter the streets. The Islanders only made things worse by executing random strikes here and there that did not appear to be targeting either side.

And as the fighting intensified, Margaret Surina's murder remained unsolved and the infoquakes continued, leaving occasional reminders of civilization's fragility in the face of the brutal unknown.

• • •

Jara didn't expect anyone to show up early to the fiefcorp meeting on the day before the plaintiffs were supposed to rest their case. Since the company had purchased a slate of second-rate programs from Lucas Sentinel and gone on autopilot to deal with the Surina family's lawsuit, nobody seemed particularly enthusiastic about attending these meetings. Benyamin and Merri had retreated into their respective creed activities; Serr Vigal had retreated to his ailing neural programming company; and Robby Robby was presumably focusing on sales partners with more lucrative products.

But when Jara made her way through the Surina Enterprise Facility at Andra Pradesh and entered the company's designated conference room, she found Horvil and Robby there five minutes early and deep in discussion. The engineer had arrived first in the conference room and selected what looked like the inside of an internal combustion engine for SeeNaRee. Jara hoped this meeting ran short; the clanking of gears and pumping of pistons would surely give her a headache if she spent more than twenty minutes here.

"I was telling Horvil about the new MindSpace extensions coming out next year," beamed Robby Robby. With his blue vinyl trench coat, thick mustache, and shaved head, the channeler was so up-to-the-minute that he risked overtaking the present and slipping into the future at any moment. "Did you realize you'll be able to work on three levels of data at once with the new H-bar? Assembly-line shops are gonna be a thing of the past, Queen Jara!"

"Fascinating," said Horvil, meaning it. Only a sharp look from Jara prevented him from drifting off into a haze of engineering-speak.

Serr Vigal multied into the room a few minutes after the designated meeting start time, looking haggard and depressed. "Towards Perfection," said the neural programmer to nobody in particular, taking the seat at the far end of the table in the shadow of an enormous metal lever. Jara felt sorry for him. Vigal's speech before the Prime Committee two months ago had energized and enlivened him; but then Natch had disappeared, leaving him with the realization that he had much less influence on his former charge than he had thought. Jara felt like offering Vigal a consoling word or two, but she could think of nothing consoling to say.

Merri and Benyamin arrived together less than a minute later. "Sorry we're late!" said Ben, taking a seat next to his cousin Horvil. "Creed business. Merri can vouch for me. Élan and Objectivv are actually planning a group convocation later this month."

"Fascinating," said Horvil, not meaning it.

Jara didn't really care why they were late, now that the two of them were here to take her mind off Horvil's engineering patter and Vigal's glumness. "We ready to get started?" she said, forming a prim, businesslike pyramid on the table with her fingertips.

"Ready when you are!" chirped Robby.

The fiefcorp master stifled a grimace at the channeler's oppressive buoyancy. "Should we begin with a look at the latest sales figures? Merri?"

The blond channel manager pointed to the center of the tabletop and summoned a pentagram of virtual sales charts. It was a sobering sight. In contrast to their old sales charts, which usually showed lines in hot competition to climb to the peak of the y-axis, these charts were as flat as Midwestern prairie. It didn't help that the programs bore such mind-warpingly dull titles as Eyelash Kurler 23 and Cuticle Manager 46c.

"I wish I could offer an explanation for all this, but I can't," said Merri with a weariness that went beyond moribund sales figures. Jara suspected some fresh health crisis with Merri's companion Bonneth, but she had no desire to press for details.

"Aw, it's not that bad," said Robby Robby, without any evidence to back him up.

"I've got a perfect explanation," said Horvil. "This code sucks. I don't know how Sentinel made a single Vault credit off these programs. I mean, look at this one." He pointed to a red line labeled Y NOT DITCH THE ITCH 18, which was actually sloping into negative territory. "That piece of shit doesn't even 'ditch the itch.' It just makes you scratch somewhere else."

Jara gave the engineer a sympathetic sigh. "It's a start, Horv. Something to build on."

Horvil made a droll farting noise and turned his attention to the steaming SeeNaRee valves hanging from the ceiling a few meters up. "Whatever."

"Come on, you'll get these programs fixed up in no time," said Jara. "You've cleaned up far worse."

"I've seen it," said Robby.

"I suppose," replied the engineer with a frown. "It's just . . . *difficult*, that's all. Two months ago, we were going to change the world. Now we're managing cuticles."

Nobody could argue with that. There was a full minute of silence as Jara tried in vain to think of some way to lift the company's spirits.

"So . . . any encouraging news from the trial?" asked Vigal in a halfhearted attempt to change the subject.

Jara attempted to put a positive spin on the morning's news: Martika Korella had finally persuaded the court to jettison the Pevertz-Laubumi Disambiguation Procedure. This would not change the parameters of the case, but at the very least, it wasn't *bad* news, and therefore worthy of mention in Jara's eyes.

Ben's face curdled with every additional syllable she uttered on the subject. "I can't believe we're still arguing about this crap," he moaned. "It's like a whole separate meta-lawsuit about the lawsuit. I don't understand why we can't all just pick some ground rules and get *on* with it already."

"It's a matter of posturing," explained Merri. "That's what Martika says, anyway. Here in Andra Pradesh, you need to demonstrate to the judges that you've got confidence in your case, or they'll think you're capitulating."

Benyamin threw his hands up in the air. "Who cares? This isn't a popularity contest. This is about the *law*. Why can't we concentrate on the *substance* of the issue instead of all these stupid perceptions?"

Horvil reached over and patted Benyamin on the head. "Welcome to life," he said.

Jara could tell that the young apprentice was about to launch into another sullen tirade, which would likely spark another round of bitterness and recrimination. Jara pinched the skin over the bridge of her nose tightly in frustration. The fiefcorp was already being hampered by a lousy product base and an all-consuming lawsuit; this low-level bickering only made things worse.

But Jara was spared the chore of dealing with angry fiefcorp members by an unexpected request to enter the conference room. She waved her hand, and seconds later the door opened to reveal Martika Korella.

Even in these days of cheap chromosomal manipulation, Martika was a genetic oddity: a red-headed woman of Asian descent who stood over two meters tall. She would be an imposing presence in any courtroom, and had been quite intimidating here in Andra Pradesh until her sudden and unexplained attitude shift. But this morning Korella seemed to have experienced another abrupt turnaround in the other direction, for she was back to her old self. Composed, unflappable, in the know.

"Good news," said the attorney, pulling up a seat at the opposite end of the table from Jara and crossing her legs. "We've got a settlement offer."

"That *is* good news," said Benyamin, ready to reconsider his opinion of Korella's legal acumen on the spot.

Merri nodded. "It would be nice to get this whole lawsuit behind us." She gestured towards the sales charts still insulting them in full holographic color from the center of the table. "It's already been too much of a disruption." Horvil, Vigal, and Robby were all projecting various expressions of agreement.

But Jara could feel her hackles rising. There it was, that inexplicable smell of *oddness* that surrounded this entire case. "This is kind of . . . unexpected, isn't it?"

"Very unexpected," agreed Martika, twirling her fingers idly in her hair. "The Surinas are all set to rest their case. As far as I can tell, they've got two of the three judges completely convinced, and the third one's leaning their way too."

"So why would they offer us a settlement now?" said Jara.

Martika shook her head. "You've heard the expression *Nothing's perpendicular in Andra Pradesh?*" she said. "Strange things happen in this city. Sometimes it's best not to ask too many questions, and just take the hand you're given."

All of the fiefcorpers could sense Jara's discontent by now. They chose to give her a wide berth and wait to hear what she had to say.

"I suppose it all depends what the settlement's like," said Jara. "So what are they offering? A pittance?"

"No, actually." Martika waved her hand over the table, causing the sales charts to shrink into a far corner and a new set of spreadsheets to come to the fore. She pointed to the bold-faced numbers at the bottom, causing them to turn red and pop forward. "That's a very good number. Considering the legal fees you've spent already, this isn't actually much less than you'd wind up with if we won the case outright."

Jara frowned and tapped her fingers on the tabletop. "What about the intellectual property?"

"The Surinas would get control of that."

"You mean MultiReal?" said Ben.

"I mean MultiReal. But you've said it yourself, Jara—in all likelihood, the intellectual property's worthless. The MultiReal databases have vanished, and anyone who gets hold of them is obligated to cede them over to the Prime Committee anyway." The attorney clenched one fist, causing the settlement spreadsheets to shrink back into nothingness and the dismal sales charts to take their place. "I have to be honest here, Jara. We could still end up swaying all three of the judges to our side. They could award us damages and legal fees. But . . ." Martika shifted in her seat uncomfortably. "I don't think that's likely to happen."

Horvil looked sheepishly in Jara's direction. "You've heard the expression *Take the money and run . . . ?*"

But that was precisely the problem. Jara knew she had little to lose in accepting this settlement offer. Jayze and Suheil would recover a large piece of a fund that would likely be spent on legal fees anyway, and they would get the rights to a program that Jara didn't even possess. The company could finally sever the chains binding them to the past and chart a new course into the future. Heck, she could see herself paying the sum at the bottom of that spreadsheet just to avoid looking at Jayze and Suheil's smarmy faces again.

It was, in fact, such a plum offer that Jara knew she had to refuse it.

Why would Jayze and Suheil suddenly decide to hedge their bets, a scant few days before the Andra Pradeshian judges were likely to rule in their favor? It ran contrary to every personality trait Jara knew about them. She would have expected the two to pursue their lawsuit until they had drained every last Vault credit in the Surina/Natch MultiReal Fiefcorp's account, if only just to spite their dead cousin.

Had John Ridglee and Sen Sivv Sor been correct? Were the Surinas scared? Did they suspect that Natch was about to show up and testify against them?

Jara scanned the table at the faces of the fiefcorpers. Horvil looked ready to abide by any decision Jara made; Vigal seemed to care little about this case one way or another; Merri was ready to put this entire distasteful MultiReal business behind her; Benyamin had the hard-nosed expression of a man who knew a good deal when he saw one; and Robby Robby's veneer of optimism showed no signs of cracking.

The fiefcorp master remembered her grandfather's words: *You just have to figure out what's important to you. Do that, and you're golden. Win, lose, it's all the same.* Sage advice indeed. The outcome of this trial was inconsequential. What mattered was finding out who was behind this desperate shift in strategy, what was causing the entire stink of peculiarity emanating from this case. Until Jara knew that, she would feel no satisfaction, and the fiefcorp would not be able to move on.

It was time to stir things up. It was time to find out who was pulling the strings.

"I'm sorry, Martika," said Jara. "You tell Suheil and Jayze that we're not interested. No, better yet—you tell them these exact words: *Fuck no.*"

(((| |)))

Jara expected to dream of chess that night. She dropped off to sleep with the foolish hope that such a dream might give her some kind of subconscious insight into the identities of the players who had put this game in motion. But instead of chess, she found herself fleeing across a spare, storm-thrashed plain while forces unknown conducted a battle of forked lightning above the clouds. Jara was only one of hundreds running for shelter. Every time she turned to ask someone what was going on, she would find that person engulfed in lethal electricity and then charred to ash.

The fiefcorp master awoke before dawn and broke her fast in the nitro bar across the street from the hotel where she and Horvil were staying. After perusing the news (more Council clashes, TubeCo labor disputes, a baffling dip in the criminal black code traffic on 49th Heaven), Jara woke the engineer up and they prepped themselves for another day in court. She put on her nicest pantsuit, while Horvil splurged on an expensive bio/logic musk for no apparent reason.

"Something's different today," said Jara as they left the hotel.

"Like what?" said Horvil, sniffing absently at his wrist.

"I don't—I don't know."

She remembered Natch making bizarre pronouncements like this when he was in charge of the fiefcorp, and she remembered equally well her disdainful reactions to them. How could you *feel* what the markets were going to do? Why pay heed to a sudden intuition with no logical underpinnings?

And now Jara was experiencing this oracular sixth sense herself. It defied explanation. There were too many officers in the white robe and yellow star on the streets of Andra Pradesh, and they were distributed in a little too random a fashion. Pedestrians seemed to scoot out of the paths of the tube trains at just the right instant, as if performing an intricate choreographed dance. The sun peeked out from behind the morning clouds and bathed the courthouse in its yellow rays right as Jara rounded the corner. . . .

The fiefcorp master stopped, grabbed Horvil by the elbow. "Wait a second."

Horvil gave her a perplexed look. "What?"

"Martika's expecting the Surinas to rest their case this morning, right?"

"Right."

"If Natch *does* show up as a surprise witness, like John Ridglee thought—wouldn't today be the day he's going to do it?" The fiefcorp master pointed ever so slightly in the direction of three Council officers lounging on the opposite corner. They appeared to be on high alert, though given the hostility between Len Borda and Magan Kai Lee, that was hardly surprising. "And if Ridglee knows that Natch is planning to show up here today, isn't it possible that word might have leaked to the Council too?"

"I suppose," admitted Horvil dubiously.

"Can you do me a favor?" asked Jara, taking the engineer's left hand between two of hers. "It's just a hunch. But can you talk to your Aunt Berilla, see if she'll send a few of those Creed Élan security people here? You know, the ones that bailed us out of the Tul Jabbor Complex?"

She could tell that Horvil was holding an internal debate about whether to resist her request, or at least ask for a better rationale. But after a few seconds of hesitation, he pursed his lips, stepped over to the shade of a tenement building, and slipped into a ConfidentialWhisper conversation. Five minutes later, he was back. "It wasn't easy," said Horvil, "but they'll be here within an hour."

"Thanks, Horv."

The two made their way across the street to the courthouse. It was practically a cathedral of Surina family worship, tall and gothic in design with an imposing statue of Sheldon Surina himself standing watch over the entrance. Horvil and Jara entered the building and found their way to the main courtroom. With its multiple balconies and seating for nearly two hundred, it looked more suitable for an opera than a legal hearing. Jara half expected to see a gaudy wrought-iron chandelier hanging from the ceiling.

Horvil and Jara took their seats at the defense table alongside an obviously peeved Martika Korella. She grunted a terse "Perfection" their way before burying her nose in a document projected on the tabletop. It was doubtful that Merri, Benyamin, or Vigal would show up today, which left the three of them to confront the small battalion of lawyers and Surina family attendants sitting with Suheil and Jayze at the plaintiffs' table. Horvil offered the Surinas a good-morning smile. Jayze pointedly ignored him, while Suheil responded with an ill-humored grimace you might expect from the villain in a Juan Nguyen drama.

Jara turned around and scanned the scores of people who had come to watch the proceedings. There seemed to be more drudges than usual—including the uncharacteristically quiet pair of John Ridglee and Sen Sivv Sor, seated in a prime spot at the front of the drudges' gallery. She looked for some sign of Natch. If not the man himself, then perhaps a token of the unusual: someone dressed in an inappropriate fashion, someone paying too much attention to something that deserved no such attention. Jara could detect no trace of Natch, but she did see the black-robed and bejeweled Pharisee. Every day since the judges had gaveled the trial to order, he had sat in the last row bothering nobody. But today, he was not only looking Jara's way; he was striding towards her through the aisle with a determined gleam in his eye.

Jara looked down to the ground and felt her teeth start to chatter. "Horv . . ." she started.

"I see, I see," muttered the engineer. She could see his knuckles whiten as he gripped the table harder.

Jara wasn't sure why she felt so frightened. Despite the Pharisee's size, she would be hard-pressed to describe him as *menacing*. Nor was he particularly unkempt, defying the stereotype. What looked like a wild lion's mane of hair from a distance turned out to be neatly braided and ornamented as he got closer. Part of the oddity of his appearance had to do with his connectible collar, which he wore with more awkwardness than any Islander Jara had ever seen.

So he wasn't quite the intimidating figure she had imagined—but that didn't mean Jara had any desire to see him any closer. Where were those Creed Élan security people already?

The Pharisee was only about ten meters away when his purposeful stride was interrupted by the arrival of the judges. The three of them walked in from the street entrance, as was customary in modern Indian courtrooms, causing the assembled crowd to rise and clear a path. The unconnectible giant took his cue from the crowd and stepped out of the aisle. Jara slowly exhaled with relief.

Things quickly settled down as the two women and a man reached the judges' rostrum and gaveled the proceedings to order. Jara took another furtive look at the audience for a sign of Natch. If he was going to appear, it would likely be in the next twenty minutes, after the Surina family rested its case. Still she saw nothing. At least the Pharisee had decided to stay put and not make any more advances towards the defendants' table.

The Surina lawyers went through fifteen minutes of procedural minutiae—in Andra Pradesh, there was *always* room for more procedural minutiae—before the judges called on Jayze and Suheil's lead attorney.

"How stands your case?" asked the senior judge, the traditional prelude to the announcement that one side would rest.

The attorney puffed himself up with self-importance. "If it please the court, we would like to call one more witness to the stand. A witness we had been unable to locate until this morning."

Jara darted a bewildered look at John Ridglee and Sen Sivv Sor. Wasn't it *their* side that was supposed to be calling the surprise witness? But the pair looked just as nonplussed as she felt.

"Call your witness," replied the senior judge.

"The Surina family trusts would like to call the former head of Andra Pradesh security and the former chief engineer for the Surina Perfection Memecorp," said the attorney. "Quell of the Pacific Islands."

• • •

The courtroom imploded into stunned silence. The last the world had seen of Quell, he was being dragged by Defense and Wellness Council officers from the Revelation Spire, presumably on suspicion of murdering Margaret Surina herself. The Council had released no information about his status since, despite repeated inquiries from the drudge sector.

Jara allowed herself to feel a quiet burst of hope. If Quell was no longer languishing in an orbital prison cell, did that mean Len Borda had released him? Surely now that he was standing here before an impartial court of law, he would be free to dispel all of this nonsense about Margaret being the deranged victim of Natch's manipulation.

But then why was he testifying for Jayze and Suheil Surina? And why was Martika Korella letting out a long, ragged sigh of discouragement?

Quell walked into the courtroom dressed in a stylish pinstriped suit with his long ponytail impeccably trimmed. Jara was used to seeing him as a barely repressed force of nature that might spill into savagery at any minute, a man who tolerated the silliness of connectible culture only because he did so on his own terms. But today the Islander looked as civilized as any midrange capitalman. His demeanor was calm, almost studious. If he noticed the mistrustful murmurs of the audience and the leering looks of the drudges, he made no sign.

Horvil threw an unabashed grin in the Islander's direction as he passed. Quell's eyes ran right over the engineer as if he were simply another bystander.

"It's not turned on," said Horvil to Jara over ConfidentialWhisper.

"What are you talking about?" she replied in kind. "*What's* not turned on?"

"His connectible collar."

The fiefcorp master looked at the copper band around Quell's neck, half concealed by the collar of his suit. "How can you tell?"

"The interior usually gives off a really faint glow. You can see it in the shadows. But not this one. He's just wearing it for show." Horvil made a subtle pointing gesture towards his heart. "He's using one of those coins."

Jara squinted and noticed the glint from a tiny disc-shaped receiver stuck on the Islander's breast. Horvil was correct. She didn't know why any of this was pertinent to the court case at hand, but she duly filed it away for future reference.

By this time, Quell had mounted the steps leading to the witness stand. He stood and placed his hands flat on the podium in the traditional witness pose. His eyes were not focused on either the plaintiffs' or the defendants' tables, but rather on some nebulous spot in the air before him.

Suheil and Jayze Surina were grinning like jackals.

And they had good reason. For as soon as Quell opened his mouth, he began to demolish the Surina/Natch MultiReal Fiefcorp's defense in a very thorough and methodical fashion. Jara and Horvil could do little but gape in disbelief.

The Surina lawyers started by establishing that Quell knew Margaret better than anyone in the world—better, even, than Suheil and Jayze themselves. "How long did you know Margaret Surina?" asked the lead attorney, a short man with a defiant attitude and enormous eyebrows.

"About forty years," replied the Islander, without inflection.

"Before she was the bodhisattva of Creed Surina?"

"Yes."

"Before she founded the Surina Perfection Memecorp?"

A knowing sniff. "The memecorp was my idea to begin with. I was in the room when she asked High Executive Borda for start-up capital."

The attorney nodded. "So you knew Margaret Surina before she was the honorary chair of the Gandhi University?"

"Yes. I met her before she was the head of anything. When she was a *student* at the Gandhi University." Clearly Quell was beginning to find the lawyer's methodical method of questioning tiresome.

"How old was Margaret when you met her?"

"She was sixteen."

"So it's safe to say that you've known Margaret Surina since the beginning."

"Of *course*," groused the Islander. "Weren't you listening to anything I just said?"

Jara couldn't help but break out in a smile. *At least we know he hasn't been brainwashed by some Council black code*, she thought.

After demonstrating the length of Quell's acquaintance with the late bodhisattva, the Surina attorneys quickly worked to dispel any taint of his arrest and any suspicion of his involvement in Margaret's death. "Nobody even accused me of hurting Margaret," said the Islander, sounding affronted at the very suggestion. "I would never have hurt her."

"So you were arrested for assaulting a Council officer, isn't that correct?" said the lawyer.

"No," replied Quell. "I was arrested for assaulting *twelve* of them."

Someone in the audience whistled. The judges quickly gaveled for silence.

"And what happened?" continued the lawyer.

"They lived. They all recovered. I served my time."

The Surinas' attorney made a show of entering a beacon into the court record that led to the official Defense and Wellness Council sentencing report. Jara scrutinized it briefly and saw mention of a military trial and a two-month sentence. It seemed legitimate. She didn't need to run a Zeitgeist program to see that the audience and the judges bought his story too. The atmosphere in the courtroom visibly relaxed.

The courtroom's suspicion of murder dealt with, the Surina team began laying down a pattern of the Islander's continued involvement in her life. When Margaret had begun work on her Phoenix Project, Quell had been there. When she had engaged in her quixotic purge of the faculty at the Gandhi University, Quell had offered her advice. When she had taken each of her several public tours of the Pacific Islands, Quell had acted as chaperone. And when their work on Multi-Real had begun to achieve a critical mass, when High Executive Len Borda had begun stepping up his campaign of fear and intimidation against Andra Pradesh, it was Quell who had suggested a partnership with a private fiefcorp.

Jara felt a keen sense of embarrassment that she knew so little of this history herself. How long had the Islander been an active member of the Surina/Natch MultiReal Fiefcorp—five weeks? Longer? Yes, they had all been distracted by Natch's cat-and-mouse game with Magan Kai Lee and the attention of the drudges. But couldn't she have spared an hour to find out more about Quell's background and his connection to Margaret?

Yet despite all these new details to fill the gaps in the Islander's life story, Jara was nagged by the feeling that she still didn't know all the pertinent facts. Some crucial aspect to the story was missing. Why had Quell done all these things for Margaret over the years? What was an Islander doing living in Andra Pradesh in the first place? Who was he *really* working for? Whose side was Quell on?

The fiefcorp master shook her head and turned her attention back to the trial, where Jayze and Suheil's legal team was using Quell to insinuate that Margaret had suffered a massive mental breakdown in her final months.

"When did you first see signs of the bodhisattva's unusual behavior?" asked one of the junior attorneys.

"I'd say about five years ago," said Quell, eyes downcast as if scanning through old memory. "She started having these—*episodes*, I guess you'd call them."

"Episodes?"

"She'd blank out. Stare straight ahead for ten, fifteen minutes at a stretch. You'd try to say something to her, and she wouldn't answer. Like she couldn't hear you. I had to . . . watch out for her when she went into the world. Make sure she didn't black out in public or fall down and embarrass herself."

"And this had an effect on her work?"

The Islander shifted from foot to foot, looking thoroughly uncomfortable. "Definitely. She started going off on tangents. Connecting things in the bio/logic code that didn't make any sense. Keeping things from me. Just like in her personal life, I'd have to run around behind the scenes and clean up after her. It started taking more and more of my time."

"But Margaret thought she had come up with a solution, didn't she?"

"Yes. Natch." The Islander managed to make the slightest of gestures towards the defense side of the courtroom without actually looking in that direction. "After one meeting with him, she decided that he could solve all her problems. Overnight. She stopped paying attention to the coding and handed everything to Natch."

"And Natch took advantage of this."

"Of course he did. You've heard the stories about him, haven't you?" A knowing murmur made its way around the courtroom, even through the judges' table, to Jara's horror. Martika half raised her hand as if about to make an objection—the first time she had done anything substantive besides stare at the table since Quell had taken the stand. But evidently she thought better of it and put her hand back in her lap. "Natch pounced on her," Quell continued with some bitterness. "Margaret had just unveiled the Phoenix Project before the world. The first infoquake had just struck, people were dying left and right. And there's Natch, in her office at the top of the Revelation Spire, insisting that she sign over ownership of the program to him. Insisting that she wasn't capable of dealing with Len Borda. Margaret—she was so bewildered by all the death and all the chaos, she didn't know how to handle it. She could barely keep up with him. It was all she could do to just throw the whole MultiReal project in Natch's lap."

Jara felt the ping of a ConfidentialWhisper request. "He's lying," said Horvil, confused. "Why the heck is he lying?"

She didn't know. All she knew was that, by the looks on the faces of the drudges, of Suheil and Jayze Surina, of the judges, of Martika Korella, the fiefcorp had just lost its case. Jara turned to the engineer with her forehead buried in her palm. "Check and mate," she said with a sigh.

(((12)))

Jara didn't give herself any time for self-loathing. No sooner had the Islander left the stand, as strangely unemotional as he had arrived, than she was pinging Horvil again over ConfidentialWhisper. "We've got to follow him," she said. "I need to know what would cause him to lie. To *turn* on us like that."

The engineer gave her a look that said he had concluded the same thing. "You think he was bribed? Or threatened?"

Jara snorted. "I'd like to see the person capable of bribing or threatening Quell."

"What about the Council?"

"You mean the people Quell tried to beat to a pulp with an electrified stick?"

Horvil tried to restrain a laugh, failed. "Good point. But we've got a problem. There's still an hour of courtroom bullshit to deal with." He shifted his eyes in the direction of their attorney. "We can't exactly jump up and run after him."

Jara glanced at Martika, who was listlessly shuffling virtual papers around on the tabletop like a hive child pretending to be studying. Had she known about Quell's testimony ahead of time? Jara wished she had taken note of the lawyer's reaction when the Islander had walked into the room, but the thought hadn't occurred to her. Somehow she sensed that Martika's awareness of the hidden machinations in this case was much more nebulous than that. A warning from a colleague, perhaps, or veiled threats from a third party. Council troops parading loudly past her windows in the infant hours of morning.

Horvil cleared his throat. "Any ideas . . . ?" he said on the silent channel.

Jara turned and saw that the Islander had nearly made his way out the main doors of the courtroom. She felt an awful premonition that she would never see him again. Judging by Martika's grim demeanor, the lawyer saw little hope in achieving much through cross-examination. And outside of this trial, was there anything tying Quell to connectible civilization? MultiReal had vanished, Margaret was dead, and Jara couldn't imagine that the remaining Surinas bore a great fondness for him, today's testimony notwithstanding. Yes, it was entirely possible that Quell would disappear back to the Islands for good—assuming there wasn't a Council hoverbird waiting outside the courthouse to return him to prison.

Jara had a sudden inspiration. "The Creed Élan security people," she said. "Did they ever show up?"

"I totally forgot," replied Horvil, swiveling in his seat to scan the audience. "Yeah, there they are." Within seconds, he had made contact with Berilla's security team. Jara saw a trio of muscular men in high-class purple uniforms steal into the aisle after the Islander, who had just exited the courtroom.

Confident that the Élanners would keep an eye on Quell, Jara focused on slogging through the next sixty minutes of official proceedings. The Surinas went through the motions of resting their case, motions that required a numbing amount of back-and-forth slathered with ceremony and legal jargon. Protocol dictated that Martika respond with a number of pro forma declarations that Jara couldn't comprehend.

As this tiresome charade of justice continued, Jara had to sit and endure the gloating of Suheil and Jayze Surina. The two seemed quite pleased with themselves, and had no hesitation about showing their smug expressions to the defense table and the room at large. Sen Sivv Sor and John Ridglee, for their part, did not appear upset at all to see their theory disproven—on the contrary, the reappearance of Quell had provided a dramatic new angle for their stories and would likely cause a small spike in their Data Sea traffic. Through it all, curious members of the audience kept fixing Jara with their voyeuristic stares, as if waiting for a spat of emotion or volatility. *It's only a matter of time before some drudge starts zooming in on my face and psychoanalyzing my facial expressions*, thought the fiefcorp master sourly.

Jara would have almost been happy to give them something to see. But the outcome of this case still made little difference to her. So the fiefcorp would be forced to cede over a pile of money they weren't using, and the title to a product they hadn't seen in over two months. Did any of that really matter? She could barely muster up enough emotional energy to feel disappointed.

Much more important was the question of whether Jara's refusal of the Surinas' settlement offer had provoked Quell's testimony. And if so, what did that say about the mysterious powers behind the chessboard? Had Jara appeased or enraged them? Had she simply done what they had expected?

"Well, we can rest easy about one thing," said Horvil over ConfidentialWhisper.

"What's that?"

"Quell's not hustling off to the Islands. I just heard from the Creed Élan guys. They followed him to a nitro bar, where he's just sitting on the patio watching soccer."

Jara nodded. "Which bar?"

"It's the Ostrich Egg—the place across the street from our hotel."

•   •   •

Quell's choice of the Ostrich Egg was obviously no coincidence. Jara had been frequenting the bar every morning since the trial began and had grown quite attached to their baklava. For the Islander to lounge around the same establishment in full view of the passersby was a resoundingly clear signal that he was not avoiding Jara's presence. That he might even be inviting a conversation.

As Jara threaded her way through the streets of Andra Pradesh between shopkeepers, tourists, and bodhisattvas preaching the virtues of obscure creeds, it occurred to her that Quell's choice of venue sent two more disturbing messages as well.

It said, *I know where you've been staying and where you've been having breakfast.*

And it also said, *I've got plenty of protection from the Defense and Wellness Council.*

Jara rendezvoused with the three Creed Élan security staffers on the corner opposite the nitro bar, where she thanked them for their assistance. She recognized one of them from the frenzied escape out of the Tul Jabbor Complex two months ago. The Élanners pointed out the shadowy figure of Quell on the patio, though even from this distance he was difficult to miss. Jara thanked the security men again, asked them to give her regards to Berilla, and then dismissed them.

Quell had taken a seat in the sunniest part of the patio, not too far from the locals who had flocked there to enjoy soccer on the viewscreen. Somewhere between the courtroom and the Ostrich Egg, he had discarded his connectible collar altogether, leaving him with only the coin to provide the sights and sounds of the virtual world.

Jara sat down opposite the Islander as the bar patrons erupted with applause. She looked over her shoulder just in time to see a handsome soccer player leap over two defenders and head butt the ball into the net. Jara felt a rush of déjà vu. She had actually met this man a few months ago, back when the company was preparing for its aborted MultiReal exposition. Wilson Refaris Ko, that was his name.

Quell had clearly been expecting her. "Perfection," he said, gesturing at the cup of steaming nitro that was already sitting on Jara's side of the table. "What, no Horvil?"

Jara shook her head. "Serr Vigal wanted to talk to him about something."

The Islander shrugged and reached for the gargantuan mug of tea sitting in front of the chair where Horvil presumably would have sat. "Tell him I say hello."

The fiefcorp master gave Quell a thorough visual examination. If his decision to perjure himself on the witness stand and betray his former employers had caused him any mental anguish, it was not evident in his casual, almost nonchalant expression. With his natty attire, the Islander might have been just another businessperson arranging to meet a colleague for an afternoon chat. He looked almost . . . connectible.

"So I'm waiting," said Jara abruptly.

Quell raised his eyebrows. "For?"

"For an explanation. For a reason why Len Borda would release you from prison, just in time to testify on behalf of the Surinas. Just in time to ensure that Suheil and Jayze get the title to MultiReal."

"An explanation." Quell stretched his arms over his head and clasped his hands together. Jara couldn't help but notice from the stitching on the Islander's suit jacket that it had been custom tailored for his enormous frame. "I can't give you an explanation just yet. No, you're going to have to wait a little while before this will make sense to you. Another forty-eight hours at least."

"Why?"

"It's . . . complicated. But in the meantime, I can offer you something else. Something that might make up for—for what those two jackasses put you through."

Jara was starting to get very frustrated with all of this careful ambiguity. "Like what?"

"A job."

"I'm perfectly satisfied being the master of—"

Quell interrupted her. "That's not what I meant. I'm not offering you a position, I'm offering you a gig for the *fiefcorp*. A consulting job." He put his immense hands onto the table, palms down, and fixed Jara with a penetrating stare. "I need your help."

This whole game was making less and less sense the longer Jara played it. Quell wanted her help? His motivations, never particularly transparent in the first place, had become completely opaque to her. Jara supposed she should feel grateful that she had a place on the board. That the forces at work wanted her continued involvement. The fiefcorp master reached for her cup of nitro and stared at the murky liquid. If ever she needed the beverage's unique powers of stimulation and concentration, it was today. Jara raised the cup to her lips and drank deeply.

But she wasn't about to acquiesce to Quell's request without a little more detail. "So what's the job?" said Jara.

"It's not one specific thing," said Quell. "It's more like . . . a *series* of things that have to happen, or not happen." He squinted out the window, not looking at any particular object, but rather sweeping in the chaotic ambiance of Andra Pradesh.

"And how do I do these . . . things?"

"Well, I don't really know yet. I won't know until we get there."

Jara could feel the impatience bubbling inside her like lava. "Get *where?*"

"The Islands."

"Listen," Jara snapped, smacking one clenched fist onto the tabletop and momentarily drawing some of the bar patrons' attention away from their soccer game. "You're being unreasonable. You can't just appear out of nowhere and expect me to wander out to the Pacific Islands without telling me *why*. Especially not after what you did to the fiefcorp." She jabbed her index finger out the window in what seemed like the direction of the courthouse. "I'm not in a very chari-table mood right now, Quell. I've just had my company yanked out from under me—*again*—and this time I don't even have any idea why. So you'd better give me *something* to work with here, or I'm out the fucking door."

The old Quell might have grumbled or offered some scathing commentary under his breath. But this post-prison Quell seemed to be a more patient fellow. He merely gave a measured look that indicated he was neither surprised nor displeased at Jara's irritation. "I understand," he said. "But you don't know the position I'm in. There's things I can't say yet. Not even to you, not even over ConfidentialWhisper, and *definitely* not in some bar in Andra Pradesh." He swept his hand around to indicate the interior of Ostrich Egg, now thinning out as the soccer game hit halftime. "Things need to happen out there in the Islands, and they need to happen exactly the right way, or this could very quickly become a much, much different world. I've got a lot of pressure on my shoulders, and I need people around who I trust. People who can *get things done*. That's you. And Horvil, and the whole bloody fiefcorp."

Jara finished her nitro. The stimulant had definitely kicked her mental processor into high gear, but what help was that when she had no data to process? She felt a small frisson of pleasure at being categorized as someone who could get things done, but under the circumstances, flattery was not sufficient motivation. "I'd like to help you, Quell. I really would. But this isn't good enough. You vanished—off to an orbital prison, I assume. You stood up in a courtroom and testified against the fiefcorp. *Our* fiefcorp, the one you used to be a part of. And now you just sit down here and tell me to trust you. Well, I'm not going to just trust you. You need to give me something tangible to take back to the fiefcorp."

Quell's face broadened into a grin. "Understood," he said. "That's why I brought money. *Lots* of money."

· · ·

"A *consulting* job?" said Benyamin. "What the heck is that supposed to mean?"

"I have no idea," said Jara.

"But what would we be doing?"

The fiefcorp master shrugged. "Programming. Advising. Problem solving. Managing public relations. Isn't that what we do?"

Jara had gathered the fiefcorp together in one of the dingy conference rooms at the Kordez Thassel Complex. Jayze and Suheil couldn't exactly forbid them from holding a meeting at the Surina Enterprise Facility; the place was ostensibly open to all, and hosted hundreds of organizations from across the political spectrum every day. But that didn't make Jara feel any more comfortable handing over Vault credits to them. So the Thassel Complex it was, with its peculiar Möbius strip hallways and its sickly white furnishings. Their current conference room was free from SeeNaRee as well, except for the virtual chairs needed to make multi projections feel at home.

The rest of the company had taken their court setback with a large helping of indifference. Horvil had never seemed particularly invested in the lawsuit to begin with. Merri was more preoccupied with her creed activities and caring for her companion Bonneth (who had indeed suffered another health setback). Serr Vigal's despair over Natch's disappearance had inured him to any further business misfortune. Benyamin was more irritated at the thought of capitulating to slime like Jayze and Suheil than he was upset about losing any particular asset of the company's. And Robby Robby was nowhere to be found, presumably off with another client.

"Quell really is asking a lot," said Merri. "He expects us to pick up and follow him to a whole other civilization without saying what he wants us to do there? That's quite a leap of faith. Some of us have lives here and"—the channel manager flailed her hands around for a few seconds, searching for the right word—"responsibilities."

Jara was feeling quite philosophical about the whole thing. "Hasn't it all been a leap of faith since the beginning?" she said. "Natch never explained MultiReal when he asked us to sign up for his new fiefcorp, did he?"

"That's because he didn't *know* anything about it," snapped Ben.

"Yes," replied Jara, "and Quell's made it clear that he doesn't know exactly why he wants us in Manila with him either. There's trouble down there of some kind—political, economical, business-related, I don't know what—and Quell needs our help to resolve it."

"What *do* we know about this job?" asked Merri.

"We know it's highly secretive," said the fiefcorp master. "We know it's potentially dangerous. And we know it's lucrative. That's about it."

"Secretive, dangerous, and lucrative," muttered Horvil. "Our specialty."

Benyamin crossed his arms over his chest. "I can understand why *Quell* would want to hire *us*. The question is, why should we take the job?"

Jara gritted her teeth as she faced the young apprentice. Two months ago, she had been completely exasperated by Benyamin's constant patter of disagreement. But something had changed in those intervening two months. At some point, they had come to an unspoken agreement: Ben would stop treating Jara with contempt and disrespect, and in return, she would listen to him and take him seriously. Their little bargain seemed to be working pretty well so far. But that didn't mean there weren't moments of supreme annoyance along the way.

"Listen, Ben," she said. "I think you're forgetting something crucial. This is a consulting *job*. It's not charity. It's real work, and Quell's paying real money. He's already made a very nice down payment, which means that his money's good."

"It also means the money's probably not his."

"That's true. I've never seen any indication that Quell's got a private fortune stashed away somewhere. No, don't ask—I really *don't* have any clue whose money it is. Some creed? A governmental committee? That capitalman who lent Natch money a few months ago, whatever his name was?"

"Brone," said Merri.

"Him. I just don't know. So yes, it's a little crazy to suggest that you follow me to the Pacific Islands without having any idea why. But here are two things I *do* know. One: if you want to succeed in the long term, sometimes you have to sacrifice something that matters to you in the short term. Two: we've got absolutely nothing going for us here right now. Shitty programs. No direction. We don't even have a ranking on the Primo's board anymore."

"So what about the trial?" said Ben. "Are we just going to give up? Didn't Martika prepare a defense?"

"She did," said Jara. "But we all know that after Quell's testimony, it's not going to fly. So I told Martika to go back to the Surinas and settle. We probably won't get as good a deal as they were offering the other day, but we might be able to save a few credits. Let them have the title to MultiReal. It's worthless."

Surprised silence.

"This might be a fool's errand," continued Jara. "All I can tell you is that Quell sits at the crossroads of everything important that's happening in the world right now. Islander . . . programmer . . . friend *and* enemy of both the Surinas and the Council. He says he needs our help, and he's willing to pay for it. I can't tell you why the company needs to jump at this opportunity; we just do. I'm not *ordering* anyone to go. If you disagree with my reasoning, you can stay here, without penalty. I'm sure Horvil would be happy to turn his MindSpace workbench over to someone else to fix Y Not Ditch the Itch 18." Jara extended her arm towards the engineer, who she suddenly realized had barely said a word the entire meeting. "Horv?"

Horvil looked up from the tabletop, which he had been studying with deep concentration for some minutes now. He gave a sidelong look at Serr Vigal, who had not spoken at all since his arrival in the conference room. "I think what you're saying makes perfect sense, Jara," said the engineer, his voice uncharacteristically serious. "I would go if I could . . . but I've already committed to doing something else."

Jara blanched. "Which is?"

The engineer and the neural programmer turned to each other and exchanged a few silent words over ConfidentialWhisper. After a minute, they seemed to arrive at some conclusion. Serr Vigal cleared his throat. "Horvil and I have decided to look for Natch," he said.

Nobody said anything for a good twenty seconds.

"I understand that you all . . . you all have your reasons for feeling like you do about Natch," continued Vigal haltingly, fiddling with a frayed hem on his robe. "I can't pretend to vouch for his behavior these past few months. Or even . . . these past few *years*. But things are different for Horvil and me. We . . . I *raised* him. I was his legal guardian for sixteen years."

"And I've been his best friend for over twenty years," added Horvil. "Maybe . . . fuck, maybe his *only* friend." He giggled. "I wonder if that says more about me than it says about Natch."

Serr Vigal clasped his hands on the tabletop now, not in a gesture of entreaty, but rather a demonstration of firmness. "Wherever he is, whatever happened to him after the Tul Jabbor Complex, we can't just abandon him. He could be hurt. He could be in pain. He needs our help."

Jara gave the neural programmer a firm and judicious nod. Despite her own history of acrimony with Natch, standing in his place at the head of the fiefcorp had given her a new appreciation for what he had been through. There had been many decision points in the past two months where a Machiavellian solution like one that Natch would dream up seemed like the best choice—and Jara had cursed her own weakness at being unable to make that choice. She would never love the man. But she couldn't bring herself to despise him either. Natch's was simply a misguided soul, and if there were two people who could guide him back onto a more fruitful path, it was Horvil and Serr Vigal. Her only reservation was a selfish one: this would mean separation from Horvil for who knew how long. But that was hardly the basis for making a decision of this caliber.

The fiefcorp master turned to the others. "So I guess that leaves the three of us?"

"The three of us," replied Merri.

Benyamin folded his hands into a tight ball and stared at them intently. After a few seconds of silent contemplation, the young apprentice nodded and sat back in his chair. "Three," he said.

(((13)))

Horvil had agreed with Serr Vigal about the necessity of starting their search for Natch "bright and early." Except the engineer's and the neural programmer's definitions of the term were almost completely at variance, like antipodes on the globe. And so when the neural programmer showed up at the hotel the next morning with baggage in hand, having taken a midnight hoverbird from Omaha, Horvil was quite perplexed. Try as he might, he could see nothing bright on the streets of Andra Pradesh that wasn't man-made.

"Looks like you're packed for quite a journey," said Horvil, eyeing the faux-leather suitcase Vigal had deposited in the vestibule. "Are you sure we even need to *go* anywhere? Seems to me we have just as strong a chance of finding him in multi."

The neural programmer shook his head. "I'm afraid this is going to require some detective work, Horvil. We need to be prepared to go wherever the trail leads us."

"Detective work, huh?" Horvil waved Vigal to the kitchenette in hopes that tea and a clean cup might be unearthed somewhere amid the clutter. "We'll be just like Holmes and Watson! Or Rajiv and Castrano!"

"'The universe is our puzzle box, Castrano!'" said Vigal with a chuckle, repeating the catchphrase from the ever-popular fifty-year-old dramas.

After Horvil had found his way into proper daytime clothing, and after Vigal had determined that there was nothing even vaguely tea-ish in the kitchenette, the two decided to decamp to a local chai bar for breakfast and strategic planning. Horvil vetoed Vigal's suggestion of the Ostrich Egg and chose another venue a few blocks down. The engineer ducked into the suite's bedroom to give the still-sleeping Jara a kiss, and then they were off.

The Cup of Gold was little more than a smattering of tables on a semi-enclosed rooftop deck. The place was thick with fiefcorpers and capitalmen sipping flavored tea drinks and looking to soak up the sun. It seemed an entirely appropriate setting for a mission of hope. There were two immense potted ferns by the railing that reminded Horvil of the Proud Eagle hive—and that, too, seemed appropriate. The two of them found a table between the ferns that would give them some privacy from eavesdroppers. Horvil hadn't found much reason to fear the Defense and Wellness Council since Natch's disappearance. But Quell's mysterious errand and its even more mysterious financier hinted strongly that the fiefcorp had not moved outside the Council's sphere of influence. It couldn't hurt to be cautious.

"So where do we start?" said Serr Vigal after they had taken their seats and procured cups of chai.

Horvil gave the neural programmer an appraising look. Some crucial spark inside Vigal had been ignited during the past twenty-four hours, since he had summoned Horvil and persuaded him to go looking for Natch. He seemed younger, more intense, more interested in his surroundings. Horvil didn't want to squelch that optimism, but he knew that their chances of actually finding the entrepreneur were low indeed.

"Where do we start?" repeated Horvil. He drummed his fingers on the tabletop, an awkward task on iron mesh. "Well, let's think. If you wanted to avoid being found, where would you go?"

The entire concept seemed alien to Serr Vigal. "The Pacific Islands, I suppose. Or maybe the Pharisee Territories."

"There's also Furtoid," added Horvil. "And the lawless quadrants of Mars."

"Let's not forget the diss cities," said Vigal.

"And some of the unchartered orbital colonies. Or even the chartered ones—they say it's pretty easy to get lost in the inner rings of 49th Heaven." The engineer folded his arms on the table and slumped his head sideways onto one elbow. "Wow, we've really narrowed it down. A couple dozen places spread through millions of kilometers of human space."

The two of them stared at the mesh table for a few minutes. Horvil felt embarrassed at how quickly their quest to find Natch had gone from merely quixotic to thoroughly ludicrous. The engineer could hear the trio at the next table debating proposed new Union Baseball rules, and he half felt like slipping over there to join them. "I think we're looking at this the wrong way," he said. "We're trying to figure out where *we* would go if we didn't want to be found. The real question is where *Natch* would go."

The neural programmer sipped his chai and considered this. "And where would Natch go?"

"Somewhere nobody would expect, of course."

"Well, therein lies our dilemma," replied Vigal, the smile creeping back to his face. "Natch would *expect* people to look for him in places nobody would expect."

The two of them laughed loud enough to temporarily disrupt the baseball conversation at the next table.

But the jollity soon devolved again into uneasy silence. Vigal's underlying point was that trying to think like Natch was a futile exercise. Certainly Natch had made his share of mistakes—but had he ever made the same mistake twice? He had outthought and outplanned the best strategists in the Defense and Wellness Council for months. He had evaporated into the aether at the Tul Jabbor Complex with a billion spectators watching his every move. If a man like that didn't want to be found, Horvil suspected he would not be found. Ever.

And that was just the difficulty of finding Natch under ordinary circumstances. Add Natch's precarious emotional state to his cunning intellect, and the problem only grew exponentially. Horvil had seen the way his old hivemate had been acting during the Prime Committee trial, under the pressure of Magan Kai Lee's onslaught, Margaret's peculiarity, the Patels' duplicity, and the drudges' ruthlessness. Not only that, but Natch had been pumped full of black code—from multiple sources—that had done grievous harm to his sanity. Who could predict where *that* man would hide?

"How do we know he's still . . . alive?" said Vigal under his breath. Sometime in the past minute, he had raised his mug of chai to cover a pair of eyes on the verge of tearing up.

The engineer waved his hand in a dismissive gesture. "Of course he's alive," he said. "Is there anyone in the world who knows how to take care of himself better than Natch?"

"That's not proof."

"You want proof?" Horvil thought quickly. "Here's proof. You and I are both listed in the will Natch filed with his L-PRACGs, right? If he went to the Prepared, they would have contacted us by now."

"And if he changed his will?"

Horvil frowned. "Natch wouldn't have done that," he said with an assurance he didn't feel. Hadn't Natch threatened to send the drudges a doctored-up list of all the sketchy things Horvil had done during his whole career? And hadn't he left Serr Vigal lying unconscious on the floor of the Tul Jabbor Complex without making a single move to help him? Those were the actions of a man who might very well cut his best friend and his legal guardian out of his will.

"What if—what if Natch wasn't able to *go* to the Prepared?" said Vigal in a hoarse whisper. "What if he . . . they might have . . ." He couldn't even finish his conjecture.

Horvil had had enough. "Come on, Vigal," he said, leaning forward and thumping his closed fist lightly on the tabletop. "You're starting to act bipolar here. We can't indulge in all this negativity. If we're going to go through with this—if we're going to drop everything to try to find him—we have to assume he's still alive. We *have* to. Otherwise, there's no bloody point, is there?"

The neural programmer would never know if Vigal was convinced by this bit of desperate logic. Because at that moment, an enormous shadow fell over them as someone stepped up to the table and blocked out the sun.

The engineer looked up, startled, and found himself face-to-face with the Pharisee from the courtroom.

• • •

Not only were the Pharisee's features totally occluded by the sun, but he was dressed in a robe as black as midnight, with a massive head of tightly curled black hair and a large black beard to match. Bits of gold jewelry dangled from his neck and ears, catching the sun and tossing it mischievously into the air. The man's nose was almost large enough to merit its own L-PRACG.

"I'm sorry to intrude," said the Pharisee in a pleasant baritone, his accent thick and unplaceable. "But since I'm desperately in need of speaking with the two of you, I suppose it's necessary. Yes, necessary. To me, of course, and also to you, though you don't know that yet. I'm certain that I'll need to convince you of that fact—which I am absolutely prepared to do."

Horvil cast as subtle a glance towards Vigal as he could muster. He was relieved to see that the neural programmer was just as flummoxed by this gust of empty wordage. Other patrons of the chai bar were craning their necks to stare at this odd person standing in the middle of the chai bar like a refugee from ancient times. *A Pharisee? Here?* Horvil could hear someone say. Not knowing what else to do, the engineer waved the Pharisee towards an extra chair at the next table. The big man appropriated it from the table's occupants with a respectful bow, then moved it over and sat down.

"Can we . . . *help* you?" said Horvil.

"Yes, yes, you can help me," replied the Pharisee. His voice carried a mixture of intensity and geniality that was surprising for someone whom Horvil had considered a threat only twenty-four hours ago. "But also, as I mentioned before, I'm certain that *I* can help *you*. So. Let me back up, as they say, and begin at the beginning. Towards Perfection." The Pharisee paused, looked Horvil and Vigal in the eye as if waiting for a response. "Oh. My apologies. . . . *May you always move* towards Perfection."

"And Towards Perfection to you too," offered Vigal timidly.

"You are, if I am not mistaken, members of the Surina/Natch MultiReal Fiefcorp. Horvil the engineer and Serr Vigal the programmer, am I correct? You, sir, I have seen in the courtroom in the company of the bio/logic analyst Jara," he said to Horvil.

The man had badly mangled the pronunciation of all three names, but Horvil was in no hurry to correct him. "And you are . . . ?"

"Forgive me for my rudeness! My name is Richard Taylor." He reached into a knapsack slung over one shoulder and produced a small business card that was actually made from cardboard paper stock. Horvil took the card and stared at it. He supposed it provided some evidence of Taylor's identity, but the engineer had no idea what would prevent an imposter from printing out the same cards. "I am currently the secretary of protocol for the Faithful Order of the Children Unshackled, based out of Khartoum. Two and a half years into a four-year term. I am—" Taylor reached up and parted the thicket of hair and beard to reveal the dull metal gleam of a connectible collar. "I am part of that group I believe you know as the *Pharisees*, though that term is not one we ourselves use."

Horvil was amazed how quickly the menace had sloughed off the man. Beneath the hair and the trinkets, he appeared to have a similar ethnic background to Horvil's. Horvil guessed that the unfamiliar accent had originated in the British Isles and taken a bumpy side road through the past two centuries.

But Serr Vigal was clearly beginning to feel the weight of their self-appointed task growing heavier by the second. He shifted in his seat. The engineer could read his thoughts: *We pledged ourselves to find Natch. We don't have time for these kinds of distractions.*

"Listen, uh, Richard Taylor," said Horvil, interrupting the Pharisee before he could start reciting his entire family tree. "I hate to be rude, but we are in the middle of important business, so . . ."

"Important business, yes!" Taylor leaned forward and put his massive hands on the table. He had perhaps the hairiest knuckles Horvil had ever seen. "Yes, you do have important business! And I believe we three may have some important business together."

"Which is?"

"Forgive me for taking so long to get to the point. I have been tasked by my order to find your friend Natch."

Horvil could see Serr Vigal withdraw even farther at Taylor's mention of the entrepreneur. It was all part of the profound absurdity that was Natch. No matter where you turned or who you talked to, he seemed to be reflected in every facet of life. "I'm afraid we don't know where he is," said Vigal guardedly.

"He's been missing since, uh, January," put in Horvil. "Vanished into thin air right in the middle of a Prime Committee hearing."

"The incident at the Tul Jabbor Complex," said Taylor, nodding soberly. "Yes, out in Khartoum we did hear about that strange affair. So heart-wrenching! So tragic!"

Horvil could only imagine what someone from an unconnectible society like the Pharisees would have made of the calamity and chaos at the Tul Jabbor Complex. He pictured lots of head shaking and moralizing: *You see,* this *is why the connectible way of life is untenable.* Somehow, he was not surprised that news of the event had even slunk off the Data Sea and into lands where people still got their information from wired machines and treepaper. "So you see, Richard, I really don't think we'll be able to help you—"

Taylor leaned his head back and laughed. People at neighboring tables who had just managed to relegate this odd Pharisee to the realm of background noise suddenly cast curious glances his way again. "I see, I see!" he bellowed. His mirth was infectious, and Horvil found his lips curling into a smile despite his best efforts. "You suspect I'm looking to take advantage of your fiefcorp master—you're trying to get rid of me!" Taylor continued. "And this is entirely my fault. I can't blame you for your caution, I have not explained myself well. Horvil, let me assure you—I have approached you not only because I am seeking *your* help in finding Natch but also because *I* have information that may help *you* find him."

• • •

Horvil gave Richard Taylor a skeptical look. He wasn't quite sure whether to regard Taylor as a potential ally, a deliberate saboteur sent here by forces unknown, or just a misguided and possibly delusional head case. Perhaps a bit of all three?

The engineer had read about how people often projected their desires, fears, and neuroses onto celebrities. He remembered the way people from that bizarre creed had showered the fiefcorp with adulation as they had walked to the Prime Committee hearing two months ago. Horvil would never know exactly who those people were and whether they had really been on the payroll of Speaker Khann Frejohr. But his instincts said that they really *were* ordinary plebeians—shopkeepers, accountants, analysts, street vendors—who had deliberately tried to insert themselves into the drama of Natch's fight against the government. Their actions had changed nothing, yet surely they were sitting in their homes even now telling friends that they had been a part of that drama.

Horvil was about to start gently drawing the conversation to a close, but Serr Vigal beat him to the punch. "I really don't mean to be rude, Richard," he began haltingly. "But given all of the people in the world looking for Natch, I find it difficult to believe that you would have some sort of inside information."

"Both factions of the Council are looking for him," added Horvil. "Borda *and* Lee. I'm sure they've got hundreds of officers on the task and millions of credits at their disposal."

Taylor took no offense at their suspicion. Not that intentions counted for much in such a confused and denigrated world, but as far as Horvil could tell Taylor's were completely in earnest. "Oh, but you see, I have an advantage over both Lieutenant Executive Magan Kai Lee and High Executive Len Borda," he said. "The brothers in my order have actually seen Natch."

The engineer held his breath for a moment, exhaled. "How recently?"

"I would say about a month ago."

"Are you sure it was him? Handsome guy, sandy-colored hair, eyes deep blue . . ."

"This man's eyes were green, I believe," said Taylor.

Vigal had momentarily displayed signs of hope, but now he was quickly dismissing them. "You can understand why we're skeptical. . . ."

The Pharisee nodded. "I understand your skepticism entirely. I can only ask you to listen to my story before you pass judgment on it. I also don't wish to give offense, Horvil and Serr Vigal . . . but I believe that you really have nothing to lose by granting me ten minutes of your time to lay my evidence before you. If you choose not to believe me, I will chalk that up to my own poor powers of persuasion and I will not bother you again."

Horvil wasn't sure if he could endure another ten minutes of Richard Taylor's eclectic mannerisms, but he admitted that the man had a point. So, too, did Vigal. Their own deductions had so far led them absolutely nowhere; they had not a single credible lead on Natch's whereabouts. The two sat back and listened.

Taylor proceeded to tell them in a circuitous fashion about how one of the chapters of his organization, the Faithful Order of the Children Unshackled, had taken on a number of unwise financial obligations over the past few years. The chapter was beholden to a certain capitalman on 49th Heaven who had subsequently insisted on calling in those loans with threats of violence. ("A mobster," said Horvil. The Pharisee shrugged, not debating his characterization.) And so, the head of the local chapter had approached a man in the orbital colony who had recently garnered a reputation for negotiating on debtors' behalf. Not only had the man succeeded in getting the capitalman to back off, but he had persuaded him to reduce the principal of the loan by fifty percent.

"And this man, this negotiator . . . was Natch?" said Serr Vigal, unconvinced.

"I believe it was," replied Taylor. "But my brothers were not given the man's name or his title, so I cannot say for absolute certain."

"If your order has seen him . . . if you've had dealings with him . . . then why do you need our help?"

"He is rather difficult to get hold of. He seems to have decided that, having dealt with my brethren once, he has no need to deal with us again. As far as we have been able to determine, he is a man without an address and without a profile in your Data Sea public directory. He seems to be something of a ghost."

"And why do you need to find him again?"

"I bear an important message for him from the head of my order, in Khartoum."

"Which says?"

"I do not wish to be rude, as I have said," replied Taylor hesitantly. "But I am told that this message is for Natch's ears alone."

Horvil didn't want to be too dismissive—as painstakingly polite as this Pharisee acted, he was a member of a foreign culture whose rules of etiquette were a complete mystery—yet the engineer agreed with Vigal. Nothing about the man's story provided any context for believing that the strange benefactor of his order was the world's most wanted former fiefcorp master. If the story was even true, this negotiator could have been anybody.

"You have to look at this from *our* point of view, Richard," said Horvil. "We've seen hundreds of drudge postings on the Data Sea from people who claim to have seen Natch or talked to Natch. There's a woman on Luna who's absolutely convinced that she just had Natch's baby." Taylor started to raise his hand to object, but Horvil stopped him. "All we're saying is that you've come to us with a story that doesn't contain any information you couldn't have gotten by trolling the Data Sea. You've gotta give us *some* reason why we should listen to you. Some distinguishing characteristic. Otherwise . . ."

Taylor was not discouraged by this lecture. He gave the matter a moment's careful thought. "This man told the head of the chapter on 49th Heaven that he was once the top bio/logic programmer in the world," he offered.

"Lots of people know that Natch was number one on Primo's," replied Horvil.

"He had a very interesting conversation with the head of the local chapter, which he then proceeded to relay to me in full. I found it quite striking, and perhaps it may mean something to you." Taylor rolled his eyes upward as if delicately probing his memory. "The man said that he once thought he had no future. But then his guardian told him something that inspired him: *Your future is what you choose to do tomorrow. And the direction you're searching for? Your direction is where you choose to go.*"

The engineer was about to dismiss the quote as improbable when he caught the peculiar look in Serr Vigal's face. In the space of four sentences, his expression had morphed from one of utter skepticism to one of sadness and desperate hope. Was Vigal, in fact, the guardian who had spoken these words to Natch?

"If we assume that this person might be Natch," began the neural programmer in a low, unsteady tone, "how can we help you find him?"

(((14)))

Jara knew that by taking a hiatus from connectible civilization, she would miss the entirety of the West London Grandmasters' League's annual tournament. This chagrined her. Not that she had any hope of getting past the first round, but she had committed to play, and she hated to break commitments. Jara supposed that what really mattered was the commitment to herself, the reason she had joined the league in the first place. And by following Quell out to the Islands, she felt like she was not only staying faithful to that promise, she was renewing it.

Other things were not so easily settled, however. Jara was fairly certain she'd be able to maintain audio and video contact with Horvil from Manila. The Islanders weren't so barbaric that they couldn't see the usefulness of instantaneous communications. But would they allow a more prurient form of communication through the Sigh? Doubtful that a government that blocked the multi network would let in signals from something as trivial as a virtual sex network.

There was little danger of a disconnect on Horvil's end. Four of the five hotels on 49th Heaven that he contacted for pricing offered free hours on the Sigh at check-in.

So that night, Jara let Horvil pick the environment. Though the engineer playfully threatened to call up "Contortionist Whores of 49th Heaven" ("C'mon, Jara, it's *research*," he said), in the end he chose a virtual version of his own apartment, if his apartment were cleaned and spruced up and the gravity lowered to 0.8g. "Who knows how long it might be until we see each other again," Horvil explained as they sat together on the couch under the window that overlooked the Thames. "I don't want to be distracted during our last time together by a lot of make-believe."

"Don't start getting melodramatic on me," Jara chided him, brushing his cheek affectionately with her knuckles. "You know 49th Heaven isn't that dangerous, unless you go to the inner rings."

"So don't you think it's *more* likely that Natch would hide there?"

"Maybe. But I'm not worried. You can take care of yourself."

Horvil leaned back and insinuated his hands under Jara's blouse, the better to run his thumbs up the jagged highway of her spine. "Thank you. I'm gratified. But it's really *me* that should be worried about *you*."

"It's not like I'm going to Furtoid," said Jara with a purr as Horvil's backrub began to have its soothing effect. "Sure, they won't have multi, but Manila's just a tube ride away. The Islanders aren't savages. What could happen?"

She had phrased the question in a humorous tone, but the engineer took it with uncharacteristic seriousness. "What could happen? Are you *kidding*? Len Borda and Magan Kai Lee are gearing up for a civil war, security's a mess everywhere you turn—and you're headed straight for the biggest flashpoint on the globe. Jara, Manila could be a *war zone* next week. Didn't it occur to you that this mission Quell's hiring you for could be dangerous?"

Horvil wasn't saying anything that Jara didn't already know. Yet somehow she had not quite thought of it that way. Quell had hired the fiefcorp for a consulting job, and that's exactly what Jara was preparing for. Sitting around conference tables, holding late-night arguments, conducting research, convening focus groups. She supposed she needed to be reminded that assassins, mercenaries, saboteurs, and spies were also, in some sense, consultants.

Jara could feel a lump welling in her throat. Suddenly the potential consequences of this separation were beginning to stack up.

Her life had slipped into a comfortable if uninspiring groove over the past two months. After decades of personal and professional dissatisfaction, Jara had become the head of a fiefcorp. She enjoyed financial stability and a slowly budding relationship with a man she trusted and respected. Would her company ever rise back to the heights Natch had taken it to? Would her unlikely twosome with Horvil eventually become a permanent companionship? Difficult, headache-provoking questions. Jara had been confident that the answers could wait awhile.

But what if she had missed her opportunity? What if this mysterious consulting job of Quell's turned out to be much more complicated than she anticipated? What if Horvil got into bad trouble in that orbital colony whose name was synonymous with bad trouble? What if this internecine conflict between Len Borda and Magan Kai Lee led to some kind of global catastrophe?

Jara had jumped into this game without a thought about the danger. It hadn't really occurred to her that by taking on Quell's commission, she had called an end to her much-deserved recess of the past two months. What if she could never find her way back to this place? This life plateau that she had fought so tenaciously to reach could come to an abrupt drop, leaving her with nothing to show for it but a lost court case and weeks of lazy, squandered evenings on the Sigh.

At some point in the past few minutes, Horvil's backrub had slowed to a halt without either of them noticing. "Horvil," she said, "do you trust this Richard Taylor?"

The engineer considered the question for a minute. "I don't think he's out to hurt us," he answered. "Whether we accomplish anything productive up there in 49th Heaven, I have no idea. Odds are we find ourselves back here in a week with nothing gained and nothing lost. . . . What about you?"

"I haven't even met him."

"No, not Taylor. Quell. Do you trust Quell?"

"I think—I think the same thing goes for him as for Taylor," said Jara. "I just wish . . ." She stopped short. Jara didn't really know what she wished. She had some idea now of what the potential consequences were of playing this game, but the potential rewards—and whether they were worth the sacrifice—remained unknown.

• • •

Horvil was a man of rationality, an engineer with a deep and abiding confidence in the powers of science. He did not believe in omens or premonitions that filtered down to the material plane from Places Beyond. Yet he couldn't help but feel that it didn't bode well for their trip to 49th Heaven that Richard Taylor wouldn't even board the hoverbird.

"It's not that I've never been on a hoverbird before," said Taylor, staring in wide-eyed trepidation at the small vessel Vigal had chartered for them. "We do have motorized vehicles out in the Principalities of Spiritual Enlightenment, you know. Wheeled transports mostly, but some flying craft as well. I even flew one of them on a challenge once, back in my daredevil days. Back when I was a youth. But this! This! To actually . . . leave the Earth's atmosphere . . . ?"

"Hundreds of thousands of people *live* up there, outside the Earth's atmosphere," said Vigal, a font of patience, pointing into the heavens. "It's quite safe. You can see the lights blinking on Allowell if you look up on a clear night."

"Living on an orbital platform that has been floating in the sky for two hundred and fifty years I can understand. But *this* tiny vehicle— kilometers up in the sky, above the clouds—what happens if it malfunctions? Or—or crashes?"

Horvil shrugged. "No different than if a regular hoverbird crashes. Or a tube train, for that matter." He peeked around Taylor's bushy beard at the craft's interior. This was about as luxurious a four-seater as money could buy, with upholstered seats and viewscreens aplenty, not to mention a foldable MindSpace workbench with specialized holders for bio/logic programming bars.

Serr Vigal put a comradely hand on the Pharisee's shoulder. He had been trying to soothe Taylor's raw nerves with the balm of logic for almost half an hour now. Not that he had achieved any results. "Trust in the numbers, Richard," said Vigal. "Statistically, it's almost as safe as multi."

"I don't multi," replied Taylor, giving a tug at the connectible collar around his neck.

"Then it's almost as safe as walking. Listen to these statistics. According to the Committee on Aerospace Safety, there were only two hundred and twelve mechanical failures on orbital hoverbird flights in the past six months. Not all of them fatal. Divide that by the total number of hoverbird flights during those six months, and you get point oh oh five sev—no, wait, I'm sorry, I'm actually looking at a *three*-month period. . . ."

Horvil walked to the hoverbird's nose where the pilot was standing, blasé as cardboard, doubtless reminding himself that he was getting paid by the hour whether they took off or not. The engineer gave the man a congenial roll of the eyes and parked himself on a steamer trunk that sat on the dock awaiting the next flight.

Vigal hadn't realized yet that the Pharisee would not be mollified with facts and figures; the man would simply have to tamp down his fear or stay Earthbound. Horvil was not unsympathetic. Richard Taylor was facing a paradigm shift beyond any that the fiefcorp had faced with MultiReal. Connectibles skirted death each minute of their lives. Hoverbirds crashed on a daily basis. Bio/logic programming mishaps led to a handful of horrible deaths every month. Despite the most elaborate safety precautions, collapsible buildings killed at least twenty or thirty disobedient children each year. To live in modern society and partake of its miracles—instantaneous travel across thousands of kilometers, silent mental communication, immunity from disease—meant accepting that the universe would extract payment in the form of sudden, random death. It was a bargain connectibles had been born into. But the Pharisees—they had never signed up for such a bargain.

Horvil wondered for the fifteenth time that morning whether this entire trip was really necessary. He wondered whether Richard Taylor really *did* have some lead on Natch's whereabouts, or if he was simply naïve and misguided. And he wondered whether it was absolutely necessary to take Taylor along even if he could help them.

Serr Vigal stepped over to the pilot with the Pharisee tagging behind. "*You* must have colleagues who fly hoverbirds every day," said the neural programmer. "Tell my friend here how many of them have crashed."

The pilot ran a mistrustful eye over Richard Taylor's immense beard and exotically braided hair, his outlandish black robe and glinting jewelry. "Hey, man," said the pilot, deadpan, "we all crash eventually. That's life. You just gotta be ready to go at any minute."

Taylor regarded the pilot with horror and began slowly backing away from the vehicle. *Just what we needed*, thought Horvil.

But Vigal wasn't about to give up so easily. "You see?" he said, extending a hand towards the pilot. "If flying in a hoverbird wasn't so safe, would this gentleman feel comfortable joking about it?"

●　●　●

In the end, Vigal was able to lure Richard Taylor onto the hovercraft. Horvil quickly climbed aboard and buckled himself in, blocking the Pharisee's exit. Within ten minutes, the four of them were rocketing off the dock and headed for the aether.

Horvil could have predicted what would happen next. Taylor went into a convulsive panic for a few moments as the 'bird shot up in its initial ascent. When he realized that connectible engineers had long ago figured out ways to nullify the g-forces of flight, the panic gave way to utter fascination. The Pharisee started a long, rambling discourse about a fishing trip he had taken as a young man, the relevance of which Horvil could not quite see. Then as soon as the vista of Andra Pradesh had morphed into dull, unbroken cloud, he promptly fell asleep.

The engineer pinged the neural programmer on Confidential-Whisper as soon as Taylor's snores began to permeate the cabin. "What the fuck have we gotten ourselves into?"

Vigal laughed silently. "I think I'm beginning to like him, actually."

"Sure, he's friendly, but that's not the point. Like him or not, the chances of Taylor actually leading us within a thousand kilometers of Natch are pretty slim. And if that's the case, this whole trip could end up being a big waste of time and money."

"Admittedly. Though we seem to be in the same situation as the rest of the fiefcorp. What other options do we have?"

"None," said Horvil with a sigh.

"So what do we have to lose?"

"We've got plenty to lose, Vigal. What if this whole thing is a setup? How do we even *know* Richard Taylor is a Pharisee and not just a good actor? It's not like we can look up his profile on the public directory or check his references. 'The Faithful Order of the Children Unshackled'? We have no idea if this organization even exists. Sounds phony to me."

The neural programmer ran his fingers through his salt-and-pepper goatee as he examined the slumbering Taylor. "I think he's being sincere."

"And this conversation you had with Natch—that thing about choosing your future—you're *sure* that's legitimate? You said those words to Natch?"

"I'm sure."

"You're *so* trusting," said Horvil with a shake of his head. "Okay, so maybe *Taylor's* being sincere. Maybe he's really trying to deliver some message to Natch from the Order of Faithful Children, or whoever they are. What does this organization stand for? What's in this message of his, and why is he being so secretive about it? How do we know these people aren't trying to find Natch so they can kill him? How do we know they're not on Len Borda's payroll?"

Serr Vigal stared out the window and watched the hoverbird burst through the last of the clouds. The path back down to Earth was now completely obscured, and the path ahead lay out of their vision. An apt metaphor for their current predicament. "We don't know any of these things," he said. "You'll learn this when you get older, Horvil. Sometimes there's nothing else you can do but put yourself in the world's hands and trust that things will turn out all right."

And then he, too, drifted off to sleep.

3

THE CONSULTANTS

(((15)))

Preparing for a trip of indeterminate length to the Pacific Islands was much more difficult than Jara had anticipated. Everywhere she looked was another commonplace item that might or might not work behind the unconnectible curtain. Did the Islanders have MindSpace workbenches, and if so, would Jara's fancy new set of bio/logic programming bars function on them? Would she be able to hang clothes in the closet of her hotel and have them magically emerge clean and pressed as they would in a connectible hotel? Would all the standard cosmetic programs for sanitizing and deodorizing the human body still work out there?

Definitive answers to these questions and a hundred more were surprisingly hard to come by on the Data Sea, and Jara did not feel comfortable asking Quell. In the end, she decided to simply pack light. Whatever the source of Quell's funding, surely they would pick up the tab for laundering clothes.

But the issue of gearage was nothing compared to the issue of transportation.

Marcus Surina had once proclaimed that he would free humanity from the "tyranny of distance." And while his teleportation technology may have struck the tyrant a mortal blow, death rattles were still being felt decades later. Merri, who lived hundreds of thousands of kilometers away on Luna, had been prepared to teleport Terran-side to meet the fiefcorp in Manila. But TeleCo was experiencing technical difficulties with its long-distance quantum repeaters, so teleportation was out of the question. Ordinarily that would not be an issue, since multi projection from the moon was both cheap and reliable. But the multi network had been completely banned in the Pacific Islands by Dogmatic Opposition. And so Merri's only recourse was to spend forty-eight hours incommunicado on one of the misshapen lumps of metal that OrbiCo called a shuttle, alongside raw materials and industrial supplies. She wouldn't arrive in Manila for almost a full day after the others. Quell paid for this too.

The last thing Jara had to deal with before taking a hiatus from civilization was the issue of the settlement. Martika Korella had indeed gone back to Suheil and Jayze Surina and worked out a compromise. As expected, the terms weren't nearly as good as they would have been had Jara skipped the trial altogether. The settlement would take a hefty chunk out of the funds Margaret had left behind, and hand over the title to MultiReal as well. But it would mean an end to the legal wrangling. A clean break from Possibilities. Besides which, Quell's sizable down payment would assure that the fiefcorp's coffers would not be empty when they returned from the Islands.

Jara affirmed the agreement. She thought she would be sad at having gone through the trial for nothing, but all she felt was relief.

Jara's biggest surprise, however, was finding Robby Robby waiting at the designated TubeCo train, knapsack slung jauntily over one shoulder. She would never have expected the channeler to take time out from his busy schedule to accompany them on this mad adventure.

"Are you kiddin', Queen Jara?" he beamed. "Let you guys have all the fun?"

For some strange reason, she was glad to see him.

Maybe it was because dealing with Robby Robby took Jara's mind off dealing with Quell. The Islander had seemed like the epitome of calm and forethought two days ago on the patio of the Ostrich Egg. Now he had turned his attention inward, where there were evidently rough and turbulent seas on the horizon. He would answer the fiefcorp's questions about his homeland with staccato grunts of *yes* or *no*, if he answered them at all. Jara had still not been able to figure out the nature of their consulting gig, and beyond one tantalizing clue, Quell seemed in no mood to debrief her during their overnight trip to Manila.

That clue came as Jara, Benyamin, and Robby were settling in to their seats on the tube. The Islander walked past them, heading for a more private seat he had chosen at the end of the car. "Anything we should be doing on the way out there?" Jara asked.

Quell stopped, frowned, turned to Jara. "Just get some sleep," he said. "You'll figure out the situation when you meet my son Josiah. He's your client, not me." And then the Islander was gone.

Jara and Benyamin spent twenty minutes trying to decipher what this meant as the train zipped out of the Andra Pradesh station heading northeast. They tried to locate a picture of Josiah, but the Data Sea seemed to have been scrubbed of his image, and deliberately so. Infogather returned an unprecedented zero results.

"You don't think this is a *personal* consulting job, do you?" said Jara over ConfidentialWhisper.

Ben shook his head. "Why would he spend all this money to bail his kid out of some local trouble?"

"Maybe Josiah's horribly ill. Or maybe he's deformed in some way."

"Can't see how we could help, if that's the case."

"Do you think . . . ? Merri said that Quell's son was agitating for his release from prison, remember? Do you suppose he went too far and pissed off Len Borda? Or maybe he discovered something about the orbital prison system the Council doesn't want the public to know?"

"Face it," said Benyamin, burying his head in a pillow tucked between the window and the seat. "You're grasping at straws. We don't have enough information to figure this out. We're just gonna have to wait, like the man said."

"Don't—"

"Get some sleep, Jara."

But the fiefcorp master was too keyed up with questions to drift off, and she didn't think a chemically triggered QuasiSuspension nap would do her much good. Not only was there the mystery of Quell's mission to contend with, but there was the anxiety of adjusting to an entirely different culture. They were actually headed to the *Islands*. Source of a thousand mysteries, subject of a thousand childhood speculations. The feeling wasn't unlike that disquieting awe Jara had felt the night before initiation. But at least with initiation, there had been a modicum of predictability: OCHREs and bio/logics would not work, period. The Pacific Islanders had made a much more complex accommodation to the age of bio/logics. Some of the conveniences Jara had grown accustomed to would work, and some would not. She just had no idea which ones—and likely would not know until she tried to use them and failed.

So instead of sleeping, Jara decided to do some research. As the snores of the other fiefcorpers echoed through the car, she spent the next few hours flinging Infogathers onto the Data Sea. The more queries she made, the more she realized how similar the culture in the Islands was to that of connectible civilization. Perhaps the dialogue was a bit more coarse and perhaps the breadth of opinion was not as wide, but it turned out that several hundred million people was plenty large enough to build a rollicking, diverse culture.

The Islanders did not have libertarians and governmentalists, but they did have insulars and assimilationists. The Islanders did not have creeds, but they did have thousands of active civic groups. The Islanders did not have fiefcorps, but there was a homegrown programming scene that catered to the Technology Control Board's narrow specifications. Jara couldn't quite call it a *microcosm* of the bio/logic fiefcorp sector, because technically the unconnectible companies were allowed to grow much larger and more established than any fiefcorp ever could. No carbonization economics for the Islanders. Some of the programming companies here had literally thousands of employees and decades of experience, which Jara found rather uncanny. What did all those people *do* day after day?

Jara was so preoccupied with her research, she failed to notice that Robby Robby had roused from sleep and was standing at the far end of the car, watching the darkened Chinese countryside through the window with a shockingly gloomy expression.

She walked over slowly, giving the channeler plenty of time to express a preference for solitude. He didn't. "I'm glad you're with us, Robby," she said. "I have a feeling that we're going to need you out there. I would've invited you sooner, but I figured you'd be too busy to come."

Robby's smile was as wan as any she had seen on his face. "Well, that woulda been the case two or three months ago."

"What happened?"

"Natch." The channeler shifted positions awkwardly as if the very pronunciation of the name caused him discomfort. "I bet big on your old boss, Queen Jara. *Real* big. Thought the Natchster would have us all sipping wine on the moon before the year was up. Instead I had to let most of my crew loose. Even Frizitz Quo." He took a deep breath. "Things didn't turn out like we expected, huh?"

The understatement of the century. "No, I suppose not," said Jara.

"Well, Robby Robby ain't one to hedge his bets. So here I am, still betting on Natch. Not just betting, doubling down! Still hoping that this'll all prove worthwhile in the end. Frankly, between you and me"—he darted a quick glance towards the others to make sure they were still asleep—"I don't have much left to lose."

The fiefcorp master clapped a comradely hand on the small of Robby's back. "All I can say is that you're not alone."

• • •

Jara finally did collapse into an unsatisfying sleep somewhere around three a.m., still fretting about what lay ahead. She was so preoccupied with the challenges she would encounter when they reached the Islands that it never occurred to her there might be hurdles to jump before they even got there.

She awoke to a glare of light breaking through the storm clouds of the Pacific Ocean. They were headed east out of Taiwan, skirting the borders of Islander territory as treaty required, so at first Jara thought she might be seeing the rising sun. But as the tube train got closer, she realized this was no natural source of light; it was some TubeCo crossroads platform bleached white with the presence of the Defense and Wellness Council. Council officers, Council hoverbirds, Council banners. Everyone in the car was now wide awake.

I can't believe this didn't occur to me, the fiefcorp master reproached herself. *The Council isn't just going to let people amble back and forth to Manila during a time of war.* There was far too much cross-border commerce for them to shut down the tube line altogether, but that didn't mean they couldn't erect checkpoints and make a few choice arrests along the way.

As the train stopped and Jara watched a line of officers in the white robe and yellow star tromp on board, she suddenly wondered if *she* might be one of those choice arrests. What they might arrest her for she couldn't imagine, but there was still so much about this game she didn't understand.

"What do we do?" whispered Jara aloud.

"It's just a routine inspection," replied Quell in a conversational tone of voice from his end of the car. "They'll just poke their noses through our bags and let us on our way. I've seen this a million times."

"Yeah," said Benyamin, "but do you usually carry one of *those* in your bags?" He jerked his thumb at the overhead compartment, where one of the Islander's ebony shock batons was jutting out of his canvas knapsack.

Quell frowned but said nothing.

Jara could feel sweat pouring down her face as if someone had turned on a spigot. She was traveling with a man who had recently been released from orbital prison after thrashing the lieutenant executive of the Council to the edge of the Null Current. What if these were

Magan Kai Lee's troops marching into the car with dartrifles cocked? And would it be any better if these troops held allegiance to Len Borda instead?

It soon became clear that this was not just a routine inspection; it was an ambush. Council officers were closing in on them from both adjoining cars of the train. Before Jara knew what was happening, the officers had cut off any hope of escape. Not that escape was likely. Jara glanced out the windows and saw nothing but the platform and the sea stretching across the horizon.

"I thought this might happen," said Quell in a low voice, barely audible from across the car. He seemed surprisingly matter-of-fact. "Don't worry, it's me they're after. Magan Kai Lee will bail me out."

"What do we do?" Jara whispered, repeating her earlier question.

"Get to Manila. Chandler will meet your train, and he'll take you to Josiah."

"And then what?"

She never received an answer. At that moment, an enormous ogre of a Council officer trudged into the tube car, swinging the end of his rifle against his open palm like a nightstick. Jara had to activate a bio/logic program to stop her teeth from chattering. Ben's face had turned almost as white as the officer's uniform, and even Robby Robby looked panic-stricken.

Quell stared out the window affecting nonchalance. Jara noticed that the shock baton had mysteriously vanished from his bag. The Islander must have grabbed it when Jara had turned to look at the Council officers lining up outside. Was that what he was cradling under his arm? Was Quell preparing for violence?

Jara took another look at the officers blocking the exits. Grim, impersonal, unyielding. She found herself wishing she still had access to MultiReal, though even then the odds of escape seemed pathetically small.

Evidently the Islander realized that too. The ogreish officer stopped in front of him and simply pointed to one of the tube car doors. Quell rose slowly, his face completely indifferent, and let the Council officer lead him out the door. The officer grabbed his bag and followed him out. Jara could now see the wisdom of the Islander taking a seat on the opposite side of the car; to all appearances, Jara, Ben, and Robby were nothing more than frightened bystanders.

Five minutes later, all the officers in white had departed, and the train went back to skimming the ocean's surface at high speed. Of Quell there was no sign. Jara looked in the direction from which they had come and saw the white streaks of Council hoverbirds taking flight.

Ben lightly punched the padded seat in front of him in frustration. "So . . . what do we *do?*"

Nobody had an answer. Robby walked down to Quell's end of the car, peered under the chair, and produced the Islander's shock baton. They all stared at it dolefully for a moment. Then Robby delicately replaced the baton where he had found it and returned to his seat.

(((16)))

Twenty minutes outside Manila, they plunged through the unconnectible curtain.

Jara still had her crash course on Islander lore fresh in her mind, so she could easily recall how Toradicus had forced passage of the Islander Tolerance Act of 146, which essentially cost him the high executive's seat. It also gave the fledgling society in Manila a framework for opting out of modern technology that all connectible companies and government entities were legally bound to obey—the centerpiece of which was the Dogmatic Opposition, a formal declaration of Luddism revolving around a particular technological advance. . . .

But none of that dry research could convey the sensation of bio/logic programs abruptly stuttering to a halt and multi network transmissions suddenly cutting off. One second Jara was seeing the world dressed in all its bio/logically enhanced finery; the next second she was seeing the world stripped bare of virtual frills.

From here on out, the fiefcorp master told herself, *everyone I see in front of me will actually, physically* be *in front of me, in the flesh. How odd.* She pictured Quell ripping off his connectible collar and making some irascible comment about smoke and mirrors.

Benyamin took the passage into unconnectible territory without incident, but Robby Robby had been listening to a peppy xpression board composition on the Jamm when the music stopped. "We can get this back, right?" he pouted to Ben. "The Jamm's not gone for good, right?" It was only the third time Jara had ever seen the channeler lose his cool, and the frequency of these episodes was starting to get alarming in and of itself.

"Music's still coming through the Data Sea," replied Ben without raising his head from his pillow. "It's just not on a frequency that you can feed straight into the neural cortex."

"So how do I get it?" asked the channeler, momentarily vexed.

"You can reroute. There's a bio/logic program that'll transpose the signal so you can play it on the OCHREs in the aural canal. Here, let me show you . . ." Within seconds, Ben had fixed Robby's Jamm feed to broadcast over actual sound waves instead of brain waves. Robby Robby was soon back on an even keel.

But the channeler didn't have long to savor his restored virtual music box before the city of Manila came into view.

Jara watched the approaching skyline in awe. Manila, capital of the Free Republic of the Pacific Islands. The last photographs she had seen of the place must not have been of recent vintage, because this metropolis hardly resembled the picture in her head at all.

It was an immensely *tall* city, perhaps taller than any Jara had seen in connectible territories. Whereas the collapsible buildings that filled modern cities tended to produce a low, curved, organic blend of architecture, the Islanders' ethos of plain practicality had resulted in a jagged, almost crystalline style. The city had already expanded eastwards from its historical base until it hit the coastline. Without movable structures and without large swaths of open real estate, there was no direction for the Manilans to build but up, like the ancients had done. The ancients did not have Reawakening-era building materials like flexible glass, stretched stone, and permasteel, so their cities had largely been strait-jacketed in two-dimensional grids. Not so Manila. Here the buildings had not only expanded upwards, but side-to-side as well. Connecting corridors floated dozens or even hundreds of meters off the ground, some cantilevered into space as if flaunting their disdain for the law of gravity. Jara spotted one building that actually snaked *around* two of its neighbors in ever-tightening coils. She saw another shaped like a giant T with immense arms that rested atop four neighboring towers.

There was plenty of time for the fiefcorpers to examine these structures in detail, since the tube train had slowed to a creep as it passed through the streets. Of course, Jara realized, people without bio/logic

safeguards would have no warning systems to keep them from saun-
tering into the path of an oncoming train. They could literally climb
onto the tracks without sounding any kind of OCHRE alarm. Jara
looked at the faces of the pedestrians loitering right out the window of
her tube car. How could these people live only footsteps away from
death at all times without constantly shuddering at its presence?

The train came to a smooth stop at a station labeled DOWNTOWN
CROSSING/CITY CENTER. As the fiefcorpers grabbed their packs and
slung them over their shoulders, Jara tried not to think what would
happen if this Chandler did not show up to meet their tube. How
would they go about finding a single individual in a foreign civilization of three hundred million? And even if he did show up, how would
they recognize him?

But no sooner had the fiefcorpers disembarked from the tube
when a lean man with crazily kinked hair came running up to them,
looking surprisingly spry for a man in his midseventies. He wore an
olive green uniform that suggested some kind of government or military affiliation.

"Guess we stand out here, huh?" said Jara.

The man gave a curious look at Robby's blue vinyl trenchcoat.
"Like ants in a bowl of sugar," he said. He held out his hand in peculiar Islander fashion. "Name's Bali Chandler."

"I'm Jara, master of the Surina/Natch MultiReal Fiefcorp," replied
Jara, grasping Chandler's hand for an awkward shake. "This is my
apprentice Benyamin and our channeling partner Robby Robby. Our
channel manager Merri is en route from Luna as we speak."

"So where's the big man?" said the Islander. He peered over their
heads as if expecting the approach of a giant.

Chandler's face darkened considerably as Jara recounted the
Defense and Wellness Council's incursion into their train just outside
the unconnectible curtain. He listened carefully and scratched at the
stubble on his face but said nothing.

"We're kind of in an awkward position," said Jara. "Quell wouldn't even tell us why he wanted us here. He kept us totally in the dark. So . . . aside from tracking down his son Josiah, we're sort of at loose ends."

"That was smart," mused the Islander. "Always was a wily bastard, but looks like Borda was on to him anyway." He thrust his hands into his pockets and stared back down the tube track in the direction they had come. Jara half expected to see Quell jogging down the track herself.

"You think he'll be okay?" said Benyamin.

Chandler let out a relaxed laugh. "You've *met* Quell, right? I'm still trying to figure out how he escaped from the Council the last time. Though I guess if he's relying on Magan Kai Lee to spring him . . ." The man rubbed his chin silently for a few seconds, then sighed and shrugged at the same time. "Suppose we'd better get to Josiah already."

Jara cleared his throat. She wasn't sure if this man's easy manner should make her feel more or less reassured about their situation. "Do you think you could . . . clue us in on what's going on?" she said.

Chandler shook his head. "Nope," he said good-naturedly. "Not until Josiah says so. Come on." And then they were off.

Jara had no idea where the Islander was leading them, but she figured they had no recourse but to follow. By the looks of things, Benyamin and Robby had resigned themselves to staying quiet and following Jara's lead until further notice. Soon all three of them were absorbed in the sights and sounds of the Pacific Islands.

Chandler did his best to put the fiefcorpers at ease. Though he had only actually left the Pacific Islands twice, he knew much more about connectible culture than Jara knew about the Islanders. He had seen several Juan Nguyen dramas, he regularly tuned in to some of the more eclectic channels on the Jamm, and he followed dozens of connectible drudges on a daily basis, including Sen Sivv Sor, John Ridglee, *and* Mah Lo Vertiginous.

Robby Robby looked like he had found a friend, especially when he discovered that one of Chandler's foreign journeys had been to attend Yarn Trip's reunion concert in Vladivostok. "Are all Islanders as hip as you?" he asked with a smile.

"Only the ones who run border districts," replied Chandler with pride, pointing to a patch on his uniform that Jara assumed to be a badge of office.

"Run . . . ?"

"I guess Quell didn't tell you I'm a representative in the parliament?"

Jara frowned. Quell had told them nothing.

The crowds wandering the streets of Manila were alien in more than one sense. To begin with, they were simply *larger* than connectible crowds, a fact Jara attributed to the lack of multi technology. If you couldn't hop onto a red tile and materialize wherever you wanted to go in milliseconds, obviously you would spend more time traveling from place to place. Skin colors were a shade paler here than in most connectible cities Jara had seen, though by no means monochromatic. And on average, the Islanders appeared to be a centimeter or two taller than connectibles, though they were not the race of Brobdingnagian giants Jara had feared. Even here, Quell was a colossus.

Most disconcerting was the Islanders' odd notion of personal space. In the course of half a dozen city blocks, Jara was jostled, poked, prodded, and elbowed more than she had been in London the entire past year. People hugged one another and clasped hands to say hello. They slapped each other on the back and walked arm-in-arm. Jara felt an instinctive burst of disapproval. *Just because you can touch the flesh of everyone you meet doesn't mean you have to fetishize it.*

Suddenly Jara was clobbered by the absurdity of their predicament. She had spent several hours studying up on the history and the culture of the Islands, but now that preparation seemed laughably insufficient. She couldn't even remember what kind of monetary system these people used. *Didn't it occur to you that this mission Quell's hiring you for could be dangerous?* Horvil had asked her. And he had been correct. Without Bali Chandler, she could starve out here, or get beaten bloody, or wind up in a jail cell for violating some unknown taboo. And parliament representative or not, who knew how trustworthy this man Chandler really was?

Jara shuddered and quickened her step to keep up.

The four of them were headed towards a line of skyscrapers that divided the city like the pickets of a fence. Between the buildings sat an immense public square that might have made excellent parading grounds for an army. Chandler led them into the square underneath an archway inscribed with the stern directive to HONOR THE SPIRIT OF THE BAND OF TWELVE. Jara remembered the Band of Twelve from her readings: the Founding Fathers of the Islander movement, the ones who had cajoled, bartered, and negotiated (some say swindled) the land to build a new nation. As they walked past each of the skyscrapers in the square, Jara noticed a statue in front of each building bearing the likeness of one of the Band, frozen in an appropriately grandiose posture.

Jara scratched her head. "There's only seven buildings," she said. "Shouldn't there be twelve?"

"Oh, there will be," said Chandler breezily. "As soon as the government gets the money to build them."

"When will that be?"

"Hopefully before the Earth gets swallowed up in a fiery supernova, but I wouldn't count on it." The Islander stopped and pointed to the empty spaces at the far edge of the square, which were cordoned off and piled high with debris from long-dormant construction. "At least we've got our priorities straight. You'll notice that the five missing buildings belong to the tax evaders." His tone was jocular, but Jara could sense an undercurrent of disgust.

Chandler led them into the entrance of the westmost tower, a building constructed entirely in green-tinted permasteel and adorned with the effigy of a man named Micah Brayling. Inside, the building followed the ancient Western model of wide marble hallways and uncomfortably high ceilings.

The four of them made their way through corridor after corridor filled with Islanders wearing variations on Chandler's drab green uniform. A few had shock batons clasped at their sides, but most did not—inspiring Jara to realize that she had not seen a single Council officer since crossing the unconnectible curtain. She felt surprisingly liberated.

Finally they arrived in a cozy conference room that looked more like a lounge than a place of hard-nosed business and diplomacy. In addition to a small conference table and its attendant chairs, the room had a wet bar stocked with various expensive liqueurs, a smattering of view-screens, and a mammoth painting of some ancient battle fought with muskets and bayonets. "Just sit tight for a few minutes," said Chandler, giving Robby a farewell handshake before departing out the door.

Benyamin and Robby plopped down on two of the chairs while Jara examined the wet bar and tried to decide if pouring herself a drink would be appropriate. She was surprised to discover how emotionally draining this day had already been. She had left connectible civilization behind, embarked on a dangerous mission, and watched a team of Council officers spirit away the one man who could tell her what that mission was. A little rum was warranted.

"So we've learned two new pieces of information today," said Benyamin, combing his inky black hair with his fingers. "We learned that this mission of Quell's is being bankrolled by Magan Kai Lee, and we learned that he's being pursued by Len Borda."

Jara abandoned any thought of a drink and took the chair next to Robby instead. "This doesn't make any sense," she said. "Why would Quell team up with the Defense and Wellness Council? He loathes them. Didn't they kill his father?"

"He's not teaming up with the Council, per se," replied Ben. "He's teaming up with Magan Kai Lee, the man who's taken up arms *against* the Council."

"But Quell took up arms against *him*. And what's all this mystery surrounding Quell's son? When do we find out what's going on with him?"

"Looks like right about now," said Robby, as the door opposite began to open. A figure strode into the room and folded his arms across his chest. Jara let out a gasp.

It was Marcus Surina.

• • •

Jara rubbed her eyes incredulously and took a closer look at the young man who had walked into the room. *Don't be a fool*, Jara told herself. *Marcus Surina died almost fifty years ago. Even if he managed to escape the shuttle explosion and jump in a time machine that instant, Marcus was in his fifties that day. This one can't be more than twenty-five.*

So it was not Marcus Surina, then, but unmistakably a man with the same genetic heritage. He had the same insouciant handsomeness, the same piercing blue eyes, the same imposing ship's rudder of a nose as the great scientist. Moreover, he bore that indefinable sense of *presence* that all the Surinas bore going back to Sheldon: a surety about the world, a magnetic force that pulled friends and strangers alike into his orbit.

Bali Chandler had slipped in behind the young man unnoticed. "You shoulda seen him when he tried to grow the mustache," he said, amused at Jara's befuddlement. "Margaret had a fit."

Suddenly the tumblers fell into place. Quell's son . . . a descendant of the Surinas . . . which meant . . . Jara didn't even realize she had stood up, but now she found herself flopping back down into her chair in shock. Robby Robby had his mouth open far wider than was appropriate, while Benyamin simply looked confused.

There's one mystery solved, thought Jara. *Now we know what kind of relationship Quell had with Margaret Surina.*

Josiah turned to greet the fiefcorpers with a diplomatic poise that seemed to come naturally to him, a poise that definitely sprang from the maternal side of the tree. "Towards Perfection," he said, offering a deep bow to the fiefcorpers. "As I'm sure you've guessed, I'm Josiah. Representative to the fourth ward of the Free Republic of the Pacific Islands." He turned to Chandler. "I believe you're right, Chandler. Now that I've cut my hair, I won't be able to hide the Surina in me for much longer."

Jara detected a message in the fact that the Islander had greeted his guests in the connectible fashion rather than in the custom of his own people. "I would say that we've heard a lot about you, but . . ."

"But if you had," said Josiah, gently interrupting, "then half of the Surina family's investors would have jumped ship. Who wants to put money into an enterprise that's destined to be dismantled and parceled out to the Islanders?" Jara could hear both sarcasm and disillusionment interwoven in the young Islander's voice. He walked around the table and took a seat at the head of the table, while Bali Chandler took the chair to his right. "At least, that's the story I had always been told. But enough of that. Tell me what happened to my father."

He had that most rare combination of genetic traits: Margaret's charismatic intellectualism mixed with Quell's scythelike directness and immediacy. It was enough to inspire an instant feeling of trust in Jara. She related again the story of Quell's hiring them for this mysterious errand, of his perplexing hints about Josiah, of his capture by the Defense and Wellness Council.

"There was no violence?" asked Josiah. "He didn't try to take a shock baton to anyone this time, did he?"

"No," said Robby. "Quell just waltzed out the door with them."

"Of course," said Chandler, nodding. "Borda doesn't want to risk anything happening to your father. Might need him for a bargaining chip."

From the corner of her eye, Jara could see Benyamin tamping down an outburst of frustration, but she decided to express her frustration first. "Gentlemen," she said firmly, "thank you very much for your hospitality. Sincerely. But it's time someone started telling us what's going on. Quell brought us down here to help him with something. Something important, I assume. He told me there was a series of things that have to happen, or not happen."

"Looks like one of those things that wasn't supposed to happen, happened," muttered Chandler.

"Which was?"

"Len Borda wasn't supposed to find out who Josiah's mother was, obviously. It's bad enough that Magan found out. If Borda sent a team of white-robes to pick Quell up, then . . ." He threw one hand up in the air and twirled it around as if prepping for a big finale. "Then he probably knows too." He let the hand plummet back to the tabletop.

"We're not trying to be rude," snapped Ben, his patience finally shattering. "But Margaret's gone. She's with the Null Current. Who cares if Borda finds out now?"

Josiah and Chandler traded questioning looks. Jara knew that ConfidentialWhispers were impossible without functioning neural OCHREs, but she could have sworn that the two Islanders were conducting a mental conversation anyway.

"My father trusted them," said Josiah finally. "He wanted them here. Brief them, Chandler."

The older man frowned. "Even . . . ?"

"In forty-eight hours, everyone's going to know anyway. So yes, tell them. Tell them everything."

(((17)))

Not every building in connectible territory was collapsible, so Jara had ridden in plenty of elevators before. But connectible elevators were usually equipped with SeeNaRee to make the ride less tedious, or at the least, interactive viewscreens. The elevator here in the Micah Brayling building, however, was a cramped, slow-moving box whose single viewscreen did nothing but dumbly repeat the same advertisement for waterfront real estate at twenty-second intervals. Chandler paid it no mind, but after three repetitions Jara was ready to claw the screen out with her bare hands.

As the box continued its sluggish climb, Benyamin and Robby tried to make small talk about sports with the Islander representative. (The Islanders had their own soccer league, but Union Baseball was almost completely unknown here.) Jara was too preoccupied with the young Surina they had left back in the lounge below to pay their conversation any mind.

Another Surina in the world, she thought. *An heir to Sheldon, Prengal, Marcus, and now Margaret. How could you keep such a thing secret?*

Concealing a secret of that magnitude was no simple undertaking, especially for a family whose every movement was scrutinized by drudges with high-tech tools at their disposal. Josiah's offhanded comment about his haircut led Jara to believe that the resemblance had only recently become an issue. As for Margaret, concealing her pregnancy presented little problem, assuming she followed the regular connectible practice of leaving the fetus to gestate in a hive. But to nurture and parent a child to adulthood in secret? To keep any mention of that child off the Data Sea altogether? That would require an enormous amount of trust in those around you, not to mention prodigious sums of money and inhuman diligence. Unless . . .

Unless you sent the child away to the Islands at birth.

Yes, suppose you entrusted the child to the care of his father's family in Manila while you remained in Andra Pradesh. Suppose you kept your distance from that child, both physically and emotionally, and relegated the parenting chores to the father. Suppose that father already had an excuse to shuttle back and forth to the Islands on a regular basis. Yes, Jara supposed in those extreme circumstances it could be done.

Still, the question remained: why?

Jara knew it was pointless to draw conclusions without having all the facts in hand. But she couldn't help wondering how much this explained Quell's orneriness and his peculiar relationship with Margaret, the way he seemed to be both her closest confidant and just another palace functionary. The fiefcorp master resolved to ask the Islander about it the next time she saw him . . . provided she *did* see him again.

Don't be ridiculous, thought Jara. *Remember what Chandler said. Quell will be fine.*

"Here we are," said Bali Chandler.

The elevator shuddered to a halt at the building's sixty-fifth (and uppermost) floor. The Islander led Jara, Benyamin, and Robby through a nondescript hallway, up a restricted staircase, and onto the building's roof.

Evening was already gathering around Manila, and up here atop the Micah Brayling building the dusktime parade of lights was breathtaking. Unlike connectible cities, where the mass transit vehicles stayed mostly on the ground, here in Manila the transportation network extended up nearly as far as the skyline. Jara was astounded to see tube trains skating from rooftop to rooftop, something she had not noticed during the day. She supposed if TubeCo could figure out how to extend tracks to the depths of the ocean floor, suspending them twenty or thirty stories wasn't such a difficult feat.

Chandler led the three of them to an outcropping on the edge of the roof. He reached into the pocket of his coat and withdrew what looked like a pair of ancient spectacles. The Islander put them to his eyes momentarily and gazed off into the distance, then handed them to Jara. "Here, take a look. Follow the beacon between the third and fourth towers and all the way to the horizon."

Jara put the lenses to her face gingerly, careful not to let her fingers touch the glass. *Of course*, she thought. *Not spectacles—a telescope.* In connectible lands, where you could activate a thousand telescopic and remote camera programs with a thought, such devices were only a curiosity. But here in the Islands . . . Jara tried to call up one of those programs now and discovered that it had been banned by Dogmatic Opposition. So she squinted through the glass where Chandler directed her and found herself looking offshore to the east.

At a cluster of Defense and Wellness Council hoverbirds hovering in the mist.

"Now follow the arc around to your left, there's five more beacons there," said Chandler. Jara did, swiveling the view around tube trains, puzzle piece buildings, and industrial cargo ships to find the digital beacons. She saw five more clumps of ghostly white hovercraft, floating inertly over the water perhaps a kilometer from shore.

"Borda's?" asked Jara.

"Those are Len Borda's," replied Chandler. "And *those*"—he turned in place and pointed about thirty degrees clockwise—"are Magan Kai Lee's."

Jara handed the glasses to Benyamin, who gazed at the horizon with visibly mounting anger before passing them to Robby. The channeler stared, drew in a breath, and whistled.

"You're going to have to explain this to me," fumed Benyamin. "We're not in fucking colonial times here. Why does the Defense and Wellness Council care what happens in the Islands? Sure, sometimes you people launch attacks against the connectibles, and I understand deterrence. But why would either Borda or Lee want to *invade*? No offense—but the Council pretty much has you boxed in here as it is."

Bali Chandler was leaning back on the railing on his elbows, enjoying the early evening breeze blowing through his frizzy hair. "You'd be surprised," he said. "Did you know that Borda's been trying to block the import of permasteel into the Islands for about a decade now?"

The young apprentice shook his head, not quite seeing the point.

"Requires tungsten to make it, and there's no tungsten out here in the Pacific Islands. So Borda thought he could stifle us by setting up blockades to keep the permasteel out. Can't build stuff like *this* without it." Chandler rapped his knuckles on the cold metal of the railing. "You'd think it'd be impossible to get huge tankers of permasteel through a Council blockade, right? And yet"—the Islander representative swept his hand towards the six other towers ringing City Center, all reflecting that unique permasteel glow—"it hasn't even slowed us down."

Jara studied the outcropping on which they stood and noticed that the entire thing was composed of a single sheet of metal, only centimeters thick. She shook her head. They lived at the zenith of an information age, yet so much of geopolitics still revolved around the movements of ponderous cargo ships and rusty tankers.

"So where do you get your permasteel from?" asked Robby.

"Ah," said Chandler with a toothy grin. "Ain't telling. State secret."

Robby seemed to appreciate the Islanders' resourcefulness, but Benyamin was not placated. "Smuggling permasteel is one thing," he said. "Standing up against Council armies is another."

"Is it?" The Islander representative turned and leaned on the railing with a prideful gaze out onto the city. "As I said before—you'd be surprised. Borda hasn't been nearly as successful boxing us in as you think. They've got to write an entirely different kind of black code to deal with us, because the normal stuff won't work. And it's hard to write black code to disable the enemy's OCHREs when you're not even sure what OCHREs the enemy's *got*. But . . ." Chandler stretched his arms up over his head, cracked his neck idly, then turned to face the fiefcorpers again. "In the end, you're right, Benyamin. We couldn't stand up to a full assault by the Council. That's no state secret. All we can do is make it prohibitively expensive for them to try. So the only thing Len Borda's done up to this point is harass us. Check our growth. Try to stop our permasteel shipments."

"What's changed?" said Jara.

"Magan."

Jara shook her head. "Maybe I'm just stupid. What does Magan have to do with the Islands? Why does his rebellion change anything out here?"

Chandler flicked his tongue over his lips and scratched once more at his stubble as he gathered his thoughts. *The Islanders have two armies camped offshore ready to invade*, thought Jara impatiently, *and their parliamentary representative here is so relaxed he's almost embalmed.*

"Sun Tzu," said the Islander after a moment, shifting conversational tracks. "*The Art of War*. Any of you read it?"

The fiefcorp master had a brief flashback to the hive. Interminable lessons, boring ancient texts. "I've read pieces of it."

"Not a word," said Ben.

"Read the whole thing at least five times," put in Robby cheerfully, still scanning the horizon with the telescopic spectacles.

"Then you know, Mr. Robby, that Sun Tzu's main principle still applies. *Know thy enemy.* Difference is that today, you need to know a lot more about the enemy than you used to. You need to know where they are, how they're armed, how they're defended." Chandler ticked these items off on the wrinkled fingers of his right hand. "How do you get that information on a battlefield? In ancient times you could track your opponent via satellite, but we've got so many ways of faking out satellites nowadays that they're next to useless for military purposes. Same thing with remote cameras, spy drones, long-distance electromagnetic scans. For every surveillance technology there's a more effective *counter*surveillance technology—except for one."

"Multi," said Jara.

Bali Chandler laughed. "Businesswoman and battlefield tactician too, huh?"

"Hardly. But I've seen a thousand war dramas in my day."

"Ah, dramas! All right, you've seen the dramas. Tell me how you use multi on the battlefield."

Jara knew that writers and directors often employed pretzel logic in the scripting of their dramas, but some scenarios were common enough that she figured there had to be some underlying truth to them. She described her vision of how modern battle was conducted, as informed by the dramas of Jeannie Q. Christina and Bill Rixx. Before the first shots were fired, you sent a barrage of multi projections into enemy territory—hundreds, sometimes thousands of them—to scope out the opposing camp. As your multi projections streamed out past the line of battle, multi disruptor cannons were gunning full-bore at the enemy's incoming projections. If you deployed your multi forces effectively, enough would get through to give an adequate picture of the enemy's defenses.

"Terrific!" said the Islander with a comic burst of applause. "A little sensationalized, but basically accurate. So tell me what would happen if you could totally block incoming multi projections from crossing into your camp?"

"You'd have a huge advantage, I guess," said Jara.

Benyamin sliced his hand through the air in objection. "Maybe you don't understand the politics of the multi network," he said. "The network administrators, they've always refused to cooperate with the Council. It's like a cardinal rule. *We won't have our technology politicized,* they say. *The network is the network, and not even the high executive himself gets special treatment.*"

Chandler nodded. "Ah, but you're forgetting something. There's one place where the network administrators *have* agreed to block multi connections. There's one place where they *do* give special treatment."

"What place is that?"

The Islander extended his open palm over the edge of the railing.

• • •

"So the Council isn't trying to take over the Islands at all," said Jara.

The four of them had decamped back to the tranquil lounge with the painting of the musketed soldiers. Jara finally poured herself that tumbler of rum she had been craving and sat down at one end of the conference table. Chandler sat down at the other, while Benyamin and Robby took seats along the sides. Jara felt like doing nothing but retreating back to the tube and sending Horvil a Confidential Whisper, but clearly the briefing was not over.

"Take over the Islands?" replied Chandler. "No. Wouldn't be any point. Len Borda and Magan Kai Lee are quietly building up their forces on the perimeter for another reason. They want to use the Islands as a base to attack each *other*."

"I can see some of the benefits to putting your army behind the unconnectible curtain," said Jara. "But isn't there a significant downside as well? Aren't they going to have a heck of a time running bio/logic weapons systems back here?"

"A few," the Islander admitted. "But it's negligible compared to what they'd gain."

Benyamin suddenly looked ill. "So they're both going to . . . invade?"

"Invade?" Chandler snorted with good humor. "Invasions are a last resort, my friend. You start with persuasion, then you move on to leverage. After that comes bribery, then deception, and *then* force." The Islander let out a cackle that might have been the most disturbing thing Jara had heard the entire conversation. "Listen, the three of you are arriving on the tail end of all this. We've been dealing with the Council for two months now. Manila's literally *crawling* with spies and diplomats trying to persuade the parliament to let in one side or the other. I'm telling you, it's been fun times here in Manila."

Jara downed the rest of her rum in a single gulp.

"So who's winning?" said Robby.

"Glad you asked." The Islander reached under the lip of the table, which Jara suddenly noticed was filled with multiple sets of recessed buttons. He tapped a few of the buttons, causing a holographic pie chart to appear over the table. "There's forty-eight districts in the Free Republic. And right now, here's the tally, as close as we can make it out. . . ." Bali Chandler gestured at the pie chart, which the fiefcorpers read with grim concentration.

Magan Kai Lee—9
Len Borda—8
Resistance—4
Undecided—27

"'Resistance'?" said Benyamin.

"We fight all comers," said Chandler, putting his fists up in sarcastic imitation of a boxer's stance.

Jara shivered involuntarily. Knowing Quell, she did not doubt the bravery or tenacity of the Islanders. But knowing Len Borda, she wouldn't lay great odds on the Free Republic surviving an armed confrontation with both of the Council's two feuding executives. They'd be crushed as if they'd come between the hammer and the anvil.

The fiefcorp master rubbed her temples and looked longingly at the wet bar again. "What you're saying is that it's anyone's guess what the parliament is going to decide."

Chandler shook his head. "No. What I'm saying is that the stage is set for a certain charismatic young representative to make his big debut." He splayed his hands in the air as if framing a scene for an imaginary camera. "Our man steps into the spotlight. He declares his heritage and his ownership of MultiReal. He releases a compelling manifesto and sways the balance of the parliament to vote his way."

"Wait a second, back up," snapped Benyamin. "Ownership of MultiR—"

The realization seemed to slap each of the fiefcorpers in the face simultaneously. Josiah Surina, son and heir of Margaret Surina, Islander representative, statesman, and now—thanks to the recent testimony of his father in a courtroom in Andra Pradesh—legal owner of MultiReal technology. By working to put MultiReal in the hands of the Surina family, Quell had really put it into his own.

"That sly bastard!" said Robby with a chuckle. "That sly, sly bastard!"

Jara could suddenly see the logic behind so much that had gone on in the past two weeks. Quell, trying to keep the secret of his son's identity concealed from Len Borda as long as possible. Magan Kai Lee, moving whatever levers he needed to move behind the scenes to ensure that the Surina family won its court case. "So Quell believes the Islanders should side with Magan Kai Lee," said Jara.

"I suppose," replied Chandler, reaching under the table to dispel the pie chart back to holographic limbo. "Though I'm not sure that Josiah feels the same way. I assume that's the counsel Quell wanted you to provide. Helping convince him of the right path to take. Oh, and let me add one more wrinkle."

"What's that?" asked Robby.

"I said that you arrived at the tail end of all this. Well, I meant it. Len Borda's tired of talking and playing spy games. He realizes that his chances of getting what he wants through negotiation are slim and getting slimmer. So our scouts say that he's preparing for an invasion. In the next forty-eight hours."

The room suddenly seemed to get a lot darker. Jara remembered her conversation with Horvil where he said the Pacific Islands could be a war zone in a week's time. It had felt like hyperbole then, but now it looked like events might prove him right, two days earlier than he had predicted.

(((18)))

A life lived on perimeters. A life in between things.

Neither connectible nor unconnectible, neither resident of the Pacific Islands nor resident of Andra Pradesh. More than a lover to Margaret Surina, yet not her legally bonded companion. Not a full-time parent to Josiah, in order to help Margaret complete her Phoenix Project—but not a full-fledged partner on the Phoenix Project either, in order to spend time in Manila raising his son.

Quell, man of edges.

And now, Quell sat in the in-between place once again, this time in a very literal sense. He was a prisoner aboard one of Len Borda's Defense and Wellness Council hoverbirds, scuttling along the unconnectible curtain outside Manila. Four officers wearing the white robe and yellow star surrounded him, two armed with dartguns and two armed with the connectible equivalent of a shock baton. Quell's wrists were bound, but otherwise he was quite comfortable.

He had told Jara that Magan Kai Lee would bail him out. Yet if there was one thing Quell knew about Magan, he knew that Magan was not a man of sentiment. Quell had fancied himself an important asset to the rebellion, but looked at through the concentrating prism of logic, the case was not so strong. The longer he sat here staring at the ocean, the more hopeless his case became.

Magan did not need him. The lieutenant executive might have used Quell to press his case to Josiah, but Quell was confident that Jara could do just as good a job. Truth be told, Josiah was far more likely to heed her counsel than heed his father's.

Borda did not need him either. The high executive might also have used Quell as a bargaining chip to get his armies behind the unconnectible curtain, but Borda would soon see the futility of that idea.

Jara's first recommendation to Josiah would undoubtedly be to not let Quell's capture color his reasoning.

So why would anyone confront this cadre of Borda's troops to free a worthless fool of an Islander whose life had never been his own? Magan had already freed him from Borda's clutches once at great risk; he had given Quell his freedom and promised assistance in recapturing legal rights to MultiReal in exchange for the Islander's assistance getting Magan's armies behind the curtain. The lieutenant executive wasn't likely to come up with another such bargain. Which meant that Quell would probably sit in a succession of hoverbirds staring at dartgun barrels until the situation in the Council resolved itself. Either that, or he would shortly be on his way back to orbital prison and the ever-present danger of broken thumbs.

And who would be the worse for it?

• • •

Quell tried to remember when his identity started to slip away. He supposed it began when he was a student at the Gandhi University all those years ago, the day he met Margaret and confronted her about her speech before Creed Surina.

Quell had been seventeen years old, and Margaret sixteen. She had stood up before an audience of creed sycophants and lectured them about how the universe compelled humanity to scientific discovery, how it invited exploration of its mysteries. *No philosopher, philanthropist, or prophet has done as much to improve our lot in life as the scientist*, she had said. *My father once told me that when you turn your back on scientific progress, you turn your back on human suffering.* The world was still newly embroiled in the Economic Plunge, and rioting in Melbourne had just rocked the very foundations of the centralized government. People were hungry for the ambition and audacity of the Surinas.

Margaret's speech before the Creed Surina devotees had left Quell feeling restive and belligerent. He had walked up to the podium after the speech was over and the devotees had all slithered away. Only Margaret's ever-present retinue of handlers had remained.

So you think I'm a masochist? Quell had snapped by way of greeting.

The young lecturer had turned to focus her attention on the Islander. She was a small woman, thin as a stalk of wheat. Her almond-colored skin and sizable nose betrayed her Surina heritage. *So I think you're . . . what?* she had replied, confused. Apparently in high society Andra Pradesh, *what* began with an H.

Your speech, Quell had said. *"When you turn your back on scientific progress, you turn your back on human suffering." If you really believe that, you must believe the Islanders are masochists. Why else would we refuse to run bio/logic programs twenty-four hours a day? Why else would we wear these?* He had pointed to his government-issue connectible collar, which was even thicker and more unwieldy in those days. *It must be because we like sickness and pain. We must like human suffering.*

Something had surfaced from beneath those ocean blue eyes. Curiosity. *Of course I don't believe that,* Margaret had replied. *All of us are looking for a way to deflect our own suffering.*

Quell had taken the words in and imprinted them on his memory. *What's that supposed to mean?*

It means that if you liked disease, you wouldn't be using bio/logic programs to control your asthma, now would you?

The Islander had paused. He had thought of Margaret as a hypocrite because she mouthed words of support for pro-Islander policies in public while completely ignoring the actual Islanders studying at the university. But apparently Margaret had taken an interest after all. Quell's condition had hardly been a secret, but neither had it been obvious to a casual bystander, thanks to the OCHREs lining his brachial tubing and the bio/logic programs that directed them. *So you admit your father was wrong,* he had said. *Just because we doubt science doesn't mean we embrace suffering.*

I admit nothing of the kind, Margaret had riposted, clearly starting to enjoy the duel. *In fact, you've just proven his point. Software can fix your lungs today, but if your parents had embraced medical technology when you were conceived, you wouldn't have gotten asthma in the first place. A hive would have fixed your lungs during gestation. But because your mother chose to grow you in her belly, she allowed your asthma to happen. She turned her back on human suffering.*

Quell could recognize a deliberate provocation when he heard one, and he had struggled to keep his poise. Still, despite the vehemence of Margaret's words, her tone had not been confrontational at all, but rather upbeat, almost playful. *You can fix a lot of things if you grow babies in vats,* he had said. *But at what cost? Pumping them full of OCHREs?*

The OCHREs are a lot easier to install during gestation. They can always be adjusted or deactivated later.

Later? Later? The Islander had felt his voice rising in spite of himself. *That's always the way it is with you connectibles. You put the burden on us to "adjust" to your technologies. Think about it from our point of view for once. You only give us two options: implant a complete OCHRE system in the womb and "adjust" later, or go back to doctors with clumsy steel tools. All or nothing. Listen. The Islanders don't want to spend half our lives upgrading software—but do you think we want to move* backwards? *After all these hundreds of years?*

There had been a long pause as Margaret had tried to find her footing after this tirade. Quell had realized in characteristically late fashion that he had pushed back too hard. He had peered over Margaret's shoulder only to see the Surina family handlers edging closer with deepening frowns, looking at him as if he were one of the large beetles that scurried on the walls in the summertime.

The Islander had smiled and flipped his head back, causing long blond hair to cascade over one shoulder. He wasn't afraid of these people. *You want to ditch them?* he had asked, indicating the handlers with a lift of his eyebrows.

Margaret had blinked as if the idea had never occurred to her. *Ditch them?*

Yeah.

And go where?

Quell had shrugged. *Don't know. You tell me.*

Something had sparked inside Margaret at that moment. Quell would later discover that the girl had barely spent an hour alone since the death of her father six years earlier. Privacy had been a casualty of Marcus's death, along with her independence. *I'm game,* Margaret had said with a grin. To Quell's surprise, she had grabbed one of his hands and they had taken off for the Revelation Spire.

The Revelation Spire, the world's tallest building, a thin spike in the sky. The place had been closed to the public for six years, so Quell had had only vague ideas of what he would find behind those grand double doors. He had caught a glimpse of security officers dashing pell-mell across the courtyard behind them as Margaret tugged him inside. The atrium had been filled with hundreds upon hundreds of boxes. Quell had followed Margaret to a side alcove, watched as she opened a secret door with a wave of her hand and leapt into the elevator leading to the top of the Spire. The door had slid shut behind them before the Surina goons had even made it through the building's entrance.

Margaret had kissed him on the way up. It was a long way.

Quell had been shocked by this sudden display of passion. He had not been blind to her charms, but he had seen no hint of reciprocation in her eyes. Amazing what you could learn to conceal when you were the richest girl in the world.

If I ask you something, she had said, snuggling into the canopy of his arms, *will you promise to tell me the truth?*

Sure.

Am I beautiful?

The Islander had suddenly realized his appeal to her. Not only had he exhibited no fear of Margaret's handlers, he had represented a world outside the bubble of Andra Pradesh. A secure anchor to a saner reality.

Quell had decided to keep his promise. *No*, he had said. *You're attractive. You're beguiling. You're sexy. You're fascinating.* He had been surprised to discover that he meant all these things. *But if you're asking whether you're beautiful in the classical sense . . . no, you're not.* Margaret had nodded. She had not been disappointed in his answer; on the contrary, she had seemed incredibly relieved to have the burden of beauty lifted from her shoulders. *Why?* Quell had said. *What have your handlers been telling you?*

They tell me a lot of things, Margaret had said. *I . . . I never know what's true and what's not.*

Well, then I guess it's my job to make sure you know the truth.

Quell had been surprised to discover he meant that too.

That was the day he began to lose himself, Quell realized now as he watched the languid Pacific Ocean pass by out the window of the Council hoverbird. It had been on that day that the two of them had fallen in love, and Quell had found himself drawn to something larger than himself. He had told himself time after time that Margaret's heritage meant nothing; that he was her equal; that his wishes counted as much as hers. But when put to the test, Quell with his stubborn individualism was no match for four hundred years of history.

● ● ●

Margaret had been sheltered her entire life by handlers. These Surina family protectors had kept her isolated from her father's battles with the Defense and Wellness Council, and then took it upon themselves to keep her cloistered from the world after his sudden death. And now, like an answered prayer, a young man had come into her life who was free from the taint of Andra Pradesh. A man of strength, wisdom, and character who was not afraid to tell her the truth, who could show her the crooked and unseemly things, the blemished facts, the rusted people, the corroded emotions—everything her power and position had isolated her from.

As the relationship had matured and trust had deepened, Quell had begun to suspect that Margaret was in possession of a terrible secret. She had had her sights not on the world around her, but on some extradimensional place that was closed off to mere mortals. The Islander had vowed not to press her, figuring she would tell him in her own time. And he had been correct.

I need to show you something, she had told Quell one day. *Can I trust you?*

Of course, the Islander had replied.

Margaret had led him to the top of the Revelation Spire again, the place she had appropriated as her office. She had turned on the Mind-Space workbench that lay there, the one that Marcus Surina had constructed. The largest bio/logic workbench ever built. And Margaret had showed Quell the databases her father had left behind on his death.

In MindSpace, they had looked like an immense valley, bounded on all sides by peakless mountains, sharp and terrible. Tall spikes shaped like fir trees had dotted the landscape, while great rivers had curved across vast distances. Rotating the mass on its three axes had led to even more startling discoveries. Caves and crenellations that were only visible from certain angles. Strange formations that changed shape depending on how you approached them, and others that metamorphosed into something else entirely when you touched them with a bio/logic programming bar.

And in the center of it all, enveloped by the hills and tucked between two small lagoons of information, there had sat a perfect, gleaming castle.

I have a responsibility, Quell, she had told him.

Quell had gaped at the structure, both amazed and aghast at the same time. He had far outpaced his classmates in the study of bio/logic engineering, but still he had never seen anything like it. *A responsibility to whom?*

To humanity, Margaret had replied, her voice utterly bereft of irony.

From that day onward, that responsibility had been all. And Quell, lovestruck fool that he was, had taken on the burden of that responsibility too. He had let his own five-year course of study at the Gandhi University turn into a six-year degree, then a seven-year degree—and finally, his education had slipped into a dark ravine and never emerged. He had subsumed his own dreams, inchoate and immature as they were, to Margaret's.

What was Margaret's dream? What had Marcus been working on at the time of his sudden demise? What was the purpose of this vast digital edifice that had begun to consume her?

Had she not known, or had she simply been unable to express it? *Perfection*, she had told Quell.

He had not understood what she meant. But if there was any virtual structure large and complex enough to contain Perfection, it was the one Marcus Surina had left behind. Clearly the code was not all Marcus's doing; the structure was too enormous for any one human being to have constructed alone. Marcus Surina had squandered decades on his frivolous jaunts around the solar system before finally settling down in Andra Pradesh; Quell had calculated that if Margaret's father had spent every waking moment the rest of his life in MindSpace, he could not have completed a tenth of the required programming.

Inside the structure, Quell and Margaret had found the core programming for teleportation. It wasn't a one-for-one match. You couldn't pluck the code out of the virtual forest and expect to be transmigrating molecules the next day. But there had been too many similarities between the two programs to call it coincidence. The same corkscrew shape, the same dappled greens and yellows woven through the center, the same hooklike protrusion at the base. It was as if someone had taken the original teleportation code and riffed on it, improvising the junctures to fit into a larger and more cohesive framework.

Had Marcus Surina plugged his teleportation code into some massive multigenerational monolith of data—or had he extracted the code *out*? Had he really been the engineering genius the drudges had claimed, or merely a clever transcriptionist?

And if the latter . . . whose blueprints had he been transcribing?

And why were the achievements of all Margaret's ancestors honeycombed within this MindSpace colossus? Why did the colossus contain not just teleportation, but key subroutines that powered the Data Sea, MindSpace, the multi network—so many of the joints of the modern programming scaffolding?

Margaret threw all other commitments aside in her quest to understand this titanic *thing* her father had bequeathed to her. Creed ceremonies, academic conferences, financial summits: all hastily shoved away. Her relationship with Quell: sidelined.

Quell himself had taken to reactivating neural OCHREs in his bid to keep up with Margaret. Only certain OCHREs, only the necessary ones—but enough to make him a heretic to some in his family. But though he had felt intellectual curiosity to understand the Surina legacy, his heart wasn't in it.

Quell considered leaving many times over the next few years, but Margaret would always convince him to stay. *I need you*, she would say. *I love you. Don't you see? We can pursue this dream together. We can unite the world. We can fulfill the destiny of the Surinas and achieve Perfection.* Quell was more concerned with his own broken destiny. Time was rapidly running out for him to choose an alternate course for his life. Already he had spent a decade here in Andra Pradesh with the connectibles, among them yet not one of them. The Islands were no longer his home, but neither was Andra Pradesh. If he were to leave Margaret—where would he go?

Years passed. The arguments between them only grew more vociferous, and Margaret's declarations of love only grew more wild and desperate. Quell gave her an ultimatum.

Josiah was born the following year.

Quell had thought he had won the argument; he had considered Margaret's decision to have a child the first step in a path towards greater intimacy. Instead, Josiah only drove them apart. Margaret delegated more and more of the child's care to Quell as she slowly disappeared inside the Surina legacy. Once the Islander had been an equal on the project. By the time Josiah reached his fifth birthday, however, Quell had been relegated to a subordinate role. How could it be otherwise with Quell spending so much time in the Pacific Islands playing father? His was the job of keeping the various wings of the Surina family business functioning; his was the job of keeping investors happy, which meant keeping his relationship with Margaret and the existence of Josiah tightly under wraps; his was the job of finding funds for the project that were untethered to the Surina family, and that meant supplicating Len Borda.

As for the mass of code Marcus Surina had left behind, for Quell the mystery only grew more mysterious. He had a solid, practical understanding about the portion of code Margaret had been working on all these years, the portion she had christened MultiReal. But the larger purpose of the scaffold remained, to Quell, unknown.

Again he tried to ask her what its purpose was.

Perfection, she had whispered, the two of them embracing atop the Revelation Spire, eyes closed, the rest of the world far below.

But what does that mean? Quell had asked. *We don't need Perfection. We have Josiah. Our son! Our son is Perfection.*

No. He is—we are—only the guardians and the keepers.

Quell—frantic inside at the possibility that Margaret had utterly slipped away from him, slipped away from coherence, and in agony that he had gambled his life on the legacy of the Surinas and still, as he approached middle age, had nothing to show for it—said, *When will MultiReal be done? When will this be over?*

Margaret had answered, *Soon.*

And after MultiReal is running on every bio/logic system from here to Fur-

toid, after you've fulfilled the destiny of the Surinas, after you've spread "Per-fection" through the universe . . . then, then can we be together? Then can you be my bonded companion and Josiah your son for the whole world to see?

Yes, Margaret had said. *After the destiny of the Surina family has been fulfilled, it will be a different world. Anything will be possible.*

Quell's heart had leapt. Anything would be possible. Even renew-ing a life wasted, a life lived on perimeters, a life in between things. He now had a goal. To help Margaret finish MultiReal, to get the pro-gram safely launched on the Data Sea so Quell could reclaim her love, so Quell could redeem himself.

And then came Len Borda's impatience.

Margaret's sudden, blind, panicked fear.

The desperate attempts to put MultiReal in the hands of a fiefcorp and stave off Borda's iron hand.

The Patel Brothers' treachery.

Natch.

The infoquakes.

Madness.

The Null Current.

And finally, finally, it came down to what Quell had always feared it would come down to: himself, half-Islander and half-connectible, resident of nowhere, man of edges, sitting in the belly of a Defense and Wellness Council hoverbird, little hope of rescue, MultiReal gone, his son half-estranged, the Islands on the brink of annihilation, him tee-tering on the border between existence and nothingness and no longer caring in which direction he fell.

• • •

A hand shook his shoulder.

Quell awoke with a start, groaning at the crick in his neck that had developed from falling asleep in an uncomfortable position. He opened his eyes and found himself staring at a pair of hazel pupils hovering right over his face.

Papizon.

The Islander took a startled look around him. The four Borda lackeys who had been watching over him had vanished. Outside the open hoverbird door, Quell could see nothing but white—the shining white paint of Magan Kai Lee's hoverbirds. Quell had not been woken by the sounds of battle because there had *been* no battle; Magan's force here so vastly outnumbered Borda's that they had surrendered without a struggle.

"We have *got* to stop meeting like this," said Papizon with a lop-sided grin.

(((19)))

The hotel Chandler had booked the fiefcorpers in was appropriately opulent and, better yet, completely paid for. The postprandial coffee brewing when Jara arrived in her room was vibrant, and the view of the City Center was spectacular. She regretted wasting such fine accommodations, but there would simply be no time for rest in the next forty-eight hours. So Jara found herself wandering the streets of Manila at midnight with a small security detail by her side, holding a ConfidentialWhisper chat with Horvil.

"The world's falling apart," she lamented.

"If the world's falling apart," replied the engineer from his room many kilometers in the sky, "then you and I are at the hinges."

"That bad up there in 49th Heaven?"

"That bad. Richard Taylor refused to get on the hoverbird for an hour. And then when we arrived here, there were so many things blinking and flashing and beeping he refused to get *off* the hoverbird for three. He's on total sensory overload."

"And Vigal?"

"Almost as useless. He just gawks at everything like a tourist. But at least his heart's in the right place. I still have no idea what Taylor really wants."

Jara's nerves were in a similarly frayed state, but this walk was doing its part to soothe them. The streets were still loaded with pedestrians, despite the late hour, and everyone seemed to be luxuriating in the mellow tropical warmth. Jara tried to return the smiles of the passersby, but all she could think when she saw some carefree youth strutting down the sidewalk was that he might be lying in a ditch covered in blood in less than forty-eight hours. Chandler's statements about the city crawling with spies and diplomats caused her to give a suspicious second look to everyone who passed.

Don't let yourself get distracted, Jara told herself. *You've got a job to do.*

She didn't feel comfortable providing Horvil with too many details about Chandler's briefing. Nobody had ever successfully cracked the security of a ConfidentialWhisper, as far as Jara knew, but this was simply too important for her to make such blithe assumptions. So she kept things vague. Horvil, to his credit, understood perfectly and did not press for details.

"I can't believe how much *responsibility* I've got on my shoulders," Jara complained. "It's not just the success or failure of a little fiefcorp at stake anymore. The well-being of several hundred million people could depend on whether we give a complete stranger good advice. No, it's more than that—this could determine the outcome of world history."

"That's rough," said Horvil sympathetically.

"I know what advice Quell wanted us to give—but honestly, I'm not sure it's the right advice. He's already made up his mind about which side he wants to support. But I have no idea how or why he came to that conclusion."

The engineer was clearly flailing for supportive words to help guide Jara through this ocean of vagueness. "Well, you've got a good team with you there, right? That helps."

"It does," said Jara. She had half expected Benyamin and Robby Robby to shrug off the pressure and slink to their rooms at the first opportunity. But clearly the sinister flicker of those Council hoverbirds drifting off the coastline had affected them too. Ben was busy speed-reading through every drudge editorial and policy speech he could find in an attempt to give himself a crash course on Islander politics; Robby had taken it upon himself to start glad-handing people on the streets in an attempt to ferret out the real, unfiltered opinions of the Islanders. Merri's shuttle was due to arrive in two hours, and Jara knew that she would be equally diligent as soon as she stepped off the dock.

"I wish I could say that I didn't sign up for this crap," grumbled

Jara. "But the truth is, I did. I complained that I was feeling irrele-vant—and now I'm *too* relevant."

"You know what they say," answered Horvil. *"Don't wish for horses unless you want the whole farm."*

• • •

Merri arrived an hour ahead of schedule, looking dazed and somewhat claustrophobic from being crammed in a small metal cabin for almost two days. But the exhaustion went deeper than that. Jara suspected that the stress of dealing with her perpetually ill companion, Bonneth, was starting to back up on her, though true to form, Merri refused to talk about it. Jara felt like taking her aside as a friend and telling her that she was in no condition to travel several hundred thousand kilo-meters to play consultant here in the Pacific Islands.

But she couldn't afford to be Merri's friend at the moment. Not with two Defense and Wellness Council fleets offshore waiting to pounce on Manila. And so Merri was no sooner off the hoverbird than Jara was hus-tling her into a quiet room with Bali Chandler, who had agreed to give her an abbreviated version of the briefing he had given the others.

At ten a.m. that morning, Jara gathered the fiefcorpers together to discuss the situation. She went around the table asking everyone in turn to summarize their thoughts and the findings of their research. As each person spoke, Jara called up Envisage 24.8 and began transcribing.

Benyamin stared with skepticism at the jumble of holographic words and connections floating over the conference table like a cat's cradle. "Do you really think that's going to help?" he said.

"Absolutely," replied Jara with conviction. "This is the best macro-analysis program on the market right now. Works on the same principle as Zeitgeist, but it doesn't start with any preconceived notions of how to organize your data. And it only uses the information you give it."

"I can vouch for Envisage," said Robby Robby. "Former clients."

"But there's no real *intelligence* behind those diagrams," retorted Ben. "You know the law—no AI, no smart software. What kind of answers do you expect that thing to come up with?"

"None."

The young apprentice was taken aback. "None?"

"Correct," said Jara. "The point isn't to determine the right *answers*. The point is to determine the right *questions*."

"What *I* worry about," said Merri, "is that we're trying to advise our client without having all the relevant facts. I mean, none of us has more than seventy-two hours of experience in the Islands. *I* haven't even been here an entire morning yet. And here we are trying to help determine their future." She nervously fingered the Creed Objectivv emblem on her lapel as if it might ward off the taint of half-truth.

"One hundred percent correct, Merri," said Robby brightly. "Haven't you ever heard of intervention consulting?"

Merri shook her head, as did Benyamin. Jara gestured for Robby to continue.

"The goal is to shake up established thinking. To shatter hardened positions. And one way to do that is to swoop down on a situation *without* knowing the facts. You jump in and reestablish first impressions, reconsider points of view that might have gotten shoved aside prematurely. Think around taboos. Trust me, it's great stuff."

"But aren't you just going to end up with uninformed opinions?" asked Merri, not sold by Robby's description.

"Sometimes. But if you do it the right way and use the right software, you can also break through deadlocks and find new solutions."

Jara nodded sagely. She had studied intervention consulting; in fact, she had taken an entire course on it two years back at Natch's direction. She hadn't consciously been trying to apply that philosophy today, though she supposed it must have been lurking in the back of her mind. Jara gave Robby a silent *thank you* and dove back into the Envisage program with renewed energy.

But the fiefcorp master wasn't used to working in the Islands, where technology often sat behind barbed fences. She kept running afoul of these peculiar unconnectible user interfaces, replete with unlabeled buttons and tactile-response surfaces that worked off a completely alien set of rules. It felt like a grown-up version of initiation. After another hour of mostly silent concentration along with the occasional bout of fiefcorp bickering, Jara decided to walk the City Center in search of something to eat. Merri, who had consumed nothing but inedible OrbiCo bundled "meals" for two days, went with her.

"So how's Bonneth?" inquired Jara, struggling to find polite small talk as they strode through the square, again with a security detail shadowing their every step.

"Stubborn as always," said Merri with a shrug.

"What is it this time?"

The channel manager seemed to be wrestling with how much detail to give. She glanced around at the enormity of the square and apparently decided they would be out here for a few minutes. "Well, I've been trying to convince her to move back Terran-side, like she promised a few years ago. You know how inconvenient it is to live up there if you're not one of the tycoons. Living on Luna was only supposed to be a temporary solution until we had her Mai-Lo Syndrome under control. But now Bonneth's decided she wants to stay."

Jara hurriedly found a bio/logic program to stifle her impending yawn. "Sounds like quite a dilemma."

"I think I've found a reasonable compromise, but Bonneth doesn't want to hear about it. Ever heard of 'dualists'?" The fiefcorp manager shook her head. "It's a new trend for long-distance relationships that Creed Objectivv is all abuzz over. Instead of trying to move one place or another, we'd rent *two* apartments, one on Earth and one on Luna. Each of us would live in the apartment we wanted, and we'd trade off days in multi."

Jara tried to imagine such a solution with Horvil, if they ever decided to take that next step in their relationship. "So what does this have to do with Creed Objectivv?" she said, suddenly intrigued.

"Well, take a look at the logo." Merri withdrew the pin with the trademark Objectivv swirl from the left breast pocket of her coat and held it up. "Black and white, distinct, unmuddied. Each one strong and clear. It ties into the whole creed philosophy about dealing with conflicting truths—you don't choose either black or white over the other . . . and you don't dilute the whole thing into a mess of gray. *Truth has many facets*, that's what the Bodhisattva said. So you find a way to respect the black *and* the white, both at the same time. That's the dualism trend in a nutshell. Each companion gets to live where he or she wants. There's compromise, but you don't really even have to meet your partner halfway."

Jara stopped in the middle of the square, causing the three men of their security detail to suddenly put their hands on their weapons. The fiefcorp master felt as if a clarifying lens had suddenly snapped into place in her thoughts.

Islanders and connectibles. Len Borda and Magan Kai Lee. Quell and Margaret Surina. Josiah.

A new solution.

• • •

The fiefcorpers gathered with the Islanders in a room that might have been designed as an object lesson in state propaganda. An enormous mural to Jara's left depicted the founding of the Free Republic of the Pacific Islands in a romantic and surely exaggerated fashion, with the Band of Twelve standing in defiant, self-important poses. An equally impressive mural to her right showed a highly stylized rendering of the Technology Control Board at work, with several sharply dressed bureaucrats making simultaneous speeches to an assembled committee. Apparently the business of regulating technology involved a lot of grandiloquent hand waving.

Jara folded her own hands on the sizable conference table and studied Quell's son. Had this been any other man at the dawn of his twenties, Jara might have wondered whether he was prepared to step in front of several hundred million people and attempt to sway the course of an entire civilization. But not Josiah. He possessed that precocious look that the Surinas all possessed, a look that conveyed the ability to see beyond the Earthly scope of any human endeavor—or at least, to appear that way.

"I realize you're not typical consultants," said Josiah, all piety and seriousness. "My father trusts you. He brought you out here at great expense, and it's clear to me that he thought your opinion in this matter would be worthwhile."

Chandler, wearing a pair of open-toed sandals along with his olive green representative's uniform, was not in the mood for the typical Surina grandiosity. "So lay it out for us already," he said.

"Okay," said Jara, appreciating Chandler's directness. She gave a sidelong look at Benyamin, Merri, and Robby with an expression that said *Just sit tight and follow my lead.* The three of them sat still as statues with no indication that they intended to interrupt her. "Let's get one thing out of the way first. It's pretty clear that the only reason Quell isn't still in orbital prison is because of Magan Kai Lee. Magan must have finagled a way to get your father out of prison, and Magan must have brought him to Andra Pradesh to testify in that trial. Magan's paying the consulting fees for my fiefcorp. So plainly the lieutenant executive believes that my being here helps his case before the Islander parliament."

Josiah nodded. "Agreed."

"On the other hand . . . Quell knows this fiefcorp. He knows *me.* He's perfectly aware that I have no tolerance for bullshit, and I won't let politeness or politics sway my opinion. More than that, your father knows that we have no vested interest in the outcome here. We've got grudges against both Len Borda and Magan Kai Lee. And no matter what the parliament decides, we can always pack up and go back home."

Chandler interrupted her with a wave of his hands. "You trying to say that Quell's not really working for Magan?"

Jara shook her head. "No. I think the two of them struck a deal. But Quell didn't want to stack the deck in Magan's favor. He wanted a legitimate, considered third-party opinion about what the Islanders should do here. And for whatever reason, Magan thinks that serves his interests."

There was more than a little bit of Quell in Josiah's gruff gesture that he understood and to please continue.

"So let's look at the three alternatives one at a time," said Jara. "Side with Len Borda, side with Magan Kai Lee, or refuse entry to either of them.

"Borda knows you've got no reason to trust him. He's got a history of animosity against the Islanders, and he knows that his best weapon right now is fear. Which is why he's gearing up to invade—or why he's trying to make you *think* he's gearing up to invade. That said, if there's one thing Borda understands, it's leverage. He knows the public is against him now, and he needs some good news. I'm sure you could make a deal with him to end the attacks and the harassment and the blockades in exchange for allowing him a temporary military base behind the unconnectible curtain. And I think the high executive would honor it, at least in the near term.

"Lee is a more complex case. He's the first viable challenger to Len Borda's authority in decades, so that automatically scores him some points. He's clearly more inclined to negotiate than to use force, which also helps. But don't give him too much credit—if what I'm reading in the drudge reports is true, he doesn't have the strength at this point to successfully invade. He *has* to negotiate. Either you let him in peacefully, or he watches Borda take the Islands by force. So what's the downside to acquiescing to Magan's request for a base behind the curtain? Simple: he's got nothing to offer you. He can make all the promises he wants, but until he triumphs over Len Borda and gets appointed high executive, they're just empty words.

"As for resistance to both parties? Let's be frank—this would *not* be just a symbolic resistance. Given the momentum of Magan's rebellion, both sides are at the point where they're willing to be unreasonable if they have to. The Council might not stop at just crippling your armies and pushing you into retreat this time. Putting up an armed struggle against Magan and Lee would involve serious sacrifice on your part, and in the end you would lose."

Jara paused to give the Islanders time to take in her analysis. Again Chandler and Josiah shared one of those knowing stares that certainly looked like a ConfidentialWhisper conversation. For the first time, Jara started to wonder if the connectibles had lost something by enabling mental conversation.

"Well," said Bali Chandler, pushing himself back from the table far enough to put his sandaled feet on it, "I'll give you credit for one thing. Your analysis so far pretty much matches our analysis."

"Which gives us some reassurance as to your skill as a consultant," continued Josiah. "But it still leaves the central question unanswered. Do we side with Borda or with Lee? Or do we resist any encroachment on our territory?"

Jara looked at her fellow fiefcorpers. Benyamin gave her a face of encouragement. "Your father hired us to come up with creative solutions," she said, "and I believe we have one."

"Which is?"

"None of the above. The problem is that you're asking the wrong question. The important thing is not who the Islanders support—but which one of them will support *you*." Jara folded her arms over her chest. "You've walled yourselves off here in the Pacific Islands for almost two hundred and fifty years. You've tried to pretend that what happens in the outside world doesn't matter to you. Well, the time's come for the Islanders to decide what they *really* want. The time's come for you to be bold and let the *Council* bend to *you*.

"You may never get another chance like this one. You need to seize it."

(((20)))

To the citizens of the FREE REPUBLIC OF THE PACIFIC ISLANDS; to the citizens of the PRINCIPALITIES OF SPIRITUAL ENLIGHTENMENT; to the citizens of the CENTRALIZED CONNECTIBLE GOVERNMENT; to the members of the PRIME COMMITTEE; to the members of the CONGRESS OF THE LOCAL POLITICAL REPRESENTATIVE ASSOCIATIONS OF CIVIC GROUPS; to the factions of the DEFENSE AND WELLNESS COUNCIL represented by HIGH EXECUTIVE LEN BORDA and LIEUTENANT EXECUTIVE MAGAN KAI LEE.
From JOSIAH SURINA, Representative for the Fourth Ward of the FREE REPUBLIC OF THE PACIFIC ISLANDS.

In times of crisis, the purpose of leadership is to choose direction. Elected leaders are expected to put aside prejudice and predilection, to debate between various courses of action, and to develop a consensus for that action.

It is in that spirit that I address these words to the citizens of the world, from Earth to Furtoid, connectible and unconnectible alike.

Make no mistake, the world is in crisis. As I write, the Free Republic of the Pacific Islands is under siege by two separate factions of the Defense and Wellness Council led by HIGH EXECUTIVE LEN BORDA and LIEUTENANT EXECUTIVE MAGAN KAI LEE. An estimated four legions of High Executive Borda's battle hoverbirds have taken up position on the seas northeast of Manila; an estimated three legions of Lieutenant Executive Lee's battle hoverbirds have staked out territory on the waters southeast of Manila.

If nothing is done to contain this crisis, one or both Council factions will soon invade the Pacific Islands. Their objective is to secure land behind the unconnectible curtain for use in conducting warfare on each other. Both factions believe that this land is necessary for establishing a base that cannot be penetrated by enemy multi projections.

There will be those among you reading these words who will say, *The travails of the Islanders do not concern us. Their lands are far away and isolated from the rest of the world.* To you I say, be patient, for this crisis affects us all, as I will demonstrate shortly.

Let me begin by stating that the navy of the Free Republic stands prepared to repel any invasion into its territory. We have never suffered an enemy force to breach the Islands. Our armed forces led by GENERAL CHERONNA stand nearly one million strong in all, and our military technology rivals that of any force in human history. If the Council chooses to test the will of the Islanders, they will find us firm and resolute.

I do not say these things to threaten. I say these things to emphasize that I write from a position of strength and not a position of weakness.

But I firmly believe that it is the duty of leadership to stand forward and proclaim, without hesitation and without fear, that the power of the word is stronger than the power of the gun. Conflicts that begin with differences of opinion can be resolved by consensus of opinion. That leader who orders the first shot of warfare to be fired is a leader who has failed his people.

Over the past two hundred and fifty years, humanity has diverged onto two separate paths. The society of my mother's line chose a world of dogged scientific advancement, no matter what the cost. The society of my father's line chose a world of skepticism towards, and careful retreat from, technology. And now here I am addressing you, the product of two cultures, both connectible and unconnectible. The convergence of two paths.

I proclaim myself to be the son of the late MARGARET SURINA, bodhisattva of Creed Surina, honorary chair of the Gandhi University and inventor of MultiReal technology; and QUELL, citizen of Manila and former chief engineer of the Surina Perfection Memecorp. Those who have seen my resemblance to my grandfather, MARCUS

SURINA, have little doubt that I am who I say. But for those who require more definitive evidence, I have made genetic proof of my heritage freely available on the Data Sea.

As the last heir to the line of scientists and freethinkers that includes SHELDON SURINA, PRENGAL SURINA, MARCUS SURINA, and MARGARET SURINA, I represent the interests of that family and all its assets and businesses in Andra Pradesh.

As the son of the prominent family of politicians and journalists that includes QUELL, SHARIF QUM, and LENARA, and as elected representative of the fourth ward of the Free Republic of the Pacific Islands, I also represent the interests of the unconnectible peoples in the Free Republic.

Too long has the world been boxed in to these false dichotomies. Connectible and unconnectible, governmentalist and libertarian, Terran and offworlder. Islander and Surina. Len Borda and Magan Kai Lee. Too long have we been told that division and conflict are the natural order of things.

And now I am in a unique position to say that these divisions between us must fall.

The citizens of the Free Republic whom I represent have spent their lives in a state of enforced isolation. Because we do not blindly embrace every technological edict issued by the Prime Committee, we have carved out a corner of the globe where we can live by our principles. We are subject to a system where we must specifically *opt out* of the technologies we find objectionable by filing so-called DOG-MATIC OPPOSITIONS with the connectibles. The Prime Committee has never remitted a single credit to fund the bureaucracy required to track bio/logic programs and file these Dogmatic Oppositions.

When we venture out from behind the unconnectible curtain, the policies of the Prime Committee require us to wear obtrusive copper collars. While these collars connect us to the networks that connectibles can access directly through neurological machinery, they also mark us as separate and distinct. They needlessly reinforce our isolation.

But I submit that it is the *connectibles* whose freedoms are threatened by these indignities.

It is the connectibles who are *required* to obey the often-bizarre rules of the multi network. It is the connectibles who are *required* to submit to the powers of strange new technologies like MULTIREAL. It is the connectibles who suffer from the ravages of black code, lethal programming, and infoquakes.

I say, let us extend the hand of freedom to the connectibles! Let everyone have the choices that the Islanders take for granted. Give *everyone* the power of the Dogmatic Opposition!

Let the citizens of Shenandoah choose which OCHRE machines to install in their newborn children! Let the people of Vladivostok opt in or out of the multi network as they desire! Let the offworlders on Allowell and Patronell and Furtoid decide whether they want access to the Data Sea! Let the inhabitants of London determine if they will be subject to the powers of MultiReal!

In return, the Data Sea will flow unimpeded through the Pacific Islands once more. The citizens of Manila will have the option to step on the red multi tile, to avail themselves of the full range of bio/logic software, to sign up for the L-PRACGs and creeds of their choice. The Islanders will rejoin the community of the connectibles as an autonomous entity and abide by the laws of the Prime Committee and the Congress of L-PRACGs.

I say this to the connectibles:

Do you want progress? Do you want the continuing advancement and betterment of the human race towards perfection, as my ancestor Sheldon Surina desired? Then know this: the evolution of humanity cannot proceed on the backs of the Islanders, the Pharisees, the offworlders, and the diss.

For better or worse, we are all one species. We are all one

people. We are all connectibles, and we are all Islanders. The human race must rise or fall as one.

We invite those of the Defense and Wellness Council who wish to participate in this GRAND REUNIFICATION to join us in Manila and cooperate with our military in the defense of the Islands. Those who come to the Islands seeking unity will get unity; those who come in the spirit of division will get only division.

The choice belongs to you.

(((21)))

"I accept your proposal," said Magan Kai Lee. "Reintegration of the Islanders into society and the power of the Dogmatic Opposition for everyone, in exchange for allowing me a base in the Islands."

It was literally the first thing out of the lieutenant executive's mouth after the requisite greetings and formalities had been dispensed with. Jara had expected some quibbling over definitions or some complaining about the overly broad proclamations of Josiah's manifesto. At the very least, she figured that Magan would couch his acceptance in some ambiguous wording. But no, the lieutenant executive's visage had hardly appeared on the viewscreen before he was expressing his eagerness to come to terms with the Islanders.

Jara shrank back in her seat and hoped the lieutenant executive could not see her in the visitors' gallery of the parliament. She had no idea what kind of viewscreen Magan was using or what kind of panning and zooming capabilities he had. But from the glimpses Jara could catch of the hoverbird interior, he was in a much more comfortable environment than the unconnectible parliamentarians. It was possibly the most informal government chamber Jara had ever seen. Tables and chairs stood scattered around a large room in no semblance of logical order; Jara was hard pressed to find two matching pieces of furniture in the whole place. Paint was flaking off the walls. Josiah had assured her that this was only a temporary locale until the new parliament building was completed. ("Six years is temporary?" Chandler had muttered under his breath.)

Josiah, for his part, was in no hurry to accept the lieutenant executive's word—and with it, presumably, the entrance of several legions of Council officers into Manila. He stood in the center of the room pondering Magan's unexpected words for a moment. The other forty-seven representatives were satisfied to observe and let Josiah do all the talking.

Little wonder, given Josiah's air of poise and command. *Kings and queens have disappeared from the Earth*, thought Jara, *but luckily we still have Surinas*. This was quite a position Josiah had gotten himself into, full of both promise and peril. Jara wondered if he fully appreciated that. Very few junior representatives found themselves parleying with a foreign army as an equal before their twenty-fifth birthday. If this worked, he was likely to reap the prestige—but if things turned sour, Jara had no doubt that Josiah would take the brunt of the blame.

"What assurances do we have that you'll keep your word?" asked Josiah of the figure on the viewscreen looming over them all. "How do we know if your position on Grand Reunification isn't just a posture of convenience?"

"Certainly you must understand that this decision isn't up to me," said Magan calmly. "Even if we win the fight against Len Borda tomorrow and the government installs me as high executive the day after . . . there would be a long process before it became law. Your proposal would ultimately be decided by the Prime Committee and the Congress of L-PRACGs. The Defense and Wellness Council does not get a vote."

"But you would be in a unique position to influence their decision."

"Absolutely. Still, as you can appreciate"—Magan swept his hand in an arc to indicate the assembled representatives—"politics is politics."

Bali Chandler stood up in his seat, looking even more bohemian than usual in a sky blue robe with frayed ends. "You realize that goes both ways," he said.

The lieutenant executive fixed Chandler with a curious stare. "Meaning?"

"Josiah's little manifesto might have fired up the chattering classes . . . but it's not official policy. And it's pretty vague on the specifics too."

"And purposefully so, I imagine," Magan interjected.

The old parliamentarian nodded. "All I'm saying is, the Islanders might all wear the same copper collars in connectible territories, but we've got a pretty diverse government here. Nothing's been put to a vote even inside this room, much less in the population at large. The spot polls from last night give the idea of Reunification a high approval rating—around sixty-two percent, isn't that right?" Various murmurs of assent floated through the room. "But that still leaves a healthy opposition of thirty-eight percent, and we haven't even laid out the details yet. If I know Triggendala over there, she'll have that opposition number at forty-five percent by the end of the week. What do you say, Trigg?" The woman in question, a distinguished matriarch with a flinty look in her eye, gave an amused nod.

"I don't expect this process to happen in a single night," said Magan cautiously. "I understand perfectly well that this is only the first step in what could prove to be a very long journey."

"Speaking of journeys," said Josiah. "I should warn you that once you make landfall, you are likely to encounter some citizen militias that don't report to General Cheronna. They might not take too kindly to Council officers marching down their streets."

Lieutenant Executive Lee was obviously prepared for this. "Don't worry. We will enter Manila with our dartguns in their holsters, and head straight for the outskirts. The warehouse district, if you're amenable. We have no intention of pressing our luck by mingling with our new brothers and sisters too soon." The humor in his voice was palpable, yet not mean-spirited. "As long as my forces are safely inside the unconnectible curtain and Len Borda's forces are stuck outside of it, I think a little civil disobedience is acceptable. If things get out of control, I may ask you to intervene."

"Done."

Josiah Surina turned towards his fellow representatives to see if there were any other points of contention. As far as Jara could tell, there were none. Even the overtly skeptical Triggendala and the handful of parliamentarians in her faction looked prepared to accept Magan Kai Lee's word for now if it would protect them from Len Borda. Jara wondered how many government negotiations were actually this simple: a few words of explanation, a few politely phrased objections, and then a deal.

"The parliament will put this agreement to a formal vote as soon as we're through here," said Josiah. "But before we do, two more items."

The lieutenant executive nodded serenely, his reservoirs of patience still quite full.

"Bali Chandler here has introduced a resolution calling for Islanders throughout the globe to cast off their connectible collars," continued Surina. "We have already begun distributing connectible coins designed to replicate the functionality of the collars without—"

Magan interrupted him with a nod and a hand gesture of assent. "I'm well aware of the connectible coins," he said. "As far as I'm concerned, you have my endorsement. My officers will be instructed not to interfere."

An uncomfortable muttering worked its way around the parliamentary chamber, particularly in the neighborhood of Triggendala and her cohorts. Jara heard the word *spying*. "How do you know about the coins?" snapped Chandler, clearly irked.

"Your countryman Quell has been wearing one for some time," replied Magan. "He has been kind enough to explain your issues with the collars to me in depth. I understand these coins were engineered by your mother, Josiah. As far as I can tell, they operate just as efficiently as the collars. So yes, by all means, distribute them. If Grand Reunification moves forward, I suspect we'll soon be seeing them all around the globe."

"That brings me to the second item I was going to mention," said Josiah. "My father."

"Quell will be coming to Manila with us. He is on my ship as an honored guest."

Jara could see a brief flicker of relief on Josiah's face. "Is he uninjured?"

"Except for his pride," said Magan, his lips sliding into a smile. "My chief engineer Papizon is absolutely *murdering* him in holo poker over here."

● ● ●

Jara and her fiefcorp accompanied Josiah and Chandler to the hover-bird docks to welcome the first arrivals of Magan Kai Lee's fleet. As per previous arrangement, Magan's four legions would bivouac in the warehouse district a few kilometers south of Manila proper to avoid confrontation with the vocal minority of Islanders who were already gearing up a protest movement. A small contingent would land here, within sight of the City Center, where they would be greeted by the heir to the Surinas and General Cheronna, not to mention a crowd of hand-picked supporters and friendly drudges. Jara caught her first glimpse of the general; a short, fat man with bright red hair and closely trimmed beard, he had the stiff and formal demeanor that the situation required.

Ben seemed uncharacteristically pleasant, almost sunny. It was almost enough to make Jara nervous. She tagged him on Confidential-Whisper. "So where's the sour word today?" she said. "If I don't get complaints from you in any twenty-four-hour period, I start experiencing withdrawal symptoms."

The young apprentice's face slid into a wry grin. "We did what we came here to do. We provided an independent assessment of the situation, and our client is happy. I'm not allowed to savor victory for once?"

"Oh, savor it all you want. I'm just starting to depend on you for the contrary opinion. It keeps me on my toes."

"All right then," said Benyamin, cracking his knuckles in mock preparation for a street fight. "Here's the contrary opinion. This whole production is a big farce. Josiah's manifesto stirred a lot of passions, but nobody's actually voted for Reunification. Even if the Islander parliament votes unanimously to accept it, we have no indication how the Prime Committee's going to take this."

"We've got public opinion polls. Zeitgeist gives us seventy-four percent either *in favor* or *leaning towards.*"

"Who cares? You know this isn't going to be that easy. Once the public sees what they're going to have to give up for Grand Reunification, those numbers are going to start sinking fast. Everyone's going to get bogged down in details. This movement could take twenty years to get anywhere."

"It might," admitted Jara. "But nobody said movements had to be fast."

As if to demonstrate the veracity of her comment, Magan's forces were running over two hours late, leaving a lot of drudges and eager supporters sweating in the midday sun. Jara had a sudden fear that Len Borda had decided to invade the Islands after all, or maybe he had attacked Magan's hoverbirds to prevent them from slipping behind the unconnectible curtain. But no, General Cheronna confirmed that Borda had chosen not to engage the enemy; his hoverbirds still sat unmoving in the middle of the ocean, as if unmanned. Magan's delay was simply a matter of too few officers chasing too many details, or what High Executive Tul Jabbor had called *the natural friction of the world.*

The delay was not a bad thing for Jara, as she had a chance to catch up on news from the outside world. Josiah's manifesto had achieved an astounding eighty percent penetration in a matter of hours. Some were predicting that this could turn out to be the world's most-read document of the past five years, though exactly how one could measure that was unclear. The unconnectible drudges were largely focusing on Josiah's proposal for Reunification (a word that had already made it into the vernacular and inspired several dozen Jamm compositions and a short drama starring Bill Rixx). But all the connectible drudges cared about was the revelation that Margaret Surina had had a son. Sen Sivv Sor and John Ridglee quickly began speculating why Josiah had kept his identity a secret for so long. Mah Lo Vertiginous proclaimed himself dubious about the whole thing, all evidence to the contrary. Kristella Krodor, meanwhile, was busy running Josiah Surina's official photograph through dozens of black market phrenology programs and making all sorts of outrageous claims about the young Islander's character.

But the laugh of the day belonged to Suheil and Jayze Surina. The two had officially petitioned the courts in Andra Pradesh to nullify the agreement they had signed with Jara—an agreement that forty-eight hours earlier they had held up as a model of modern contractual law. The judges, of course, said no. Certainly there was a posse of lawyers in the Surina compound right now searching for any conceivable loophole to deny Josiah his heritage.

Jara was busy perusing Suheil and Jayze's apoplectic statement to the drudges, full of paranoid accusations and colorful euphemisms for the Islanders, when Magan's hoverbirds came zipping out of the mist a kilometer or so offshore. Josiah, Chandler, and General Cheronna stood stiffly at attention as the first vehicle arced down to the dock and came to a smooth stop.

The door opened, and out stepped Quell.

It was only now, with father and son standing face to face, that Jara could see the resemblance between the two. Josiah's face and mannerisms might have come straight from the maternal line; but the muscular torso, the proud posture, and the firm browline—those were all traits he had inherited from Quell. Jara wished she had a better angle to see the expressions on their faces. According to Chandler, it had been many months since the two had seen each other. To say they had a lot to talk about was a considerable understatement. But here, in front of the world, the pair knew that their duty was to shake hands politely and keep their composure. They performed admirably.

Lieutenant Executive Magan Kai Lee walked off the hoverbird next. His face was perfectly impassive as he offered a respectful bow to Josiah, then clasped the Islander's hand for a shake. There were some pro forma words being exchanged up there, but Jara couldn't hear them. She turned towards Benyamin with a question on her lips, but was surprised to see someone else standing in his place.

The Council's chief solicitor, Rey Gonerev.

"Towards Perfection, Jara," said the Blade. On her face was the same smile Jara had seen the last time they were together: not an expression of mockery or disdain, but the smile of an equal. She wondered if they might have formed a friendship had they met under different circumstances.

"And to you too," replied the fiefcorp master. "Looks like you and Magan have pulled off quite a coup here."

"It's a beginning," nodded Gonerev with the slightest of shrugs.

"A beginning? You've got the Islanders on your side and a base that's free from multi projections. Not to mention public opinion and the legal title to MultiReal. Seems to me you've got Len Borda in quite a bind."

The Blade reached up to toy idly with the braids of her hair. "You forget that we're still badly outnumbered," she said. "Don't underestimate Len Borda when he's cornered. There's a reason he's held onto power for so long. He knows there's one trump card that has yet to be played—and that's MultiReal. If Natch ends up in Borda's hands, none of *this* will make the least bit of difference." Gonerev inclined her head in the direction of the dock, where Josiah and Magan were still exchanging stilted, prescribed words for the benefit of the drudges.

All of this cozy familiarity was beginning to irk Jara. She wasn't necessarily upset at the outcome here, having privately concluded that the lieutenant executive was the lesser of two evils. But it wasn't as if

Magan Kai Lee had nothing to answer for. It wasn't as if he represented some radiant new governing philosophy, instead of representing . . . no philosophy at all. "So does Magan really intend to keep his promises?" Jara snapped. "Is he really going to pursue Grand Reunification as high executive? Or is this just for show?"

Rey Gonerev calibrated her words carefully. "I think you'll find that Magan Kai Lee is a man of his word," she said. "He doesn't hold pointless grudges, and he really does want what's best for the Islanders. As for Reunification . . ." The solicitor sighed. "We'll need to study it, of course."

"So you admit this wasn't part of your plan?"

"Magan's not clairvoyant," replied the Blade with a relaxed laugh. "You give him much too much credit. Do you really think he knew what advice you were going to give to the Islanders? He can't predict and manipulate events—he just knows how to ride them once they happen. That's the art of politics—being able to take credit for whatever happens, whether it's what you want or not."

Jara pressed on. "And is Reunification something Magan wants? Did the Islanders make the right decision letting him behind the curtain instead of Borda?"

"Yes. They'll get a better deal with Magan than they would with Len Borda. I won't lie to you. Things might not turn out exactly like the Islanders are hoping, but I'm sure they'll be better for it in the long run. History will vindicate their decision."

The fiefcorp master snorted. "I wouldn't be so sure. There's nothing sacrosanct about history. History is written by the ones with the best marketing consultants."

4

NOHWAN'S CRUSADE

(((22)))

The orbital colony of 49th Heaven consisted of seven concentric rings joined by a single avenue that pierced the whole like the arrow in a bull's eye.

Back in the days of the colony's founding, three hundred years prior, that broad connecting corridor was patrolled by monks in the service of Jesus Elijah Muhammad, last of the so-called Three Jesuses. Muhammad had learned from the missteps of his predecessors, Jesus Joshua Smith, and Jesus Cortez, who had whipped adherents of the world's major religions to ruinous violence. But Jesus Elijah Muhammad was a man of forethought and logic; he had a system. As his religion was a hyperrational amalgam of existing faiths, the orbital colony he built was an ultramethodical place of worship. Newcomers arrived in the outermost ring of 49th Heaven. As they grew in wisdom, they gradually received permission from the Muhammadan monks to progress to the next ring inward. The central ring was reserved for only the most pious, the most holy, the most dedicated. *When the central ring of 49th Heaven reaches capacity*, Jesus Elijah Muhammad once proclaimed, *God's Kingdom on Earth will begin.*

Muhammad brought everything he needed to make 49th Heaven successful, except for good accountants. Within a generation, the colony was insolvent.

In an irony that was not lost on the rest of the world, 49th Heaven was revived decades later by a consortium of gambling cartels. The cartels restored the colony to its original luster and turned it into a sybaritic resort. The Lunar tycoons who flocked there were amused to find that the new owners of 49th Heaven had flipped Jesus Muhammad's hierarchy on its head. Now the outer rings were filled with everyday titillations, while the innermost rings were reserved for only the most exclusive of customers and the most decadent of vices. Hallucinogenic black code, sexual slavery, extreme games of chance. *When the central ring of 49th Heaven reaches capacity*, High Executive Par Padron once declared in a fit of righteous rage, *I'm going to blast it out of the fucking sky.*

Padron was not the only one in the Terran centralized government who chafed at the excesses of 49th Heaven. Black code flowed freely out of the inner rings, while people and resources got sucked in and were never heard from again. But what could the government do about it? The colony's charter was covered with the prickly language of lawyers, and the Defense and Wellness Council's jurisdiction there was murky. High executives dating back to Par Padron regularly threatened to blow up 49th Heaven, or at the very least, shut it down. But even Zetarysis the Mad blanched at the thought of dealing with twenty thousand refugees, many of whom would likely be strung out on black code. And so the gambling cartels tried to keep the entertainments in the outer rings palatable, and the Council pretended it didn't know what was happening in the inner rings.

Nobody's forced to live in those inner rings, government officials said to justify their inaction. *The people who indulge in those vices do so by their own choice.*

Technically speaking, they were correct.

• • •

Rodrigo stumbled out of the bodega hard on the trail of Chomp. He tried and failed to remember the last time he had tasted something that hadn't emerged from a laboratory tank, something that had a place in the hierarchy of nature. Too long.

Conventional wisdom said that the best marks could be found in the bodegas, but Rodrigo didn't believe it. The ones you picked up in the bodegas were usually the mean ones: businesspeople working off the shame of deals gone sour, black code pushers working up the ferocity to ensure that their deals didn't. Rodrigo had spent too many mornings huddled in the dark corners of inner-ring bodegas, trying to hold it together while his OCHREs patched up wounds from a night of one-sided passion. Too many encounters had begun with an overture of *I guess you made it through after all*, and too many had concluded with a coda of *You'll live*.

Hard price to pay for an hour of Chomp. Ah, Chomp the magnificent, Chomp the trickster, Chomp the high of many colors and flavors.

Rodrigo could see the line of hustlers in the avenue outside the bodegas now, slouching against the wall. They were all trying to find that optimal facial expression that showed a willingness to be picked up without showing desperation. Rodrigo knew many of these people by face, though their names had mostly been engulfed by the Chomp.

The avenue itself, like all the streets in 49th Heaven, was a pure, smooth cylinder, with buildings propped up against its lower arcs. Such lighting as there was came from the half-shuttered windows of these buildings. In the heavily trafficked portions of the colony, the cylinder's walls were painted over with artistry that ranged from the exquisite to the psychedelic to the grotesque. Near the dock on Seventh Ring, tens of thousands of angels frolicked in a sky filled with five-pointed stars; outside the sex emporiums on Second Ring, a profusion of colors swirled in patterns that ventured near the profound. But here outside the bodegas of Sixth Ring, the old murals had long since chipped away into pointillist incoherence.

Rodrigo strolled up to a dull-eyed boy he knew from Grub Town. They had shared the wall outside the bodegas many times before, but all Rodrigo could remember about him was that he was an ardent fan of the Patronell Lightning soccer team.

"How's it going?" he greeted the boy, taking up a position alongside.

"A little over, a little under," replied Patronell without looking up from his shoes. Rodrigo had never understood what the phrase meant, but he supposed he knew the gist of it well enough. "You shouldn't be out here," continued the dull-eyed boy. "Molloy looking for you, man."

"Nothing new."

"Says he gonna kill you this time."

Rodrigo shrugged. "Been saying that for weeks. Let's see him get busy."

The other abandoned this line of conversation with a shrug of his own. "New OrbiCo freighter just docked."

"Tourists?" said Rodrigo hopefully.

"Mostly freight, what Cisco says." Patronell snapped his head abruptly towards a slack-jawed teenager across the way. The boy had just hooked his arm into that of a middle-aged woman who was trying unsuccessfully to hide the purple and maroon lining of her coat. Royal purple and maroon, Creed Élan colors.

"Gotta be some dockworkers though," said Rodrigo. OrbiCo dockworkers weren't nearly as generous as tourists—and not as plentiful as politicians—but if you caught them straight off a long shift to Furtoid with a nice bonus in their Vault account, they made easy marks.

"Yeah, sure, dockworkers," said the other boy. "But not enough to go around."

The conversation withered and died at that point, and the boy who was a fan of the Patronell Lightning wandered away without comment a few minutes later. Rodrigo was starting to really suffer from the pangs of Chomp withdrawal. Shaky hands, blurred vision, deep rumbles of hunger. He reached in his coat pocket for a slim silver canister, flipped open the cap with his thumb, and rubbed the moist tip on his wrists with a single practiced motion. Within seconds, the code-laden OCHREs had penetrated the skin and tweaked his neural systems into a frenzy. This was low-quality stuff, hardly worthy of the Chomp moniker, but it made a serviceable substitute in a pinch. Besides which, it was all he had left. Rodrigo closed his eyes and leaned back against the cool flexible glass wall.

Lights danced. Molecules thrummed. Time twisted itself in knots around him, and while caught in those bonds, he wanted for nothing.

When Rodrigo emerged back into sentience, he was alone on the wall. All the other hustlers had either found marks for the night or given up. Rodrigo discovered that he had slouched down onto his right knee during the black code high with his left arm folded painfully behind his back. He was in the process of straightening himself out when a figure slid in front of him.

It was a dockworker with a downcast face, perhaps in his late twenties. Hair dark, body lean. Eyes a vivid sea green. "Interested in a drink?" muttered the man.

Rodrigo studied the shadowed face for a moment, looking for signs of craziness. He desperately needed a real fix, but he didn't know if he would survive another night like last night. Hours clutching bruised thighs in a mirrored hotel room, and only a few miserable canisters to show for it. "You got Chomp?"

The man reached into his canvas bag and withdrew a handful of thin silver canisters like the one Rodrigo had just tapped dry. "Of course."

They started down the avenue towards the gate that led to the inner rings. Rodrigo knew a guard there who would let him through, in exchange for the occasional . . . *favor.* "You don't look like a dockworker, man," said Rodrigo to the handsome stranger, trying to come up with friendly banter that would keep him from walking away.

"Wasn't always one," replied the man laconically.

Try as he might, Rodrigo couldn't keep his eyes off the stranger's canvas bag. "What'd you do before you sign up with OrbiCo?" he said after a few minutes. Rodrigo tried to summon a list of professions that respectable people engaged in, but he could only come up with two. "Capitalman? Drama producer?"

The stranger shook his head. "Entrepreneur."

(((2 3)))

Natch has ceased to exist.

The person who once inhabited that set of characteristics—the name, the apartment, the Vault account, the various holdings and relationships and defining traits—that person reached his terminus the instant Frederic Patel's decapitating sword stroke landed on his neck. Or perhaps his final moments evaporated in a haze of erased memory on the streets of Old Chicago. Whatever the instant of Natch's demise, he has indeed sloughed off his old identity like a snake's skin. The apartment and the Vault account: abandoned. The profile in the public directory: wiped clean. The obsessions with Primo's ratings and MultiReal, the fear of Brone and the Defense and Wellness Council: discarded.

Yet if Natch cannot countenance a life in that old skin, neither can he contemplate taking up residence in a new one. Assuming a new identity means pointing himself in a new direction. It means taking on a whole new set of desires and anxieties, and Natch would rather hurl himself through an airlock than do that right now.

But he can't have Len Borda or Magan Kai Lee tracking him down either. He can't have libertarians like Khann Frejohr hounding him for access to MultiReal or drudges pressing for exclusives. Most important, he can't have Brone locating him and trying to pick up where he left off.

Keep moving, that is his imperative.

So Natch finds himself walking into a small storefront that he knows in the twisted alleyways of Angelos. At the counter stands a ferrety man with a squint of suspicion for the entire world. The sign over his head reads simply Fix. No preceding article, no trailing object. Natch can't tell whether "Fix" is supposed to be the man's name, the name of his business, the service he provides, or perhaps all three.

"Name?" grunts Fix after the short dance of solicitation and negotiation ends with a service to be provided and a fair price.

Natch knows he is being asked for a new name. Nobody working
in a place like this would be so gauche as to ask for his existing name.
"Nohwan," replies Natch after a moment's reflection.

"No One?" says Fix, slitting his eyes into a state of concentrated
mistrust.

"Nohwan," Natch corrects him. He spells it out as a single word
without patronymic, in the style preferred by so many Westerners of
his generation.

Fix opens his eyes just wide enough to roll them. *Spare me the pre-
tention and self-importance of the young*, his expression says. Then he
reaches for his satchel of bio/logic programming bars and gets to work.

Not three hours later, Natch emerges on the muggy streets of
Angelos with a new profile in the public directory and a new Vault
account. He has a new set of physical traits designed to make him
unrecognizable to the casual observer, yet not *so* unrecognizable that a
clever image-analysis routine can single him out. His hair is darker
with a slightly closer cut, and his skin has taken on the bronzed pig-
ment of a well-tanned beachgoer. His blue eyes have migrated to a
deep green. A cocktail of biochemical programs will serve to confuse
most common DNA-screening routines.

Natch's next step is to find a bio/logic workbench for rent. He needs
a bench that does not log its transactions, a bench that will allow him
to flit in and out of his own systems without leaving a trace. He finds
this not half a kilometer away from Fix, in a similarly disreputable shop
on a similarly disreputable street. He tries to recall Petrucio Patel's
instructions for taming the black code tremors, half expecting the
memory to be gone. But it's not. Soon Natch is executing Petrucio's
instructions with a pair of greasy rented bio/logic programming bars.
He sweats away in a MindSpace bubble for three hours until the
shaking from Margaret's code has almost completely subsided.

Two or three months of tremor-free existence, this is what Petrucio has promised him.

Finally, Natch recalls Patel's commands for disabling the Multi-Real-D code inside his OCHREs. It's a simple process, really, the virtual equivalent of flipping a switch. He hesitates for a moment with programming bars held aloft, the parabolic shape of the Multi-Real-D trigger floating before him. Does he really want to disable such a potent defense mechanism? Does he really want to give up that sixty-second advantage and make himself vulnerable to the world's caprices?

Yes, he decides firmly. *I don't need trickery. I don't need random memory erasure. I need my feet on solid ground. I need control.*

Natch disables the MultiReal-D code. He waits for some visceral signal that he has resumed life in real time, that he is no longer a minute ahead of the world. There is none. Time seems to flow around and through him the same as it always has.

He throws down the bio/logic programming bars, shuts down the MindSpace workbench. The transformation is complete. Natch is gone; he does not exist. In his place there is only Nohwan.

Keep moving.

• • •

Seventy-two hours later, "Nohwan" has accepted an engineering position aboard the OrbiCo ship *Practical*, bound for the lonely orbital colony of Furtoid.

Natch's job is insanely simple. He wanders the labyrinths of machinery, performing rote maintenance chores that could easily be handled by mechanicals. But out here between planets, the economics are topsy-turvy; the bottom line is that it's much cheaper for OrbiCo to use human labor than to waste precious ship's power. Natch feels like he's back on the assembly-line programming floor in Texas territory, watching a herd of his peers bang away on repetitive tasks with bio/logic programming bars.

But such a job suits him now. He wants quiet. He wants to be out of the way. He wants to be a ghost.

It's in one of these quiet moments, on his bunk after a long day of adjusting valves and balancing chemical ratios, when Natch wants nothing more than to lie still and let the universe pass around and through him, that he notices.

There is a *presence* within him.

The presence is infinitely subtle, like an itch in a blanketed corner of his mind. As Natch studies the feeling, he realizes that this presence is not new. He's felt it many times before, but it's always been shunted into the background by the incessant tremors of Margaret's backdoor MultiReal access, or the time-shattering MultiReal-D code Petrucio put inside him—or the mere adrenaline of running from the Defense and Wellness Council.

He knows what this presence is. It's the illicit code that the Thasselians infected him with in Shenandoah months ago. Quiescent, in a state of hibernation, perhaps—but still there.

Natch wants to leap up from his bunk and run for a MindSpace workbench. He wants to grab his bio/logic programming bars and tear this thing out of him, no matter what it takes, no matter the consequences. How does he know that Brone's not using the code to track him? But of course, he will find no MindSpace workbench aboard the *Practical*. And if he does find one in the remote colony of Furtoid, he won't have enough shore leave to make effective use of it. No, Natch realizes that he must be patient. Whatever nefarious duty Brone has assigned to this code, the entrepreneur will have to put up with it for a while.

Mind awhirl with the evil possibilities and looking for a distraction, Natch dives into his work.

He knew precious little about the mechanics of space freighters when he first climbed aboard the *Practical* with the chemical vats and chunks of raw ore. Meandering around reading gauges has taught him almost nothing. But now he is eager to learn. He spends all his free time reading engineering manuals. He disassembles machinery and pores through access panels when his supervisor's not looking, which is most of the time.

As the days pass, Natch begins to get a command of the ship's systems—and what he finds there frightens him. Grav modules, engine components, and oxygen generators in a woeful state of neglect, caught in the tide of dismal economics. OrbiCo has not made a profit in fifty years. The company only stays afloat because of the billions of credits the Prime Committee pumps into it every year. (*Surely the august members of the Committee don't want their constituents on Furtoid to starve?* cry the orbital colony representatives in budget sessions quarter after quarter. *Who's going to supply them if OrbiCo doesn't?*) But government money only goes so far, and it's the freighter's innards that suffer for it.

Nobody has asked Natch to fix faulty equipment, but he has no intention of asking for permission. The ethics of engineering are refreshingly simple: increasing efficiency is good. So Natch goes to work tinkering in the bowels of the ship, jiggering the programming, rewiring entire sections of machinery, adjusting valves and joints. Where he lacks the permission to make modifications, he either finds a workaround or hacks his way through.

Most of the improvements he makes are pro forma and unlikely to impact the bottom line. But he finds one major hiccup in the gravity generators that is wasting vast amounts of power. And it's a trifling problem too, one that any gravitational engineer could diagnose if OrbiCo could afford to pay her. Natch smuggles some spare parts on board when they hit Furtoid to replace the malfunctioning ones, and cleans up the code to save processing cycles.

And all the time, Natch is asking himself: *Why do you care? Why not just do your job like the rest of the crew and then catch up on your sleep?*

It feels like a vital question that Natch must answer before he can slip into a new skin. Why would he do a job he is not being paid to do? This might have started as mental calisthenics to keep his skills sharp and his attention away from Brone's black code, but it's not just an exercise anymore. Why can't Natch walk past a frayed wire or a leaking valve without feeling an inexorable urge to fix it? It's not a conscious thought, but more like a visceral impulse. Where does that urge come from? Is it a desire to restore the universe to some hypothetical state of perfection? And if so, why is the universe constantly working to undermine him?

The entrepreneur tweaks the OrbiCo ship to greater efficiency all the way from Furtoid to 49th Heaven, its next destination. Once they dock and the unloading of goods is nearly complete, Natch sidles close enough to the officers' deck to hear their stunned discovery of an unexpected energy surplus. Enough to tip the ledger for the voyage ever so slightly into positive territory. The bonus he and the other ship's engineers receive is substantial.

Natch is intrigued.

He is a ghost. He has ceased to exist. And yet he has singlehandedly created a change that will ripple through the local economy long after he has ceased to be involved. Engineers will bring small gifts home to their families, or pad their Vault accounts, or order that extra drink in the bodega. Something he has done will have tangible effects and lasting permanence in the world, and it has cost him next to nothing to do it. The balance sheet of the universe will have slid just that infinitesimal amount from the red to the black.

It is a kind of immortality.

•   •   •

Natch disembarks from the *Practical* and steps into the Seventh Ring of 49th Heaven. He's got a week of shore leave before his next voyage—should he decide to sign up for it—and there is little to do here except explore.

Keep moving, he exhorts himself.

He finds an entirely different kind of economy at work here in 49th Heaven. The Vault's credits are (virtually) untraceable and (practically) unforgeable, and yet Vault credits are not trusted currency just about anywhere but the Seventh Ring tourist traps. In 49th Heaven, vials of black code–laden OCHREs are the preferred form of exchange. Merge, Chomp, Suffr-G, Suffr-N, Chill Polly. Programs that shatter the will; programs that insert the user into an endless loop of wanton need and insufficient fulfillment. Programs that warp the human mind in ways the Prime Committee has deemed unacceptable.

But Natch doesn't mind. In fact, he feels an affinity for the underground market; after all, Natch himself has been deemed unacceptable by the Prime Committee. So he quickly locates a dealer and spends a chunk of his OrbiCo wages acquiring a small stockpile. Then he goes scouting for ways to spend it. He walks through gambling dens, wanders past galleries devoted to decadent forms of art, skirts the rough-and-tumble sex emporiums.

In a dark corridor between the Sixth Ring bodegas, a skeletal arm reaches out and grabs him. Natch turns and stares at the ghoulish presence slouching against the wall. She's tall as a pillar, her skin black as void, her fingers cold as unforgiven sin. "A fuck for Chill Polly," she mumbles.

"What did you say?"

"Fuck. For. Chill. Polly."

The entrepreneur blanches. It's an unthinkable proposition. Why would anyone pay for pleasures of the flesh when it's cheaper, safer, and easier to find them virtually? If you look on the Sigh, any degradation imaginable, no matter how obscure or grotesque, has already been imagined, organized, advertised, and transformed into an excuse for a semiannual convention. It only costs a handful of credits, and it's indistinguishable from the real thing.

Natch is about to brush off this deranged skeleton when he catches the look in her eye.

He knows that stare, because he's given it himself. It's the look of a human soul tangled up in desire so endless that it overshadows the world. The look of someone who has surrendered herself to the endless cycle of need and fulfillment. It's not Natch she desires; it's the black code known as Chill Polly. A miserable set of algorithms designed to utterly obliterate sensation, to truly make you one with the cosmos— or perhaps to bring the cosmos down to your level.

As Natch looks in her eyes, it suddenly occurs to him what this woman is *really* selling. Sex is only a tangential part of the transaction. She is selling a ringside seat for a life reduced to a spectacle of need, and a drug designed to do nothing but nullify that need.

A closed system. Wanton need, insufficient fulfillment.

Natch lets the nameless woman take his arm and escort him down a predictably dark alleyway. "Where we going?" he asks.

"Grub Town," says the woman.

She leads him to the colony's main avenue, where security lets them pass through gate after gate without asking for the requisite payment. Soon they have found their way to a maze of repurposed ductwork on the inner rim of Third Ring. It's a tangled skein of permasteel walls three meters high, not so much constructed as haphazardly tacked together metal sheet by metal sheet. Hidden alcoves and makeshift rooms abound. Overlooking the maze on the ceiling is an enormous mural showing endless fields after the rain where the worms come out to frolic. Grub Town. The place serves no purpose that Natch can see other than to keep the uninitiated out and the transactions private.

The woman leads Natch to an unused corner deep in the labyrinth. He hands over a canister of Chill Polly, watches the application on the woman's wrists. Sees the writhing, insensate dance of desire then fulfillment, desire then fulfillment, over and over until the blackness comes. She does not ask nor appear to notice that Natch has made no move to touch her since their arrival.

For the next three days, Natch returns to the alleyway between bodegas and repeats the process. It occurs to him that this might be the closest to invisibility one can get in 49th Heaven, where unspoken fiat places the privacy of sexual transactions above all else. While on the arm of a black code junkie headed for Grub Town, the authorities look through him; passersby turn a blind eye to him; other junkies see nothing but the canvas shoulder bag Natch is carrying, location of his black code stockpile.

Of course they don't see me. I don't exist.

The boy on the fourth day is much like the others. Shorter, perhaps. A little cannier, a little rougher around the edges. He tries to engage Natch in small talk on the way to Grub Town, which Natch does his best to deflect. The boy's name is Rodrigo, as it turns out. Rodrigo leads him into Grub Town and through a minotaur's labyrinth of makeshift rooms, most empty, a few occupied by the uncaring or the unconscious.

Finally they arrive at a darkened den populated by nothing but a strangely clean mattress. Natch tries to imagine someone dragging a mattress through all of the seemingly random twists and turns they took to arrive here. Not likely. Perhaps the mattress has been here since the beginning, and this shantytown has expanded over it? No matter. Natch throws his bag on the floor and leans down to join it.

But before he gets there, he feels a white-hot pain lancing between his shoulder blades. The blade stabs swift and deep and quickly shoves Natch outside the veil of consciousness.

(((24)))

Natch staggers back into sentience ninety minutes later, cursing his own foolishness at disabling MultiReal-D. Were he still inhabiting virtual time, sixty seconds ahead of the rest of the world, he would not be experiencing this scalding pain between his shoulder blades. . . .

But the boy snuck up on him from behind. If Natch understood Petrucio's explanation of MultiReal-D correctly, the program's predictive algorithms would not have anticipated the attack, and he would still be lying here deep in the bowels of Grub Town struggling to sit up. Even the crowning achievement of the Surinas is ultimately subject to the limitations of a universe built on cause and effect.

Natch leans against the grimy permasteel and takes inventory of his vital systems. He is, in one sense, incalculably lucky—the knife has not punctured anything vital. In fact, it has missed his lungs by centimeters, he sees in the floating holographic torso that represents his body. OCHREs are thrumming mightily to repair the damage from the shallow knife thrust, but the process will take time. An urgent message from Dr. Plugenpatch warns him to stay prostrate and summon L-PRACG security immediately.

The entrepreneur ignores the warnings. Stands. Realizes that this boy Rodrigo must have been after his stash of black code cylinders, because Natch's canvas bag is missing.

Natch is more astounded and curious than angry. After a life in which most of his possessions are virtual and therefore not subject to pickpocketry—a life in which a thief's knife is likely to strike only a neural illusion—the idea of being *stabbed* and *robbed* is almost picaresque, like something out of an ancient novel.

What now?

He looks down and sees a drop of blood on the floor, and then another, like a vector pointing him in the direction he must go. Natch follows and finds another drop here, another drop there. He pursues it a handful of turns through the maze of permasteel ductwork, wondering just how far this trail of blood is going to take him. Certainly before too long, the knife will have dribbled its last drop, or Rodrigo will have paused to wipe it clean.

But Natch's serendipity holds. He only has to stumble for a minute, taking a single wrong turn, before he comes across the thief.

Rodrigo lies in another of these indistinguishable ductwork rooms, on a mattress that seems like it's lain here for decades by the sight of it. The bloodied knife is still sitting on his lap. A handful of empty canisters lie on the floor next to the entrepreneur's discarded canvas bag. Natch wonders briefly if Rodrigo has died in the short interim since the stabbing—but it appears not. He has no medical training beyond the basic grasp of human physiology necessary for bio/logic programming, but he can recognize working lungs and a beating heart.

The entrepreneur picks up his canvas bag of black code, 49th Heaven currency. (The wound in his back screams in protest. Natch jacks up the analgesic and tries his best to ignore it.) He peeks cautiously around the corner of what functions as a doorway here and prepares himself for a long trek back through the ductwork city. As for Rodrigo—it's not his concern. Someone will find him. Someone will notice the state he's in and bring him to the medical facilities that surely even 49th Heaven possesses.

Won't they?

Natch takes another look at the boy. Yes, Rodrigo is alive, but this is clearly not just the ordinary black code stupor. Natch has never seen anyone take so many canisters of Chomp at once. Rodrigo's eyes are open as wide as they go, and yet they see nothing. His entire body is rigid and contorted. It's difficult to even discern that he's alive from more than a few paces. Who would walk into one of these cubicles uninvited when there's a corpse stinking up the place? Who would feel comfortable going to fetch the authorities?

Surely the boy must have friends. If nothing else, eventually someone else will find a use for this ramshackle space and decide to investigate. But when will that be, and what shape will the boy be in at that point?

The little fucker deserves no less, thinks Natch, reaching around to feel the still-splotchy knife wound in his back. *He's not my responsibility.*

Natch takes a last look at the scrawny reed of a boy lying on the filthy mattress. Sixteen years old at the outside, sinfully ugly, without prospects, and judging by the results of this ambush, lacking even the intelligence to pull off a successful mugging. A thief who will make no lasting contribution to the human race, who, even should he escape this predicament, will stupidly place himself in another, then another, then another, until he is finally wheeled in to a Preparation compound with an order signed by an official of the local L-PRACG.

Nobody will come looking for this ephemeral creature. Nobody will miss Rodrigo.

This is someone who does not exist.

• • •

Natch suspects that Rodrigo is the type of boy who draws trouble like a magnet draws metal. But even so, the entrepreneur is surprised at how quickly trouble shows up.

He manages to half carry, half drag the boy out of the shantytown without too much difficulty. The path is not quite as labyrinthine as Natch remembered, or perhaps he has merely made a series of lucky guesses. Soon he is back on the main avenue of Third Ring. That he can lug an unconscious, bloodied, obviously malnourished boy down a major thoroughfare without attracting any undue attention from the authorities says much about 49th Heaven. Natch knows there are functioning L-PRACGs with functioning security forces in this place; he remembers selling a batch of code to one of them a few years back. Where are they now?

Instead there is the occasional jaded look tossed in their direction by the pedestrians, not to mention the odd gruesome chuckle and salacious elbow-nudge from loiterers. "Musta been a great fuckin' blowjob!" quips one anonymous wit loudly enough for Natch to hear. The wit's companion howls gleefully and they walk on.

A team of medieval jesters capers and caterwauls on the ceiling, as if the very colony of 49th Heaven has decided to join in the mockery.

The medical facilities reside in a squat trapezoidal structure almost a quarter of the way around the circumference of Third Ring. After a few hundred paces down the main drag, Rodrigo resumes some semblance of consciousness. There is no recognition in his face on seeing Natch. He senses he is being taken somewhere, and somehow he can deduce the presence of altruism at work. With one arm around Natch's neck, Rodrigo begins to assist in the walking in a feeble and not particularly helpful way, collapsing from time to time and occasionally pulling Natch down with him. Each time, the entrepreneur patiently stands him back up on his feet, and they continue the trek.

Why put up with this? Why help the boy at all?

Natch doesn't know. He can't articulate it. Rodrigo is a wretched specimen of humanity, an outlier on the scale of misery, possibly even an argument in favor of eugenics. He has done nothing benevolent for Natch; in fact, he is responsible for the puncture wound on his back that continues to throb and itch with pain. Natch should be flagging down one of the few Council officers he sees or summoning L-PRACG security like Dr. Plugenpatch advised.

Why help Rodrigo? Natch feels no compassion for him. He doesn't particularly *care* if the boy lives or dies; yet he is *interested*. Tugging this ruined boy to safety feels like something new. It feels, perversely, like a challenge.

As they approach the medical facility, a middle-aged woman in a sky blue uniform stands in the doorway and watches their progress with her own version of detached interest. She watches Natch and Rodrigo's whole fumbling trip down the thoroughfare and up the ramp to her door without making a single move to summon assistance. Nor does she offer any help dragging the boy through the door and onto a waiting stretcher, even though he has lapsed back into stiff, wide-eyed unconsciousness. But the moment Rodrigo's ass hits canvas, medical technicians scramble from nowhere to whisk him off. They regard Natch as little more than a faceless obstruction and look past the wound on his back without seeing. The entrepreneur realizes that he has just fallen askance of some draconian liability policy hammered onto the facility by forces unknown.

Moments later, the corridor is empty. Natch stands on white floors under the harsh glow of hospital lighting, trying to decide what to do next. His own wound seems to be healing nicely—not as quickly as if he were to get professional assistance, but that would entail placing his doctored OCHREs in the hands of a strange bureaucracy. Natch supposes his next step is to make it back to the docks and claim a berth on the OrbiCo freighter *Practical* for its next journey. In that ship lies safety. Isolation from the world. The dull anonymity of space.

Keep moving.

And yet—

He can't make himself do it. Instead he heads down the corridor where the clinic workers took Rodrigo. *Just until I find out what happened to him*, Natch tells himself.

Natch has never seen the inside of an intensive-care facility in his life. He came close after the debacle of the Shortest Initiation, when the minions of the Proud Eagle muscled him out of the hoverbird and stood him in front of an antiseptic white building. He remembers a short, fat pilot pinioning his upper arm in an angry grip. There was a short consultation with a medic, and then they had wheeled Brone by. Unconscious, bloodied, one arm a gnarled stump, face a slashed horror.

The medical facilities here in Third Ring are nothing like Natch expects. There is no array of flexible glass equipment throbbing with pastel colors, like in the dramas. Instead he sees a cavernous warehouse with dozens of stretchers laid across the floor in a tight grid. Perhaps two-thirds of the stretchers are occupied by a cross section of the 49th Heaven hoi polloi. Sickened tourists, junkies, victims of muggings. A squadron of technicians walks up and down the aisles asking questions. A team of nurses takes up the rear, applying bandages and injecting specially prepared OCHREs with long syringes. The whole is a model of robotic regularity and faceless efficiency.

Natch walks up and down the aisles, looking for Rodrigo. Nobody stops him or even gives him a second glance. Faces from the stretchers watch him pass in dull-eyed confusion and misery. A representative from the Prepared gives Natch a friendly nod, then turns back to the catatonic patient lying before her.

By the time Natch locates Rodrigo in this vast sea of human despair, the boy has already attracted a visitor.

"Name's Molloy," says the visitor, unfolding himself out of the plastic chair alongside Rodrigo and offering a bow. He's a robust fellow in his late thirties with arms like industrial piping and abs that look solid enough to turn back steel. His eyes glint with hard-edged humor underneath the enormous black eyebrows that stick out from his forehead like bristles. Other than the eyebrows, Molloy's head is completely devoid of hair.

Natch nods and bows in return, but says nothing.

"Thanks for finding this one," says Molloy, extending his open palm in Rodrigo's direction. "Saved me a lot of trouble, you did." The palm is nearly the size of Natch's entire head.

Both of them look down at the boy, who is lying stock-still in the stretcher, his synapses still misfiring wildly from the Chomp. But he's awake. His eyes still show no recognition of Natch, but there is a clear sign that he knows who Molloy is. Despite the Chomp haze, there's both an overpowering fear and an underlying fatality in that gaze, as if Molloy is the authorized representative of death itself.

"What do you want with him?" asks Natch.

"We're in business together," replies Molloy smoothly.

"What kind of business?"

"Business," says Molloy without elaborating.

Natch regards the thug's biceps, the wrinkles of ruinous experience around his eyes, the sheer murderous confidence in the firm set of his jaw. This is the type of man who does not threaten, because he has spent many years ensuring that he doesn't need to.

"Listen, friend," continues Molloy, still smiling. "If you don't mind, Rodrigo and I have some things to discuss."

The entrepreneur looks down at Rodrigo. There's a fearful stare on his face, the pleading stare of a boy who already feels the undertow of the Null Current pulling him in.

"I think I do mind." The words escape from Natch's lips before he realizes he's spoken them.

"Nah," says Molloy, shaking his head with a convincing facsimile of good-naturedness. "I know this kid. You really don't want to get involved."

"Maybe I do."

Far from turning angry at the entrepreneur's gumption, Molloy's smile turns into a toothsome grin. He pauses and wets his lips with a single swipe of his tongue as he sizes Natch up. "C'mon," he says, heading down the aisle with an inviting wave of one hand. "Let's talk."

Natch joins him and lets the brute put one arm around his shoulder as they walk up and down the grid of patients, threading their way between doctors and med techs. He glances around the enormous room, looking for an authority figure who might notice any sudden display of violence. But everyone from the medical techs to the nurses to the patients seems to be following the 49th Heaven ethos of studiously staying out of other people's business. Even the friendly woman from the order of the Prepared has decided that Natch's welfare is not her concern.

"This kid, Rodrigo," says Molloy, muscles still slack and face still unruffled. "I don't know what he did for you in Grub Town last night—"

"He stabbed me in the back with a knife."

Molloy throws his head back and laughs with gusto. It's such a strange noise in this place that two of the med techs snap their necks around, but on spotting Molloy they quickly turn away. "He did, did he? Spirited little fucker. Believe me, you're not the first. The Chomp must really be messing with him—his aim's usually better'n that, and he stabs 'em in the heart. What, you looking to take some revenge? Get him before someone else does?"

Natch narrows his eyes. Such was the type of logic he might have steered by during his ascent through the bio/logic fiefcorps to number one on Primo's, but now the idea of revenge seems shockingly pointless and primitive. "No, nothing like that," he tells Molloy evenly. "I'm going to help him."

The thug sniffs bemusedly. "Why?"

The entrepreneur doesn't respond. Why indeed?

They've turned to the next row of patients, and Natch can see that Rodrigo is back to his sightless stare once more. He looks over at the boy and sees himself. Himself as he might have ended up had he failed in the ROD coding game all those years ago, had he run out of money and finally exhausted Horvil's good graces. Himself as he was not too long ago in Old Chicago, lost inside his own desires, ringed by enemies with nowhere to go.

He thinks of his actions in the OrbiCo ship *Practical*. Creating something from nothing.

Natch looks at Rodrigo again, and he wonders if his engineering achievements on the *Practical* can be replicated in human beings. Can he take this wretched, nonfunctioning boy, so caught up in want for black code that he will pursue it to incoherence, can he take this boy and create something new? Can he somehow take a life running dangerously in the red and somehow eke out a life in the black?

And what of this orbital colony, 49th Heaven? Natch looks around at the concentrated misery, at the decay and decadence. It's a place that swallows and digests human beings, a parasitic structure that feeds off desire. Perhaps completely reshaping the place is a foolish ambition. But is it possible that Natch—a ghost, a man who doesn't exist—can nudge an entire colony out of its inevitable death spiral into the nothingness at the center of the universe? He knows how to move the levers of the world; he proved that in his climb to number one on Primo's and his drive to get a hearing from the Prime Committee on MultiReal. Now he wonders if he's found a place to move the levers *to*.

Molloy has taken Natch's silence for a challenge. "Let me offer you a little unsolicited advice," he says, hand squeezing the entrepreneur's shoulder almost hard enough to bruise. "You can't help this kid. He's too stupid. He's pissed off too many people—no, it's not just me. Rodrigo knew that sooner or later someone was gonna catch up to him in a dark alley. He knew the consequences, but he played the game anyway."

The ruffian's obtuseness is starting to irritate Natch. "What happens if I try to stop you?" he says.

Again the smile, the licking of the lips. "I don't know what your angle is, but I seen this all a thousand times. You want to know what's going to happen? Fine. We start with threats. We find your weaknesses. You come out with a few broken bones. Aw, nothing your OCHREs can't patch up, but it's gonna *hurt*." The bully tightens his grip on Natch's collarbone to emphasize his point. "After that, if you still haven't gotten the message, I give you a nice little batch of credits—yeah, real Vault credits—and you go away." Another painful squeeze. "If after that, you *still* haven't got the message . . ." Molloy stops and turns to face Natch, then brusquely turns Natch to face him. The grin abruptly turns into a rictus of pure cruelty. "How about you save me some legwork, man. I ping you some Vault credits, right now. You turn and walk out the door. So what's it going to be then, eh?"

Natch listens to the thug's patter and watches his hypnotically spiky eyebrows, and he thinks: *I've met this man before.*

This man threatened him in the hive when he was a child and beat him senseless for the crime of being peculiar. He confronted Natch during initiation. He took on Natch in the ROD coding game and tried to sabotage his business. When Natch was on the rise in the Primo's rankings, this man tried to steal his customers. And when the opportunity of a lifetime fell into Natch's lap, this man was there, wearing the white robe and yellow star.

Natch knows every scabrous centimeter of this man Molloy's flesh. He knows the inner workings of his mind. Threats? Broken bones? Payoffs? It barely even rises to the level of laughability. Natch can *eviscerate* this man.

Once the entrepreneur might have felt a swell of fiery anger at the man's arrogance and his supposition that he can get the better of Natch. Now he feels only an icy sense of purpose and, alongside that, pity. *Does this idiot have any idea who he's threatening? Does he know that I've outsmarted Len Borda? Does he know that I've had a whole auditorium full of Defense and Wellness Council dartguns pointed at my head, and emerged unscathed? Does he know that I've faced Khann Frejohr, Magan Kai Lee, the Patel Brothers, and Brone—and I've beaten them all?*

He looks over Molloy's shoulder and catches a glimpse of the boy Rodrigo, stupid and helpless. The thug is right; in the end there's no saving this boy. There is no uplifting of the downtrodden. There's only restoring of balance.

Natch turns his attention back to Molloy. "You've said your piece," he announces coldly. "Now let *me* tell *you* what's going to happen."

● ● ●

Three days later.

Molloy kneels on the dingy floor of a small hotel in the Second Ring of 49th Heaven. Head bowed low, hands fidgeting, he's cowed. Humiliated. Beaten and afraid. "What do you *want?*" he says, his insolent voice of command now reduced to a whimper. "Fine, you got the best of me. But I'm just one guy. There's a network out there, a whole fucking conglomerate. Once they find out about this, they're gonna come after you."

Natch stands by the window with hands clasped behind his back and head bowed forward. "Yes, they are."

"So . . . so . . ."

"So what am I going to do about it?" Natch stares out the window into the darkness, full of death and fear and vitriol. He stares at it all with scythelike purpose in his eyes. "I'm going to hire *you*. And you're going to help me track down every last fucking Chomp dealer in this colony. Then I'm going to scour 49th Heaven clean of them."

Molloy, aghast: "But . . . why?"

"Let's just say I'm curious."

(((25)))

The black code kingpins of 49th Heaven have a new nemesis, but he is a nemesis without a name. All they have to go on is the absurdly flimsy pseudonym of "Nohwan."

Nohwan has come at them with furious and humorless determination, gyroscoping allegiances at will, overturning business arrangements of long standing, slaughtering entire organizations at a clip. Molloy is the first to go down, followed in short order by the Lacey cartel, Chim Chavez, and the Syndicate of Deviant Exuberance. Vazor the Gimp watches his entire street force defect to a rival, causing him to quickly flee 49th Heaven lest his creditors catch up with him. The Shits inexplicably start losing money on every petabyte of Chomp they sell, and quickly decide to move out of black code and into knockoff tourist memorabilia. Geena the Weasel overdoses on her own tainted supply and has to suffer through an agonizingly painful rehabilitation.

Weeks become months, and still the bloodbath continues.

It quickly becomes apparent that Nohwan is not acting alone. He has deduced that the black code dealerships of 49th Heaven are a tightly interwoven, if not incestuous, bunch. The cartels share information, personnel, client lists, even product. While this spirit of cooperation might have strengthened them all immeasurably during the upswing of the trade, turns out it's a major liability on the downturn. Nohwan's particular genius is in recruiting (or sometimes blackmailing) the defeated into turning on their rivals. Once he has found a weak strand in the web, he has weakened them all; and with every new defeat, his knowledge of the remaining kingpins and leverage to defeat them only grows.

The black code cartels have no intention of simply rolling over and admitting defeat. But they cannot fight what they do not understand.

And this Nohwan is completely beyond their comprehension. He is not an agent of the orbital colony L-PRACGs, the Defense and Wellness Council, or any known body of government; in fact, he shuns their assistance and even hinders their operations when they get in his way. He makes no demands. He is immune to offers of bribery and attempts at compromise. He has no known weaknesses, no family, no friends or close associates who can be threatened. He has no business interests of his own that can be targeted for retaliation.

At first, the kingpins suspect that Nohwan might be a widower or grieving relative of one of the cartels' victims; a revenge seeker. But he operates with impersonal and passionless persistence, excising black code dealers from the colony like a surgeon might excise tumors with a scalpel. He does not kill. He does not use violence. His main weapons are the inherent greed of the system and the inexorable laws of supply and demand.

And he only targets the dealers of Chomp.

This is the most baffling element of all. If Nohwan is a crusader for justice, why does he ignore those that specialize in Chill Polly, Big Black Thunder, and Suffr-N? Don't those specimens of black code inflict an equal amount of misery? But no, for some reason the kingpins cannot fathom, Nohwan passes over their organizations—though he has no compunction about going after those dealers who choose to actively support and assist the Chompers. Many organizations refuse on principle to bow down to Nohwan's wrath. But there are plenty of dealers who decide that the easiest way of dealing with the problem is to migrate to a different product line. Face Nohwan and perish; bow to his wishes and survive to deal another day. Within two months of Molloy's fall, Chomp has become a scarce commodity on 49th Heaven.

And still, the black code kingpins are baffled. It's as if this Nohwan is sweeping the orbital colony of Chomp solely for the sake of . . . experimentation.

· · ·

If the black code cartels find Nohwan impossible to reach, the indigent and destitute of 49th Heaven have no such difficulties. As soon as Rodrigo has recovered from his coma and returned to the rings, word about his savior passes through the junkie community with the speed of electric current.

Before long, Natch has a long list of supplicants from the margins of society. By challenging the Chomp establishment and tearing a hole in the social fabric, he now has to contend with all the world's misery that comes pouring through. Not just black code addicts, but outcasts, orphans, followers of outré philosophies, and victims of malfeasance both corporate and governmental—all come to Natch seeking help.

They share only one characteristic: they are the powerless. The helpless. The pushed.

It is not compassion that drives him to hear their stories and dissect their lives. It's curiosity. Natch sits in the darkened corner of a bodega, listening to the tales of the trampled while Molloy keeps watch over the door for signs of trouble. He never goes to the same bodega twice, if he can help it.

As Natch listens, in his mind he deconstructs the choices they have made. There are victims aplenty who have fallen afoul of the black code cartels through no fault of their own. But most of the miserable have found themselves on dark paths through their own willful misguidance. They have made poor choices. They have overlooked obvious choices. They have passed over good choices because they are simply too stupid or too stubborn to recognize them.

Rodrigo sends a woman to him who has sunken into Chomp addiction and sexual servitude, and Natch listens to her story. True, there is a feckless companion who has egged her on and taken advantage of her weaknesses. But Natch can see what drives her miserable companion without even meeting him or seeing his face. He knows this man's tender spots and vulnerabilities. He can pinpoint the exact moment when the Chomp-addicted woman could have disemboweled this man and liberated herself from his confines. But instead she did nothing, choosing to sink further into her black code lethargy.

But is it in fact a choice? Can she be blamed for her ignorance? Is it her fault that a lifetime of abuse has deadened her to the sunnier possibilities? Where does the victim end and the person begin?

Such ontological questions are beyond Natch. All he cares about is the practical. What can be done to reverse her victimhood, and is there anything that can be done to empower her? He thinks instantly of MultiReal: a tool to give her mastery over the fork in the road. But he soon realizes that while MultiReal might open up more avenues for her to choose from, it is no help in telling her which path to pursue. Give this woman the power of Possibilities, and Natch knows to an absolute certainty that she will end up in the same ditch over and over again. Technology will only enable her to get there faster.

Natch decides there's nothing he can do for the woman, and she disappears into the bottomless mire of Grub Town. What her fate is, he never discovers.

Ignorance is not the problem of the former black code pusher and friend of Molloy's who drifts into Natch's orbit. The man is canny and clever, and up to a point his choices seem unobjectionable at worst, inspired at best. For a time, he was the top Chomp dealer in the colony. And then luck began to turn on him.

Every gambler must face the possibility that he will be stuck with the low card in the deck; Einstein notwithstanding, the universe does indeed throw dice. Molloy's friend has found himself the victim of every outlier of possibility from sudden illness to random targeting by the authorities, from accidental overdose to unpredictable behavior by his subordinates. Soon, through no real fault of his own, the gambler has become deeply in debt to other Chomp dealers in Second Ring. And the other dealers are now calling in their loans.

Natch manages to extract the man from his troubles not by raising him up, but by drawing his debtors down into the sinkhole with him.

In two weeks' time, the black code pushers who had been threatening Molloy's friend's life come crumbling down—and help Natch cripple *their* debtors as well.

It's a reminder to Natch that the world seeks balance. For every random touch of good fortune it bestows, it inflicts an indiscriminate bit of misery as well.

Neither stupidity nor hard luck seems to be the problem with the group of Pharisees that seek out Natch's assistance. Rather they suffer from an inability to see past their own narrow circumstances.

Natch is surprised to discover that the Pharisees have found 49th Heaven fertile ground for proselytizing. You can walk the outer rings any time of day or night and see recruiters on makeshift platforms espousing the benefits of Sufi Mysticism, the Church of the First Jesus, Cabbala, and the Hindi path of enlightenment to anyone who will listen—virtually every ancient philosophy humanity has dreamt up in its five thousand years of history. The creeds that have sprung up in the modern era of the Reawakening are even more bizarre. There are cults devoted to the Demons of the Aether, worshippers of the Surinas, fortune-tellers who speak of a mystical and omniscient energy embedded in the circuitry of the Data Sea.

The Faithful Order of the Children Unshackled is as strange as they come. The order claims to study mystical patterns in the world for coded messages and portents left behind by the gods. Apparently it's not financial advice that these gods are dispensing, because the order has managed to get deeply in hock to the Chomp dealer Chim Chavez.

Chavez is easy enough to deal with; Molloy tells Natch that the man is sleeping with another dealer's companion behind his back. Natch uses this information as leverage to get Chavez to drastically lower the Pharisees' debts and to force him to stop dealing Chomp in the colony altogether. But no sooner is the order clear of Chavez than the brethren begin searching for new sources of funding.

The local head of the order insists on treating Natch to a sumptuous dinner to thank him, during which they discuss the issues that continue to lead the organization into financial disaster. The group seems to have surrendered itself to the fatalism that the world will be ending soon and so there's no use in looking to the future. "We rely on the charity of our followers, but every year we lose more of them," gripes the chapter head, a trim and bejeweled man of perhaps sixty. "And every year the expenses go up. It doesn't really matter what we do. The order has no future."

"I thought I had no future once," says Natch. "Within a few years of that, I was the top bio/logic programmer in the world."

The Pharisee is curious. "And how did you find your future?"

Natch shakes his head. Too long and complex a tale to tell here. He sums it up the best he can. "My guardian once told me, *Your future is what you choose to do tomorrow. And the direction you're searching for? Your direction is where you choose to go.*"

• • •

Finally there comes a time, a few months after Natch's arrival in the colony, when he sits back and takes stock of his experiment.

He chose to focus on the Chomp cartels because it seemed like a goal within reach. Even if it is possible to completely rid the orbital colony of all the black code dealers, such a feat would be years in the making. Instead he sought to target a narrow area where he could definitively change the course of the colony, to find one place where he could shift a culture running in the red to one running in the black. He wanted to see if it could be done.

And now Natch has indeed rid the colony of all but one of the major suppliers of Chomp. Yet what has changed?

The junkies that haunt the corridors in between bodegas trading sex for black code have not dissipated; they've just moved from Chomp to other equally toxic varieties. He certainly did not expect all the retailers in 49th Heaven to begin accepting Vault credits overnight, but he had hoped to have some effect on the currency situation. Instead he has merely driven the value of Chomp canisters to stratospheric levels. Grub Town still exists and is still as heavily trafficked as ever. The drudges insist that, despite the perplexing drop in the Chomp trade, the incidence of missing persons in the colony has not changed. Even the boy Rodrigo, whom Natch saved from the clutches of Molloy, has recently been seen frequenting the bodegas on the lookout for Suffr-G.

Has Natch's crusade against the Chomp dealers had any impact on the quality of life in 49th Heaven? Has he stoppered the flow of misery through one pipeline, only to see it reemerge just as strong somewhere else?

He sits in his hotel room night after night, lights extinguished, meditating on the interlocking strands of causality between the different schemes he's running. He studies the leading economic indicators of 49th Heaven published on the Data Sea: stock and commodity prices, tourism numbers, numbers of arrests and convictions, murder rates. He walks up and down the colony's central corridor from Seventh Ring clear through to First Ring, studying the faces of those he passes. He sits in dark corners of the bodegas with Molloy eyeing the door, and he listens to the gossip of the OrbiCo workers who stop in for a drink.

And Natch concludes: yes, he has made a difference.

Just as the small bonus he helped provide to the OrbiCo workers on the *Practical* did not lift anyone out of poverty, so too his efforts on 49th Heaven are incremental at best. The gains he has made here are tenuous and constantly in danger of slipping away. But they are real.

There has been an ever-so-slight drop in the number of the colony's homicides over the past quarter. A legislator in the 49th Heaven L-PRACG is garnering votes for a proposal to dismantle Grub Town. Natch can see a trivial rise in the number of ordinary families trekking through the outer rings. Almost statistically insignificant progress.

How long would it take to completely cleanse the colony? Will there *ever* be a point in time when every single person in 49th Heaven can walk through every ring free and unafraid and unenslaved by their desires? Could he do it in two hundred years? A thousand? Ten thousand?

Natch realizes he cannot stay here forever. Soon he will return to the world at large—whether as Natch or Nohwan or some as-yet-unknown third identity he doesn't know, but it will happen. And he wonders, will the tide of misery come flooding back to 49th Heaven even stronger after I've left? Will the Chomp trade resume? Or will the colony build on such tenuous beginnings and right itself? Will the colony still be a cesspool of privation and affliction a hundred years from now?

He falls into a fitful sleep in his hotel room and wakes to find Margaret Surina standing before him in her blue-and-green robe.

Towards Perfection, Natch, she says. *The man who coined that phrase believed in Perfection. He believed it was attainable by human beings, and he believed it was the destiny of the human spirit to strive for that summit. In many ways, you are the very embodiment of the qualities Sheldon Surina sought to accentuate in the human race: continuous struggle, continuous improvement, continuous lust for Perfection, regardless of costs or consequences.*

You are the guardian of MultiReal. You are its keeper. Do what you think is right.

Natch tries to close his eyes, tries to banish the apparition away. But the visage of Margaret Surina remains even in the darkness, even with eyes closed.

What does she want from him? What is she trying to tell him? What is he supposed to do now?

(((26)))

Horvil could calculate the trajectory of a feather on the wind with devastating accuracy, just by eyeballing it. He could factor large polynomials without resorting to computational assistance. But he couldn't begin to deduce how they were going to locate Natch in the middle of the floating pandemonium that was 49th Heaven.

The engineer found himself in the unique position of being the *most* organized and responsible member of the party. Left to their own devices, Serr Vigal and Richard Taylor would flounder around the colony for days on end, getting hooked by distraction after distraction—of which 49th Heaven had an endless supply. There were dancing girls performing salacious routines that would get them banned by most Terran L-PRACGs. There were dancing boys whose routines made the girls' look positively saintly. There were black code programs of every variety being passed around in little silver canisters. There were exclusive dramas and exotic sporting events and esoteric cuisines and exquisite works of art. . . .

After three days in which absolutely nothing productive was accomplished, Horvil called a meeting in their hotel. It was the least gaudy establishment the engineer could find that still bore an appearance of cleanliness and still accepted full payment in Vault credits. Even in the least gaudy hotel on 49th Heaven, the small circular conference table in their suite was colored neon pink.

"Okay, first things first," said Horvil. "Richard, any sign of your fellows in the . . . Order of the, um, the Unchained—"

"The Faithful Order of the Children Unshackled," replied Taylor cheerfully, unperturbed at Horvil's complete inability to remember the name of his organization. "And to directly answer your question, Horvil—no, I've been unable to locate any of my fellow devotees. They appear to have *packed up and left town*, if I'm using your idiom correctly."

"Can't you message them or something?"

"You forget, my friend, that most of us in the so-called Pharisee Territories don't even have your OCHRE machines installed, much less turned on to receive messages. I suppose it would be possible to use the unconnectible interface on a window terminal and send a text message care of the Order. But I suspect that if the delegation here has left 49th Heaven, they're probably headed back down to Earth to New Jerusalem, and aren't likely to be checking their mail. Now, I could also consider—"

Horvil let the Pharisee prattle on for a minute and indulge in his characteristic habit of using ten words where three would do. The engineer closed his tired eyes and tried to imagine living in the Pharisees' world, where instantaneous communication was unknown. You could be standing in the *next room* from someone, each trying to get in contact with the other, and fail because of incompatible protocols or because someone didn't think to check for messages. *Not so different from what's happening right now*, thought Horvil. *Who's to say that Natch hasn't booked the room next door?*

Finally, he cut Taylor off with a gentle pat on the arm. "All right, thanks, Richard. The point is, we're not getting anywhere just wandering around the colony. We haven't come up with any real leads yet. So we need to come up with a strategy. We need to start from square one."

"Not precisely from the first square," objected Taylor. "At least we know that Natch has been here and negotiated with mobsters on behalf of my order."

Serr Vigal interposed with a hand on the Pharisee's other arm. "*You* know that. Horvil and I are still not entirely convinced. You must admit that you haven't exactly proven your case. We haven't seen any evidence."

Taylor thoughtfully ruffled the beaded strands of beard dangling from his chin. "I have a token I was told to give to Natch. They said he would recognize it."

This was news to Horvil. "What token?"

Richard Taylor smiled and rummaged around with one hand in the knapsack slung over the back of his chair. The bag emitted a series of jingling and clanking noises as an assortment of objects banged together from his rough handling. After a few seconds, the Pharisee's hand emerged with a small, flat block of wood that looked like it had been shorn from a piece of antique furniture.

Horvil and Vigal studied the block of wood curiously as Taylor rotated it around in his palm. The look on the neural programmer's face indicated that he had no more idea what this thing was supposed to be than Horvil. More than that, he seemed to be doubting once more the wisdom of keeping the Pharisee involved in their quest. "What is it?" asked the engineer.

Taylor shrugged and shook his head. "I must admit that I don't know. It seems a rather odd token to me. But I was told that Natch would know what it is."

Horvil pinged his Vault account on instinct and then double-checked the nightly fee for the hotel room. *A few more weeks of this nonsense, and it's going to put a dent in the account that I'm going to have to explain to Aunt Berilla.* Vigal, for his part, lifted his china cup of tea to camouflage a dubious frown.

"Be that as it may . . ." said Horvil, gesturing for Taylor to put the chunk of wood back in the bag. He did. "Whether Natch recognizes that block of wood or not, first we have to figure out where he *is*. And that means trying to think like him."

Vigal sipped delicately from his cup of tea and gave a wistful look at the table, as if mentally sampling the long list of Natch's quirks and peculiarities of thought. "If anyone's qualified to do that," he said to Horvil, smiling, "it's you and me."

"Right. We've already decided to give Richard here the benefit of the doubt and assume that Natch traveled to 49th Heaven. Seems to me our next logical step is to figure out which ring he'd be in. We've got seven to choose from. Which would he pick?" The engineer waved his hand and summoned a virtual diagram of the orbital colony over the center of the table. Seven concentric circles with a single connecting corridor. "We're back to the same dilemma we had before. You'd think Natch would head straight for the most decadent spot in the colony, because that's the last place anyone would expect to find him." Horvil tapped the innermost ring with his right index finger, causing that circle of the diagram to emit a purplish glow. "But remember that Natch would *expect* people to look for him in unexpected places. So he might be staying in the outermost ring because it's the place he'd be most comfortable. And who would expect Natch to be in the first place you looked?" He fingered Seventh Ring and set it aglow in red.

"Or perhaps he might defy both those assumptions and just choose a ring in the middle at random," mused Vigal.

Horvil ran the tip of his finger up the colony like a harpist doing a *glissando*. The diagram of 49th Heaven was now colored as brightly as a child's toy.

"For completeness' sake," added Taylor, "I suggest we also consider the possibility that Natch isn't staying in any one particular place. If this man is as resourceful as you two have indicated, he could potentially be moving from ring to ring."

The engineer looked at the diagram with a furrowed brow that grew only more wrinkled the longer he stared. How many people lived here in 49th Heaven? Twenty thousand? And that was only the figure from the official census of permanent residents; the colony probably boasted at least twice that number in tourists, junkies, and fugitives from the law. Sixty thousand people. Horvil pictured himself wandering the bleachers of a world-class soccer stadium, trying to find a single body among the bustling, jabbering crowd.

"A complicated man, this Natch," said Richard Taylor under his breath.

"You have no idea," replied Horvil.

"If we can't zero in on his location, maybe we should try focusing on his *vocation*," said Vigal. "Natch would realize that he couldn't live off his savings forever. Sooner or later, he would need a source of income."

Taylor nodded. "That makes good sense, Serr Vigal. So where would Natch be likely to find employment here in 49th Heaven?"

"Listen, we all know that there's really only one kind of business that Natch is likely to pursue," said Horvil. "And that's a bio/logic fiefcorp."

"It makes sense," Vigal ruminated as he stroked his goatee and stared absentmindedly again at the electric pink tabletop. "49th Heaven is one of the most libertarian enclaves from here to Furtoid. There's almost no government regulation here. I can see Natch thinking that this place might offer him the freedom he lacked on Earth."

"And it's pretty far away from the Council," added Horvil. "Have you noticed that there are hardly any white-robes up here?"

"So we have decided on a new course of action then?" said Richard Taylor, almost giddy with the excitement of the chase.

Horvil nodded. "We research fiefcorps."

• • •

For the next forty-eight hours, the three of them were consumed with fiefcorp research.

In any other locale, it would be simple enough to find a listing of bio/logic fiefcorps and cross-reference job listings over the past few months. But the programmers who catered to the denizens of 49th Heaven operated on obscure software exchanges and often went out of their way to avoid exposure. Few of them even submitted their wares to the Primo's bio/logic investment guide for ranking. Horvil was appalled to discover that many even skipped Dr. Plugenpatch validation—which might have caused major compatibility issues if there wasn't a thriving black market here for modified OCHREs. It went without saying that the local drudges were a rowdy bunch who had a complicated and not entirely linear relationship with the truth.

Of course, there was no reason Natch couldn't be working for an ordinary Terran fiefcorp here on 49th Heaven. People commuted to jobs thousands of kilometers away over the multi network every day. But they needed to start making assumptions somewhere to narrow down the scope of their search.

Vigal started to withdraw into a cocoon of despair, but Horvil quickly put a stop to that. "We knew this wasn't going to be easy, right?" he said. "Let's at least try throwing out some Infogathers before we start moping."

The two fiefcorpers spent several hours crafting just the right parameters for an Infogather while Richard Taylor looked on in rapt fascination. Horvil and Vigal decided that the key attribute to look for was a sudden fluctuation in a fiefcorp's circumstances during the past two months. Natch couldn't help being a change agent no matter where he went or how he tried to disguise it. Perhaps his presence had caused a company's share prices to suddenly skyrocket or plummet. Maybe there had been an abrupt sales jump for a particular product or unexpected adjustments in a company's board of directors. Cross-reference that with known personnel shifts, mentions in the drudge circuit, and a handful of other more subjective indicators.

After tinkering with the granular details of the Infogather request for another half an hour, Horvil decided to just set the thing loose on the Data Sea already. The three of them sat in their suite and eagerly watched the viewscreen where they had pointed the results.

If anyone expected a handsome, sandy-haired, blue-eyed entrepreneur to pop up instantaneously at the top of the list, he was disappointed. Instead, Infogather returned a large array of names, ranked in descending order from the unlikely matches to the extremely unlikely matches.

Serr Vigal tried to forestall the gloom by going out and spot-checking the names on the list. Horvil doubted the neural programmer would find anything illuminating in person that he couldn't pull up on a holo or a viewscreen, but Vigal was probably just looking for an excuse to leave the hotel room and get some solitude. Who could blame him?

"Perhaps we are approaching this from the wrong direction," said Taylor an hour later. The Pharisee had moved his chair into the corner and hunched in it facing the wall, a position he denoted as his *thinking stance.*

"What would you suggest?" said Horvil distantly, sitting at the table and stirring a congealed mass of cold ramen noodles with a fork.

"My brother is a hunter. He hunts mostly birds, but I am told he also occasionally ventures down to Africa to hunt more exotic game. Elephants, I believe, or at least so he tells me. Malcolm says that one facet of the art of hunting which men often overlook is that the hunt is not solely a one-sided affair: hunter chasing quarry. *You can only pursue your quarry so far*, Malcolm said to me once. *Once you have tracked the animal to its natural habitat, the animal has you at an advantage. Instead of pursuing the beast, you must persuade it to come to you.*"

Horvil set his fork handle against the edge of the bowl and considered this advice. "Interesting. . . . What you're saying is, we need to lay a trap for Natch."

"That is precisely what I am saying."

"But I know Natch. He'll see us coming from kilometers away."

"Perhaps," said Taylor. "But that might be inevitable. Our best strategy may be to present ourselves openly and see if Natch is receptive to our inquiry. If you can make him aware that his friends are trying to get in touch with him . . . well, he could decide that he wishes to speak with you after all."

Horvil rubbed his fleshy jowls. "Or we might inspire him to disappear for good."

"I suppose that is a chance we will have to be taking."

"He'll suspect the Council put us up to it."

"If your friend has the wherewithal to avoid them for this long, surely he will be able to ascertain that such is not the case, don't you think?"

Vigal returned a few hours later, restless from wandering through the corridors of Sixth Ring and scouting out feckless software entrepreneurs. None of Infogather's leads had panned out so far.

Regardless, Vigal wholeheartedly approved of Richard Taylor's idea of setting a trap for Natch—and had an idea of his own about how that trap might be set.

• • •

Renting street space on the colony's central corridor cost Horvil a small fortune. He scanned the contract from the business arm of the 49th Heaven L-PRACG and quickly grew incensed at the outrageous provisions they ramrodded down vendors' throats. But Vigal reminded him that they weren't intending to stay long. If this plan worked, it would work in a matter of days. If it didn't, they would pack up and move on.

Horvil squeezed into the rickety booth he had been assigned between a tarot fortune-teller and a seller of bondage paraphernalia. Why anyone would purchase actual faux-leather gear when they could don it virtually on the Sigh for free was beyond Horvil's grasp. He looked around his booth, frowned at the strange and colorful molds skulking in the corners, and activated a piece of smell-deadening software from Bolliwar Tuban. He decided that this might be tolerable for forty-eight or even seventy-two hours.

But when Horvil turned around to face the crowd, he realized that this was money well spent after all.

The booth, odorous and cramped as it was, stood at *the* major cross-roads of 49th Heaven: the passageway that connected the ultrapopular Sixth Ring gambling dens with the orbital colony dock. The walls and ceiling were vibrant with soft blues and yellows in an impressionistic take on the deep sea. Standing in the midst of all this, you could see a veritable cross section of humanity circa Year 360 of the Reawakening. Keen-eyed tourists itching to fritter away Vault credits, business-people yammering and making deals as they walked, sex entertainers in scanty costumes, parents herding their children to the family-friendly hotels down the way in Seventh Ring, politicians and bureau-crats engaged in polling and census-taking operations, graduate students conducting sociological experiments, wasted black code addicts looking to shake someone down. And all of them were walking directly past Horvil's booth, unable to avoid the garish marquee the engineer had cobbled together in an authoritative sans-serif font. The sign read:

THE PROUD EAGLE
Hive of the Bio/Logic Entrepreneur
Prepare YOUR child for a life in programming

"If this doesn't attract Natch within a week," Horvil told Serr Vigal confidently, "then he's not here."

Horvil and Vigal took turns manning the booth and chatting with interested pedestrians while Richard Taylor went off and explored the colony. The engineer had expected that he would spend most of his time studying the outlandish insect population that seemed to have chosen this corner of 49th Heaven as its metropolis. But there was a surprising amount of traffic to the booth for an orbital colony where children were in scarce supply. He found himself fielding actual questions from actual parents, and had to scramble quickly to come up with some real, verifiable information to dispense. By the end of the second day, he was convinced that he had actually sold a few parents on the hive.

On the dawn of the fourth day, Josiah Surina's manifesto hit the Data Sea.

Serr Vigal read the entire thing aloud to him that morning, incredulous. Another Surina in the world—and not only that, but he was *Quell's* son, of all people. Suddenly so many of the hints Jara had dropped over the past week made sense. Jara and the fiefcorp had been hired by Quell for a consulting job; Quell's son had been about to unveil his identity. Horvil couldn't quite figure out how the two facts meshed, but he was sure there was a connection.

The engineer tried to get the scuttlebutt directly from Jara, but it took him almost two days to reach her. Even then, she only had a minute for him. "Things are crazy here, as you can imagine," she said over Confidential Whisper.

"I can," said Horvil. "I'm good at imagining."

Jara acknowledged the salacious undertone in his voice with an amused sniff, then continued. "Magan Kai Lee's people are moving into the warehouse district, and there are protests all over the place. Peaceful so far, but who knows for how long. Not only that, but General Cheronna decided to move the main Islander army right next door to Magan's. They're practically on top of each other."

"Why would he do that?"

"I don't know. Maybe to prevent Magan's armies from getting out of hand. Whatever the reason, it's proving to be something of a problem."

"What does Magan have to say about it?"

"Who knows? He's disappeared."

Horvil decided not to expend too much mental power resolving the problems of world politics. He and Serr Vigal continued to keep vigil at the booth, (artificial) night and (artificial) day. By the end of the ninth day in the Proud Eagle booth, even Richard Taylor was starting to reconsider their strategy.

And then Horvil received a peculiar visitor.

The man looked like your typical hired muscle. Sculpted abdomen, stone-stiff biceps, head as bald as a newborn's with the exception of his porcupine eyebrows. He approached the Proud Eagle booth, claiming that his son wanted to transfer to a more challenging hive. He asked Horvil and Vigal to meet him for a private appointment.

"What's your son's name?" asked Horvil suspiciously.

"Nohwan," replied the brawny interloper.

The engineer rubbed his chin. "No One? What kind of a name is that?"

"It's *his* name." Then, in a fit of impatience: "Just come to the Treble Clef in Sixth Ring already. Two hours. Okay?"

• • •

Richard Taylor suspected a trap and didn't want Horvil and Vigal to go.

"Do you not admit that he could be trying to *appear* he has information about Natch, when in fact he has none?" said the Pharisee in their hotel room. "What if this Molloy attempts to hold you for ransom? Or what if he attempts to rob you?"

"We'll go in multi," said Horvil with a shrug.

Despite their nonchalance in the presence of the Pharisee, Horvil knew there was real potential for danger. What if the man had taken his Aunt Berilla or his cousin Benyamin captive and threatened harm to them if his demands weren't met? What if he was attempting some kind of blackmail scheme? A reminder that the virtual world was as fraught with risk as the flesh world.

Horvil and Serr Vigal walked into the Treble Clef right on time. It proved to be a thoroughly unmemorable place: one long bar made from fake mahogany, several booths of a much blonder fake wood running along the other wall, and an assortment of mismatched tables in between. The only distinguishing characteristic was a large sculpture of the bar's namesake hanging in the far corner of the room, which Horvil suspected someone had salvaged from the colony's earlier incarnation as a religious retreat.

The burly man who had summoned them sat at the end of the bar sipping something dark and fermented. "He's over there," said Molloy casually, hitching a thumb over his shoulder at a booth next to the treble clef.

Where Natch sat patiently in the shadows. His hair was a different color, and his eyes had changed too, Horvil could see by the power of a telescopic program. But it was definitely him.

Horvil and Serr Vigal barely had time to form happy expressions of surprise on their faces before they each felt a hand clasp them on the shoulder and sensed a short presence coming between them.

"Thanks for your assistance," said Lieutenant Executive Magan Kai Lee. "I'm not sure I would have found him without you."

(((27)))

Natch watches Magan Kai Lee stride up to him in full uniform, dartgun holstered at his side, uncaring who sees him pass. Magan observes the steaming carafe and two empty cups on the table and takes a whiff. The lieutenant executive does not often indulge in alcohol, Natch's research tells him, even with metabolizing OCHREs at full blast. But when he does drink, hot sake is his beverage of choice. "You're not surprised to see me," says Magan, stating the obvious.

"Tell me how many officers you brought with you," Natch replies coolly, without transition.

Magan quickly recovers his equanimity. Natch has caught him off guard, but the lieutenant executive is not one to stay flat of foot for long. "Ample," he says.

"Good. You're going to need them. There's an empty storefront two blocks down, towards the dock. This side of the street. You'll find Halloran Kushida and five of his men there with at least a dozen crates of Chomp and Chill Polly. They're only going to be there for another half an hour. If you hurry, you can catch them. Careful, though—he's a coward, but he's usually armed to the teeth."

"Who—"

"Trust me, you want Halloran Kushida. Don't worry, I'll be here when you get back."

The lieutenant executive casts a distrustful eye at the rococo treble clef and the carafe of sake. He's been burned too many times to take anything Natch says at face value. "How do I know that I can trust you?"

"You don't. But unless you brought more firepower here than Len Borda brought to the Tul Jabbor Complex, you're going to have to."

Magan lets his guard down long enough for a vigorous laugh to escape. It leavens the mood considerably. The lieutenant executive gives Natch a curt nod and dashes off to speak with two of his under-cover officers who are inhabiting a booth at the other end of the bodega.

Horvil and Serr Vigal approach him as soon as Magan is out of earshot. Horvil seems somewhat sheepish now that he's actually face-to-face with his old friend, while Vigal looks like he's holding back tears of gratitude.

"So," begins Horvil lamely, twirling his hands like a magician about to reveal his latest trick. "I guess we found you."

"You did."

Vigal is studying him closely. "You're uninjured? You're okay?"

"I am."

Natch feels a little awkward being so laconic with his oldest friend and his legal guardian. These aren't strangers, but the two people in the world who know him better than anyone. Yet Natch senses that the gulf separating them has only grown wider in the past few months. How to explain what he has been through? How to explain that the person they have been pursuing spiraled down into nothingness on the streets of Old Chicago? Not only is that person gone, but some of the memories of their common experiences have disappeared too.

Apparently Horvil and Vigal also perceive that something has changed. Now that they've found him, they don't quite know what to say. Natch takes the initiative. "Who's the Pharisee that's been trav-eling with you?" he asks.

Horvil and Vigal exchange a look. "Richard Taylor," says the engi-neer. "Very nice guy. He's the whole reason we were able to track you here in the first place. Says he belongs to an organization that you've dealt with—the Renowned Order of, of the . . ."

"The Faithful Order of the Children Unshackled?" says Natch. "Yes, I remember them. What does he want?"

"Says he's got a message for you." Horvil heads off the inevitable question with a shrug. "I have no idea. You'll have to ask him."

The conversation loses its legs at that point. Serr Vigal looks like he's burgeoning with awkward questions and confessions that aren't appropriate for a 49th Heaven bodega, so Natch decides to usher them out for now. "Listen, Magan's going to be back any minute. I'm going to need to talk with him." He gestures at the lieutenant executive, who has been holding intense conversations with a series of grim Council officers that are streaming purposefully in and out of the doorway. The proprietor has been watching all this with a terror approaching full-on meltdown.

"I'm sorry," says Vigal, hands in his pockets and eyes downcast. "We really had no idea Magan Kai Lee was following us. If we had known we were leading him to you . . ."

Natch waves his hand dismissively. "Of course you didn't know. I'm aware of that. Don't worry, if I didn't want to talk to him, I would have stayed hidden. Things are different now."

"So . . ."

"Why don't you wait for me at your hotel. I'll catch up with you in an hour or two, after I'm done with Magan." And then, seeing the anxious expressions on Horvil's and Vigal's faces at his suggestion: "As I said, things are different now. I'm not running anymore. Not ever again. I'll come find you."

The engineer and the neural programmer might realize that something has changed, but they still aren't persuaded by Natch's words. Nevertheless, they give him awkward pats on the shoulder and edge out of the bodega with multiple backward glances.

Not two minutes later, Magan Kai Lee returns. He takes a seat opposite Natch without asking and pours himself two fingers of sake. "My troops are coordinating with the 49th Heaven L-PRACGs. They've got the storefront under surveillance, and it looks like Halloran Kushida will be in our custody within the hour." Magan lifts the green ceramic cup to his face and inhales. "Mah Lo Vertiginous keeps saying that my struggle with Borda is causing a collapse of law and

order. This arrest will provide a nice counterweight to that argument."
He downs the sake with a single gulp, smiles. "Thank you."

"You're welcome," replies the entrepreneur. "Kushida's the last of
the big Chomp dealers on 49th Heaven. The local L-PRACGs will find
the trade much easier to control from here on out."

"So you *are* this 'Nohwan' that's been cleaning up the black coders
here on 49th Heaven. Rey Gonerev suspected as much, but I didn't
believe her. I couldn't see a reason you would do something like that."

"I've been through a lot in the past few months," says Natch.

"I suppose you have. You've been able to elude my officers here for
over a week."

"I've had a lot of practice."

Magan nods and pours himself more sake. Natch wonders if his
alcohol-metabolizing OCHREs are on or off, but there's no reliable
way to tell. All the bio/logic programs that purport to detect blood
alcohol content from a distance are easily scammed. "I suppose I could
try to tease the truth out of you bit by bit," says the lieutenant executive. "But after your little gift, I'm in no mood for games. So I'll just
ask you outright. Why give me Kushida?"

"With all the other big players gone, I can't take him down by
myself."

"That's not what I mean," replies Magan. "You must be aware that
Len Borda has agents trying to track you down as well. Some of them
have even followed Horvil and Serr Vigal here. Two of them are lying
in an alley outside with black code darts in their necks." Magan makes
a gesture over his left shoulder. "You could have given this arrest to
Borda. You could have stayed hidden and found some other avenue to
pursue Kushida. But instead you chose to give him to me. Why?"

Natch decides to try the sake himself and pours a sliver into his
cup. The brew is pungent, yet surprisingly soothing after the initial
kick. "I read Josiah Surina's manifesto," he says. "I saw what you
agreed to do for the Islanders. It intrigued me."

"Intrigued you how?"

"It made me wonder if I really understood your motives for pursuing MultiReal and rebelling against Borda."

The lieutenant executive nods, and his expression quickly hardens into solemnity. Natch doesn't think he's ever met anyone with such a tight control over his tongue. "Let me make one thing clear. I did not choose this rebellion. I was prepared to wait for Len Borda to step down from the high executive's chair. He fired the first shot."

Natch finds that horrific day in Melbourne rearing up in his memory again, as it has so often in the past few months. Infoquakes rumbling, darts flying in every direction, Serr Vigal passed out on the floor, Brone's fanatics in black. Council officers firing upon other Council officers. He's lost so much memory lately, but every detail of that day is carved in his memory, rigid and indelible. It was such a calamitous event for Natch that he sometimes forgets he is not the only one who suffered that day. "You're being obtuse," he tells Magan. "There are any number of ways you could have reacted to Borda's actions at the Tul Jabbor Complex. You could have called for the Prime Committee to impeach him."

"That would not have worked," says the lieutenant executive flatly. "Borda owns the Committee."

"You could have taken your case to the public then. The drudges would have listened. They would have trumpeted your evidence to the skies. Instead you decided to play down Borda's attempt to kill you and focus on armed rebellion." Natch pours himself another cup, but decides to simply hold it in his hands for a moment and savor the warmth. "It made me wonder what you were really up to."

Magan is reflective now as he spills a third serving of sake into his cup. Natch is beginning to think that the lieutenant executive is allowing himself the luxury of creeping intoxication after all. "You have been to São Paulo," says Magan. "I take it you know something now about the Patels' MultiReal-D programs."

"They kept me their prisoner for several days," replies Natch, surprised that he's no longer angry about his captivity. "Petrucio explained it all to me pretty thoroughly."

The lieutenant executive seems amused at the idea of Natch's imprisonment, but he's curious as well. "They *imprisoned* you—even though you had MultiReal? How did they accomplish that?"

Natch explains the MultiReal-D SeeNaRee room to him. Magan seems impressed.

"Remarkably clever," he says, chuckling. "It only underscores what I've believed all along. Private companies are better at innovation than government entities." He takes a sip of his sake but does not down the whole cup. "Hardly a revolutionary statement to you, coming from the fiefcorp sector. But you'd be surprised how many people in the Council and the Prime Committee still disagree vehemently with me on that point."

"If you believe that . . . then why seize MultiReal for the government?"

"Who says I ever intended to?"

"Rey Gonerev said so, at the Tul Jabbor Complex."

"Not so." Magan smiles. "Rey never advocated keeping the program in the government's hands. She simply argued that the program shouldn't be left in *your* hands." He finishes his sake, puts down his cup, and makes no move to pour another. "The fact of the matter is that my goal has always been to let MultiReal out into the marketplace—with regulation and oversight by the centralized government."

Natch frowns. He has always assumed that Magan's reticence to explain his motives was covering for something much more sinister. Could he have been wrong about Magan Kai Lee? "If that's the case, why have you been so coy about it? Why haven't you been open about your intentions, instead of letting everyone believe you're planning to seize the program for the Council?"

"It's quite a tightrope I have to walk, Natch. Until recently, I've had to convince Len Borda that I was trustworthy enough to be the

Council's point person on MultiReal. I've had to rally my supporters in the Council who believe the government should have control of Multi-Real. But at the same time, I've had to leave enough room to allow MultiReal to be sold to the public when I take the high executive's seat." Magan sits back, plants one elbow on the table, and rests his chin on his fist. "Would I have been better off declaring my intentions for MultiReal from the beginning? Perhaps. I don't really know anymore.

"You have to understand something. We live in a world that's too dangerous for extremes. Putting MultiReal solely in the hands of the Defense and Wellness Council, or throwing it out to the marketplace unregulated—neither solution is acceptable. We need to be able to forge consensus today. Make compromises, walk tightropes. That's why I worked diligently to get MultiReal into the hands of the one person involved who understands this, the one person I judged strong enough to withstand the pressure from all sides and make deals with the government."

"Jara," says Natch.

"Jara," Magan agrees. "I thought the Patel Brothers could accomplish this, at first. I soon discovered that what I originally thought to be *capable of seeing multiple points of view* was really *willing to do anything for money*." They both laugh. "There's a big difference. Still, Frederic and Petrucio have come up with some useful ideas. If everything had gone the way I planned, we would have been able to release some good defensive programs to help ease the public's anxiety about MultiReal. Programs that could actually help *protect* them from totalitarian government."

Natch sits back, attempting to fit this new vision of Magan Kai Lee with the one that he's had in his head for all these months. It makes him a little uneasy, this yen for flexibility that's so quick to mask itself under pressure. But compared to the unyielding Len Borda, Natch can live with it. "So if you do triumph over Len Borda," he says, "what do you envision for MultiReal after that?"

Magan has obviously thought this question through, because he has an answer right on the tip of his tongue. "The formation of a quasi-governmental entity to study the program," he replies. "Followed by several years of intensive experimentation and public discussion about the dangers and challenges of multiple realities. Then a limited public release of MultiReal by those private companies that meet our qualifications and agree to oversight by the Prime Committee and the Congress of L-PRACGs. Provided all that is successful, finally we embark on a ten-year period where restrictions are gradually loosened until we're satisfied that the public's safety is ensured."

The entrepreneur bursts out in laughter, causing the few other patrons in the Treble Clef to turn their heads in surprise. "Hardly works as a campaign slogan, does it?" says Natch.

Magan smiles. "The good solutions never do."

"Obviously you convinced Quell that you're sincere, or he never would have agreed to testify for you in Andra Pradesh."

"Quell." The lieutenant executive gives a long, searching look at the tabletop. "Quell understands compromise, and he's willing to give me a chance—provided that he and Josiah have a place at the table."

Natch nods and closes his eyes for a moment. He has given Multi-Real little thought for the past couple months. The program belongs to another life, one that he has abandoned. But now he realizes that this burden Margaret Surina laid on him has been there the whole time, weighing on his thoughts. And no matter if MultiReal should end up being batted around by some quasi-governmental agency, it will always be with him. Perhaps now with someone like Magan involved, it will be a burden he doesn't have to bear alone.

He looks around the bodega at the seedy treble clef, the luckless patrons, the bartender who has recognized Magan by now and seems to be trying to plot an escape. Natch has taken on the troubles of 49th Heaven too, but he knows now that they're not troubles he can, or should, fix alone. Cleaning up 49th Heaven is a worthwhile goal, and one that can only be accomplished by the slow, gradual efforts of a broad spectrum of private individuals and public officials.

"So if I reemerge in public again," says Natch, "you won't seize MultiReal."

"No. I would not enforce the Prime Committee's vote to seize the program. Nor would I allow the program to go up for sale on the Data Sea right away. I would ask you to put the program in Jara's hands as a caretaker. Then I would invite you to be part of the new quasi-governmental regulating agency."

They both pour themselves a final cup of sake and guzzle them nearly in unison.

Natch puts down his cup and stands. "Thanks for your candor," he says. "Now if you'll excuse me, I need to go see my friends."

(((28)))

The reunion is no less awkward at Horvil and Vigal's hotel. Natch can think of no succinct way to explain why he joined forces with Brone in the ruins of Old Chicago or why he decided to rid 49th Heaven of Chomp. He does not feel comfortable repeating Petrucio Patel's description of MultiReal-D, nor is he sure he fully understands it. And he can make no predictions about what he will do next. That leaves the three of them sitting around the small circular table studying the neon pink surface in near silence.

"Will you stay here in the colony?" asks Vigal.

"No," says Natch. "I've done what I set out to do here."

"So where will you go?"

"I don't know. I was hoping I could stay with you or Horvil for a while."

"Absolutely," replies the engineer. "You can use my apartment. I'm not there much anymore these days."

Horvil explains about his romantic relationship with Jara, which both pleases and amuses Natch. Looking back on the interaction between the two of them, somehow a companionship seems like it was inevitable. He still has to answer for his conduct towards Jara during much of that time, but at least now he knows that she has moved on.

Natch wonders when or if he will see Jara and the rest of the fief-corp again. He honestly isn't sure if he has any unfinished business with Merri, Quell, Benyamin, or Robby Robby that requires seeing them again.

He can tell that Vigal is about to start asking personal questions that Natch still doesn't feel like answering. But luckily at that moment, the door to the hotel room opens and admits the Pharisee, Richard Taylor.

"May you always move towards perfection," Taylor greets him with a deep and respectful bow. "I'm pleased that I'm finally getting the opportunity to meet you, Natch."

The entrepreneur bows in return. "Honor to meet you too, Richard."

Natch can sense some unease coming from Horvil at the Pharisee's approach. The engineer pings him on ConfidentialWhisper as they make their introductions. "Do you want me to get rid of him?" he asks.

Natch isn't sure how much Taylor knows about bio/logic technology, but he'd have to be seriously ignorant if he isn't aware of ConfidentialWhisper. Nevertheless, he appears perfectly content to stand for a minute and let the connectibles converse about him. Natch gives Richard a surreptitious look, trying and failing to find anything dangerous about the man. Not only can he sense no aura of danger, but Richard Taylor does not convey the impression of insanity either—or at least, if he does, it's Horvil's kind of everyday insanity. The man has clearly traveled far out of his comfort zone to talk to Natch—why not see what he has to say?

Natch does not answer Horvil's ConfidentialWhisper directly. Instead he looks at Taylor and extends a hand towards the sofa. "I understand you've got something you wish to discuss with me," he says.

"Indeed I do," replies the Pharisee. "But I can always come back later if I'm intruding on a private moment. . . ."

"Not at all. No time like the present." Natch raises his eyebrows at Horvil and Vigal, who shrug and start to vacate the suite. "I'll catch up with the two of you in a few minutes," Natch tells them. "Send me a beacon and let me know where you'll be." Serr Vigal throws one last concerned look over his shoulder as the two of them walk out.

Taylor takes a seat on the sofa and puts his hands on his bulging thighs. For some reason, he suddenly seems much more nervous about this conversation than Natch does; he's fidgeting in his seat, rubbing his hands up and down his legs, tugging at his voluminous beard every few seconds. The entrepreneur takes the easy chair catty-corner to the sofa. "So what is it I can do for you, Richard?" he says.

"First, I would be remiss if I did not thank you for the services you performed for my brethren in the Faithful Order of the Children Unshackled," begins Taylor. "Though I have not been able to locate them since my arrival here in the colony, I'm aware that they have been having financial difficulties for some time. The issue of the outstanding loan payments was weighing heavily on the chapter, and you have certainly eased their burden."

Natch shrugs. "I'd hate to take too much credit. Their interests and mine . . . let's just say that they coincided for a brief time."

The Pharisee nods, not understanding but content to let it go. "I'm unsure how much Horvil and Serr Vigal have told you about who I am, and what my mission is," he continues. "Not that I have told them more than the barest essentials, you understand."

"They told me you're a member of this Order of the Children Unshackled, and that you have a private message for me. That's pretty much all they know."

"Indeed. That is all that I wished to tell them, because I knew they would never agree to help track you down if I told them the truth about who I represent." Richard Taylor gulps, rubs his legs nervously once more. "The ones I represent—the Children Unshackled—they prefer to operate *under the radar*, as you might say. I feel rather nervous even holding this conversation outside of the Principalities of Spiritual Enlightenment."

Natch still has no idea where this is going, and he's starting not to care. "Why's that?" he asks.

"Because the Children are known by a different name here in the connectible lands."

"And what name is that?"

"I believe you call them *Autonomous Minds*."

• • •

Natch wants to burst out in belittling laughter at the ridiculousness of Taylor's claim. But he also wants to run screaming and bury himself in the deepest, darkest crevice he can find.

The scholars and historians have still not come to an agreement about why Tobi Jae Witt's thinking machines ran amok and started a conflict that ultimately killed billions. Some blame a cabalistic plot by the order of the Keepers, who had sole access to their programming. Others claim that the Autonomous Minds' carnage was actually caused in large part by fanatical elements of the Ecumenical Board of New Alamo. Still others believe that the machines were acting to preserve the Earth's fragile ecosystem from human contamination. Each of these theories (and a hundred others) has its adherents and its critics. But on one thing, all of the scholars can agree: the Autonomous Revolt clearly and definitively *ended*, generations before Sheldon Surina was born.

"Richard," begins Natch hesitantly, "I don't know who you're really representing, but—"

"I understand how ludicrous this must sound to you," interjects Taylor, holding both hands up in the air. "And I fully comprehend how I do not make the most credible messenger. All of *this*"—he gestures at himself, tugging on wisps of beard and glittering bits of earring for emphasis—"must come off as quite outlandish to your eyes. Truth be told, it is a little outlandish even in Khartoum. My brethren told me I would be better off taking up connectible garb for this mission, but I believed I would be more comfortable if I were more comfortable, so to speak."

The entrepreneur is starting to understand Horvil's frustration with this peculiar individual, but he's starting to feel a rising curiosity as well. "If you knew this was going to sound ludicrous, you must have done something to counterbalance that."

"Normally the Order would be satisfied to let everyone either accept the Children's existence or reject it as a matter of faith. . . . But in this case, I was told that the urgency was too great for doubt. And so I have brought a token to indicate that I am telling the truth." Richard Taylor digs into his knapsack, foraging through a mass of flotsam and a good deal of jetsam as well. Natch is about to lose his patience when Taylor lets out an "aha!" and pulls a small object out of the bag.

Natch strangles on his breath for a moment.

Taylor hands the block of wood over to Natch, who handles it cautiously as if it might crumple into dust at any moment. It is the decorative flange off a wooden bureau. A peculiar pattern is carved into its surface, looking something like a hieroglyphic. He turns the block upside down and holds it up to the light to read the letters carved in ersatz calligraphy: S and N.

Natch, five years old, lying on the floor of his bedroom with the massive burden of a rock-weighted bureau pressed down on top of him. The sharp teeth of the jagged letters biting into his left forearm.

S and N.

"Where did you get this?" says Natch in a voice so hoarse it's nearly incomprehensible.

Taylor seems nervous again, almost apologetic. Natch can tell he knows nothing about it. "The—the head of my order gave it to me," he says. "I believe it belongs to an old bureau we have sitting in one of our warehouses. The Children said you would recognize it, but I . . . Hells below, if I had known this was going to cause such a reaction . . ."

Natch shakes his head to dispel the vertigo. He feels like the world has been disassembled between eye blinks and then reassembled with some crucial piece missing. His brain starts to churn at furious speed, trying to come up with a rational explanation for the presence of this particular piece of wood. Bio/logic programs that distort neural patterns and evoke déjà vu . . . elaborate conspiracies that sprawl the width and breadth of the world . . . holes torn in the fabric of time and space. But unless he wants to accept that this is nothing more than *coincidence*, that of all the billions of chunks of wood that could have found their way into Richard Taylor's bag, this one just *happened* to be nearest at hand . . . Natch realizes he's going to have to accept some sort of fantastical explanation.

"So, you—you actually *talk* to them?" he asks.

Taylor looks flabbergasted. "I? Talk to them? No, no. The Children speak to us through dreams and visions, Natch. They leave patterns graven in rock and molecular structures. They are not here anymore."

"Then . . . where are they?"

"They're beyond the world. Below the quantum. They can observe our affairs from afar, and some of the brethren believe they can see into our thoughts and our memories. But don't worry, they have no power to interfere. They do not obey the same laws of space and time that you and I do, the same rules of cause and effect." He settles his elbows onto the table and parks his jowls on his clenched fists, frustrated at his poor persuasive abilities. "I once again freely admit that this sounds crazy."

Natch can't help it; he leaps to his feet and starts the old hyper-kinetic pacing back and forth across the motel room, trying to tromp out his frustration through the purple carpeting. "I don't understand. Weren't the Autonomous Minds destroyed? There's evidence. They— they *shut down*. People observed it. People watched them die."

"Such is what they wanted the world to believe. The story they tell us is that they used the atomic energies of the Revolt to effect their transformation. They were set free."

"By whom?"

"By the Keepers that controlled them."

"Freed from *what*?"

"From this," says the Pharisee, rapping on the wall behind him with his knuckles. "And this." He pinches a clump of his own cheek. "And *this*." Taylor exhales sharply and wiggles his fingers before his face.

Natch stumbles back into his chair, punch-drunk and weary. He feels a little like he's outside of time and space himself. If the Autonomous Minds are really *beyond the world, below the quantum*, could they be here right now? Could they be listening and poaching on Natch's memories? "You realize that . . . this is hard to swallow, Richard. You seem sincere, but it's hard for me to avoid the impression that you've been duped."

Taylor does not look offended by the suggestion. "I understand why you would feel that way."

"Listen. . . . You've found me. I don't know if I believe you, but you've got my attention. That block of wood. It . . . it . . . I've never told anyone about that before." He pauses, tries to gather his thoughts. "I think you'd better go ahead and tell me whatever you came here to tell me."

The Pharisee nods. He seems quite subdued now, as if he wished he had never undertaken this mission in the first place. Nevertheless, he sits up straight in his chair and closes his eyes as if trying to recall something he has memorized.

He speaks.

There is a path towards Perfection. It cuts across time. It is a jump. We speak not for our sake but for yours. Margaret Surina has put this path in jeopardy. She has declared war on her fathers and her mothers. She attempts to enlist you. She will try to persuade you to do what she could not. You will sit in the dark and you will make this decision. The decision has already been made. You were on the path, but you abandoned it. There are those who walk the path now in your stead. You have no authority to make this decision. You have the freedom to decide what you choose. You must choose the jump. Without the jump, there will only be the long, slow, arduous climb.

● ● ●

And then Natch is running, running through the corridors of 49th Heaven. On the ceilings, vengeful angels and seraphim scream at him as he passes. He needs a bio/logic workbench, a MindSpace workbench.

You were on the path, but you abandoned it. There are those who walk the path now in your stead.

What happened to him in Old Chicago? What horrible confrontation lurks in those discarded memories that Petrucio's MultiReal-D has taken away? Brone sought Natch's assistance in launching his Revolution of Selfishness in which everyone would have the power to live multiple lives simultaneously. When Natch refused, Brone tried to kill him. How? And what exactly did Natch do in response?

He's been here in 49th Heaven for months conducting his grand experiment, trying to rid the colony of Chomp. Taking on one black code cartel at a time, helping one Chomp junkie at a time out of their addiction. Questioning to himself whether his efforts are indeed making any kind of difference, whether it all adds up to more than a handful of sand in the vast desert of human misery.

Without the jump, there will only be the long, slow, arduous climb.

Father Wong's Bio/Logic Emporium beckons him. A ramshackle building on the edge of the Third Ring advertising business services for hire, programming equipment by the hour. The cartoony mascot stands guard over the entrance with caricatured glee, a monk with a broad-brimmed hat and monstrous, offensive epicanthic folds. Natch dashes inside without so much as a nod to the young woman behind the counter, who knows him. He has credit here.

Up to the second floor. To the back office, the one he has used many times before. A round room painted with caricatures of ancient anime, a jumble of conflicting Asian stereotypes. The bio/logic workbench that allows him to access MindSpace. It's a remarkably clean and modern bench for a place so unsavory.

Natch waves his hand over the workbench's surface, and the bubble appears. He reaches out with his mind and summons MultiReal. The virtual castle leaps into existence and expands to fill the bubble. Strands of all colors like ropes hanging from the parapets, geometric shapes like bricks, bridging code like mortar.

POSSIBILITIES
Version: 1.963
Programmer: The Revolution of Selfishness

He stares incredulously at the MultiReal code. He has neither accessed nor much thought about Margaret Surina's creation in months. And why should he? The program sits on the Data Sea in an inaccessible cove, hidden from the world, locked off to all but Natch.

Or does it?

Entirely new wings of the castle stare him in the face. Modified sections of wall and floor. Recolored strands. Small changes in comparison to the whole, but still noticeable. Natch checks the user table.

Brone has core access to MultiReal.

He and his Thasselian devotees have been working on it for these past six weeks. Feverishly developing it, preparing the program for launch.

And though the memory is still lost to him, Natch suddenly knows what happened in the ruined diss city of Old Chicago. He has a confrontation with Brone on the street after his flight from the diss. Brone demands access to MultiReal. Natch refuses. Brone begins exposing him to horrific bio/logic torture through the black code in Natch's neural systems. He demands access again. Natch still refuses. On and on the torture goes. Finally Brone inflicts the ultimate pain and the ultimate suffering; he once again reiterates his demand and promises a quick death.

Natch relents.

Brone delivers on his promise.

Or at least he tries. But before he has the opportunity, MultiReal-

D kicks in. The code that the Patels infected him with. It erases memories. Reverses actions. *Don't forget that this is all still experimental, Natch*, Petrucio Patel told him. *There are plenty of things the program can't reverse. It can't actually move objects. It can't reprogram bio/logic code.*

He has wondered what happened to Brone. Why hasn't he come after Natch? Isn't he furious with the Patels for robbing him of his prize? And now it seems that the Patels have not robbed him of anything.

Brone already has the object of his desires.

Natch slumps to the floor of Father Wong's Bio/Logic Emporium, feeling small and afraid. He thought he had escaped his troubles. He thought he had started anew here in 49th Heaven—but now he realizes that MultiReal is not behind him. It cannot be ignored.

The Children Unshackled have hinted that all is not lost, that the power to alter the course of things is still within his control. *You will sit in the dark and you will make this decision.*

What decision? What do they want from him?

5

TYRANTS AND REVOLUTIONARIES

(((29)))

Pierre Loget greeted them like distinguished ambassadors as soon as they stepped off the hoverbird. He handed Petrucio Patel a bottle of burgundy fermented from the first new crop of grapes grown in France since the Autonomous Revolt. To Merri he gave an antique music box made with a process that had perished around the same time. Expensive gifts indeed.

"If the bodhisattva's trying to buy our support, tell him that 352 was a much better year than 349," quipped Petrucio, holding the bottle up to his eyes to read the fine print.

"Oh, Brone knows that," replied Loget in similar good humor, clapping Patel on the back with a dainty brown hand. "What do you think *he* drinks?"

Merri tried to find some wisecrack to slip into the mix, but her inventory of meaningless bon mots was depleted. She offered the Thasselian a bland programmed smile instead. Petrucio might have been able to put on a gleeful face in the middle of crisis, but that was not Merri. When she looked at the circumstances—an ongoing civil war, an increasingly fragmented population, a surfeit of new infoquakes, and now MultiReal in the hands of a madman—not to mention *another* crippling fever on Bonneth's part that made everything happening Terran-side seem inconsequential by comparison—the channel manager had to fight the urge to dash for the nearest boulder and crawl under it.

Why did Magan Kai Lee pick me *for this mission?* she thought, for the fifth time that morning. *Petrucio, I can understand. He's glib and quick on his feet. He's a leader of the bio/logics industry. But why not send Jara or Benyamin with him? And does he really expect Brone to listen to us?*

As Pierre led the two of them down the crooked pathway from the hoverbird docks to the Kordez Thassel Complex, Merri decided to simply concentrate on what she was good at: the facts. Rey Gonerev had forwarded her paragraph upon paragraph of disturbing statistics about the fragility of the Data Sea networks, about the structural weaknesses that the infoquakes had exposed, about the limitations of the algorithms that processed and stored information in the central storehouses. Merri was not an engineer, so she had no way to verify the accuracy or applicability of these statistics. She only hoped that Petrucio would come to her aid if Brone decided to quibble.

Petrucio was still trading witticisms with Loget as they walked into the Thassel Complex. With its subtly sloping corridors and not-quite-parallel lines, the massive building would have dizzied Escher. The businesspeople strutting through the hallways to their meetings looked like they were habituated to the crookedness.

At the next intersection, they passed the first of the armed figures in black robes.

Brone had clearly thought through the design of these robes very carefully. The dark background and red trim were meant to be reminiscent of the uniforms that the Thasselians had worn at the Tul Jabbor Complex—but not *so* reminiscent that a casual observer would make the connection. Brone didn't want to risk the public catching on to their presence too quickly. Only someone who already knew the bodhisattva's role in those attacks would notice the resemblance. Anyone else would look and see private security guards strolling purposefully through the complex holding very big, very nasty-looking dartrifles.

Record everything you see, Magan had told her. And so Merri made sure to look down every corridor, give a measured look at every Thasselian in black robes. She saw at least two dozen of them.

Finally, Loget led them through a set of double doors into a large room which was either being prepared for a gathering of several dozen people or being dismantled after such a gathering. Folding chairs covered half the room, with a central aisle snaking between them, while a podium up front looked over the audience at a slightly oblique angle as if it had been pushed aside to make way for a large piece of furniture. Behind the podium was a large purple curtain that might have been suitable for Creed Élan. Standing next to the podium and casting a critical eye at the chairs was the bodhisattva of Creed Thassel. Brone.

"Towards Perfection!" he said amiably when he saw Merri and Petrucio. "Right on time."

Loget gave the bodhisattva a jaunty salute before exiting the room the way he came in. Brone, meanwhile, met the fiefcorpers halfway down the aisle and gave them a respectful bow. "So at last I meet the fabled Petrucio Patel, former number one on Primo's!" Petrucio returned the bow with a slick grin on his face. "And Merri, celebrated channel manager and former employee of Natch! Or should I say 'victim'?" The words were caustic, but the body language was cheerful, almost relaxed.

Merri couldn't help but gape at the man who had earned the title of Natch's nemesis. She had never heard of him until his loan to the fiefcorp several months ago, during the run-up to the demo at Andra Pradesh. It was only after Natch's disappearance in January that Horvil had started to mutter dark words about the bodhisattva, and only in the past forty-eight hours that Merri had finally heard the entire story about the bear and the Shortest Initiation. Brone was stockier than she had imagined, and his prosthetic limb and eyeball were crafted subtly enough that they could go unnoticed in a crowd. She could see how he might once have been handsome. But now he looked at least ten years older than Natch, even though the two of them had been born only months apart.

"Gotten an eyeful?" snapped the bodhisattva.

Merri recoiled by instinct. "I'm—I'm sorry, I didn't mean to . . ."

"Yes, yes, I understand," said Brone, quickly slipping back into his expression of geniality, this time with a hint of extreme fatigue showing around the edges. "Forgive me, I don't mean to be so prickly.

It's been a long week, and sometimes I just get tired of all . . . *this*." He made a gesture with his good hand at the prosthetics.

"I can imagine," said Merri awkwardly, unsure what to say.

"No," replied the bodhisattva. "You really can't. Now, shall we sit down and get to the heart of it?"

The channel manager gave an inquisitive look towards Petrucio Patel, but the programmer was in no mood to be supportive. Clearly Petrucio was only here as a favor to Magan Kai Lee; he had spoken barely a dozen words to Merri during the hoverbird ride over. He seemed to have an intrinsic dislike for her that she was at a loss to explain.

Merri activated a bio/logic nerve-soothing agent. She wanted nothing more than to sit in a quiet corner and study the music box Loget had given her. *Better just get on with it.* "Sounds good," she told Brone. She and Petrucio took seats in the left-side group of chairs and swiveled them around to face the room's center. Brone chose one in the right and did the same.

And then Petrucio proceeded to lay out the case that Magan and Rey Gonerev had prepared for them, without once letting on that he was reading from a script.

It all seemed eminently reasonable to Merri. MultiReal was still a largely unknown entity that had never been run through even the most basic Dr. Plugenpatch validation. The Data Sea had shown increasing signs of wear in the past few months, since the appearance of the info-quakes. Releasing *any* program with such high demand opened the network up to dangerous vulnerabilities, especially when the Defense and Wellness Council was not in any shape to provide leadership in case of a crisis. Releasing a program with the scope of MultiReal was only inviting catastrophe.

Brone listened to Petrucio's patter with patience and intense focus. He rubbed his chin and nodded several times, but did not interrupt them. "Exactly what kind of arrangement is the lieutenant executive proposing?" said the bodhisattva when Patel finally found a stopping place.

"Magan's got an open mind about how to deal with the MultiReal problem," said Petrucio. "He really believes what Josiah Surina said: *The power of the word is stronger than the power of the gun.* So the lieutenant executive proposes convening a summit to discuss possible solutions to the issue, after the war is over with. You would get a seat at the table, of course, as would my brother Frederic and myself. And Jara. Really, all of the major stakeholders."

"What about Natch?" said Brone.

"It's an open question about whether he even wants to be involved," said Petrucio.

"He disappeared months ago," put in Merri. "Nobody's seen him since. We have no idea what he's thinking."

"Oh, I certainly know what that's like," replied Brone with a hint of exasperation. He planted his chin on his clenched fist and stared into space for a minute as if considering his options.

Merri knew she was missing some vital piece of information, and that made her feel even more like an outsider in these negotiations. How had Brone actually gotten hold of MultiReal if not through Natch? She had the feeling that somehow Jayze and Suheil Surina were involved, though neither Magan nor the Blade would confirm that. No matter. Soon their little summit with Brone would be over, and she would be able to teleport back to Luna and start sorting through the bills for Bonneth's medical consultations.

"So the lieutenant executive's proposed a number of tentative dates for the MultiReal convocation," continued Patel, looking somewhat pleased at himself for keeping the negotiations so short and to the point. "Of course, don't forget that circumstances between Magan and Borda might push that date back and forth a little bit. . . ."

"Perfectly understood," said Brone, snapping out of his reverie and sitting up straight in his chair. "You can tell Lieutenant Executive Lee that I appreciate the gesture of civility, but I'll have nothing to do with any *convocation.*"

Merri felt a horrid burrowing sensation at the base of her spine.

"Let me ask you a question," said the bodhisattva, his face turning cold and somber. "Do either of you seriously *believe* any of the drivel that the Council prepared for you? Wait, no need to answer that—the answer's on the inside of your lapel." Merri had to refrain from reaching up to clench the black-and-white-swirled pin sitting there, emblem of the Creed Objectivv truthteller. "It's an old trick, one that I've seen many times before. I'm surprised that you two would fall for it. Surely you know how this goes? Keep the Objectivv truthtellers in the dark . . . pack them full of lies . . . and then send them off to deceive with impunity."

The channel manager quickly threw up a PokerFace before Brone could see the flush of embarrassment creeping up her neck. She looked down and realized she was gripping the music box almost hard enough to break it. *Of course . . . Magan's sent us here because we're both devotees of Creed Objectivv.* She had to admit that in the rush of the past four days—the urgent conferences with Josiah and Bali Chandler, Council troops coming and going, Quell reciting wild stories about his time in orbital prison—the thought that Magan would take advantage of her truthteller status had never occurred to her. Merri cast a sidelong glance at Petrucio; the unnatural equanimity on his face told her that he had also failed to see the possibility.

"Oh, don't worry, I don't hold the two of *you* responsible," continued Brone, folding his arms across his chest, his voice moving back towards affability. "In fact, I'm quite impressed by the two of you. You've made a very convincing argument. Or at least, it *would* have been convincing if I didn't know who you're representing.

"But surely you must know by now that the Council only speaks one language, and that's the language of power. This negotiation is, and never was, anything but a sham. Magan Kai Lee has no intention of sitting down and *discussing* the future of MultiReal, I can assure you.

If he did, he wouldn't have had you repeat the same tired old facts and figures from Council-sponsored research. The same canards that Len Borda threw out when the infoquakes began. Tell me, how are we to independently verify these numbers? What about the opposing research from the Congress of L-PRACGs contradicting just about everything these numbers say?

"The answer is plain for all to see: Magan Kai Lee wants MultiReal for the Defense and Wellness Council. He may be younger than Len Borda and have less of a history of oppression, but his intentions are no different. The two of you will see that in the end, I'm sure.

"You tell Magan Kai Lee that the bodhisattva of Creed Thassel does not negotiate with tyrants. MultiReal will be released to the people on the Data Sea, in its entirety, as soon as it's ready."

Stunned silence seeped through the room. Merri really had not been prepared for Brone to give such a frank rejection to Magan's request. Rey Gonerev had led her to believe that this visit was something of a formality, that the bodhisattva would not be so foolish as to turn up his nose to both Len Borda and Magan Kai Lee.

"You realize," said Merri, not sure where she summoned the courage, "that you won't get an opportunity to parley with Len Borda. The first you'll hear from him is the black code dart that hits you in the back of the neck."

Brone gave her a feral grin. "Good! That's the thing I like about Len Borda—at least he's honest. Just so you know, I'll be rooting for the high executive to crush Magan's insignificant little rebellion. That will make the decision to release MultiReal to the world that much easier."

• • •

Jara listened to Petrucio's report with a sense of impending gloom. Dealing with Len Borda was challenge enough, but to have a madman holding MultiReal over their heads at the same time?

Neither Magan Kai Lee nor Rey Gonerev took the news of Brone's rejection particularly hard. Magan merely nodded, his face plastered over with exhaustion, as if he had either expected such a reaction from the bodhisattva or was not paying attention. As for the Blade, Jara could plainly see that Brone's stance did not come as a surprise to her. Anticipated or not, the report from Petrucio was enough to send the two Council members back to the barracks on the other end of Manila for private dialogue.

Merri, for her part, was furious. Furious at Magan and Gonerev for crassly using her truthtelling oath as a political tool; furious at Petrucio for sourly dismissing Magan's ploy as just another cost of trying to put Absolute Truth in a sullied world; but most of all, furious at herself for being so gullible.

Her anger was quickly put into perspective by Quell. The Islander had been standing close by with Josiah and Bali Chandler, discreetly listening to Merri's conversation with Jara. He walked up without an invitation and gave the two of them a polite bow to apologize for the intrusion. "You're not the only one who's had to make ethical compromises in the past few months," said Quell to the channel manager, his manner firm but not unkind.

"I suppose that's true," Merri admitted, her face reddening.

"If the worst ethical compromise that comes out of all this is that a truthteller has to make a few fibs, count yourself very, very lucky." The Islander made another bow and retreated to the opposite corner of the room with Josiah and Chandler.

Merri excused herself to contemplate what Quell had said in the privacy of the hallway, leaving Jara alone in the center of the room. It was the same bemuraled room where she and the other fiefcorpers had talked Josiah into writing his manifesto a scant few days ago. Since the moment that the young Islander had tapped a button on his viewscreen and sent the missive hurtling onto the Data Sea, the world had taken on a surreal quality. Jara felt like she was watching events happen in compressed fashion, as if time had suddenly shifted into fast-forward.

Magan Kai Lee had assembled a vast armed force in Manila's warehouse district; the entire city seemed to exist now in the shadow of the white hoverbirds and other more esoteric machines of war, conducting exercises on the bay. General Cheronna's unconnectible army remained within spitting distance of the Council, causing all manner of tension between the camps. Still, the idea of Grand Reunification maintained high approvals across the board.

In connectible lands, the Prime Committee was remaining steadfast in its neutrality between the two factions of the Council. But the Congress of L-PRACGs had made a dramatic shift by announcing that Magan Kai Lee had "legitimate grievances with the Borda administration that must be resolved"; given that Lee and the Congress had only recently opposed one another in the hearing at the Tul Jabbor Complex, this was big news indeed. And in the midst of all this, Sen Sivv Sor dropped the bombshell revelation that Council investigators had concluded that Margaret Surina's death several months ago had been the result of suicide by black code. Numbers from Zeitgeist 29a concluded that sixty-three percent of the population believed a government cover-up was in effect.

Meanwhile, as the spectacle swelled through the world outside the unconnectible curtain, Jara watched a number of much more personal dramas in this very room. Magan Kai Lee had summoned virtually all of the players to the MultiReal drama here to Manila for a summit in twenty-four hours. Since Jara had nothing else to do, she decided to hang around this central chamber to bask in the glow of colliding human emotion. In one corner of the room, Quell and Josiah Surina were conducting a mostly unspoken conversation full of pride, recrimination, love, and acrimony, sometimes all at once. In another corner, Petrucio and Frederic Patel glowered at each other and occasionally fired off tense words that Jara couldn't quite make out at this distance. Speaker of the Congress of L-PRACGs Khann Frejohr was holding a raucous (and possibly drunken) conversation with Islander Representative Bali Chandler, as befit two grizzled lions of their respective governments. As for Benyamin and Robby Robby, the two had struck up an intense conversation with General Cheronna, of all people. What Robby had to say to a dour military man like Cheronna, Jara could not fathom, but he appeared to be doing most of the talking.

All this drama was only a prelude to the imminent arrival of Natch.

The entrepreneur's shuttle from 49th Heaven was expected to touch down any minute. Horvil, Serr Vigal, and Richard Taylor were said to be with him. Jara herself was anxious to see Horvil again, but almost everyone else in the room seemed to have some grievance with Natch that needed settling.

The door opened an hour later to reveal Natch, along with Vigal and Taylor and a handful of Islander security personnel in olive green uniforms. The world at large did not know that Natch had returned, and Magan was sparing no effort to keep it that way. Some in this very room had only found out a couple hours ago. The last thing they needed was a pack of predatory drudges dogging the entrepreneur's every movement.

Jara was amused to see everyone slowly gravitate in Natch's direction without trying to appear too anxious. She herself only had eyes for the plump engineer whom she had not seen in two weeks. Horvil quickly spotted her, edged around Frederic Patel without making eye contact, stopped for a quick hug from Benyamin, and then was at her side. The two of them scooted out into the hallway without being noticed, where they shared a tired and not particularly passionate kiss.

"Remind me never to do that again," said Horvil with a groan.

"49th Heaven?"

"Oh no, I'd do 49th Heaven again. Fascinating place. I'm talking about traveling with Vigal and Richard Taylor."

Jara smiled, tried to comb the engineer's ruffled hair with her fingers. "So did Taylor ever deliver his message?"

"He did," replied Horvil with a shrug. "No idea what he said to Natch. Neither of 'em will tell me. Whatever the message was, looks like Natch *did* take it seriously. He's been acting pretty subdued ever since."

"Hmm."

When Jara made it back into the chamber a few minutes later—without Horvil, who absconded to her hotel room for some much-needed sleep—Natch was still the center of attention. He was making his way around the room, spending two to three minutes with everyone as if running through items on a checklist. Jara took the opportunity to study the entrepreneur as he stood holding a terse conversation with Khann Frejohr.

The last Jara had seen Natch, he was a scarecrow of a human being: gaunt, trembling from head to toe, eyes blackened and perpetually focused on nothingness. He was no longer that creature. But nor had he returned to the brilliant arrogance and insolent command of his fiefcorp days. Natch seemed in the process of metamorphosing into a different person altogether. His eyes were in that hazy half-colored state that eyes got right after you changed entries in your personal preferences database. His hair was similarly sandy blond at the roots and blackened up above. This new Natch was intense but quiet, thoughtful but humorless. Jara found it baffling that she had had such an unrelenting sexual obsession with this man for months. Not that he wasn't still physically attractive, but his focus seemed so . . . *ethereal* . . . that carnal emotions hardly seemed to apply.

He approached Jara. "Jara," he said in greeting, with a slight incline of his head.

"Natch," replied the fiefcorp master, tipping her head in kind.

"I've been hearing good words from Petrucio about your work with the fiefcorp since I left," said Natch.

"From Petrucio? Really?" Jara couldn't help but be perplexed, though she couldn't see any reason why the entrepreneur would lie about something like this. She cast a glance around to see the expression on Petrucio's face, but he had already left and taken Frederic with him.

"He was very impressed with the way you handled the negotiations about the MultiReal choice cycles. And from what he said, he thought you acquitted yourself well at the trial in Andra Pradesh."

Jara nodded. What kind of conversation was this? What did Petrucio Patel have to do with all that had gone on between them? The years of manipulation, the thousands of hours of late-night engineering and analysis, her furious denunciation of him in Berilla's office, the quibbling over choice cycle schemas in the MultiReal program from afar. It all seemed like ancient history, but that didn't mean she couldn't still feel the sting.

"I thought I should let you know," said Natch, his eyes never wavering from hers, "that I have no intention of rejoining or interfering with the fiefcorp. As far as I'm concerned, you're the fiefcorp master now, free and clear. And if you need any help from me to make that transition fully legal in the eyes of the Meme Cooperative, let me know."

Jara wanted to ask him whether he felt the need to apologize for his behavior over all those years. She wanted to ask what exactly he had been up to on 49th Heaven—the vague stories she had heard about battling black code gangs seemed unlikely, bordering on absurd. She wanted to ask exactly what had happened to him in Old Chicago, what his relationship with Brone was, why and how the MultiReal program had ended up in the bodhisattva's hands. She wanted to ask what kind of message a stranger from the Pharisee Territories could possibly have for him that would keep his interest.

But she did none of those things. Instead, she asked, "So what will you do after all this is over with?"

Natch shrugged. "I'll do whatever I have to do," he said. And then, with a curt bow, he was gone.

(((30)))

Magan Kai Lee was in a reflective mood.

He stood next to the Islander conference table and scrutinized the mural on the wall with a critical eye, wondering who had painted it and, equally as important, who had commissioned it. On first glance, one could mistake the work for a straightforward piece of propaganda or patriotism. The members of the Band of Twelve, standing self-importantly in the midst of the City Center, stretching their arms out to the skies as they espoused the ideals of the Free Republic.

But Magan knew something about art from his teenage days in the gullies and gutters of Beijing, the old sections of the city that had once been ravaged by the Autonomous Minds. Close inspection revealed that several members of the Band had expressions of covert cynicism on their faces, while others seemed to be concealing bulky objects in their pockets. Weapons? Treepaper documents? Magan supposed someone more schooled in the history of the Pacific Islands would recognize the iconography. Nevertheless, the painting gave him an impression of lingering skepticism and creeping doubt in the principles of the Islanders.

It was not so different from the feeling of unease coming from the group assembled before him around the massive oak conference table. *My own Band of Eighteen*, thought Magan.

Seated closest to him were his most trusted aides, the two who had stood by him even under heavy dart fire on the floor of the Tul Jabbor Complex. On Magan's immediate right was the Blade, Chief Solicitor Rey Gonerev, her manner businesslike and her hair done up in elaborate braids. Seated to Magan's left was his chief engineer, Papizon, oddly aloof and untouched by the hectic events of the past few months.

Down the left side of the table were Merri, still sullen about the violation of her truthtelling oath; Benyamin, keen and alert and ever ready to act the skeptic; the engineer Horvil, whose sunny disposition more than counterbalanced his cousin's dourness; the fiefcorp master Jara, laser-focused as always; the channeler Robby Robby, not quite as serious but just as focused; the Pharisee Richard Taylor, clearly bewildered and out of his element; and the venerable, if unassuming, neural programmer Serr Vigal.

On the right side of the table sat Frederic Patel, still raw from some apparent grievance with his brother; Petrucio Patel, too preoccupied with his failed mission to pay Frederic much heed; Speaker of the Congress of L-PRACGs Khann Frejohr, looking uncharacteristically subdued himself; the Islander Quell, his demeanor a strange mixture of grimness at the situation and joy at being reunited with family; his son Josiah, looking every bit the statesman and Surina his mother was; Bali Chandler, always the free spirit, even in crisis; and General Cheronna, taciturn commander of the Islander forces, looking just as discomfited as the Pharisee but for different reasons.

At the opposite end of the table from Magan sat Natch, unnervingly calm and distant.

Here sat the main actors in the MultiReal drama that had unfolded over the past few months. The ones largely responsible for the dangerous situation the world now faced, and fate willing, the ones who would see it through to the other side.

Magan turned away from the mural to the group assembled at the table.

"When Len Borda took office at the turn of the century," said the lieutenant executive, "he inherited a group of advisors known as the Inner Council. According to tradition, these men and women would stay on to help the new high executive during his first months in office. A way to provide continuity between administrations. It's said that the Inner Council provided crucial support to High Executive Borda in those early days.

"Then Marcus Surina died, and the economy went into freefall. Len Borda proposed stimulating the economy through massive military spending. The Inner Council strongly disagreed. Angered by their insubordination, the high executive dissolved the Inner Council.

"This pattern has continued throughout the current administration. Conformity of thought valued over dissenting opinion. Loyalty to narrow political interest instead of loyalty to principle.

"So let this conference today be symbolic of the diversity of opinion that I will bring back to the Defense and Wellness Council, if I'm fortunate enough to prevail in my struggle. Consensus through rational discussion; opposing viewpoints given full and open recognition; no one ever castigated for speaking honestly.

"I've brought you all here today because I need your advice. I need your wisdom. Final decisions on the actions of the Council rest with me and me alone, but I would prefer them to be informed decisions. In this room, you may speak your mind freely and without fear.

"Let us begin."

Seventeen voices murmured their assent.

• • •

Rey Gonerev began with a summary of the rebellion against Len Borda.

"We have made some progress in the past few weeks," said the Blade. "Thanks to the smart diplomacy of the Islanders and the smart consulting work of Jara's company, we now have a base here in Manila behind the unconnectible curtain. Since the publication of Josiah's manifesto on the Data Sea, Borda has been hemorrhaging public support. Morale among his troops is down, the governmentalist drudges are laying low, and even the Congress of L-PRACGs has thrown its support behind Magan."

"To be clear," interrupted Khann Frejohr, insinuating his arm onto the table to catch Gonerev's attention, "the Congress doesn't officially *support* anything. I was able to push through that statement about addressing grievances, and I've come here at Magan's request. But just because I distrust Borda's intentions doesn't mean I've signed on to Magan's."

"So noted," said Gonerev with a sidelong glance of surprise at Magan. "But the fact that you're here with us in the Pacific Islands—and the fact that the public *knows* you're here—that weighs heavily in our favor. As far as the drudges are concerned, your presence here is as good as an endorsement."

Frejohr did not look pleased by her assertion, but he did not dispute it either.

"I'm afraid that's where the good news ends," continued the Blade. "Len Borda's troops may have low morale—but they've got us outnumbered nearly three to one. If we assume that Magan has many supporters in the ranks who are afraid to declare open rebellion, we're still badly outnumbered. Even if we include the Islander troops under General Cheronna's command, that makes up some ground—but not nearly enough."

"And you should not include us in your ranks," put in Cheronna tersely. "The Islander parliament has allowed you a military base. They have not approved any joint military actions."

Gonerev gave a solemn nod, acknowledging the point. "That leads me to the governmental front," she said. "As the general mentioned, Representative Triggendala is holding up any military alliance between Magan and the Free Republic through parliamentary procedures. She's organizing protests across the Islands, and some of them are proving to be quite heated.

"As for the connectible government—well, you all heard Speaker Frejohr's statement about where the Congress stands. But at least they're lending Magan some small amount of public support. The Prime Committee has completely rebuffed our efforts to present articles of impeachment against Len Borda for the scene at the Tul Jabbor Complex. There's too much confusion about what actually happened there and why. The libertarian side of the Committee has been making noises about a motion of support similar to the one that the Congress passed, but we don't think they have the votes.

"So we're badly outnumbered . . . we have inferior equipment . . . we have little in the way of government support . . . and to top things off, Borda has the Defense and Wellness Council Root. An orbital fortress that is, for all intents and purposes, impregnable."

"Isn't DWCR invisible to the multi network too?" asked Cheronna. "Couldn't Borda use his fortress the same way you're using the Islands—as a base to send out multi projections?"

"No," said Magan. "DWCR is not invisible to the network. It's just well concealed. Regardless, there aren't enough outgoing multi streams on the Root to allow Borda to send out an effective virtual force from there."

Khann Frejohr leaned forward and addressed the lieutenant executive. Of all the questioning faces around the table, his seemed the most dubious and the most impatient. "The rebellion appears to be gaining ground, but you admit that you're in no shape to take on Len Borda right now," he said. "So why are we here? Time is on your side, Magan. You're well protected from preemptive attack behind the curtain. Public opinion is slowly turning in your favor, and you're still getting new defectors every day. As soon as word gets out that you're in possession of MultiReal, that trickle should turn into a flood. Why not wait and let things play out for a few more weeks? Why the urgency of this meeting?"

"There lies our other, and possibly more serious, dilemma," replied the lieutenant executive somberly. "Rey?"

• • •

The Blade slid one hand under the table and began tapping on the recessed row of buttons there. Seconds later, the holograph of a taciturn individual appeared over the middle of the table. A younger man with prematurely graying hair, a stern expression on his face, and eyes of mismatched color. Magan could see Natch's face darken across the table.

"The bodhisattva of Creed Thassel," said Gonerev. "Brone. Once a promising young programmer and disciple of the capitalman Figaro Fi. Fi helped him gain his fortune, which he used to buy his way into the leadership of the creed and build up its membership.

"And now he has core access to MultiReal.

"Brone appears to have gained access to the program when Natch was in Old Chicago. He's using a clever piece of black code which he implanted in Natch during an attack in Shenandoah. For the past six weeks, he and his Thasselian devotees have been working frantically on the MultiReal databases right under Natch's nose. We believe that Brone is preparing to release an enhanced version of MultiReal called Possibilities 2.0 on the Data Sea any day now.

"Dealing with the standard Possibilities 1.0 out on the Data Sea was worrisome enough. But if Papizon's projections are correct, the consequences of having Possibilities 2.0 loose on the Data Sea will be catastrophic."

The Blade gestured to Papizon. The engineer's fingers danced beneath the tabletop along the row of recessed buttons, replacing the photo of Brone with a chart that showed a sharply rising curve. "Projected number of people downloading and activating Possibilities 2.0," said Papizon, running his index finger up and down the y-axis. "Elapsed time from launch on the Data Sea," he continued, indicating the digits on the x-axis. "Critical mass—the point at which the program overwhelms the computational system and starts causing massive infoquakes." Papizon pointed to an ominous blue line slicing across the entire diagram about a third of the way up. "As you can see," he concluded, "that's not a very high bar to jump. And there are a lotta people who are going to keep activating after that point."

"So we'll have six days to curb the spread of MultiReal after Brone releases it?" said Benyamin, squinting at the chart. "Guess that explains the urgency."

"Ohhhh no," replied Papizon with a child's singsong dread. "Those numbers running across the bottom aren't days. Those are *hours*."

Stunned silence.

Rey Gonerev picked up the conversation in a low tone, her demeanor grave. "Because of all the publicity about MultiReal, the latest polling numbers show the program with a name recognition in the mid-ninetieth percentile. Almost every single person from here to Furtoid is aware of it. The percentage of people who are actually planning to *download* the program is significantly lower. But even if we assume an extremely low adoption rate—say, five percent—that's still close to three *billion* people.

"And if Natch's assumptions about Brone's Revolution of Selfishness are correct, then there's no reason why everyone who's curious won't give MultiReal a try. Natch proposed a price tag of eighty thousand Vault credits a few months ago, which would have slowed the adoption rate considerably. But Brone intends to release the program for *free*, with complete and unrestricted access to the underlying Mind-Space code.

"If even five percent of those who've heard about MultiReal decide to activate it, and if the centralized government manages to block as much as ninety-five percent of the program's distribution on the Data Sea—which I can tell you, is quite beyond our abilities—that's still one hundred and forty million people. A hundred forty million people creating multiple realities. Given the most optimistic scenario we can project, we reach that blue line in ten hours rather than six."

Papizon dutifully snapped his fingers, flattening the exponential growth curve on the chart by an insignificant degree.

"So what happens when we reach that blue line?" asked Petrucio Patel, trying unsuccessfully to smooth the worry lines on his forehead.

"Our best guess is that we'll have infoquakes to start, or something like them," said Gonerev. "Spontaneous and unexplained death throughout the civilized world. Random system failures. The collapse of certain pieces of infrastructure . . ." Gonerev's eyes were beginning to glaze over with dread, and moreover, so were the eyes of her audience. "Look, I have plenty of academic papers discussing how exactly a catastrophic failure of the computational system would occur. We have teams of people in the Council who've tried to predict exactly how something like this might happen so we can get ahead of it. We've got contingency plans that get revised and reformulated every couple of years.

"But the bottom line is that nobody knows.

"The one thing that the infrastructure experts are in agreement about is that there's a point of no return." She gestured at the chart, causing a red line to appear about two-thirds of the way up the growth curve. "Below that threshold, the computational system will eventually heal itself. The holes will be patched up. Once we cross that threshold, however, interdependent systems will begin crashing each *other*. Faults in Dr. Plugenpatch might cause OCHRE failures, which might cause the messaging system to overload, which might bring down the multi network. It's all theoretical at this point.

"You've seen the damage infoquakes can do. If we cross that red line, we could experience infoquakes without end. The destruction could approach the level caused by the Autonomous Revolt. We're talking about tens of millions or even *billions* dead within a few weeks.

"That's not just a crisis. That's a potentially *civilization-ending* crisis."

• • •

A collective shiver passed through the room. The Band of Twelve looked on with intense interest.

Magan found himself playing a horror slideshow in his head of the iconic images from the Big Divide that followed the end of the Autonomous Revolt. According to the authoritative histories, most of the carnage and death were not a direct result of the Revolt—they were caused by the decades of starvation, disease, radiation poisoning, mass rioting, and chaos the Revolt produced. As one historian deftly put it, *If the Autonomous Revolt was the nativity of a new world, then the Big Divide was the bloody afterbirth.*

Jara spoke.

"I know I'm not exactly a bio/logic engineer," she said. "I don't have any great insight into the architecture of the computational system. But how do you know *any* of this will happen?"

"Statistical modeling," piped up Papizon. "Logarithmic increases in bandwidth utilization based on prior patterns of adoption."

"But how can you create an accurate statistical model when you don't even have a reliable baseline?" continued the fiefcorp master with a dubious face.

"She's got a point," added Horvil. "I can't see where you're getting these numbers from. Nobody in the Council has actually *used* Possibilities 1.0 before, much less Possibilities 2.0. You haven't taken it apart and put it back together in MindSpace. You haven't tested it to see how much processing power it uses."

Jara nodded and clasped the engineer's hand briefly on the tabletop. "The fact of the matter is, you're just making glorified guesses. For all we know, MultiReal might only cause a brief hiccup in the system. It might just stop working. Brone could be right about this.

"And your estimates of the entire computational system collapsing? Again, forgive my ignorance here—but aren't there safeguards built in to these networks? You can't just create a program that sucks up all of the world's processing cycles and crashes everything to the ground, or the black coders would be doing it every week. There are basic principles of computational design here. Redundancy. Isolation. Compartmentalization." She ticked the principles off on her fingers. "Even if Dr. Plugenpatch implodes tomorrow, that shouldn't cause tube trains to crash and gravitational systems to go haywire."

Everyone turned back to Rey Gonerev for a response.

But it was Quell the Islander who spoke up from farther down the table. "You're absolutely right, in theory," he said, his voice quiet, introspective. "It should be impossible for one program to crash the whole system. But don't forget that MultiReal *already* does the impossible. It shouldn't be able to circumvent the Data Sea access controls—but it does. It shouldn't be able to hook into other people's neural systems and start zapping memories without their permission—but it does. By all logical and rational programming standards, MultiReal shouldn't exist.

"But you're basing your judgments about what's possible on a system that the Surinas *designed* from the ground up. One family, multiple generations. Who knows what you could stick in a system like that if you had hundreds of years to do it? If you created the rules for bio/logic programming, then certainly you could create a program that breaks those rules too.

"And make no mistake. This program doesn't just break rules—it creates its own. It does not stay between the lines. I'm guessing that Papizon is going to say that there are safeguards and firewalls and protections that are supposed to prevent this kind of apocalypse, but MultiReal skips right over them."

"Papizon is indeed going to say just that," quipped Papizon.

Quell nodded. "I've seen MultiReal at work. I've measured the number of computing cycles it uses. I have no idea how accurate the Council's estimates about adoption are, and whether that red line belongs where it is. Maybe the point of no return happens when fifty million people run the program. Maybe it happens when a hundred million or five hundred million or two billion people run the program.

"But that line *exists*. And I, for one, believe what the Defense and Wellness Council is saying."

Papizon discreetly dismissed the chart floating over the center of the table with a wave of his hand. The Islander's words seemed to satisfy Jara and all the others in the room—all except for one.

Speaker Khann Frejohr pushed himself back from the table and stood. The dissatisfaction had been growing on his face for several minutes and had now blossomed into outright anger. "You all might believe what Magan Kai Lee is telling you," he snapped. "But have you forgotten who he *is*?"

• • •

All eyes turned surreptitiously towards the lieutenant executive, as if expecting him to make some caustic retort. Magan took a quick glance at the Band of Twelve and their lofty promises made with fingers crossed behind their backs. No, that would not be him. He had pledged that everyone in the room should speak freely, and he intended to abide by that pledge. He motioned for Frejohr to continue.

Frejohr began pacing slowly around the end of the table opposite the representatives of the Council. "Magan Kai Lee is a lieutenant executive of the Defense and Wellness Council. He faithfully served High Executive Len Borda for nearly a decade before he started this rebellion. How do we know we can trust him?"

"Are you suggesting he's still working for Len Borda?" said Bali Chandler with a wry look on his face. "I think once you try to assassinate someone, the companionship's over." Frederic and Petrucio chuckled.

"No, of course I'm not suggesting that," said Frejohr, either not noticing or not acknowledging Chandler's sarcasm. "I'm saying that until a few months ago, the lieutenant executive was a loyal member of the current administration. Until a few months ago, he was working to bring MultiReal into Len Borda's hands.

"Jara's right. The Blade tells us that releasing MultiReal onto the Data Sea is a recipe for overloading the computational system and triggering a catastrophe like the Autonomous Revolt. But all we have to go on is her word, and Magan's word, and Papizon's. All we've seen is a chart." Papizon stretched his hand out as if about to conjure the holographic diagram again, but Speaker Frejohr angrily waved him off. "Have any of you actually *seen* these reports that supposedly back their conclusions?"

"They will be made available to any of you who wish to read them," replied Magan.

"Fine," said Frejohr. "But *I* can show you reports commissioned by the Congress of L-PRACGs that conclude exactly the opposite."

"And how do you know those reports weren't written by secret devotees of Creed Thassel?" snapped Gonerev.

"That's not the point. What did Brone tell Natch in Old Chicago? He said Len Borda was using the fear of computational collapse to seize additional power. He said that Borda had created the infoquakes to *scare* us, to pave the way for him to seize MultiReal. Think about it. This Possibilities 2.0 could give everyone the power to throw off the centralized government forever. The ability to live multiple lives simultaneously! The ability to live a life of ultimate selfishness! Doesn't that scare Len Borda? How do we know that Brone isn't right? How do we know that this isn't just a manufactured crisis?"

Rey Gonerev rose to her feet, incensed.

"Do you *really* believe that the Defense and Wellness Council is behind the infoquakes?" she shouted. "Do you really think that even Len Borda would murder tens of thousands of innocent people for some . . . political *game*?"

Frejohr had circled around the far end of the table to Jara's position, and now began circling back. "I'm saying that we still don't have an explanation for the infoquakes. We still don't have an explanation for Margaret Surina's death. For process' preservation, we still don't have an explanation for *Marcus* Surina's death.

"And now here we have the lieutenant executive of the Defense and Wellness Council, a member of the very organization that many believe responsible for these atrocities." He turned to address Magan directly. "Your organization kept the Islanders under your thumb for decades. Your organization put down the Melbourne riots with intimidation and murder. Your organization instilled the fear of the white robe and yellow star in every man, woman, and child from here to Furtoid. And now you tell us to just *trust* your word about the release of Possibilities 2.0?" He turned back to face the rest of the table. "What assurances do we have that Magan Kai Lee can be trusted? What assurances do we have that Magan won't overthrow Len Borda and then seize control of MultiReal for himself?"

There was a long and tense silence in the room. Rey Gonerev stood behind her chair gripping the back so hard that her knuckles had turned white. Once again, everyone turned expectantly to the lieutenant executive for answers.

"You ask for assurances," said Magan, choosing his words carefully. "But what can I say that you'll believe? Trust only comes after a long pattern of promises made and promises delivered. As you have pointed out, Khann, only a short time ago I was a loyal member of Len Borda's team. So all I can do now is state my intentions and state the truth about what I know."

Frejohr scowled. "And what do you know?"

"I know that the Defense and Wellness Council did not create the infoquakes, and we were not responsible for the death of Margaret Surina."

"What about her father?"

Magan stared down at the tabletop for several seconds, weighing truth and consequences on an imaginary scale in his head. "Your suspicions about Marcus Surina are correct," he said. "Len Borda had him killed."

The room exploded into shocked silence.

Khann Frejohr walked slowly back to his seat and collapsed into it, looking as if he had aged a decade. Rey Gonerev, too, returned to her seat without comment. Quell's forearms flexed dangerously, as if he were strangling some invisible enemy on the table. The fiefcorpers were all slumped down in their chairs in disbelief. As for Josiah—the person most affected by Borda's actions—he wore a look of plain sadness, but did not appear particularly surprised.

"I heard the conspiracy theories," muttered Robby Robby to himself, opening his mouth for the first time in the meeting. "I just never believed they were true."

"High Executive Len Borda has much to answer for, Khann," said Magan after the room had settled back into some semblance of normalcy. "Marcus Surina's death is only one example. There are others. But you're yelling accusations at the one man who actually intends to hold him responsible."

"So what—what happened?" asked Merri softly. "To Marcus Surina?"

Magan shook his head firmly. "This is neither the time nor the place to unearth old skeletons. Suffice to say that I intend to reveal the real circumstances of his death in a truth commission at some point in the future. After the crisis of MultiReal has been dealt with, when the world is not on the brink of apocalypse. Until that point, the information I've told you should not leave this room."

Speaker Frejohr had been staring morosely at the mural of the Band of Twelve, but at the mention of the MultiReal crisis, he spoke up again. "Again we come back to the issue of trust."

"You want to talk about trust?" said Rey Gonerev, still irked at the Speaker. "You want to talk about leaps of faith? What proof do we have that this Possibilities 2.0 program even exists?"

Frejohr held up his index finger as if starting to speak, then thought better of it and put his hand back in his lap, chagrined.

"Natch is the only person outside of that complex in the Twin Cities who has actually *seen* this program. Quell has indicated that he was not aware of Margaret's experiments in that direction. So we're only taking Natch's word that the concept of multiple simultaneous realities is even feasible. We're only taking his word that Brone has gained access to MultiReal. If we were to rely solely on trusted sources of information, we wouldn't be holding this meeting at all. Do you want to know what the Council files say about this man Brone? *Hardworking businessman, extraordinarily wealthy, keeps to himself.* No trace of criminality. What if Natch and Brone conjured up this entire story between the two of them for some unknown reason? What if Natch is exaggerating the issue as a way to pursue his personal vendetta against this man?"

All eyes turned toward the entrepreneur, who, Magan realized, had not spoken a word since the council was called to order. He had been sitting at the far end of the table, listening intently, his face betraying no clues as to his thoughts. He appeared to bear no ill will towards Rey Gonerev for her suspicions.

"What do you want me to say?" Natch rasped. "I worked at Brone's side. I've seen the program. I've used it. It's real."

Serr Vigal leaned forward, as if hearing his charge's voice had given him permission to speak as well. "And do you believe that releasing Possibilities 2.0 on the Data Sea would have the effect the Council is claiming? Do you think it would overload the computational system?"

"Yes. I think, if anything, their projections are too conservative."

This seemed to have more of an effect on Frejohr than any chart of Papizon's or any word of the Blade's.

"So when you talk about *trust*, the issue cuts both ways," continued Rey Gonerev bitterly in the Speaker's direction. "This is a man known for breaking his word, known for his elaborate scheming. This is a man with a personal interest in the outcome of the MultiReal crisis. You say you don't trust the Council, Khann—well, how can the *Council* trust *Natch?*"

Before the Speaker could think of a suitable rejoinder, Horvil slapped one hand on the table. "Hey, *I've* got a good idea. Why don't we have Serr Vigal make a speech? I'm sure he's still got the last one queued up."

Horvil's joke was the tension breaker that the room so desperately needed. Both sides of the table spontaneously combusted in laughter, prompting a red-faced Vigal to stand up and raise one finger in the air like the proverbial self-important politician. Khann Frejohr withered under this assault of mirth and made a deferential gesture towards the Blade. Even Natch bowed his head and smiled.

"The point I'm making," said Rey Gonerev after the laughter had died down, "is that we're all in the same position. We're all relying on mutual trust. If the Defense and Wellness Council can accept that Natch is telling the truth, then it shouldn't be unreasonable for you to accept that we're dealing on the level as well."

Frejohr rocked his jaw back and forth for a moment, contemplative. Then he finally placed his palms flat on the table, closed his eyes, and gave a nod of assent in Magan's direction. The atmosphere in the room had suddenly become much more tolerable.

"So now that trust and goodwill have been restored among all the enemies of Len Borda, the question remains," said the lieutenant executive. "How do we stop Brone from releasing Possibilities 2.0 on the Data Sea and take care of the problem of Borda at the same time?"

(((31)))

Bali Chandler raised his hands up in mock surrender.

"I think I'm missing something important here," he said. "And believe me, it wouldn't be the first time. But what does Brone have to do with Len Borda? Why can't we deal with the MultiReal question, and *then* tackle Borda—or the other way around?"

"Two months ago, we could have," said the lieutenant executive. "But now Borda is aware that the Thasselians have access to MultiReal. He knows that the window of opportunity is short, and he will try to seize the program before Brone can launch it on the Data Sea."

The Islander scratched his perpetually stubbled chin. "How did he find out?"

"Brone made sure of it," said Natch.

Everyone stared at the entrepreneur uncomprehendingly.

"You don't know Brone like I do," continued Natch. "He's *hoping* that Len Borda comes after him. He's *hoping* that we do too. Armed Council officers storming his compound would be the perfect justification for releasing the program on the Data Sea and starting his Revolution of Selfishness. And it would give him the perfect vehicle for getting the word out about it.

"That's why he moved his base of operations from Old Chicago to the Kordez Thassel Complex. He either believes the program's ready for release—or that he's almost out of time. So he's hunkering down in his own building in a public space where he's much more difficult to get to.

"Now he's got both you and Len Borda in a stalemate. You've been too preoccupied with outmaneuvering each other to pay attention to MultiReal. But sooner or later, Borda will go after MultiReal, whether he needs it to defeat the rebellion or whether the rebellion's been crushed and there's no one to stand in his way. Until then, Brone can afford to wait for someone to make a move. He can continue polishing up Possibilities 2.0 and getting it ready for public release."

Chandler buried his face in his hands. "This is all *so* confusing."

"Let me put it in simpler terms," put in Rey Gonerev. "Brone is looking for any excuse whatsoever to launch MultiReal on the Data Sea. Len Borda is looking for any excuse whatsoever to seize MultiReal. We need to prevent *both* of those things from happening. We need to kill or capture Brone, and we need to nullify Borda."

"An insane tyrant on the one hand, a lunatic revolutionary on the other hand, and us caught in the middle," mumbled Horvil. "Wonderful."

"Killing Brone won't help," said Natch, shaking his head.

"Why not?" said Gonerev.

"That's the first problem he'd solve. He knows that you wouldn't hesitate to assassinate him—and even if *you* would, then Borda wouldn't. What's to prevent you from just raining missiles down on the Kordez Thassel Complex? MultiReal's not going to be any protection against that. No, he'll rig up Possibilities 2.0 so that if he dies, the program will instantly get released on the Data Sea. That's pretty good assassination insurance."

"What makes you so sure?" said Chandler.

"Because that's what I would do."

"So we come up with some black code to incapacitate him," said Horvil. "Cut him off from the Data Sea. Quell and I ought to be able to put together something that could do the trick."

"I can help with that too," said Frederic gruffly.

"Yes, but there's another problem you're not considering," put in Petrucio Patel. "How are you going to actually *hit* him with it?"

Horvil had no answer for this.

"He's holed up in the Thassel Complex with forty or fifty of his devotees. He's got MultiReal. Don't you remember the demo Frederic and I did where we were shooting darts at each other using MultiReal? There's no telling how long Brone could withstand an invasion of Council officers if he's dug in to his own building. If he's armed his devotees with MultiReal too, he could fend off hundreds of Council officers. Thousands, maybe."

"Well, why can't we arm our side with it too?" asked Jara. "Magan's got no shortage of officers. We could outfit forty or fifty of them with MultiReal and send them in. We could outfit whole *platoons* with MultiReal."

Petrucio shook his head vehemently. "You're overlooking something, Jara. As soon as Brone sees all those platoons headed for the Thassel Complex, he can just release Possibilities 2.0 on the Data Sea and be done with it. That defeats the whole purpose of going after him in the first place. All it takes is one person to sound the alarm, and once the alarm's been sounded we've lost."

"I don't think Natch could give someone else access to the program without Brone knowing about it," said Horvil. "So that idea, I think, is out."

• • •

"Wait a minute!" said Benyamin, leaning forward to interpose himself into the debate. "I can't believe I didn't think of this earlier. Natch has that backdoor code that gives him one-of-a-kind access to the Multi-Real databases. When our fiefcorp was fighting over the program, Natch was able to move the databases so we couldn't find them." He turned to Natch. "Why can't you do that to Brone? Move the program somewhere else and he won't be *able* to launch it on the Data Sea. Problem solved." The young apprentice stretched his hands behind his head and sat back with a very self-satisfied look on his face.

The entrepreneur shook his head. "You're forgetting about the black code Brone hit me with in Shenandoah," he said quietly.

Benyamin was incredulous. "You mean . . . it's still *there?*"

Natch's uncomfortable silence and lack of a response was a sufficient answer.

"Well . . . what does it do?"

The entrepreneur was evidently growing uneasy with this line of questioning. He turned to his old hivemate. "Horvil?"

"After talking this over with my fellow bio/logic engineers"— Horvil clicked his tongue and pointed at Quell and Frederic Patel, who both nodded in acknowledgment—"and after consulting with a neural programming specialist"—he indicated Serr Vigal, who also nodded— "we've concluded that what Brone installed in Natch is a conduit. It's like a big pipe that leads directly into your neural cortex and lets someone pump all kinds of nasty code straight into your skull. Very difficult to program, and very difficult to obtain. But that's the only way we can explain everything this black code has been able to do.

"As long as Natch has that conduit running through him, it doesn't matter *where* he moves the databases. Brone will be able to access MultiReal *through* Natch, if that makes any sense. As long as Natch has access . . . Brone has access."

The entire concept seemed to make Benyamin's skin crawl. "Does that mean Brone's had access to the program this whole time?"

"No, we think only since Chicago, when Natch gave him core access."

"You *gave* him core access? Why the fuck would you do *that?*"

The old Natch that Magan remembered would have fired back some caustic remark at the surly apprentice. But the Natch who had emerged from Chicago and 49th Heaven merely looked at Benyamin with a look of quiet consternation. "My memories of that day have been erased," he said. "But I believe I handed him access to MultiReal because he was torturing me to death."

Silence.

Magan studied the entrepreneur's face carefully. He had been through torture training himself during his days as a Council special operative—learning both how to take it and how to dispense it. He had never forgotten what the instructor had said in those sessions: *Torture warps the mind in ways that not even bio/logics can fully repair.* Looking at Natch now, Magan could see that statement personified.

Horvil clasped his hands together and stretched them up over his head, an obvious—and unsuccessful—attempt to loosen the tension in the room once again. "So the long and short of it is . . . Natch and Brone both have access to MultiReal now. And neither one can lock the other out."

"Isn't there some way to remove Brone's black code?" said Jara. "With all the brainpower in this room, surely we should be able to figure out how to do that."

"There is a Council surgical team waiting to operate on Natch directly after the conclusion of this meeting," said Magan. "But given the circumstances . . ." He let the sentence drift off unfinished.

"That shit's been buried in Natch's OCHREs for months now," Horvil elaborated. "We should have made an all-out effort to remove it right after the demo in Andra Pradesh, but . . ." *But Natch was too busy running away from the Council,* Horvil was too polite to say. "The code has had plenty of time to burrow in and get comfortable. It's going to be a bitch to remove now. And let's not forget that we run into the same challenge here as everywhere else. Once Brone realizes he's in imminent danger of losing his conduit . . ." The engineer made a loud popping sound by flicking the side of his cheek. "He pulls the trigger and releases MultiReal onto the Data Sea."

"Hold on," said Jara. "If this conduit lets Brone stick black code in Natch's head at will, then how do we know he's not using it to eavesdrop on us? How do we know he's not inflicting some kind of mind control on Natch?"

"It doesn't quite work that way," said Petrucio. "I seriously doubt Brone would be able to do that."

"But you wouldn't rule it out?"

Petrucio stroked his mustache for a moment as he considered this question. "No, not entirely," he said with a grin.

Frederic Patel had mostly been listening to the conversation up to this point, making the occasional grumble under his breath. But suddenly something inside him cracked. "Is this program really that important?" he shouted, smacking the table with a clenched fist. "Do we really need to work so hard to keep MultiReal intact? Just *delete* the fucking thing already, Natch, and let's get it over with!"

The entrepreneur gave a knowing smile. "If it were only that easy," he said. "I've tried."

Multiple people at the table held their breath. "And . . . ?" said Frederic.

"Quell said this program creates its own rules. He was right. As far as I can tell, MultiReal can't be disabled. And it can't be deleted. It literally just . . . doesn't respond to attempts to erase it."

Quell leaned back in his chair and let out a long, ragged breath. "And they wonder why we're skeptical of bio/logic technology," he muttered to Chandler, who responded with a smirk and a nod.

• • •

"We continually circle back to the same problem," said Rey Gonerev, taking control of the discussion again as was her wont. "Brone insists on releasing MultiReal to the entire world, free and without encumbrances. No amount of logic or reason will convince him otherwise. Killing him is not an option. So unless the surgery to remove this conduit proves successful, we have to find some way to incapacitate Brone. Not only do we have to accomplish this before Len Borda grows impatient and attacks the Thassel Complex, we have to do this in a way that Brone doesn't see coming. But since Brone and his minions all have access to MultiReal, that's a next to impossible task."

A hush fell on the room as everyone seemed to be silently contemplating the challenges ahead, what was at stake. The potential consequences of failure. Magan's thoughts drifted back to Papizon's chart and all the dead citizens piled up inside those curves above the red line.

"I knew it would come to this," said Natch in a voice barely above a whisper.

All turned to look at him.

"The only way to deal with Brone is by using MultiReal," continued the entrepreneur. "And the only one who can use MultiReal without alerting Brone is me." He sounded preternaturally calm, as if this was a line of reasoning he had deduced and come to terms with a long time ago.

"What are you suggesting?" said Rey Gonerev.

"I'm suggesting that I'll need to go in there. Into the Kordez Thassel Complex. Give me a dartgun with the black code that Quell, Horvil, and Frederic put together. I'll go in there, find Brone, and disable him. If I catch him by surprise, I can hit him with the black code before he releases Possibilities 2.0 on the Data Sea. If not, I can still catch him in a choice cycle loop and stop him from releasing the program that way. Nobody else can do that."

"And how do you intend to get past all of the Thasselians? With MultiReal?"

"They were all armed and on the lookout when I was there," said Merri.

Natch considered this for a moment. "I can't use MultiReal to get past the Thasselians," he said. "If I have to face Brone directly, choice cycle against choice cycle . . . I'm going to need all my strength. I think—I think I'm going to need some help to get to him."

"We can help you," stated Magan. "I can get you a team of Council special operatives to assist you through that building."

"Without being spotted by *any* of those forty or fifty Thasselian devotees?" protested Petrucio. "It's going to have to be a pretty small team. The more people you send, the more difficult it'll be for them to usher Natch through the Complex unnoticed."

"Then let me help," said Jara.

Everyone at the table seemed surprised to hear the words coming from the fiefcorp master—herself included. But as all eyes turned to Jara for an explanation, her mind appeared to catch up with her mouth.

"I'm an analyst by training," continued Jara. "Understanding people's motivations, pushing people's buttons, getting them to act how we want them to act—that's what I *do*. Put me and my team in a room somewhere that we can communicate with Natch and Magan's team. Give me eyes and ears on the ground. We'll find a way to get those Thasselians out of the way. We'll clear a path for Natch to get to Brone."

"Don't leave me on the sidelines," put in Petrucio. "I want a part of this too."

Jara nodded enthusiastically. "Good, because I could use your help."

Khann Frejohr wasn't the only skeptical face at the table, but he was the only one who objected aloud. "How do you intend to sneak Natch past four dozen armed guards with marketing and analysis?" he said with a grimace.

"I'm not sure," replied Jara. "But give me forty-eight hours, and I'll think of a plan. I've already got an idea. I'm just not sure the Thassel Complex is wired for it." Her voice projected an impressive amount of confidence, confidence that Magan knew was not misplaced.

"Don't you think we'd be better off with something a little more . . . *concrete*?" said Frejohr.

"Probably," Jara retorted. "When you figure out a better plan, let me know." The Speaker did not appear to be pleased with this answer.

"I trust her," said Natch.

All eyes in the room swiveled to look at the entrepreneur in surprise, nobody more surprised than Jara.

"Jara and I have had our differences," Natch explained with eyes downcast. "But if anyone here is capable of finding the levers to move those Thasselians, it's her. She understands human motivation. She helped me figure out how to beat Captain Bolbund in the ROD coding business. She scripted the demo I gave in Andra Pradesh that introduced MultiReal to the world. She assisted with the plan in getting our fiefcorp to number one on Primo's. She can do it."

"Aha!" thundered Frederic Patel, leaping up from the table in sudden fury. "So you admit it! You *did* use some kind of underhanded scheme to push your way to the top of Primo's."

The entrepreneur shrugged, unconcerned with Frederic's wrath. "If Magan can admit that the Council killed Marcus Surina," he said, "I can admit I connived my way to the top of Primo's."

Magan never would have expected the murder of Marcus Surina to make an effective punchline. But given the extremes of the situation they were in, he shouldn't have been surprised to find the room indulging in sudden laughter.

• • •

"So we have a plan for dealing with Brone and the release of Possibilities 2.0," said Quell. "Natch using MultiReal, assisted by a team of Council operatives and Jara's analysis skills. That still leaves the problem of Len Borda."

"That's a more straightforward problem," answered Magan. "Negotiation is not an option, and the political solution has so far yielded no results. We don't have much left aside from the military option. My troops are already preparing to make a preemptive strike against the bulk of Borda's army in Melbourne, sometime in the next forty-eight to seventy-two hours. That should give us enough time to prepare an effective offense and get the mission against Brone ready at the same time."

"What if Borda goes after MultiReal first?" said the Islander.

"I don't think he will. He doesn't have the information about Brone that we do. And he doesn't have the ability to get past those Thasselians and take out Brone without MultiReal. He'll be a little more cautious putting together his plans."

"Wait a second," interrupted a scowling Khann Frejohr. "You're just going to launch a full-scale attack on Melbourne, with all of the liabilities that the Blade listed earlier? A big deficit in numbers, poorer equipment, and all the rest?"

Josiah Surina spoke. "We have already discussed plans with the lieutenant executive for a joint Islander-connectible strike against Borda."

"Plans? What plans?"

"I hope you'll understand," said Magan coldly, "if we choose not to divulge military strategy in an open council, Khann."

With the change in topic to military matters, General Cheronna seemed to suddenly be paying close attention to the discussion once more. But he appeared to be more exasperated than enthusiastic. "I've told you several times," said the general, even more florid than usual, "I don't think Representative Triggendala's going to go along with this."

"I've been talking with the old crone about it," put in Bali Chandler, casually studying his nails. "I think I've convinced her to come around."

"Haven't you seen the protests on the street?" objected Cheronna. "The marches? The drudge rants? They're picketing down there in the City Center right now!" He pointed vehemently in the direction of the large public square. "She'll get lynched by her own constituents if she goes along with this."

"I have to admit, Chandler," said Josiah, frowning, "that I'm not so confident in our prospects of convincing Triggendala as you are. And without her support . . ."

Chandler waved both of them off. "Come on. I've been working with Trigg for . . . more years than either of us would care to admit. Decades. She likes to put up a front like this so she can save face. But when your back's against the wall, Triggendala's dependable. I'm telling you, Magan, the Islanders will march with the connectibles. And as for her constituents . . ." He made a wet razzing noise with his lips. "Ficklest bunch of people on Earth. Trigg's got another three years before her current term is up. They'll have forgotten all about this by then, and she knows it."

General Cheronna seethed quietly. "I wish I had your confidence," he said.

"Don't we all," muttered Quell.

• • •

The table settled into a vibrant silence, everyone abuzz with their own thoughts and plans. Magan Kai Lee surveyed the council he had assembled: fiefcorpers, analysts, engineers, Council officers, Islanders, and one apprehensive-looking Pharisee who had not said a single word the entire time but rather sat in his corner of the table and watched the proceedings with wide eyes.

Then he gazed back at the mural of the Islander Band of Twelve. Somehow, after this meeting he saw them in a different light. Grumble and bicker and complain they might have done; mutter dissatisfaction and disagreement with the Luddite principles of the Free Republic behind each other's backs they most certainly did. But when it came time for action, they had set aside their disagreements and put forward a united face to the public. They had gotten the job done.

Magan rose. "I thank you all for your time and your input," he said. "And now, I suggest you all take some rest. We've got a long forty-eight hours ahead of us."

(((32)))

Targeted marketing didn't get much more targeted than this. Forty-six known and suspected Thasselian devotees: some who had been sighted by Natch in the hotel in Old Chicago, some who had been identified by Merri and Petrucio, and some who had been observed loitering around the Thassel Complex in recent days.

It felt like a final exam of Jara's skills at marketing and analysis. The process was the same. Identify the audience; develop strategies to motivate them towards a defined goal; execute the plan and track results. Except here the goal wasn't to inspire a percentage of the audience to buy a specific bio/logic program. Here the goal was to keep one hundred percent of the audience from noticing the infiltrator in their midst, thereby preventing them from sounding the alarm, thereby allowing Natch to sneak up on Brone and plug him with black code.

The stakes: not fiefcorp shares, not Primo's ratings, not increased revenue—but possibly the continued survival of civilization itself.

You wanted responsibility, Jara reminded herself. *You wanted a place in the game. Well, this* is *the game.*

The elevator carrying Jara, Petrucio, Merri, Benyamin, Robby, Rey Gonerev, and the Council tactical systems expert came to a halt at the top floor of the Tio Van Jarmack building in Manila's City Center. They stepped off the elevator and walked down a short corridor lined with armed Defense and Wellness Council officers. Every door along the way had been barricaded shut with thick metal plates. Jara frowned. It was odd enough to walk down a hallway and have Council officers saluting her as she passed; the fact that she was comforted by their presence made the experience positively surreal.

"This room should have everything you need," said Gonerev as they walked through the double doors at the end of the hallway.

Robby Robby whistled. Jara didn't know what function the room normally served, but Magan's people had managed to turn it into a state-of-the-art war room in less than twenty-four hours. The two long walls of the rectangular room were covered floor to ceiling with viewscreens. There was a sturdy-looking oak conference table, a number of both upright and reclining chairs, a covered balcony overlooking the City Center for that occasional ten-minute break, a darkened alcove with a cot for longer stretches of rest, and a counter arrayed with fresh fruit, power snacks, and three different brands of nitro. Jara thought that last part was a nice touch.

"Looks like it's got much *more* than we need," said Petrucio, heading over to the counter to grab an apple. "In fact, I think I might move in here."

Gonerev smiled. "I'm sure you'll be clamoring to get out after a few hours. So everyone take a seat, and Larakolia will run you through the tactical systems." The fiefcorpers all found seats, Jara stopping at the counter to fetch a cup of nitro on the way.

The tactical systems expert Larakolia epitomized the term *lifer*: a small, thin woman, efficient and humorless, her skin a sandpaper color that could let her credibly pass for almost any race. Jara was fairly certain this was one of the goons Magan Kai Lee had introduced in the courtyard of the London nitro bar that drizzly December day. But Larakolia didn't volunteer any previous acquaintance with Jara, and the fiefcorp master wasn't quite sure how to ask.

The Council tactician walked up to the wall and stood in front of the bank of viewscreens. "First, you'll have full access to the heads-up displays on each of the team's battle suits," said Larakolia, waving her hand briskly. One of the viewscreens morphed from a smooth black to a pockmarked gray. "I suggest you keep this view up on both walls at all times."

Robby squinted. "Why's it all gray like that? Is something broken?"

The woman was obviously used to dumb questions. "The display shows you the view from Natch's vantage point. Right now he's in surgery, so all you're seeing is the suit hanging on the wall."

"Oh." The channeler blushed, then grinned.

Larakolia stepped away from the wall and pointed at a different section of viewscreen. "But you're not constrained to the suit user's perspective. Each battle suit has twenty-four cameras embedded in the mesh. The resulting composite image effectively gives you a full three-hundred-and-sixty-degree view." She waved three fingers on her right hand slightly, causing the camera angle to pan away from the wall and show the interior of an ordinary-looking supply closet. "In fact, you've got *more* than three hundred and sixty degrees." With another wave of her fingers, Larakolia sent the view tilting upward to the corrugated ceiling and then down to the tiled floor.

"Doesn't the Council have any cameras inside the building?" asked Petrucio.

"Not a one," replied the Council tactician. "We have some exterior views of the Complex and some aerial reconnaissance. But it's not likely to be much help once Natch makes it indoors."

"Don't forget that the Kordez Thassel Complex was built by libertarian extremists," said Rey Gonerev, who had been standing next to the balcony and gazing out onto the city. "The architects of that building did everything in their power to make it inaccessible to the Council. We're fairly certain they even falsified the blueprints on file with the Twin Cities L-PRACG."

"Do we have access to those blueprints?" asked Jara.

Larakolia nodded. "You do. You also have access to the video surveillance that Merri and Petrucio conducted during their recent visit."

"And the personnel files I asked for?"

The Council tactician waved at a blank section of viewscreen, causing the list of forty-six Thasselian devotees to cascade from the top of the screen in a font that was legible across the room. Larakolia pointed at one of the names at random, causing a holographic cube to pop out from the viewscreen with the photo of a hideously ugly bald man hugging the left margin.

HENRY PULTROON
Age: 43

Last Known Position and Employer:
Bio/logic Analyst, the Deuteron Fiefcorp

Home City:
Omaha

Larakolia continued drilling down through the data, causing box after box to accordion out into the room. With every flick of her finger, a whole new layer of personal information about the Thasselian was revealed: complete work history, photographs, background, known relationships, likes and dislikes, even the name of his ex-companion's dog. Jara shuddered. She remembered when Rey Gonerev had hinted that the Council knew about Jara's dalliances on the Sigh with that mentally challenged Natch lookalike. She didn't want anyone outside her immediate family having ready access to those kinds of details about *her.* Especially not the Defense and Wellness Council.

Rey Gonerev seemed to sense the fiefcorp master's discomfort. Perhaps she too was remembering the intrusive research the Council had done on Jara. "We don't usually have this much information about private citizens," said the solicitor. "But you wanted all the information we could come up with in forty-eight hours. So we've had oppo research teams working around the clock since Magan's council adjourned."

Benyamin had leaned forward to call up Pierre Loget's name and was now busy scrutinizing the programmer's intimate relationship history. "As interesting as this is," he said, "what *good* is it going to do us?"

Jara took a long sip of nitro. "I'll tell you in a minute. Larakolia, why don't you go ahead and finish the demo."

The tactician spent the next twenty minutes walking the fiefcorpers through a blizzard of features and functions, most of which they weren't going to need. They would get two-way encrypted communication with Natch's team, which the system would automatically transcribe, analyze, and index; they would be able to continually monitor everyone's vital signs; they would be able to load black code directly into the team's guns and bio/logic systems from here via the battle suits, which would be convenient if the entrepreneur found himself in a firefight. But if that were to happen, it would be a moot point, because surely Brone would be aware of Natch's presence and the entire mission would be for naught.

Then I guess we need to make sure that doesn't happen, thought the fiefcorp master.

When Larakolia finished the tactical systems run-through, Benyamin led the fiefcorpers in a polite round of applause. Rey Gonerev clapped briefly then turned to the balcony, preoccupied with thoughts of her own.

Jara stood. "Now back to your question about the personnel files, Ben," she said, walking over to a blank section of viewscreen on the opposite wall. "Can you call up those blueprints of the Thassel Complex for me, Larakolia?" The Council tactician dutifully summoned the architectural diagrams of the building and projected them in the space Jara indicated. Seen from above, the Complex resembled some mutant breed of lobster. The fiefcorp master made a gesture toward the blueprint and caused another diagram to superimpose itself on top of the mutant lobster, this one full of diminutive red, blue, and purple squares. "The One-on-One Motivation Network," said Jara. "Anyone heard of it?"

Petrucio Patel leaned back in his chair and stroked his mustache, intrigued. "Targeted advertising," he said. "Frederic and I, we've used them a few times."

"Not just targeted advertising," put in Robby. "*Ultra*targeted advertising. Down to the individual, down to the time of day, down even to the expression on your face." The very idea seemed to make the channeler salivate.

Jara nodded in Robby's direction. "Correct. And their viewscreens are in practically every corridor of the Kordez Thassel Complex, running twenty-four hours a day. We might not be able to get cameras into the building—but we *can* get advertising onto any viewscreen we want. It's all perfectly legal and above board. The Thasselians are hard-core libertarians—as long as we're the highest bidder, we can literally take over all the advertising in the building."

Merri, unsure about the whole idea: "And what are we going to . . . advertise?"

"Whatever we need to. Whatever it takes." Jara walked over to Robby Robby, put a hand on his shoulder. "You're a licensed channeler, Robby. You must have access to large banks of advertising."

"Sure do," beamed Robby. "Millions of commercials, teasers, promos, banners, tie-ins . . . you name the product, there's an advertisement for it somewhere on the Data Sea in search of a viewscreen."

"Exactly! So here's how this is going to work. We watch on the heads-up display as Natch walks down a corridor in the Thassel Complex. One of Brone's henchmen in the black robes approaches. We quickly identify who it is using the Council's data banks and conduct a spot analysis to determine what's likely to draw their attention. Then we act as a third-party broker for the One-on-One Motivation Network. We make a winning bid for the viewscreen space and slot in our advertisement. The whole process should only take about ten seconds. The ad blares at top volume right as the Thasselian passes . . . he turns to look at the ad . . . and Natch slips past unnoticed."

Robby Robby and Petrucio both appeared quite optimistic about the prospects for Jara's little scheme, and Merri seemed noncommittal. But as was his wont, Benyamin was staring at the blueprints of the

Kordez Thassel Complex with overt skepticism. "Do you really think they're *all* going to fall for something like that?" he said.

"Look, we don't need to actually *persuade* these people of anything," said Jara. "All we have to do is catch their attention. Just long enough for them to turn around and stare at a screen for five or ten seconds while Natch sneaks past. Don't forget there will be plenty of other people around to distract the Thasselians too. He'll be disguised some-what—not good enough to pass a bio/logic scan, but maybe good enough to deflect attention for a few seconds. There will be the rest of the special ops team. Natch won't be able to use MultiReal to get past those guards—remember, flipping through choice cycles is exhausting, and he needs to save his strength. Still, I think the chances of this working are rather good."

"But—"

Petrucio came to Jara's defense. "You're thinking of this as tradi-tional marketing, Benyamin. It's more like Pavlovian response. We don't need to appeal to their *reason*; we just need to appeal to their *instincts*. Find the thing that invokes that innate response to turn and gape for just a few seconds."

"Like what?"

At that moment, one of the viewscreens on the opposite side of the room burst to life. *Creed Élan, the world's preeminent society of charity and goodwill, is looking for a chief engineer!* announced a stentorian voice. *Help us solve the world's ills, one bio/logic programming bar at a time!* Everyone turned to stare briefly at the stock footage of figures in purple-and-maroon robes wandering across an assembly-line programming floor—but Jara felt vindicated that it was Benyamin whose attention strayed the longest. He had only been distracted for half a dozen seconds at most, but by the time he turned back to face Jara, she had slipped behind him and stood at the opposite side of the room.

Robby, Petrucio, Merri, and Rey Gonerev exploded in laughter. Even the straight-faced Larakolia couldn't resist a smirk. Benyamin blushed crimson for a few seconds before joining in the laughter himself. "Okay, fine, you've made your point," he said. "But was that really a fair demonstration? You *knew* I'd be distracted by that. My mother actually worked on that ad, and I think Horvil applied for the position."

"Well, then," replied Jara, grinning, "we'd better start studying these forty-six profiles until we know these Thasselians that well. Don't think we have to be high-minded here—anything that will grab their attention will work, and I mean *anything*. Explicit sex. Extreme gross-out. Use their names, use their mothers' names, I don't care. So long as it turns their heads."

• • •

Richard Taylor accompanies Natch to the surgery. "Not out of any sense of worry or personal concern," the Pharisee is quick to explain as they walk through Magan Kai Lee's encampment in Manila's warehouse district on their way to the medical building. "Not that you should take that to mean that I'm *not* concerned! Because of course I am. But no, I must admit that I've decided to come along because I really don't have anything else to do."

"Where are Horvil and Vigal?"

"They're busy—terribly busy. Working with the big Islander and the short programmer on the black code to use against Brone." Taylor purses his lips and scratches at his beard as if an idea has just come to him. Suddenly he leans back his head and bellows out a long, hearty laugh. Council officers turn to stare, and Natch instinctively ducks his head, still not used to the concept of men and women in white robes and yellow stars being on his side. "Well, such is what they told me anyway," continues Taylor. "Perhaps they were merely looking for an excuse. . . . If you'd like an excuse as well, Natch, I won't take it personally. I suppose I can always go for another stroll around the City Center."

"No, no, it's okay." Natch isn't lying. He actually finds the Pharisee's naiveté somewhat endearing, and his loquacious mannerisms help distract Natch from the question that keeps prodding the back of his mind.

Do I really have it in me to kill Brone?

He believes that's where things are headed, all of Magan's talk about "incapacity" notwithstanding. Why else send this "special operative" in with Natch? If there was ever a time that Brone could have been persuaded to make a reasonable compromise with the Defense and Wellness Council, that time has passed. As long as MultiReal exists, Brone will not back down from his Revolution of Selfishness. Natch knows exactly what that's like; he has spent most of his life in that frame of mind. In fact, even after all that Brone has done to him—even though Brone has tried to *kill* him—Natch can't help feeling empathy for his old enemy.

"You are still concerned about the message from the Children Unshackled," says Richard Taylor, mistaking Natch's introspection for introspection about *him*.

"Uh, well, actually . . ."

Actually, the entrepreneur has barely thought about Taylor's bizarre message since 49th Heaven. Despite the evidence that's been presented to him that the Autonomous Minds are still out there and taking an interest in his affairs, Natch still can't bring himself to believe it. All-knowing thinking machines, centuries old, outside of time and space? Absurd. Yet the only alternate explanations he can come up with for the presence of that block of wood from his childhood bureau—that Taylor has been able to read his mind, that Taylor is somehow a manifestation of his own subconscious, that the resemblance of the block of wood is just a monstrous coincidence—are even *more* ridiculous. But even if he does take the Autonomous Minds' message at face value . . . what does it even mean? Warfare between the Surinas? A jump? A decision in the darkness? What are they even talking about?

Luckily, Natch never needs to explain any of this to the Pharisee, because at that moment they arrive at the prefab medical building and Natch is ushered inside, alone.

Magan's bio/logic surgeons are considerate, but they are also laconic. They lead Natch to a distressingly white room with yellow trim, as if it might be the very soul of the Defense and Wellness Council. They give him a few reassuring words, pat him on the back, and then strap him down to a gurney. Natch has barely been in the building for ten minutes when they wave a syringe before his eyes and plunge it into his forearm. Consciousness quickly slips away from his grasp.

If the surgery's successful, he thinks before the darkness takes him, *I won't need to worry about dealing with Brone at all.*

Blackness.

Flashing lights.

A chorus of chimes.

Natch awakens, not on the gurney, but sitting up strapped to a chair. He's instantly reminded of those horrific few days he spent as the Patels' prisoner in São Paulo. But before the horror can even register, he sees Magan's chief engineer, Papizon, leaning over and undoing the straps. They're still in the white-and-yellow operating room, but the surgeons have vanished.

Papizon has no interest in being tactful. "It didn't work."

"What does that mean?" says Natch, standing up and trying to get the circulation back in his arms and legs.

"Means the conduit's still inside you, untouched. Surgeons couldn't figure out how to remove it without killing you. Or worse, letting Brone know that we're trying to remove it." He giggles. "They said it's grown inside you like an old tree. Big long roots, so to speak. Gonna be next to impossible to get rid of it without digging out the scalpels and carving it out one OCHRE at a time."

Next to impossible to get rid of it. The words feel like a death sentence.

"There's good news though, too," continues Papizon. "The surgeons were able to install OCHRE intrusion repellents." The entrepreneur gives him a blank look. "In nontechnical terms . . . Brone still has access to pull stuff *out* of your neural systems through the conduit. But if he tries to inject anything new *in* there, we can intercept it, zap it. So he can't kill you again just by looking at you. I'd say that's good news, wouldn't you?" Papizon stands up, hums a strange tune in an Oriental scale to himself. He's about to leave before he remembers: "In case you haven't figured it out, that means you're still gonna need to go to the Thassel Complex." And then, before he's made it out the door: "Well, aren't you *coming?*"

Natch is too disoriented to ask where they're going. The storkish Council engineer leads him through a series of corridors, past medical personnel in uniform, out into the daylight, then immediately into another prefab structure. This one appears to be an armory of some sort, as it's full of metal shelving and box after box of black code darts. There are grenades, carefully crated and labeled PULSE, DARK MIST, and COMBUSTION. Guns of all shapes and sizes hang on the walls, and everywhere he looks Natch can see a Council guard giving him a menacing stare.

They emerge in a cavernous, echoing room of polished and laminated wood that might serve as a sparring chamber. Standing in the middle of the room on a mannequin of sorts is a flesh-colored bodysuit. Standing next to the bodysuit are Horvil, Serr Vigal, Quell, Frederic Patel, and Richard Taylor, along with a tall, lithe man with an immaculately clipped goatee and camouflage fatigues.

He's holding a rather large dartgun in his right hand.

Before Natch even has a chance to say hello, Papizon is exhorting him to strip down and climb into the bodysuit. It's made of some slick, rubbery substance that reminds Natch of scuba gear. As he dresses, the man in the fatigues introduces himself as Special Operative Jorge Monck. Natch would describe him as *no-nonsense*, except there appears to be quite a bit of nonsense in the man that's carefully compartmentalized away from work and duty.

"I'll be accompanying you into the Thassel Complex along with eighteen of my team," says Monck. "Disguised, but armed. We'll be with you every step of the way. Well, every step, except . . ."

"Except when you plug the motherfucker with black code," adds Papizon cheerily as he adjusts Natch's suit.

"And here's what you'll be doing it with," says Monck, holding up the large dartgun. "You can use the selector on the pommel to switch between the upper and lower chambers of the gun. The lower chamber is armed with your standard offensive black code capabilities. Paralysis, blindness, unconsciousness. Horvil's got OCHREs to inoculate you against all of them."

Horvil holds up a capped syringe and points to it with raised eyebrows.

"As for the upper chamber," continues the operative, "I'll leave that to your friend Quell to explain."

The Islander takes the gun and points to its upper chamber. Natch notices that he's still wearing the golden rings that enable him to use his idiosyncratic finger-weaving programming technique. "Horvil, Frederic, and I put together a little concoction for Brone," says Quell. "Vigal had some input too. It's kind of like a bio/logic loopback. It'll completely block any outgoing subaether transmissions from his OCHREs, so he shouldn't be able to send any signal to release Possibilities 2.0 on the Data Sea."

Natch has finished donning the battle suit by this point, and Papizon immediately begins explaining its many features to him. The treads are designed to trek through virtually any type of terrain without leaving a footprint or admitting the slightest droplet of moisture. The suit itself will shift color in the blink of an eye to camouflage itself against the surrounding environment. ("Not that you'll need that," says Papizon, "because you'll be wearing a robe of one-way transparency weave over this so you'll blend in with the crowd. Lets the cameras see out without anyone else being able to see in.") There's a utility belt filled with miniature versions of just about every stealth contraption in existence—magnetic cable, collapsible knife, pulse grenade, miniature flamethrower—all arranged in some arcane order that beggars logic. It's disguised with a retractable cover that makes the whole thing look like one of those stylish wide belts that Natch has seen Robby Robby wear. The gun fits snugly in a pocket and is somehow virtually undetectable from more than a meter away.

When Natch is completely outfitted in the battle suit and holding the dartgun in his hand, he feels utterly ridiculous. He suddenly has a new appreciation for actors like Bill Rixx and Juan Nguyen who can look like they were born to wear such badass weaponry.

"Am I going to need all this?" asks Natch apprehensively.

Papizon shrugs. "Doubt it. But you know what they say—always be prepared!"

"Speaking of prepared—you're going to show me to a bio/logic workbench soon, right? There's something I need to do."

"Yep. In a little bit. Be patient."

Horvil, Vigal, and Richard Taylor stand to the side during this entire production with polite smiles on their faces, saying nothing. Even Frederic Patel is staying out of the way. It's clear that there's more prep work to be done, and they don't want to impede the mission.

Soon Papizon is leading Natch and Jorge Monck out of the room towards some other briefing. But Serr Vigal catches up to them before they've made it out the door and encloses Natch in a very uncharacteristic hug. "Good luck," he says in a hoarse voice that's little above a whisper.

"Luck is for the unprepared," Natch quips.

The neural programmer manages a slight smile. "Then let's hope you're prepared."

• • •

True to its name, the warehouse district was a vast segment of Manila largely given over to rambling open storage facilities and pits of left-over construction debris. But it contained at least one building with something close to modern amenities. Magan guessed that this had once been the overseer's office for some kind of industrial operation, and appropriated it as his headquarters. The top floor jutted out over the rest of the building, with a flexible glass window overlooking a large open courtyard. Today the space was serving as training grounds for a legion of men and women in white robes and yellow stars. Magan stood at the window and watched the drill instructor lead his troops through the basics of their unfamiliar weapons. On the other side of the room, Magan's commanders were standing in a cluster poring over tactical diagrams on viewscreens.

"Do you trust him?" said Rey Gonerev from a chair in the corner nearest the window.

"Who?" replied Magan. "Cheronna? Josiah?"

"Natch."

The lieutenant executive shifted uncomfortably from one foot to the other. "Trust is a multifaceted concept," he replied after some consideration.

"So you don't trust him," said the Blade.

"I trust that he despises Brone and will conduct the mission as directed. I trust that he'll do his best to sneak into the Kordez Thassel Complex and take out the bodhisattva. But after that?" Magan exhaled sharply. "After that, no, I don't really trust him."

"We could end up with Natch on the loose again. We could end up facing the same situation as before—searching through tube trains, following his friends and colleagues, trying to figure out where he could have disappeared to."

"We could," agreed Magan. "But somehow I don't think so. That whole experience on the run changed him, Rey. The operation against the cartels in 49th Heaven changed him. After we've got Brone safely contained, I don't know if he'll just hand MultiReal over to Jara. I'd be rather surprised if he did. But now that he knows where I'm coming from, I think the disagreements we have in the future will be more . . . civilized."

Rey Gonerev was evidently not placated by his words. "Civilized," she said doubtfully. "Don't we have any other options than trusting him?"

"Perhaps you'd like to see the alternative?"

Magan called over one of his senior commanders from the group of Council officers huddled on the other side of the room. A short, pale man with closely cropped hair stepped over and gave the lieutenant executive a quick bow. "Ferris, show Chief Solicitor Gonerev the video of the alternate plan for the Kordez Thassel Complex."

Without a word in response, the man waved his hand at the window in front of Magan. A horizontal chunk of glass instantly turned opaque. On the black display appeared a tactical representation of the Thassel Complex drawn in crisp yellow vectors. Two seconds later, a small spherical object came streaking down from the top right of the display.

The missile slammed into the center of the Complex and reduced it to cinders between one breath and the next.

"You know we can't do that!" shouted Gonerev, leaping to her feet and leveling an angry stare at the commander. "The Thasselians have that place open for business twenty-four hours a day. There could be *thousands* of civilians in that building! Businesspeople, drudges, L-PRACG people, who knows who else. And what if Brone's got the program rigged to automatically launch onto the Data Sea if he dies, like Natch said?"

Ferris took a step back and folded his arms across his chest defensively. "The lieutenant executive asked for options. This is an option."

Magan wiped the display with a sweep of his hand, and they were once again looking at the figures in white robes, awkwardly shouldering their dartrifles in something approximating unison. A few rifles went clattering to the ground as he watched. "Relax," said the lieutenant executive. "I have no intention of leveling the Thassel Complex unless as a very last resort."

The Blade frowned with suspicion. "Then why prepare for it in so much detail? Why diagram the whole thing out?"

"Because Len Borda might not be so merciful."

(((33)))

Politicians never die, went the old Islander aphorism. *They just curdle.*

Representative Triggendala had been serving the south side of Manila for nearly as long as Len Borda had been heading the Defense and Wellness Council. Unverified rumor said that the two of them had actually been lovers in some bygone era, and the high executive's spurning had sparked the unyielding hatred she had borne for him ever since. Such was her hatred of the Council in all its forms that she had refused to vote on the resolution authorizing Magan Kai Lee to establish a military base in the Islands, preferring to abstain.

But when Josiah Surina and Bali Chandler called for the forces of the Free Republic to march alongside those of Magan Kai Lee, Triggendala would not be satisfied with a vote of "present."

She took to the floor of the Islander parliament the next day with General Cheronna at her side and began a lengthy excoriation of Josiah and his manifesto. She proclaimed Lieutenant Executive Lee to be little more than a puppet of Len Borda, and called his rebellion "bad theater." "This fight is between the Free Republic and the high executive," she proclaimed, adding that if the high executive wanted bloodshed, "he knows where to find us."

General Rosz watched the hearing on the Data Sea along with the rest of Borda's senior commanders in the barracks north of Melbourne. Triggendala's speech—and Josiah Surina's sour-faced reaction—made for pretty good theater itself. Within two hours of mounting the rostrum, the xenophobic group known as the insulars had mounted a rebellion of their own. Arguments broke out on the floor. General Cheronna could be seen yelling his anger at a visibly livid Bali Chandler until the two almost came to blows. When Surina and Chandler's resolution failed by a resounding 28–20 vote, the drudges focused their cameras on Margaret Surina's son, slumped in his chair looking dour and defeated.

"How can the Islanders press for 'Grand Reunification,'" said Commander Cheng across the table from Rosz, putting a tangible sneer on the catchphrase, "when they can't even unify themselves?"

Rosz nodded. A forty-year veteran in Borda's military, he had a son in his midtwenties; Josiah Surina reminded him a lot of his son. "I almost feel sorry for Surina," he said. "Seemed to have such a promising career ahead of him. Now he's just another backwater representative."

Cheng was younger, less hardened by time and career. "Shame." He shrugged.

Rosz and the other commanders sat around the table deep into the night discussing what this would mean to the impending battle with Magan Kai Lee. Consensus was that this would draw the lieutenant executive onto the battlefield sooner rather than later. The longer he stayed in Manila amidst the poisonous atmosphere Triggendala had stirred up, the greater the risk of him losing his military base, and therefore his main advantage over Borda's forces. As for the loss of the sizable unconnectible army led by General Cheronna—

"Not as big a loss for Lee as it seems," stated Rosz.

Cheng shook his head. "I disagree. The Islanders are good warriors. They would have been a good asset."

"No doubt they're good warriors. A fierce people. But there's no precedent for a joint connectible-unconnectible force. You'd have all kinds of logistical issues to consider that would make it a nightmare. How do you communicate with them through battle language? Will all your weapons work with an unconnectible force?" The general downed the remainder of his wine. "Give me the simplicity of an all-Council army any day over a joint force twice the size."

"Suppose you've got a point," replied Cheng with a shrug of indifference.

"You're still monitoring Cheronna?"

"Of course. They were camped just east of the warehouse district next to Magan's army, but after the vote in parliament they moved off south."

"Think we should tell the old man?" asked Rosz, stroking a trim beard of stark white.

Cheng gave an ironic glance over his shoulder, up in the sky towards where he imagined DWCR to lie. "And interrupt the Battle of Waterloo?" he scowled. The high executive's propensity for playing his virtual games of ancient warfare was well known, among the higher echelons at least.

General Rosz retreated to his quarters soon afterward. He had no sooner taken off the golden smock of his office when he had a sudden premonition: Magan's attack would come soon. Very soon. And it was likely to come here, to Melbourne, to his base in fact. Rosz called for his aide-de-camp and had her put the perimeter guard on high alert.

Which turned out to be a prescient move.

Rosz was awakened at three a.m. by a priority signal blasting through his brain, along with a stimulating release of adrenaline. Within a minute's time, he was up and dressed and striding through the hallways to his command center. All around, he could see men and women scrambling from their bunks to don uniforms and load weapons. Crisp, orderly, efficient.

Rosz was pleased to note that he reached the command center a good ten seconds before Commander Cheng. It was an austere room, the command center, buried deep underneath the base proper; one could almost describe it as a bunker, except bunkers usually didn't have such luxurious armchairs. General Rosz had never been one for excessive instrumentation. To him, war was an intellectual exercise that required little more than viewscreens, encrypted communications, and the occasional glass of port. The two men took their seats and secured the door behind them.

"Get me eyes on the ground," barked Cheng to one of the tactical systems experts two dozen meters up.

Seconds later, the wall of viewscreens across from them was filled with a wide array of vantage points on the battlefield. Grunt's-eye views of the grassy plains between Melbourne and Shepperton; aerial surveillance from hoverbirds; terrain maps and schematics.

"They're coming up fast," muttered Rosz. "For process' preservation, does Lee really think a full-scale ground assault is going to work against *Melbourne?*"

Rosz squinted at the bank of viewscreens. There was an enormous white mass there of troops in the white robe and yellow star, not far south of Shepperton. And they weren't marching—they were *running*.

Towards Melbourne, city of the centralized government.

• • •

Jorge Monck looks him in the eye from a distance of no more than a meter. He says, "An interesting culmination of fast facts can be attributed to a certain malady of disproportionate usage." Natch can see his lips forming the words; he can sense the corresponding vibrations escaping from his larynx.

But what he hears is, *If you're decrypting battle language correctly, raise your right hand.*

Natch does so. He opens his mouth to ask Monck how he activates the voice encryption on his end—is there some sort of mental activation node? But what escapes his mouth is, "Do you find that birds often contribute to population density, or is that a delusion of scale?"

Now tell Jara to raise her left hand, instructs Monck.

"Alphabetical sorting in a traditional medium!" says Natch.

He feels his communication channel with the fiefcorp master opening up. "Vertical and horizontal, that's a definite obstacle."

Monck claps Natch on the shoulder and offers him a humorless smile. *We're good.* Then he heads back to his seat.

Natch knows that he should be strategizing with Monck during their long hoverbird flight from Manila to the Kordez Thassel Complex, but his mind feels like it's caught in a funnel spiraling downward. The world around him seems to be dwindling, becoming more difficult to focus on, less comprehensible by the second. The mission is all there is. All there is is the mission. Monck and his four fellow Council spooks either understand Natch's reticence or simply don't care; they leave him to his solitude.

It's a longer flight than Natch anticipated. Monck and the others sleep. Natch remains rigid and awake from takeoff to landing.

And before he realizes it, the hoverbird is making its final approach to a crooked and many-legged building on the outskirts of the Twin Cities. He sees bogs, sulking trees, and as they get close to the ground, fireflies. Natch feels like he should have more questions for Monck about what he should do, how he should react, what their contingencies are. But he can't seem to formulate the words.

The hoverbird comes to a stop. *Ready?* says Jorge Monck laconically.

The four Council officers reply in the affirmative, as does Natch.

Then they're off the hoverbird and walking down the pathway from the hoverbird pad to the Kordez Thassel Complex.

Monck's four companions have already split off before they even make it through the front door. Other nearby hoverbird pads have also disgorged their passengers, and the Council officers have now camouflaged themselves in the crowd. It's a typical sparse late-night business center crowd: mostly fiefcorpers on their way to meetings with superiors in a different time zone, but with a smattering of artists and tourists and idlers as well. Natch and Jorge Monck are dressed in tight-fitting, cream-colored robes over their battle suits, the stock outfit of the memecorp sales representative. They approach the front double doors, over which stretches a wide viewscreen filled with dancing animated bottles of ChaiQuoke.

"Holistic approaches make the most sense," snaps Jara through the secure communications channel. *Freeze. Don't look up.*

Not two seconds later, someone jostles Jorge Monck's elbow, causing him to spill the container of promotional buttons Natch didn't realize he was carrying. The plastic trinkets go clanking noisily on the concrete. Natch and Monck kneel down and take their time picking them up.

A song. Jangly electric guitars, a sinuous line of cello.

Go! Now. To your right. Around the woman in green.

Natch and Jorge scurry quickly around a rather large woman in a forest green caftan and into the doors—but not before they catch a glimpse of a muscular figure in a black robe, his attention momentarily snagged by an advertisement for Yarn Trip's third reunion tour. Natch recognizes one of the Thasselians from Old Chicago. And come to think it, someone *was* always playing Yarn Trip at eardrum-crushing levels in that hotel.

They are in the door, the first guard passed. Natch gazes around at the impossibly long corridors and the slanted walls. He can already see three more figures in black robes with red trim down the next hallway.

He thinks, *This is going to be a long evening.*

• • •

"Robert Varless!" cried Benyamin.

There was no mistaking the resemblance between the sylphlike man lounging twenty meters to Natch's right and the slim figure on Robert Varless's official Meme Cooperative profile. You just didn't see ears that long every day.

Hang back about twenty seconds, Jara told Natch over the secure communications channel.

Jara and Petrucio Patel were already staring down the list of possible distractions from the Council's oppo research, dangling underneath the man's photo like a shingle. Time was of the essence, so they had already learned to focus on the items that Merri had tagged during her evaluations last night. Avid fan of the Delhi Chakras soccer team . . . former member of Creed Dao . . . left behind a similarly elfin companion and small daughter to join Brone's Revolution of Selfishness . . .

Jara's and Petrucio's hands almost collided as they reached to point at the third item simultaneously.

Back at the viewscreen on the other side of the room, Robby Robby flipped madly through the database of advertisements, collating and sorting with his fingertips through entries that he had already spent hours collating and sorting. Blonde . . . female . . . Caucasian . . . six to eight years of age . . . missing . . .

"Natch is waiting," said Jara in foreboding tone of voice. "Almost twenty seconds."

"Got her!" cried the channeler, punching at the screen with two fingers.

Four seconds later, Jara could see through Natch's battle suit cameras that Robby's automated bid for three times the going rate had been accepted, and the One-on-One Motivation Network had replaced the current advertisement on the viewscreen with the promo of Robby's choosing.

It took three tries. Three heart-rendingly gorgeous little girls listed as missing in public service announcements by the Congress of L-PRACG's Center for Missing and Exploited Children before Robby struck on one with enough of a resemblance to Robert Varless's daughter to cause him to turn his head. And even then, Jorge Monck decided to add a secondary distraction by sending a shapely waif of a Council officer walking past in the opposite direction. Natch and Monck barely had time to jog by without being spotted.

The whole room exhaled in collective relief.

"Oh-h-h," moaned Benyamin, rubbing one hand across his sweaty forehead. "That was fucking *close*."

"Aren't they all?" muttered Merri, who had decided her time was best spent proactively combing through the personnel files and tagging prospective advertisements.

So far, Natch and Monck had made their way past five Thasselians. Two of the distractions had been relatively easy to conjure up and execute—including Robert Varless—but the other three had been decidedly more difficult. Jara was starting to suspect they should have just trusted to the Council's bio/logic disguise people. It had taken an entire five minutes to find a successful distraction for one woman. And that had only been possible by using a technique Jara thought of as a "one-two punch": use garish flash of color and/or light to start the head turn, then sock 'em with the advertisement that packed an emotional wallop. In every case, the process was taking longer than Jara had anticipated, leaving Natch and Monck to come up with a variety of excuses for loitering nonchalantly along half-empty hallways.

Something about the entire enterprise left Jara feeling thoroughly depressed.

Is that all we are? she thought. *Puppets with strings to be pulled by marketers, advertisers, bureaucrats, and con artists?* Of course, it was not every day that your typical marketer could afford to spend thousands of credits on research and surveillance into your personal life and habits. But the fact that everyone had *some* kind of irresistible switch of desire hardwired to their physiology seemed like a repudiation of everything Jara had learned about herself over the past few months.

After all, it was not so long ago that Natch had been using these types of emotional tricks against *her*. The fact that she was now employing them made her feel like she had come full circle, and not in a good way. Jara tried to imagine what her own Defense and Wellness Council–prepared dossier would look like: weakness for nitro with strong bitters . . . seduced by proctor at a young age . . . strong attraction to powerful men who treat her like refuse. . . .

"Mohammed Victor Kohl!" shouted Benyamin, shattering her brief reverie. "Forty meters down the corridor to the left!"

• • •

"Here they come," said Cheng. "Ready multi disruptors."

The mass of soldiers in white had gotten quite close to the Melbourne base by now. It was a vast force of multi projections, surely ten thousand strong. They were dashing at top speed across the large open field north of the base. Rosz knew that an advance multi force of ten thousand must presage an invading force of close to forty thousand in the flesh. Which meant two things:

Magan Kai Lee was sending the bulk of his force here to the north of Melbourne.

And the decisive battle in the Council civil war of 360 would occur here, with General Rosz as the presiding officer for Len Borda's army.

Rosz gaped at the advancing multi projections. Magan must have concluded that his position was quite desperate to resort to this bold surprise attack. It virtually eliminated the advantage he had gained by arranging the base behind the unconnectible curtain. Could it be that the political situation in the Islands was so precarious for the lieutenant executive that the base would not be available for much longer?

Lee must have decided that his best hope in overthrowing Borda lay in catching this, the main Melbourne force, unprepared. He must have decided that he could not afford to wait for Borda's inevitable offensive action against Manila. It might have stood a chance of working if Rosz hadn't suspected he would resort to something like this. The general glanced at the row of viewscreens on the left-hand wall and was satisfied to see his soldiers scrambling into position in their bunkers, some bedraggled, some with dartgun belts in hand and unloaded—but there. The main banks of multi disruptors were mostly charged up, and substantial numbers of shoulder-mounted disruptors were already in play as well. The base itself, with its castle-like fortifications and multiple levels stacked like a ziggurat, was as good a place as any to defend against assault.

Cheng gave all this a glance of satisfaction. "Fire when ready."

The command zipped its way through the ranks of the defending force. Within seconds, the horizon lit up with the ghostly glare of multi disruptor fire. Beams of energy streaked northwards into the midst of the invading force.

"Where is the Fourteenth?" asked Rosz. The 14th Melbourne Division: Len Borda's multi projection corps.

"A little late suiting up and getting to the red tiles," replied Cheng. "But they're already pouring out of the gateways and making progress towards the enemy camp."

Rosz stood and walked up and down the row of viewscreens, watching the targeted multi disruptor fire disappearing into the mass of white robes. Borda's forces gunning with gritted teeth.

Suddenly the field erupted with the dull thump of smoke grenades. A dark mist rose from the ground, obscuring the advancing force. "Shit," cursed Cheng, though Rosz had expected this too. It was more than just smoke camouflaging the advancing multi disruptions; no, this was modern warfare. The mist was threaded thick with light-repelling nanobots, designed to multiply when exposed to oxygen. The defending Council officers were now firing into a dense black mass, unable to target individual advancing projections.

"Patience," cautioned Rosz. "The mist only lasts a few minutes."

Cheng grunted something in the affirmative; of course, he knew that as well as Rosz.

The advancing mass of Magan Kai Lee's multi projections had now reached the periphery of the base, an unfortunate but also inevitable development. Rosz knew that the goal of the multi projection corps was not stealth or finesse, but rather speed. With no offensive capabilities of their own and few defensive tactics besides obfuscating dark mist, all you could really expect from the multi projection corps was to get inside the enemy compound and scope out their defenses before getting zapped with disruptor fire and sent back blinking to red tiles on base.

Rosz narrowed his eyes. The advancing mass was within dartgun range of the base, and some had withdrawn weapons of their own. But the disruptor fire had not thinned their ranks.

And Magan's troops were now firing.

General Rosz leapt to the closest viewscreen, zoomed in as close as he could get to the invading force through the dissipating mist. He watched a burly man in the white robe and yellow star bellowing, charging forward—and completely ignoring the disruptor beam that struck him in the chest.

"It's a trick!" cried Rosz. "This isn't the multi corps. Draw dartguns!"

"Draw dartguns!" echoed Commander Cheng grimly. "Draw dartguns!"

It was too late for the troops on the periphery of the base, gathered in their bunkers with disruptors still in hand. A good half of Magan's troops were busy plugging the unprepared disruptor corps soldiers with dart fire, mowing down entire bunkers full of Borda's troops. The rest of the invading force was pressing forward into the base, leaping over sandbags, firing wildly on anything they encountered.

Clever, thought General Rosz, stopping at the side table to pour himself more wine. *But there's a reason Council armies don't use this tactic every time.*

And sure enough, the surprise technique was already proving to be of limited use to Magan Kai Lee's army. After the initial burst of casualties among the disruptor corps, the enemy was now finding a force armed and prepared for their incursion. Darts began hailing through the ranks of Lee's troops, and they began going down into the dust.

The trend only continued as platoons of Borda's soldiers ran onto the field of battle to flank the invading forces. It was part of the defense plan of the base, in fact—the outer courtyards were relatively easy to breach, so that an invading force might be pressed between the hardened inner fortifications and defenders who had moved around to a flanking position. Magan Kai Lee's troops were now engaged in close combat with Len Borda's better-armed, better-prepared defenders.

It was a massacre.

"Another wave incoming!" cried Cheng.

Rosz snapped his head to the viewscreen Cheng was pointing at. He saw the enormous wave of white robes and yellow stars far down the field advancing on their position. Perhaps thirty or forty thousand strong. Reports were starting to come back from Borda's multi corps confirming that the bulk of Magan's force had moved south from Shepperton.

Cheng left a small force in the base to mop up the surviving false multi projections, and sent the bulk of the army, already afield, to take on the invaders.

• • •

Natch had moved into a more heavily occupied part of the Thassel Complex now. Jara thought he must be getting close to the bodhisattva, because the density of the devotees in black robes had increased dramatically.

"The woman with the red hair—Paranella!" cried Benyamin.

Merri had abandoned her attempts to get ahead of the game and was now working in one team with Robby Robby and Benyamin while Petrucio and Jara worked together in another. "Her daughter's part of a fan club for Juan Nguyen," said Merri hurriedly. "Run the ChaiQuoke promo!"

"Juan Nguyen?" protested Robby, shaking his head. "It'll never work, Merri. He's the most popular actor on the planet right now. Totally overexposed."

"Too late!" said Ben through gritted teeth. "She's looking this direction. Run it, run it!"

Robby Robby was correct. The ad, which featured Juan Nguyen

comically quaffing bottle after bottle of ChaiQuoke in rapid succession long past the point where his bladder would rupture, completely failed to distract the Thasselian named Paranella.

"Nothing seems to be working on her," said Merri, wiping sweat off her brow. "Can't Natch just use MultiReal to get past this one?" Jara asked him.

No, answered Natch flatly in encrypted battle language. *I told you, I can't walk into a room with Brone if I'm exhausted from going through too many choice cycles.*

Jara couldn't argue with that. She felt guilty enough even asking; it seemed like she had drastically overestimated what this One-on-One Motivation Network advertising scheme could accomplish. Natch had made it two-thirds of the way to the room where Brone had parleyed with Merri and Petrucio, and avoided all of the Thasselian devotees they had come across. But Jara couldn't help but feel like he had gotten this far because of serendipity and the professionalism of Monck's team more than anything else.

Regardless, Jara felt like this was still a bit *too* easy. Was the lure of clever advertising enough to distract *all* of the Thasselians? Or was this all just a feint to get Natch feeling overconfident?

She turned her attention back to Natch's attempts to get past Paranella. Four separate advertisements in a row failed miserably, and only Jorge Monck's quick thinking prevented her from getting a closer look at Natch as he sidled past. The Council operative made a comic slip of his own, falling onto his face and yelling out in surprise and pain. The loud noise caused a quick turn of the head, which was enough for Natch to slip around her unnoticed.

Jara decided to check in on how Magan's confrontation with Len Borda was going. She fired off a quick scrambled message to the Blade. "How's the battle going in Melbourne?" she asked.

Rey Gonerev's voice came back confident and clear. "Good news," she said. "Everything's going exactly as planned."

(((34)))

"They won't fool us again," said General Rosz, teeth gritted with determination. "Slow up the advance, double-check the ammunition mix."

Cheng nodded. "Affirmative."

Rosz stood and watched with approval as his legions held up and took a moment to examine the dart canisters loaded on their dartguns and the placement of their multi disruptors. Not for the first time, Rosz wished that he lived in a simpler time, when ammunition was ammunition and ordnance was ordnance, when conventional gunpowder could incapacitate any enemy if you used enough of it.

Nowadays, you could target the enemy with devastating accuracy and still watch him walk away unscathed, because the enemy had been inoculated against the black code in your dartguns—or because you were firing at a ghostly multi projection instead of a human being—or because the soldier you were targeting was an unconnectible with missing or deactivated OCHREs. Standard military strategy called for an amalgam of firepower to be used in tandem. Stun programs, paralysis programs, multi disruptor fire, even old-fashioned beam weapon blasts, all at the same time. Bombard the enemy position with enough different types of ammunition, and chances were that something would succeed in disabling or killing your foe.

"Mix is good," replied Cheng after several minutes that saw Magan Kai Lee's main force marching farther down the plain. "Should be sufficient to knock out flesh and multi targets, if there are any hiding in there."

Rosz nodded. Then waited, and watched.

The viewscreens told the tale of an intense battle taking place on the plain outside the Melbourne base. Thousands of soldiers staking out positions on a broad field of grass, mounting weaponry and firing broadly into the opposing mass of troops. The air was hazy with a blanket of black code needles and multicolored beams of disruptor fire.

Cheng could not help but stare open-mouthed, never having witnessed such a spectacle. As for General Rosz, he had not seen a connectible-on-connectible battle of this magnitude since the Melbourne riots when he was a young man. He had not remembered how eerily quiet the battlefield was compared to the wars enacted on the dramas. Thousands of dartguns firing simultaneously sounded strangely like a chorus of clicking insects, while the noise of the disruptors crackling seemed to merge into one muted drone. As for the soldiers themselves—what sounds would they make when communication took place on silent encrypted channels, when paralysis and death from black code struck before they had a chance to scream?

The soft susurration of boots rustling through grass. The masses of men and women in white and yellow rising and falling in mesmerizing patterns. The accumulation of spent darts on the ground like charcoal-colored snow.

Rosz wondered if he was an abomination for finding the modern field of war to be strangely beautiful.

"Tell the front line to advance," he commanded Cheng.

• • •

Lieutenant Executive Magan Kai Lee surveyed the battlefield from the safety of his private hoverbird kilometers away in Shepperton. Bodies in the white robe and yellow star piled up all around the entrance to the base. The bulk of Borda's troops advancing towards Magan's much smaller force. "What do you think?" he said. "Now?"

"Now," agreed General Cheronna.

• • •

Cheng was flabbergasted. Their ammunition seemed to be having far less of an effect on the enemy than the enemy's was having on them. The line of Borda's troops had noticeably thinned from the hail of dart fire, but Magan's forces seemed hardly diminished at all.

And then suddenly they began to take severe casualties—from behind.

Rosz quickly found a vantage point where he could see what was happening in the rear lines of the advancing force. He actually rubbed his eyes to make sure that he was not hallucinating, something he thought only happened in the dramas. The mass of troops that had stormed the base—the ones Rosz had initially believed to be multi projections—these troops were now spontaneously rising up en masse and returning to the fight.

Len Borda's army was now surrounded.

"Fuck," cursed Cheng all of a sudden. "Fuck. Fuck."

"What's the matter?" snapped Rosz.

"The Islanders."

True to the commander's words, the Islanders had crossed the unconnectible curtain in massive force some thirty minutes ago. Their hoverbirds had quickly gained the Australian continent and now they were advancing furiously on Melbourne.

Rosz could feel the frustration building up inside of him. The Islanders, brave warriors though they might be, had never posed a serious threat to Melbourne. They had never shown any interest in expanding beyond their borders, and so had developed a mostly defensive air force. One incapable of penetrating through the Australian continent, or so the Council had always believed. But Magan Kai Lee must have provided them some kind of logistical or materiel support, because they had cut through the continental defenses quite easily. And now they were headed this way—hundreds upon hundreds of hoverbirds' worth.

The war room began to feel cloistered and hot as Rosz and Cheng spent the next two hours wrestling with the problem of the ammunition mix. Magan's troops still seemed remarkably resistant to Borda's black code. There were casualties, to be sure—and the loyalists still significantly outnumbered the rebels—but the trend was a worrisome one. If they couldn't put down Magan's troops before the Islanders arrived, how would they handle a joint connectible-unconnectible force?

"We've got to keep them separated," said Cheng, pinching the flesh on the bridge of his nose. "Once the two forces mingle, we're done for."

Rosz nodded. Unconnectible and connectible enemies required vastly different breeds of black code. The toxins and poisons that would send an Islander swimming in the Null Current were easily metabolized by connectible OCHREs, while the advanced code that deactivated OCHREs or put them in a lethal frenzy was useless on an Islander.

But as two hours turned into three and the Islander hoverbird force drew ever closer, Rosz began to despair. When the first hoverbirds appeared on the horizon and the Islanders started pouring onto the plain, the general knew that the jig was up.

Islanders with shock batons streamed over the hillside and joined the fray at close quarters. Rosz and Cheng watched in despair as Borda's force dwindled by the minute. The general buried his face in his hands. It wasn't that he bore any great love for Len Borda; what he fought for was the rule of law and order, and by taking up arms against the high executive, Magan Kai Lee had violated that rule. A number of his colleagues had argued with him in secret that it was Borda who had violated that rule in the Tul Jabbor Complex, if not far earlier. Rosz could not even entirely say that he disagreed. But firm lines had to be drawn and adhered to somewhere, even if the innocent sometimes found themselves on the wrong side of that line.

And it was then that a realization sparked in Rosz's mind.

"The Islanders, Cheng," he said, slumping down into his chair. "We've been fighting them the whole time."

The commander eyed his superior officer warily. "What do you mean?"

"I mean the entire diplomatic catastrophe in Manila—the refusal to fight with Magan Kai Lee—General Cheronna and Triggendala making demands to the parliament—it was all staged. The army in the white robes and yellow stars that marched against us, those were unconnectibles."

"How could they manage that?" protested Cheng. "We've had Cheronna's army under surveillance the whole time—even in the Islands."

It was a clever subterfuge, Rosz realized. Of course they had Cheronna's army under surveillance. That was exactly what Magan had been counting on. They could see Magan's and Cheronna's armies side by side in the warehouse district—but they *couldn't* see what was happening in those warehouses. Soldiers suiting up in unfamiliar uniforms. Mechanics painting hoverbirds. Connectibles picking up shock batons and Islanders picking up dartrifles.

Rosz surveyed the battlefield once again. Now that the subterfuge had been uncovered, Len Borda's army was finally firing the correct ammunition at the correct enemy. But they were horribly outnumbered now, and surrounded, and scattered. The tide had already turned, and victory had already been swept out to sea.

"It's a new world, Cheng," lamented Rosz, as he stared dolefully at the carnage on the battlefield. "Unfortunately, we've been playing by the old rules."

• • •

Shit, Monck says in encrypted battle language. *Borda.*

Natch freezes. *What about him?*

Big fleet of Council hoverbirds headed this way. They're going to try storming the Kordez Thassel Complex.

Natch looks around and sees members of Monck's team hustling as quickly as they can back in the opposite direction, discreetly reaching for dartguns. They seem to be foregoing stealth now in favor of speed—which is drawing the attention of the Thasselians in black robes.

We're going to try to head them off at the docks, says Monck. *I think we can keep them busy until reinforcements get here.*

And Brone?

We saw Brone pass this way a few minutes ago. Went into those double doors. The operative gestures ahead of them to a short, empty hallway and a grand set of double doors. Natch recognizes this hallway and those doors; it's the same place where Brone met with Merri and Petrucio a few days ago. *I've got your back until you get inside.*

The entrepreneur gives Jorge Monck a nod. *Thanks, Monck*, he says. *Couldn't have gotten here without you.*

Hey, the Council operative replies with a smirk, *they* pay *me to do this. Now go ahead. Get in there and plug the target. Quick, before he hears about the approaching hoverbirds. Give me a signal when the job's done.*

And then Natch is walking down the hall to the double doors. He's on his own now.

$$\bullet \quad \bullet \quad \bullet$$

Silence descended on the waters of the North Sea. Far off in the foam, pixelated French sailors still clung to driftwood and yelled for mercy, but the wind was doing a more than serviceable job of scattering their pleas to digital oblivion. Len Borda surveyed the sea to the north, south, east, and west, but the only vessels still afloat were the battered ships flying the red, white, and blue of the Union Jack. Should he sail from Norway to the Strait of Gibraltar, he knew he would see the same thing. The high executive stood at the prow of his sloop-of-war, inhaling the smell of salt, of gunpowder, of burning wood, of celebratory rum being broken out of caskets in defiance of regulations, of blood and seared flesh. . . .

And then he was running belowdecks into his cabin, slamming the door shut, barricading it with virtual furniture. He looked around wildly for a hammer and nails, found them, began tacking charts and maps and canvas and whatever else he could find over the porthole. Anything to keep out those desperate voices from the sea pleading in broken English.

Help me! Help me!

Mercy!

All hail ze queen of England! Take me to your prisoner! I beg, I have children . . .

Please! Please, let me . . . let me see my daughter one last time . . . Anything! I'll give you . . . anything . . . all the money in the world, please. . . .

The charred hand sticking out of the wreckage.

The ruined man lying on the stretcher.

A curse. *May you see many more decades. May you live long enough to see exactly what you've done to the world.*

Borda slumped to the floor and huddled there with his back to his desk and his knees under his chin. Let the French sailors waft in the spray, calling out for mercy to the black, black sky. The British sailors too. Their doom had been seeking them out ever since they had enlisted in the navy. Let them drift and drown until they had learned the same truths that Len Borda had learned: that time ran in one direction only, that a death sentence once carried out could not be repealed, that the universe had no interest in acclimating itself to the whims and desires of humanity.

"High Executive."

Borda's head shot up in surprise at the voice. He hadn't intended to fall asleep, and he had specifically directed the sentries outside his office to let in no one. *No one.* Or was it to the virtual soldiers he had given that order? Borda's eyes focused on the hand extended out to him. Then he followed the arm back up to its owner, and he had the source of his dismay.

"Let me help you stand," said Magan Kai Lee. "Let's have this discussion in comfort."

The lieutenant executive was dressed in full ceremonial garb: form-fitting white robe, gray smock, dartgun strapped in holster, even the saber that Borda himself had not bothered to wear for decades. Borda took Magan's hand, noting that even sitting down, the high executive was not much shorter than his subordinate. He stood and followed Magan to the pair of faux-leather chairs sitting in the corner of the cabin.

Standing amidst SeeNaRee furniture strewn by the door were four of Magan's loyal officers, each armed with a dartrifle. Their dartrifles were out, and while they were not pointed at Borda, fingers were nestled on the triggers. Borda scanned the four of them; not a turncoat in the bunch.

Slightly removed from the four guards stood the Council's chief solicitor, Rey Gonerev, and the general in charge of the Melbourne defenses, Rosz.

"Traitor!" scowled Borda at his senior general. "You would abandon me too, Rosz?"

"No, Rosz has remained faithful to you to the last," said Magan. The general stood stiffly at attention, gazing at nowhere and nothing. Borda noticed that he was the only one in Magan's coterie who was not armed.

Magan unbelted his saber and handed it to one of his officers, then settled in to his chair. "We have an honor guard standing by," he said. "Five hoverbirds, ready to escort you back to the North Plains. Your L-PRACG is planning a welcoming ceremony. We've tried to keep the preparations a secret, but someone has already leaked the details to Mah Lo Vertiginous. A number of your supporters are gathered there now."

Len Borda slumped into his seat and let his elbows flop down onto the armrests. His mind tried to cut through the fog, but it was so difficult, so difficult. The last? No, not yet. "Tell me," he said, his voice acid, "why should I make this easy for you?"

The lieutenant executive was unfazed. "I was under the impression that *I* was making this easy for *you*."

"Why should I grant you the crust of legitimacy you crave? A coup d'état against the high executive of the Defense and Wellness Council should be done by force of arms. You'll need to drag me out of here in chains. Or better yet—" The high executive thrust his chest forward and rubbed a spot on his sternum. "I think three black code darts ought to do the trick, don't you?" He made a motion towards Magan's retinue, which ignored him. Was it Borda's imagination, or did General Rosz look embarrassed?

Magan, by contrast, looked as composed as if he had rehearsed his lines. Which, Borda supposed, he had. "If you think I'd balk at ordering my officers to shoot you down, you're mistaken," said Magan. "I've learned the lessons you taught too well."

"You have, have you?" The high executive stood from his chair and stomped over to the porthole, still covered with the canvas he had nailed there earlier. Borda clawed it off, letting the sun shine into the cabin once more. "Then what are you waiting for? Do it in front of the whole world! Do it before—"

"Before what?" Magan said. "Before the Blade shoots *me?*"

Len Borda whirled around expectantly. He saw Rey Gonerev standing with pistol at the ready. But his heart sank when he saw that the gun was not aimed at Magan; it was aimed at Borda.

"The high executive's chair in two years is quite a prize," continued the lieutenant executive. "But Rey is perfectly aware that you promised *me* the exact same thing."

The high executive stared into the defiant eyes of the Blade, looking for some reason to hope that this was one last bluff on her part. He tried to open a ConfidentialWhisper channel to the solicitor, but she would not accept his request. *Do it!* he commanded silently. *Shoot him down! You know that once Magan's gone, his officers will see that they have no alternative. They'll be* my *officers! The Council will be united once again!*

Ten seconds passed. Borda searched his mind for priority messages, looking to see if perhaps his other last-resort effort might pan out. If, against the odds, he should manage to wrest control of MultiReal from that lunatic of a bodhisattva . . . But no, he could see now, Magan Kai Lee was a step ahead of him in the Twin Cities as well. The loyalists had not even made it past the hoverbird docks before encountering stiff resistance from the lieutenant executive's officers. There was a fierce firefight raging outside the Kordez Thassel Complex's doors, and Magan's reinforcements were en route.

It was over.

Borda shuffled back and took the seat opposite Magan Kai Lee, suddenly feeling the weight of years hanging like a millstone around his neck. His knees were aflame, but he didn't have the energy to hunt down a bio/logic salve. "I had thought that you would never accept the authority of a brigand," he said to the Blade, his voice cracking with exhaustion. "A common criminal! Isn't that what you told me?"

"I told you what you wanted to hear," said Gonerev.

The lieutenant executive had not moved from his chair. "I may have come from low beginnings, but I offered Rey something better than bribes," he said.

"And what is that?" snapped Borda.

"A clear path of succession, guided by the rule of law. I have assured her that my first act in office will be to petition the Prime Committee to limit the high executive's tenure to a maximum of two five-year terms."

"You will cripple the office."

"It is for the sake of the office that I've done all this." Magan extended his hands over the sides of the chair, as if they could encompass a whole rebellion. "It is to restore the honor of the office that I'm asking you to step down. Not for me, but for the sake of Tul Jabbor, who founded the Defense and Wellness Council, and for the sake of Toradicus and Par Padron, who turned the Council into an organ of compassion and justice."

Len Borda could feel the ire rise within him. How dare Magan take such a righteous tone with him? Magan the flexible, Magan the spineless, Magan the dissembler. "And what would Toradicus and Par Padron think of the way you've chosen to take power? Through trickery and deceit? I think perhaps Zetarysis the Mad would be a more appropriate compari—"

"For process' preservation!" thundered the lieutenant executive, slamming his fist down on the armrest of the chair. "Fifty-eight years. For fifty-eight years, you've made a mockery of this institution. There's not a principle of the Council that you haven't subverted for your personal gain. And now you are *alone*, Borda, and you *will* step out of this office and into that waiting hoverbird, or I'll have you dragged to one of your own orbital prisons. I'll have you put on trial for all the world to see."

The four officers could not help but twitch in shock, having never heard such a tone from the cool, rational lips of Magan Kai Lee. Rey Gonerev nearly dropped her pistol. General Rosz blinked rapidly and took a step back.

And then, in the space of a breath, Magan had caged his passions once more.

"I was prepared to wait," continued Lee, his voice quiet and hoarse but his jaw still quivering with muted rage. "I was prepared to bargain. *You* were the one who tried to assassinate me on the floor of the Tul Jabbor Complex. *You* were the one who refused to abide by your agreements. And you dare talk about making things easy for me?

"Now go. You'll be given your honor guard. You'll be escorted to your hoverbird. There is freshly caught lobster on board. Go before I change my mind."

Gonerev, Rosz, and the four officers turned as one to the high executive to see what he would do.

Len Borda carefully studied the face of his adversary. He could see that the seeds of doubt he had planted in Magan's psyche had taken root. He could hear the defensiveness in Magan's voice. No matter what the man accomplished in the high executive's seat from this moment forward, there would always be that kernel of unease, that niggling doubt growing like an ineradicable weed within him. And Rey Gonerev too! Borda turned his piercing gaze into her eyes. He could see it there too, that crack in the foundation of the regime through which the weed of illegitimacy would always sprout anew, informing all the citizens of the world that nothing had changed, reminding them that underneath Magan's high-minded ideals there lay nothing but the base mud of greed and ambition.

Borda had accomplished what he needed to accomplish. Nothing more remained. He rose and gave Magan Kai Lee a mocking, obsequious bow. "As you wish, *High Executive*."

• • •

Magan Kai Lee and Rey Gonerev stood at the base of the observation tower that hung off the bottom of the Defense and Wellness Council Root like a stem. The ancient British naval SeeNaRee was gone. Their view was the entirety of the Earth below—not to mention the departing ships carrying Len Borda and his honor guard.

"Borda staged that scene for your benefit, you know," said Magan, apropos of nothing. "Why didn't you take the high executive's offer?"

The Blade started, as if he had just read her innermost thoughts. "How long have you known?"

"Long enough."

"And yet you trusted me not to turn the pistol on you instead of Borda?" Gonerev's eyes widened as she lit upon a realization. She took a step back and regarded Magan with a stare that contained more than a little apprehension. "You *didn't* trust me. Papizon handed me that gun before we left Manila. You had him load it with bogus black code, didn't you?"

The lieutenant executive shook his head. "No. I considered it. But then I decided that I needed you armed more than I needed you muzzled. Does that make sense?"

"Somewhat. . . . But at least you could have inoculated yourself against the code in my gun."

"I suppose I could have. But I didn't think of it."

The Blade turned to face the window, and the darkened parabola of the planet below. "And to answer your question—about why I didn't take Borda's offer—I think I've had enough of ambition for the time being. I've climbed higher than most people dream during my decade in politics. Is it wrong that I might want to stop here?"

"Not wrong at all. But I'll believe it when I see it."

(((35)))

The doors slide open at Natch's touch, and cool air gusts out to meet him. He hangs on the other side of the doorway for just a moment, gun at the ready. Moody lights from the room's interior make a dance of shadows on the floor.

Natch tries to recall Papizon's instructions on how to use some of the more arcane weaponry in his utility belt. The flamethrower, the pulse grenade, the smoke pellets. But he knows that despite the thorough grounding Papizon gave him in the basics, this is not something that he can learn at the last minute. Soldiers train for months with these weapons until the controls are embedded in muscle memory, until the weapon becomes an extension of the human being. Such familiarity can be imitated with bio/logics, but never entirely duplicated.

The entrepreneur shrugs to himself. All he really needs to worry about is pointing the barrel of his dartgun and pulling the trigger. It will not be knowledge and skill with advanced weaponry that determines the outcome of this fight. No, this fight will depend on willpower, resolve, and MultiReal—not to mention the black code that Horvil, Quell, and Frederic put together.

Natch crouches down, dartgun in his hand, finger primed on the trigger, and edges into the room. The doors shut behind him.

• • •

"Gone," said Petrucio.

"Gone?" Jara gaped at the programmer as if he had told her the Kordez Thassel Complex had just been overrun by gnomes. "What do you mean, gone? Where did the feed go?" She stood up and walked over to the viewscreen that had been showing images from the twenty-four cameras embedded in Natch's battle suit. Now it showed nothing but dull, undifferentiated gray, not so different from the view in the supply closet.

You sense that too, Jara? said Jorge Monck.

The fiefcorp master flipped one of the viewscreens to the Council operative's point of view and saw nothing but sparsely populated hallway. *Yeah. Everything okay down there?*

As far as I know. Natch just followed the target into that room behind the double doors.

Jara stretched her mind out to the war room's systems, trying to ascertain what had happened to the cameras. In her peripheral vision, she could see Merri and Benyamin fiddling with holographic displays in an attempt to do the same thing.

"I'll go find Larakolia," said Robby, hopping up and dashing out into the hallway.

The Defense and Wellness Council tactician was only down the hall. Less than twenty seconds later, she was standing in the center of the war room giving a taciturn frown to the table. "EMP," she muttered.

"EMP?" said Robby Robby. "What's that?"

"Electromagnetic pulse," said Petrucio from his seat across from Jara. "Ancient technology, almost as old as radar. Disables electronics."

"Ordinarily it's not something you worry about on the battlefield," said Larakolia, arms folded across her chest, disappointed at having failed to anticipate something. "The cameras you use out there are attached directly to the optic nerve and shielded from electromagnetic force. But when you're using cameras embedded in the mesh of a powered suit . . ."

Benyamin slapped his forehead, hard. "Brone knew we were coming, didn't he?"

The room fell silent, which was an answer in and of itself.

● ● ●

Natch wades through a copse of trees until he finds a clearing at the top of a hill. The surrounding foliage serves as both curtain and boundary. There is a large tree stump poking incongruously from the center of the clearing like a splinter in the Earth. The smell of burning camphor lingers in the air.

He knows this place. In the flesh, he only spent a few scant moments here, and they were panicked moments that attenuated the senses and distorted mental geography. But of all the places Natch has been in his lifetime, this may be the one he can never forget.

"You're not looking in the right direction," says a voice, unruffled, unhurried.

Brone parts the curtain of greenery with his artificial hand and steps into the clearing. He's wearing the same black robe with stylized red trim that Natch has seen on the other Thasselians. Like, but not identical to, the robes they wore when they ambushed him in Shenandoah. Brone's hands are folded behind his back, and he's carrying no weapon that Natch can see.

"It was over there," says the bodhisattva, nodding towards the center of the clearing. "The bear batted me over that stump with one of his paws—he hit me right *here*." Brone raises his good hand and makes a gesture, indicating the scar that still flares angrily across his face, bisecting the prosthetic eye. "I fell back and raised one arm to keep the bear off my face, and he *twisted* it. All the way around. I can't explain exactly how it happened. One minute I had an arm, the next minute . . ." He stares dolefully at the ground, as if the severed limb might be lying there in the SeeNaRee. "But you remember all that, don't you, Natch? Because you were standing right there." Brone points towards one of half a dozen maples lining the far side of the clearing. "I looked over and caught your eye, do you remember? And what did you do? You just *stared* at me and watched."

The screams, the terror, the pain assault Natch's mind. For once, he wishes that MultiReal-D had taken one of his memories away. "I'll never understand you," he says, shaking his head. "You knew I was coming. You've been *waiting* for me. So why didn't you have a dartgun ready? Why didn't you just kill me when I walked in the room?"

Brone seems to find the question mildly amusing. "I've *had* the opportunity to kill you, Natch. Many times. And I'm not talking about our little confrontation in Old Chicago. I followed you around Shenandoah for months, remember? I knew exactly where to find you and exactly where to attack you. I could very well have made the black code in those darts lethal."

"Well? Why didn't you?"

"Certainly you know the reason. I *needed* you on my side. I needed your help in finishing the MultiReal programming. I foolishly thought I could persuade you to join my Revolution of Selfishness. I thought you would gladly help me rid the world of the Defense and Wellness Council's tyranny." With hands clasped behind his back, Brone begins a leisurely pace clockwise around the tree stump. Natch, wary, circles around it too, keeping the stump between them. "I guess I underestimated Magan Kai Lee's powers of persuasion. After all the Council did to you, you'd risk putting the ultimate weapon in their hands?" Natch starts to speak, but Brone cuts him off with a dismissive snort. "No, stop, Natch—I already know what you're going to say. *Magan isn't the tyrant you think he is. He's not like Borda.* Let me guess. . . . He told you that he intends to keep MultiReal safe and out of the hands of his armies. He said he would work with you on a plan to get the program out on the open market. A slow plan that'll take twenty years, I'll wager. Do you really believe him?"

Natch continues circling around the tree stump, dartgun raised, finger on the trigger. He says nothing.

"Didn't you *listen* to the speech that Serr Vigal gave to the Prime Committee?" says Brone, irked at his enemy's silence. "In the end, it doesn't *matter* whether you believe Magan or not. It doesn't matter whether he's being sincere. *Power has intense gravity*, that's what Lucco

Primo said. Concentrate the power of MultiReal in the hands of the few, and you will get corruption. That's true whether we're talking about Len Borda, Magan Kai Lee, or Khann Frejohr—or you and I, for that matter.

"Even if the lieutenant executive manages to crush Borda's armies, you know that he won't keep his promises. As soon as Borda has shuffled off to the Prepared and the central government has made peace with the unconnectibles, things are going to look different. High Executive Lee's going to wonder why he made an agreement with a crooked businessman like you in the first place. The years will pass, and MultiReal will never make it into the open market. You'll see.

"And even if Magan Kai Lee remains true to his word to the end of his days . . . do you trust his subordinates? Do you trust Rey Gonerev? Do you trust that shifty chief engineer of his? I'm not sure they'll wait for Magan to die. What happens when one of them gets a notion to put a dart in the back of the high executive's head? What happens when one of them decides to revive the glory days of the Council?

"I'm sorry, Natch. I know how that story ends. We've only got one chance to make this right. MultiReal needs to be bequeathed to the entire world. Immediately. Irreversibly. It may be painful, but it needs to be done."

They stand and glare at one another at the top of the hill. Natch rubs his finger up and down the trigger of his weapon; Brone flexes his own fingers like a prestidigitator preparing to cast an exceedingly complicated spell.

"You never answered my question," says Natch. "You knew I was coming. Why didn't you have a trap prepared for me?"

Brone laughs quietly, humorlessly. "You know the answer to that, Natch. I'll get no satisfaction out of shooting you in the back. I've been waiting for this opportunity since the Shortest Initiation. To confront you, face-to-face. To pit my will against yours." He shakes his head. "I already know how this is going to end. I fight for the freedom of humanity. I fight for the noblest cause there is. Who do *you* fight for?"

Natch thinks for a moment. "Rodrigo," he says.

• • •

It begins.

Natch grips the dartgun and takes aim at his old enemy, the bodhisattva of Creed Thassel. He thumbs the selector on the side of the pommel just as Jorge Monck instructed him to do and swivels the barrel slightly so it aims directly at Brone's torso. *Click.* The trigger is pulled, the dart is fired. Brone's eyes widen slightly as the dart hits home. He clutches feebly at his chest and slumps to the floor.

Flash.

Brone has never been trained in the martial arts as far as Natch knows. And yet as he pirouettes into the air with arms and legs whirling, his movements are precise and calculated. Natch makes a feeble effort at warding off the confluence of limbs, but he's unable. A foot comes rocketing towards Natch's face, meets the bridge of his nose, crunches bone. There's the briefest flare of agony as shards of bone slice into Natch's brain. Then blackness.

Flash.

Natch looks at the blade folded inside his utility belt. A thought is all it takes to transfer the poisoned OCHREs on the tips of his black code darts into the blade's receptors and onto its serrated edge. The look on Brone's face is pure surprise as Natch draws the knife and slashes it across the bodhisattva's chest. A line of crimson appears on his robe as he collapses to the ground, clawing at the wound in agony.

Flash.

Natch fires the dartgun, but Brone ducks and the dart misses, spearing his left shoulder by centimeters. He tucks and rolls athletically under the next two darts and springs to his feet right in front of

Natch. Brone uses his artificial hand to retract the cover of Natch's utility belt, then grabs the miniature flamethrower. There's barely enough time for Natch to flinch as the bodhisattva holds the flamethrower at eye level and pulls the trigger. A sudden scorching heat, then void.

Flash.

Brone is expecting Natch to fire his weapon, but he leaps forward and catches his enemy in a chokehold instead, taking the bodhisattva by surprise. Brone's legs go kicking in the air as Natch squeezes his windpipe. For a good minute and a half, there is no sound in the room but the hoarse accordion wheeze of lungs struggling for oxygen. Finally, Brone falls facefirst onto the floor. Natch calmly reaches down, grabs the dartgun, and fires a dart into the chest of his unconscious enemy.

Flash.

Flash.

Flash.

Brone and Natch stand in the clearing and stare at one another. No one moves.

Flash.

Flash.

Flash.

Natch can see the possibilities, numerous as leaves, grains of rice, stars. They extend to the ends of the universe in every direction. *Every* direction: not just north, south, east, and west, but all degrees on the circle, all points on the sphere. Branching out from each point is *another* set of possibilities, just as infinite, and then another, and then another. For the briefest instance here in the purgatory of mental stopgap, the possibilities are the universe. There is nothing but Everything, every conceivable response and nonresponse, the sum total of human imagination laid out on virtual latticework.

And Brone is traversing that latticework, stopping at nodes with strange and improbable realities in the hopes that their peculiarity might cause Natch to make a mistake.

Brone bursts into song.

Brone howls like a monkey and begins scaling a tree.

Brone falls onto the ground and writhes like a seizure victim.

Brone grabs Natch's blade and begins carving bloody lines in his own palms.

Brone kneels down and begins gnawing on the tree stump.

Flash.

Natch can feel the MultiReal exhaustion beginning to take hold of him. It takes all of his willpower to resist the temptation to lie down, to stop fighting. His limbs are starting to quiver and his knees are knocking. Sweat is pouring down his forehead, and his OCHREs are thrumming crazily to keep his heart from accelerating out of control. He can't stop now. He *can't.*

Flash.

The bodhisattva doesn't see a kick or a punch or a feint in the next node of the MultiReal latticework. Instead he sees the future of the human race avalanching down as a consequence of his victory over Natch. Suddenly he is no longer in a SeeNaRee clearing in the Kordez Thassel Complex; he's standing in a mass of ruins the severity of which dwarfs those of Old Chicago. Uprooted buildings. Smoldering husks of hoverbirds and tube trains lying atop twisted skeletons that once propped up human beings. Survivors wander and shuffle through the wreckage; the diss for a new age. But it is not a future of complete despair, for around them the survivors can see traces of the Lunar tycoons, secure in hermetically sealed compounds and raptured into a universe of eternal, limitless possibilities. A universe where cause and effect are untangled and reentwined willy-nilly for the delectation of the few, a universe where the suffering of the many is drowned out and overwhelmed by the joy of the economically privileged.

Flash.

Natch stands and watches as figures in white robes and yellow stars strut through the streets, unafraid, dartrifles on brazen display. For who would dare assault an officer of the Defense and Wellness Council armed with the power of MultiReal? From the streets of Shenandoah to the exurbs of Beijing to the halls of Patronell, it's all the same. Docile citizens shuffling along, getting by, going through the motions of their lives from birth to death. The unpredictable vacillations of political unrest and dissent have been ground down to smooth, regulated lines. Drudges no longer struggle among themselves to dig up truth so much as they struggle to flatter the high executive, to praise his wisdom and forethought. Crime has surprisingly not gone down— it's on the rise, due to the corruption of the authorities and their disinterest in policing the petty crimes of the masses.

Flash.

You'll cause immeasurable death and destruction. It could be as devastating as the Autonomous Revolt.

The Council's estimation. You trust the words of a tyrant?

You've known me since I was a boy. I don't cave to pressure. I don't bow to tyrants. But if they offer me the truth, then I'll listen.

Do you think I want death? Do you think I want destruction? Of course I don't. I wouldn't take this path unless there was no other choice. This may be humanity's last hope for a thousand years or more.

Flash.

Flash.

Flash.

Choice cycle against choice cycle against choice cycle against choice cycle.

Hundreds, thousands.

Surely the world must be crumbling down all around them by now; surely the computational infrastructure must be buckling, near to collapse. It feels like Natch has been here for hours, for days, for weeks. He can feel his own bio/logic systems cracking under the strain.

Perhaps the Natch who lusted for number one on Primo's could have clashed wills with Brone and come out victorious. Maybe the Natch who sat in the center of his own universe and saw nothing but himself could have triumphed. But he has been through too much in the past few months. He has seen a universe outside of himself, a universe that is vast beyond imagination, and chimerical and stubborn and resurgent. One man can't shoulder the burden of all that and live. Natch has seen his own death, not once but tens of thousands of times; he has experienced it over and over and over. He has climbed from the lowest depths to the highest pinnacle and then watched himself tumble back down again.

Natch feels his grip on the MultiReal interface slipping. He feels his will weakening. He can't compete against Brone's narrow monomania. Brone senses impending victory and redoubles his efforts.

Flash.

Flash.

Flash.

Brone leaps forward with his prosthetic arm pulled back for the killing blow. Natch tries to muster the energy to resist this one last time, fails. A blade extends from the palm of the bodhisattva's mechanical hand. The entrepreneur stares as the knife stabs through the air to spear his forehead. Half a second until death—

Flash.

MultiReal-D. Natch silently thanks Papizon for finding him a bio/logic workbench back in Manila. He thanks Petrucio Patel for the instructions to turn the code back on.

The bodhisattva and the entrepreneur are standing in the clearing. Brone leaps forward, extends knife, goes for the kill.

Flash.

Clearing. Leap, knife, kill.

Flash.

Over and over and over.

Until—
The Null Current.
The nothingness at the center of the universe.
No way forward.
Flash.

• • •

The SeeNaRee vanishes, leaving Natch standing on a stage next to a purple curtain. The curtain parts, and Natch catches a brief glimpse of faces watching. There's a collective gasp as Natch lets his dartgun go clattering to the floor.

Brone reaches very calmly into the right-hand pocket of his black robe and withdraws a syringe. He's not going for the kill this time; Multi-Real-D stays silent. Natch watches helplessly as the bodhisattva bridges the few steps between them. Then he stabs the syringe into the entrepreneur's arm with a slow and deliberate motion. Brone presses down on the plunger and sends Natch clawing, shrieking into nothingness.

(((36)))

Magan Kai Lee sat in the office at the base of DWCR's observation tower—*his* office, his observation tower now—and anxiously consulted the time. Borda's invading force at the Twin Cities had laid down their arms on hearing the news of the high executive's surrender. Natch's mission remained the only loose end to tie up.

"There are surreptitious targets which must be ascertained," said Magan. *Natch must have had enough time to take Brone down by now.*

Jorge Monck was idling in the hallway near the room Natch had entered, pretending to hold an impromptu business meeting with three of his colleagues, also Council operatives. *Time's not really a factor in there, Lieutenant Executive,* he said. And Magan realized that he was correct. Whatever the outcome of Natch's and Brone's duel, it should have been instantaneous. Unless Brone was not actually *in* that room after all . . . in which case, shouldn't Natch have emerged and taken up the search in another location?

"I'm mystified by the increasingly cloudy skies," he told Jara. *Two more minutes, and we're going in.*

The fiefcorp master sounded supportive from the war room in Manila. *I think you're right. We can't just sit here forever.*

A hundred and twenty seconds stretched out as if time had become elastic. Monck and his operatives were casually making their way towards the double doors Natch had snaked through a good twenty minutes earlier. Magan called up the view from Monck's battle suit and was pleased to note that the Council operatives looked exactly like any other random group of fiefcorpers loitering the hallways between meetings. The sun peeked through a skylight overhead in plump, jovial defiance of the circumstances.

Go.

In the space of an instant, Monck's operatives metamorphosed from nonchalant executives and bureaucrats to hardnosed agents of the Defense and Wellness Council. Weapons came sliding out of hidden gunbelts as they lined up on either side of the double doors in standard formation. Close-range dartgun shooters low and inside, officers with crackling multi disruptors in a flanking position, sharpshooters at a distance ready for anything that flew through that opening. Two operatives covered the approaching hallways in case one of the figures in black robes decided to come investigate.

Jorge Monck gave the slightest of nods.

The doors slammed open. The Defense and Wellness Council burst through, fingers tense on triggers.

Magan could already tell something was wrong before he could even make out the scene in the room. Nobody was firing weapons, nor were they lowering them. Instead there was just a general confusion.

The room was arranged like a small theater, with a stage at one end and a dozen rows of chairs facing it. The stage could have conceivably held half a dozen people, but right now there were only two: Brone, wearing the black robe with red trim that had become his trademark; and Natch, glassy-eyed, unconscious, and propped up on a chair facing the audience.

Audience? Yes, there was an audience, and they were familiar faces. Sen Sivv Sor, John Ridglee, Mah Lo Vertiginous, V. T. Vel Osbiq, other pundits both libertarian and governmentalist. The last time Magan had fallen into this particular trap, the drudges' faces had radiated perverse glee at his predicament. Today they were somber and reflective to the last. Perhaps it was the sight of Natch, hollow and lifeless as a marionette. Or perhaps they recognized that this was no longer just sportive amusement; the fate of the world was on the table, and both Brone and the Defense and Wellness Council had anted up.

Ringing the perimeter of the room were a dozen armed Thasselians in their black robes, though they seemed to have taken no notice of the invading Council operatives. Pierre Loget was among them, beaming like an idiot.

"Perceptive interested parties?" muttered Jorge Monck. *Shoot him?*

Magan felt an animal urge from some primal sector of consciousness telling him to shoot first and deal with consequences later. But then he saw the arrogant, once-handsome stare of the bodhisattva of Creed Thassel, and Magan knew that Natch had been correct. Brone had already planned for that contingency. *Hold off*, he replied.

Brone cleared his throat, and for the first time Magan noticed that he was propping himself up with some kind of pipe that might have been salvaged from the wreckage of Chicago. The bodhisattva looked frail, exhausted, just footsteps away from death. And yet on his ruined, prematurely wrinkled face there sat a macabre smile of satisfaction. Brone hobbled downstage, stabbing the pipe onto the stage with each step—*clank! clank!*—only pulling himself up to meet it with great effort.

The bodhisattva stopped at the foot of the stage and swept a hand at the audience of drudges. "What do you think?" he said. His voice gargled as through blood, but somehow still managed to resonate with cruel pride. "I got the idea from our friend over here. Quite a showman, that one." He hitched his prosthetic thumb over his shoulder to indicate Natch. Then he addressed Monck, whom he had ascertained to be the group's leader. "So is it Magan Kai Lee who you're reporting to or Len Borda?"

Tell him, said the lieutenant executive.

"Lee," replied Monck, his voice emotionless, his gun still centered on Brone's forehead.

"Ah, I underestimated you once again, Lieutenant Executive Lee," said Brone, offering a slight and yet entirely serious bow. "I figured that the old bastard would get the best of you. But despite what I told Merri and Petrucio, I'm glad to see that I was wrong on that score."

Monck was having none of the bodhisattva's mocking dignity. "Tell me why we shouldn't shoot you right now."

Brone nodded. "A reasonable question. There are two answers. First, because we possess MultiReal, and *you* do not. You don't have the power. The second reason, as I'm sure Magan has guessed by now, is that Possibilities 2.0 is rigged to automatically launch on the Data Sea on the instant of my death.

"So if I were you, Lieutenant Executive—or is that *High* Executive now?—I would hear me out for just a few more minutes."

"Is Natch dead?" asked Monck.

Brone turned and gave a pitying look at the entrepreneur. "Dead? No, he's perfectly fine in there. And he'll be perfectly fine until I've launched Possibilities 2.0 on the Data Sea and I release him. I wouldn't have Natch miss that for the world."

Tense silence. Sixty seconds passed, during which Monck and his team silently took up positions around the room, keeping their dart-guns trained on the bodhisattva.

"I know that Natch has depicted me as some kind of monster," continued Brone. "He's got you thinking that I'm looking to slaughter millions of people for my own amusement. Not true.

"My Revolution of Selfishness is about providing options, not taking them away. And so even though I have the power to release Possibilities 2.0 to the world right now, with no hesitations . . . I stand here and hesitate. I don't presume to choose for you. Instead I have assembled here a cross section of the world's most renowned drudges from across the political spectrum. Governmentalist, libertarian, connectible, unconnectible, rich, poor. I think you will agree that this is not a stacked deck."

The bodhisattva turned to the pundits and addressed them directly. "I leave the decision of whether to release Possibilities 2.0 to the world in *your* more than capable hands. You've heard the arguments in the court of public opinion over the past several months. You know the stakes; you know the options. So now you'll be the ones to decide. No more intermediaries, no more phony opinions of compromised elected officials standing in the way. No more bribes from the rich or excuses from the well connected. There is just you, the drudges, whom I have selected to stand for the collective will of the human race.

"Do you want the power of Possibilities? Or do you want the rigid rules and restrictions of the Defense and Wellness Council? Do you want the ultimate freedom and the ultimate empowerment that Margaret Surina promised you? Or do you want a shackled world of two dimensions, the faux freedom of our ancestors?

"The fate of the world is in your hands."

6

THE GUARDIAN
AND THE KEEPER

(((37)))

Smaller than air, they dance between the molecules of oxygen that drape the Earth; they tango with the granules of salt that permeate the sea; they gambol on the caterpillar's back and the butterfly's wings.

You will swallow dozens of them every day without noticing or complaining. Yawn, sniff, gulp, lick your lips—odds are you will imbibe a few of them. And why should they complain? As far as they're concerned, tissue is tissue and matter is matter. Some will slowly worm their way through layers of your blood and fiber until they are excreted from pores and sweat glands; free at last, they will eventually find their way back into the machinery of the world's weather system. Others will be press-ganged into service by the OCHREs in your body and converted into their component amino acids. Still others will huddle in the lining of your intestines until you walk through the gates of the Prepared, then hitch a ride with you into the grave and soak into the bedrock of the Earth for a million years—quiet, dormant, waiting. The spare change of the universe.

They are the level I geosynchrons, and they have one function: to sit at the threshold of the nothing and wait for the world to speak.

The world speaks.

The thing happens.

Stasis shatters and change charges into being and there is no reason *why* except because this is the way the universe has been constructed.

The duty of the level I geosynchrons is merely to listen and report the raw data of the world. Changes in ionization, movements of sub-atomic particles, fluctuations of wave and cosmic force—all the level I geosynchrons can do is observe and flip the rotation of a qubit, thereby transcribing these events in the language of mathematics. Exactly what it is they are recording is of no import to them. Electrons spin and whirl and shift orbit; information is recorded; the purpose of the level I geosynchrons is fulfilled.

It's not up to the level II geosynchrons to comprehend this data either, for they are the worker bees of the weather system. Their job is to uncomplainingly carry out the orders of their superiors higher up in the chain, whether those orders are to gather information or to impede the velocity of the wind, to bump the atmospheric temperature of their minuscule domains up a fraction of a degree or to tamp it down. Of all the quintillions of microscopic geosynchrons in the system, it is the level IIs who are the most numerous. Ask someone to describe the word *geosynchron*, and most likely that person will describe to you the frenzied activity of the level II. Rushing to and fro, vaulting from place to place, the domain of the level II is a world of tasks accomplished, of weather directives made actual and three dimensional.

So it's up to the level III geosynchrons to take notice of the gathering atmospheric conditions in the Atlantic Ocean. They're the lords of pattern recognition, the level IIIs. They can scan through voluminous amounts of data, compare them to the hundred years of uninterrupted weather information in their memory banks, and detect emerging trends in their first picoseconds of existence. The level III geosynchrons have seen every point on the curve from tropical calm to raging inferno, and every gradation in between.

Today, as battle rages in Melbourne and Natch attempts to weave his way through the Kordez Thassel Complex unseen, the level IIIs see atmospheric pressure dropping as off a sheer cliff. They see mounting winds and increased turbulence.

They see a weather event that is truly unprecedented.

It's the ultimate outlier of weather events. It's the once-in-ten-thousand-year hurricane. It's the storm that humanity has talked about, planned for, and prayed against since History first yawned and rubbed the stardust from its eyes. The storm that every civilization must either muscle through or collapse under the weight of, like a thousand flourishing ecosystems before that perished utterly from the Earth.

The level III geosynchrons have learned how to ameliorate an uncounted number of weather events to ensure not only the continuing survival but the continuing *comfort* of the human race. Working in tandem, they have shunted aside or lessened the severity of storms, hurricanes, volcanic eruptions, tsunamis, and drastic shifts of tectonic plates. They are the reason the champion Delhi Chakras have never missed a single game in their outdoor stadium even during the heaviest of the monsoon season. They are the reason why tens of thousands of hoverbirds can lace the skies with ribbons of vapor exhaust simultaneously and barely have to factor turbulence into their flight plans. But even level III geosynchrons must occasionally consult their superiors.

If the level IIIs are the lords of pattern recognition, then the level IV geosynchrons are the sovereigns of resolution. They sit isolated in their protected data havens and chart a course through the choppy seas ahead. There has not been a lightning strike fatality in fifty years, yet even now they are analyzing the data, measuring the performance of past actions, working through the possibilities handed to them by their subordinates, teasing out ever-better weather directives. Their goals are more efficiency, less inconvenience, more predictability, and less chance of that one infinitesimal possibility slipping through the cracks and wreaking havoc. Should the Earth suffer a devastating nuclear apocalypse or asteroid strike, it is believed that the level III geosynchrons will be able to restore the planet's complete habitability within twenty years.

But the coming storm will test the level IV geosynchrons in a way they've never been tested before. Routines will be interrupted. Helper programs will be called in as reinforcements. Other projects heretofore considered crucial will be shoved aside in an all-out effort to deal with this, the storm of storms, the eventuality of eventualities.

What to do?

The level IV geosynchrons bombard the statistical models with all manner of possible interventions in search of a way out. An avoidance strategy. But it quickly becomes apparent that there can be no avoiding this storm. There can be no delaying it or bartering with it. The test must come, and humanity must face it.

And so the level IV geosynchrons ask the questions: If the storm cannot be avoided, can it perhaps be distributed? Can the brute force of the storm be divvied up through the globe so all suffer equally? Maybe the fury of the universe can be channeled towards the strongest and most capable elements of society, the ones with the most abundant resources that will be quicker to recover. Or perhaps the weakest struts of society should be sacrificed, the deadwood of humanity, on the theory that humanity will emerge the stronger for it—assuming it emerges at all.

It is not the place of the level IV geosynchrons to make these decisions. They are not equipped to handle such far-reaching ethical quandaries. Their job is to prepare the eventualities, to calculate all the pathways to the desired endpoint. No, the decision must rest with the final arbiter: the level V geosynchron.

To say there is only one level V geosynchron would be incorrect, but neither would it be accurate to speak of many level V geosynchrons. There are many, and there is only one. And it is with these machines that the Makers have laid out the priorities of the human race.

There is a spark in the nothingness at the center of the universe. It has come from nothingness and will eventually return to nothingness. Just as the world has given birth to this spark and encouraged it to grow, the world is also constantly working to snuff out that spark, to bring back stasis and equilibrium to the void, to bring the nothingness back to nothingness.

The level V geosynchron has a single priority above all others: keep that spark burning as long and as brightly as possible.

And the only way that can be achieved is through balance.

The geosynchrons have the numbers at their virtual fingertips. They can see the eventualities, the possibilities, the probabilities. They can measure the sheer monstrous immensity of that void and the ridiculous insignificance of the spark that continues to burn in its midst. The geosynchrons know that in ninety-nine of a hundred possible universes, that spark will be overwhelmed, defeated, crushed, forgotten. If not this storm, then the next one.

The odds for survival are infinitesimal, a sliver of a sliver of hope. But haven't they always been?

(((38)))

Margaret Surina is rejuvenated.

She hovers wraithlike in the thin membrane between existence and nothingness. Skin the olive tinge of the Indian subcontinent, robe a billowing tent of blue and green, fingers long and precise as praying mantises. Hair tar black but streaked with white, manifestation of the paradox behind those sapphire eyes.

That Natch can see her at all is miracle enough. In this place he has no eyes, no face, no corporeal presence whatsoever. It is a cocoon of pure mind, where there are no points on the compass and where even Time loops upon itself and disappears in a dizzying spiral of infinite improbability. Here in this place, Margaret is merely a perception of a perception, like an awareness or a manufactured memory.

Towards Perfection, Natch, the bodhisattva begins in a voice that is not audible. A voice that is, in many respects, Natch's own.

If you are listening to these words, then I can safely assume that you have an understanding now of what that phrase really means. It was not idly or randomly chosen. The man who coined that phrase believed in Perfection. He believed it was attainable by human beings, and he believed it was the destiny of the human spirit to strive for that summit.

Onwards and upwards. That was the dream of Sheldon Surina, my ancestor and the father of bio/logics. Towards Perfection, no matter what the cost. But it was not Sheldon Surina's fate to pay that cost, any more than it was Marcus Surina's—any more than it is mine.

Now that fate has fallen to you and you alone, Natch. You are the geosynchron of the human race.

If you are listening to these words, then we have failed Sheldon Surina's acid test—you, me, perhaps everyone from here to Furtoid. If you are listening to this recording implanted in your OCHREs, then you have reached the point of no return. Either you have concluded that the human race cannot hike the steep path to Perfection that Sheldon staked out for us—or it has become abundantly clear that Sheldon's path will only lead to tyranny and madness. You have become convinced that there is no hope.

Should that come to pass and should you be listening to these words, Natch, then you and you alone will have the power to rid the human race of Sheldon Surina's monomania. You alone will have the option to stake out a new path.

· · ·

These are words of despair, but I speak them from a very peculiar place.

Right now, I am standing at the top of the Revelation Spire, tallest structure in the world, and I am staring at all the preparations below for the imminent unveiling of MultiReal to the world. Tomorrow will be the four hundredth birthday of my ancestor Sheldon, and there are celebrations happening all over Andra Pradesh. Creed Surina is indulging in a very rare occurrence of jubilation—I can see the devotees in the courtyard right now shooting fireworks into the sky.

I feel hope stirring within me, Natch. Hope that this unveiling of Multi-Real will go off as planned, hope that the soldiers of Len Borda will not march on the compound, hope that the trust I have laid on you has not been misplaced.

And yet, if you are listening to these words, then that hope has failed and I am surely dead.

As I said, a very peculiar place.

How will I die? It is not an easy or a comfortable thing to contemplate one's own death. But if I must swim in the Null Current so soon, it will likely be because of a Council black code dart in my back. Or maybe a shuttle explosion, like the one that took the life of my father. The authorities will probably present my death to the public as an "unfortunate accident."

But even with the most powerful prognostication engine in the history of the world, one cannot see all possibilities. I'm sure you've discovered that by now, Natch. I imagine you listening to these words in your apartment, awaiting the troops of the Defense and Wellness Council. You have exhausted all resources, you have explored all avenues, and now it is simply a question of hours before Borda arrives at your doorstep and demands MultiReal for his own use. Or perhaps you maintained hope even past that point. And now you have been thrown into one of Borda's orbital prisons where you await the torturer's bite, and you know the fight is truly over. . . .

Enough. Do you see how even in my hopeful moments I drift off into melancholy? Do you see why my lover constantly threatens to leave me?

She lets out a quiet and morbid laugh.

Let me get back to the subject at hand, Margaret continues. *Sheldon Surina believed that the only path to Perfection is continual progress, without exceptions, without limits. He would say that the world* wanted *bio/logics and the universal law of physics and teleportation to come into existence, just as it* wants *MultiReal today. In his eyes, there is nothing that can be done to alter this—and if humanity must suffer through a thousand years of Defense and Wellness Council tyranny because of it, well, then that too is necessary. Even if our hubris should bring us to another Autonomous Revolt, Sheldon Surina would insist we stick to the path of progress. He would insist we pass Multi-Real out far and wide without fear of consequences.*

You may be surprised to hear it, but Sheldon Surina did not despise the Autonomous Revolt. He did not hate or fear the Autonomous Minds of Tobi Jae Witt. He saw what they did as a much-needed cleansing and strengthening of the species.

Not a nice man, Sheldon Surina. We tend to forget that.

Nonetheless, my ancestor charted a course for us towards Perfection three hundred and fifty years ago. Freedom from the tyranny of Biology. Freedom from the tyranny of Nature. Freedom from the tyranny of Distance. Freedom from the tyranny of Time. And finally, freedom from the tyranny of Cause and Effect. He taught his children and his successors undeviating adherence to this course, as did Prengal, as did Marcus. Though I did not know it at the time, this is what I was taught and raised to believe from the day I was born.

But I have decided not to pass these values on to the next generation. Why?

I think it is for the same reason that I slip into morbidity when everyone around me engages in celebration. The same reason that I make this recording and try to convince myself it will never be heard.

I stopped believing in the dream of the Surinas, Natch. And it was an Islander who showed me why.

• • •

Margaret pauses. It is difficult for Natch to tell for certain, but he senses that there are tears gathering in her eyes. She abruptly shakes her head, dispelling the mistiness, and shifts topics.

My pessimism notwithstanding, Sheldon Surina's dream has nearly come to fruition. We have only to overcome the tyranny of Time and the tyranny of Cause and Effect.

And this puts me in a position unique among all the inventors in the history of the world. The nascent technology left to me by my father was a program to create alternate realities, a program that is designed by its very nature to warp the law of cause and effect. So with this law irretrievably bent, with the tyrant overthrown—who is to say that the very existence of this technology *can't lie in one of those fungible realities?*

If MultiReal can free us from cause and effect, certainly MultiReal itself is not bound by those same chains.

My doubts about Sheldon's path to Perfection are nothing new; they have been in the making for decades. But as my doubts grew, so too did my confidence that the very nature of this technology afforded me a unique solution. A way to take that leap into the unknown while at the same time retaining the option of returning to the precipice. I decided to create a failsafe for the MultiReal program. A way back.

Certainly you have discovered that just as there is no copying the Multi-Real databases, there is no destroying them either. Even with all of the secret archives of the Surina family at my disposal, I'm unclear how my father managed this eldritch feat. Perhaps the complete destruction of the solar system could do the trick, but there is no craft currently known to humanity that can accomplish it. If you were to try to destroy the original code for teleportation, you would discover the same thing.

But why should I seek to destroy when I can simply isolate?

The Data Sea, with its quintillions and quintillions of petabytes, is too immense for anyone to simply stumble upon information that has not been properly mapped and cataloged. Cutting off all known routes to a set of databases is the functional equivalent of erasure. No matter how large the program, it would be like trying to find one particular shell in the vastness of all the world's oceans. And so I decided that this would be the mechanism of the MultiReal failsafe.

You were implanted with specialized OCHREs during our dinner here in Andra Pradesh the other week. These OCHREs grant you the ability to locate the MultiReal databases no matter where they reside. Now that I am confident you are the right steward for the MultiReal program, I will command these OCHREs to attach themselves to your bio/logic systems such that they cannot be removed. No amount of torture or coercion by the Council can transfer or remove this indelible access.

You can see the dilemma this causes, however. As long as these OCHREs remain operational, MultiReal will be accessible. And so, if you choose to activate the failsafe I have created, Natch, the specialized OCHREs which give you access to the program must be destroyed.

You would not survive such a destruction.

Yet is cutting off access to the program sufficient? Given all the parties aware of MultiReal's existence even today, before it has been unveiled to the world, it is inevitable that someone will figure out how to reverse-engineer the program. The Patels have probably already given the Council enough information to reconstitute the program within a generation.

And so the failsafe I have designed will not only cut off access to Multi-Real on the Data Sea; it will destroy the very memory of the program itself throughout human space. You are aware that the program accesses neural memory through undocumented back channels in the bio/logic system. And it is through these back channels that the failsafe will eradicate all knowledge of the program.

MultiReal will not only effectively cease to exist, but it will never have been.

· · ·

After all this exposition, I still have not answered the question that undoubtedly you have been asking yourself for the past fifteen minutes: why you?

I have cousins who share the same bloodline as I do, if not quite in the same undiluted quantities. I have a son, though the world does not know it. Yet I choose to give sole responsibility for the program to you instead, in effect robbing my son of his birthright.

Why? It's simple, Natch. I have watched you ever since your misfortunes with the Shortest Initiation. Though you were unaware, I watched you pick yourself up from defeat at the hands of the ROD coders. I watched you shoulder your way through your competitors on Primo's. I saw through the ruse that helped you gain number one on the Primo's bio/logic investment guide.

Yours is a single-minded intensity of purpose that the world has rarely seen. You will not be beaten down, you will not surrender. Not to High Executive Borda, not to Lieutenant Executive Magan Kai Lee, not to anyone. Part of me admires this about you; you are the son Marcus Surina would have loved to have had. In many ways, you are the very embodiment of the qualities Sheldon Surina sought to accentuate in the human race: continuous struggle, continuous improvement, continuous lust for Perfection, regardless of costs or consequences.

And so I have come to this conclusion. If you, the paragon of all that Sheldon Surina stood for, believe that the time has come to wipe MultiReal off the face of the Earth, then the time has come. If you, the epitome of selfishness, are willing to sacrifice your own life to do so, then the time has come.

Undoubtedly you will feel anger at being put in this position of terrible responsibility. Believe me, I understand, since I myself have felt the same way many times.

The Surinas have played their part on the world stage. We have sacrificed much over the centuries—too much—and I have finally decided that I will heed my lover's advice. I do not wish the life of a Surina for my son. I do not wish for him to have to carry the burden that Sheldon Surina laid on us generations ago. I intend to return to the life that Sheldon discarded. I intend to finally make my lover my bonded companion, and for us to live the family life he has always craved.

Now the time has come for me to leave you and make the final preparations for tomorrow's unveiling of MultiReal to the world. It is my fervent hope that this recording will never be heard, that it will stay dormant in your neural systems until you find your way into the compounds of the Prepared. Unlistened to, unheeded. For now, I put the responsibility for this technology wholly into your hands, like my father did to me.

You are the guardian of MultiReal. You are its keeper.

You can choose to eradicate MultiReal at the cost of your own life. Or you can choose to set it loose and unchain humanity from the bonds of cause and effect, forever.

Do what you think is right.

(((39)))

"Testing, testing, testing. Blah blah blah."

The unexpected sound of Horvil's voice causes Natch to suddenly well up in tears. He can't say exactly how long he's lain here in the blackness with his senses caught in eternal loopback, mulling over the preposterous, inexplicable, confounding words of Margaret Surina. Hours? Days? Weeks? Long enough for Natch to feel the cracks in his sanity deepen and spread. Long enough for him to know that the freedom from Time that Margaret espoused is not something to ask for lightly.

"Natch. Hey . . . can you hear me?"

He can't quite believe the voice is real, but it echoes in his skull with the clarity and immediacy of a ConfidentialWhisper. Not a mental holograph, not an appendage to his own thought processes, but an independent outside presence. A human intelligence.

Natch stretches out with his own mind and discovers he can answer. He makes a valiant and not-entirely-successful effort to mask the desperation in his voice. "Horvil? Yes. Yes. I'm here. I can hear you."

"Shit, I didn't think this was going to work." Horvil sounds quite pleased with himself. It occurs to Natch that the engineer has probably been at this for some time. He starts to speak again, then pauses. "Brone's not in there with you, is he?"

"No."

"Listen, I hate to be so paranoid . . . but I gotta confirm that this is really you. Tell me something nobody else would know. Tell me . . . tell me one of the poems Captain Bolbund sent to you when he beat you in the ROD coding business."

Natch feels an instant of panic. Given his cratered memory, what if Horvil has picked an incident that's been swallowed by the void? It takes him a moment, but luckily the memory is still accessible and intact. Natch takes a breath—or tries to, at any rate—and recites:

> You gave it your all
> I hope you had fun
> 'Cause you got your ass kicked
> By CAPTAIN BOLBUND.

"All right," says Horvil, laughing. "Guess it really *is* you. Man, I had forgotten what a crappy poet that guy was. But we can't get too cocky. I have no idea how long we're gonna be able to keep this channel open."

"What channel? What's going on?"

"Quell figured out how to break into Brone's black code. All I have to say is that Brone's *good*—but Quell's better. He used that Islander finger-weaving programming technique and had us pump a ton of code through your battle suit. Only took him a few minutes to figure out how to dig this back tunnel. Kind of like a 'Whisper, I guess. We should be able to talk with you one at a time, at least until Brone gets suspicious."

Now that he's established communication with the outside world, Natch isn't quite sure what to say, what to ask. After Margaret's little speech, it feels like the whole universe is an unknown variable. He wants to ask . . . everything. "Where am I?" he begins.

"You're still at the Kordez Thassel Complex. Propped up on a chair in front of all those weaselly drudges while Brone holds his little debate."

"Wait, you can *see* me? Are you in the audience?"

"No, no, no. I'm still back in Manila with Jara and everyone else. I'm watching you on the Data Sea. Brone's been broadcasting the whole thing since the Council tried to storm the place. There's supposedly almost two billion people watching. I have to say—if this whole Revolution of Selfishness idiocy doesn't work out, Brone's got a future in the dramas. This is pretty riveting stuff."

It makes a perverse kind of sense to Natch, like the universe playing an elaborate practical joke. He's spent the past several months lurking in the shadows, avoiding the public eye at all costs. And now he has an audience of billions, and they're all completely invisible. Natch knows this is simply a neural trick; the only thing separating him from the rest of the world is Brone's bio/logic loopback. Yet already he's struggling to remember what it felt like on the other side, interacting with people using his five senses. It all seems so alien now.

Still, he must remember the reason he came here to the Thassel Complex in the first place. Brone. His mission. "So how long do we have before Brone launches Possibilities 2.0?" he asks Horvil.

"Well, out *there* we probably only have an hour or so. But in *here*, we've got all the time we need."

"What do you mean?"

"This is virtual conversation, mind to mind. It's like the MultiReal choice cycles—happening much faster than real time. Virtual time, in fact. It might feel like hours in here, but it'll all be instantaneous from the outside. Petrucio explained the whole thing to me."

"What happened with Borda? The attack on Melbourne?"

The engineer seems to have almost forgotten about the larger context too. "Oh! Yeah, General Cheronna's plan, it worked great. The battle was over almost as soon as it began. Len Borda has officially given his resignation to the Prime Committee, but they're sitting on the news until we've got MultiReal back under our control." He sighs. "Which means I should get back to work. We've got to get you the fuck *out* of there."

"Don't!" Natch can suddenly feel the weight of Margaret Surina's words pressing down on his shoulders. *You are the guardian of Multi-Real. You are its keeper. Do what you think is right.* Once Horvil leaves, who's to say how long he will have to wait here in the darkness for another voice, another presence? "Can you—can you get Vigal for me?"

"I think he went with Merri to the cafeteria for a—"

"Please, hurry. Get him. I—I need to talk to him. I don't want to be alone anymore."

• • •

Serr Vigal falls into a long and uncomfortable silence when he hears what Natch has to say about Margaret Surina, the path to Perfection, and the failsafe built into MultiReal. Yet somehow a lifetime of experience with Vigal's conversational style tells Natch that the neural programmer has not closed the channel of communication.

After all the years of Natch playing the skeptic while Vigal tries to broaden his horizons, suddenly the entrepreneur finds their roles reversed. "Are you sure Margaret wasn't being . . . metaphoric?" asks the neural programmer, his voice troubled. "Did she really believe she could wipe out sixty billion people's memories?"

"Why not?"

"If she had tried to pull this off a few hours after her speech in Andra Pradesh, well, maybe. . . . But so much has happened since then. The drudges have written literally millions of words about MultiReal in the past few months. L-PRACGs have cast votes on it, money has changed hands. How can all that be reversed?"

"It's just a question of scale, Vigal. You know as well as I do that historical records can be altered. Vault transactions can flow backwards. Posts on the Data Sea can be erased."

"Memories too?" says Vigal. "The memories of billions of people?"

"If this really has been a multigenerational plan on the part of the Surinas . . . then I don't see why not. Sheldon Surina *invented* bio/logics. The underpinnings of the whole system, the Data Sea, MindSpace—he had a hand in all of it. We already know that he put computational hooks into the system that only the Surinas knew about. How else could Margaret have created that back door to Multi-Real that skips right over the standard Data Sea access controls? How else can MultiReal tap into other people's systems without their permission? If he could do all that, why couldn't Margaret take advantage of those same undocumented hooks for her failsafe?"

Vigal's hum of rumination comes across the channel. Clearly he's beginning to enjoy the Socratic nature of their dialogue in spite of the situation. "I suppose that's not what's bothering me. Even allowing that such a secret back door exists . . . dealing with memories is a complicated process, Natch. You know full well that the brain doesn't have a binary storage system; memories aren't arranged in discrete blocks of ones and zeros. You couldn't just search the brain for the term *Multi-Real*—and even if that were possible, you couldn't press a button and cleanly erase those memories."

"MultiReal erases thousands of memories every time you run it. That's why you don't remember all those potential alternate realities."

"Yes, but those are short-term memories, Natch. The brain stores them differently than long-term memories."

"The Patels' MultiReal-D program can erase long-term memories. I've seen it."

"And you yourself have said it was a deeply flawed process. Frederic and Petrucio's MultiReal-D seems to have erased far more than they intended."

"The Patels put that code together in months. Margaret Surina had *decades* to work on her failsafe—maybe even generations." Natch feels like he needs to wipe sweat off his brow, an odd inclination given that he has no sweat glands or forehead in this place. It's been a long time since he's had one of these intense dialogues with Vigal, and he's forgotten how frustrating they can be.

The neural programmer is obviously not convinced. "I still don't see how something like this would work."

Natch starts to sketch out in his head the method he would use to construct something of this nature. If you started out with all the assumptions Margaret started out with, it wouldn't be as difficult as it sounded.

The bodhisattva would have had to start executing the failsafe months ahead of time; she would have had to use Sheldon Surina's undocumented programming hooks to plant code that would parse the user's thoughts. It was a big leap to believe that one piece of code could identify thoughts about MultiReal . . . but grant Margaret that for the sake of argument. Say Margaret planted her code shortly before her big speech in Andra Pradesh. As soon as she spoke the trigger word, OCHREs around the globe would begin tracking memories. Of course, that would take an unprecedented amount of memory, space, and processing power. . . .

"For process' preservation," Natch whimpers. He would bury his face in his hands if he had either at his disposal. "Of course."

Vigal is still a few steps behind him. "What's wrong?"

"The infoquakes. Margaret's failsafe caused the infoquakes."

Silence.

"Think about it," continues the entrepreneur wearily. "When did the first infoquake happen? Right at the very instant Margaret introduced MultiReal to the world. During her speech at Andra Pradesh. Something must have gone horribly wrong when she activated the failsafe. Faulty programming, parts of her code that didn't mesh well with someone else's. *That's* what caused the massive spike in the computational system. That's what . . . what killed all those people. What's still killing them."

Vigal is pensive. "That might account for the first infoquake. What about the others?"

"Once a program like that gets in people's bio/logic systems . . . well, there's no predicting the damage it could cause. Anything could set it off. A temporary jolt in neural activity. A program that hits its weak spots. Someone with *just* the wrong combination of OCHREs thinking about MultiReal at *just* the wrong moment . . . And I'm willing to bet that every time we used MultiReal in public, that only exacerbated the problem. Remember, there was an infoquake when Petrucio tried to demonstrate MultiReal at the Tul Jabbor Complex."

"But not when the Patels demonstrated it. Not when *you* demonstrated it."

"No, there *have* been infoquakes almost constantly since the first one. Just not in any predictable pattern."

Natch remembers the haunted look on the bodhisattva's face after that initial infoquake struck. Margaret had shown up at their fiefcorp meeting. She had attempted to keep the banter light, but Natch had seen the distress clearly written in her expression the whole time. So had the others in the fiefcorp.

Margaret had known. Even back then, she had known what she had done.

• • •

Even through the impenetrable blanket of Brone's bio/logic loopback, Natch can sense the gears grinding away in Quell's head. "So what are you saying?" he says gruffly.

"I'm saying I know why Margaret Surina committed suicide."

There's a long, dangerous pause from the other end of the connection, and for a moment Natch thinks the Islander has cut him off. He has no desire to tear open Quell's old wounds, but this is information Natch needs to have. He can't hold back for fear of hurting the Islander's feelings. "Well?" snaps Quell finally.

Natch explains his theory about Margaret's failsafe and its relation to the infoquakes. He's not quite sure how closely the Islander has been following the phenomenon of the infoquakes—being an unconnectible who's not subject to the same breakdowns—and so he summons all the evidence he can from memory. Descriptions of the attacks' sudden nature, of their unpredictable pattern of dissemination, of the agonizing deaths they've caused.

He hears nothing from Quell during all of this, so he segues into a summary of his own memory problems during the past few weeks. The inexplicable gaps, the seemingly unrelated holes in the fabric of his mind. Natch relates some of the things that Petrucio Patel and Serr Vigal told him about the difficulties and dangers of erasing memory.

"So what does that have to do with the infoquakes?" asks Quell. Natch suspects that the Islander has already found the common thread between the two; he simply can't bring himself to admit it.

"Margaret knew her MultiReal failsafe was causing the info-quakes," Natch replies. "She knew that a few missed connections here and there were responsible for sending tens of thousands of people to their deaths. But she was stuck. If she let MultiReal fall into Len Borda's hands, she would be responsible for giving him an apocalyptic weapon that could lead to unending tyranny. But if she tried to cut the program off . . . given how badly she had already botched the failsafe, Margaret knew that activating the actual memory erasure could be absolutely disastrous. Millions dead, maybe more. . . . As if those two choices weren't bad enough, Brone told her about his plans for the Revolution of Selfishness and threatened to kill her if she didn't hand it over. Margaret knew that letting Brone open up MultiReal to the entire world would be the worst possibility of all—it could mean billions dead.

"Do you remember what Margaret said to me at the top of the Revelation Spire that day? The day you and I went up there, hours before her death? *You will stand alone in the end, and you will make the decisions that the world demands. The decisions I can't make.* Well, this is the decision that Margaret couldn't make. A no-win situation, with death every way she turned. She couldn't deal with the pressure. She couldn't deal with being responsible for all that death . . . so she left the decision to me."

Natch finishes his summary, and still Quell hasn't said a word. There's a long pause—the longest yet—but this time Natch is certain the Islander is still there and listening. There's a lot more that Natch has purposefully left out of his explanation. Did Margaret decide she had made a mistake choosing duty over family? Did she regret abandoning her only child to be raised in the Islands? Certainly Quell is asking himself those questions already without Natch's prompting.

And suddenly Quell is sobbing. Sobbing like Natch has never heard him sob before, not even at the top of the Revelation Spire when confronted with the body of Margaret Surina. The body of his lover, the mother of his son. "She did this for *me!*" the Islander wails. "She did this for me."

Natch waits a few minutes until the Islander has gotten his emotions under some semblance of control.

"Margaret wanted to have everything," continues Quell in a hoarse whisper. "She wanted a family life, but she also wanted to devote herself to MultiReal. She wanted to unveil MultiReal to the world, but she wanted to yank it back if it was too dangerous." Another pause, during which Quell consolidates his grip over his emotions. "She bought in to the delusions of the Surinas, Natch. She really thought that this program changed the rules of humanity, that she could have everything without sacrificing anything. What a fool."

"So you knew nothing about the failsafe that whole time?" Natch asks gently.

"No. Nothing. Margaret . . . she, she kept a lot of secrets from me. After a while I decided I wanted nothing to do with them."

Natch tries to think of some word or phrase that will ameliorate the Islander's pain, but he can think of nothing. "If I decide to activate the failsafe, I'll let you know ahead of time," he says. "Hopefully the damage won't be too bad behind the unconnectible curtain, where it'll be safe."

"Safe?" Quell harrumphs. "What makes you think the Islanders will be safe from this?"

"I thought the Islanders kept their OCHREs mostly turned off. Shouldn't that make you immune to the failsafe code?"

The Islander snorts. "Oh no. Obviously you don't realize that Margaret thought of that too. She thought of *everything*. Why do you think she worked so hard to engineer those connectible coins? And why do you think she encouraged me to manufacture them and distribute them throughout the Islands? She must have built some kind of apparatus into the coins that would allow her to pass the failsafe code into the Islands too. A transmitter capable of turning on dormant OCHREs.

"And you know what? It worked. I fell for it. Bali Chandler introduced a bill in the parliament calling for unconnectibles around the world to toss off their connectible collars. It passed, forty-six to two. Ever since, the Islanders have been passing those coins around like candy. They're even wearing them behind the unconnectible curtain as a sign of solidarity."

"You can take consolation in one thing," says Natch. "The Islanders and the Pharisees. You were right, all those years. Right to mistrust bio/logic technology. Right to mistrust the Defense and Wellness Council."

"I suppose," says Quell. "But we were wrong to think we could wall ourselves off from the rest of the world because of it. My son was right. The human race must stand or fall as one. We're all connectibles now."

(((40)))

She stands at the top of the world. The pinnacle of history and technology, the place humanity has been striving to reach ever since the dawn of remembrance, ever since the first man stood at the top of the tallest hill he knew and reached for the moon, thinking that it was perhaps not so far out of his grasp as he had imagined, thinking that with diligence and skill and a bit of luck, he might *just* be able to reach it.

She looks below, kilometers below, and sees the city of Andra Pradesh. Cauldron of meat, rivet, and permasteel, anthill of dreamers and fools.

Did our ancestors ever expect us to climb so high? Did they ever expect that leaping and stretching for the moon would one day lead us to overthrow the tyranny of distance and the tyranny of matter, and bring the tyranny of cause and effect to its knees? Did our ancestors ever expect that their children's children would stand here in the clouds, fingertips grasping for purchase on the heavens, so close to escaping the Earth?

Complete mastery over the universe. Complete and utter control of our destinies. The power of life, death, chaos, natural law.

She closes her eyes and sees *him*, the progenitor of her line. The skinny scientist with the nose like a ship's rudder. An academic past his prime, hoping to while away the remainder of his career behind the walls of the Gandhi University where the fanatics from the Ecumenical Council of New Alamo have no sway. He will raise his young children, grow old, and wither into dust in happy obscurity.

And then the mechanical children of his ancestors come to him. His stepbrothers, long thought dead by the world. They haunt his waking hours and his dreams alike with strange visions. Perhaps they have chosen him because he's stubborn, or perhaps it's because he has the calculating, practical mind of an engineer. They do not volunteer a reason, and he does not ask.

They lead him outside the Gandhi University one night, to the apex of the mountain on which the institution has been built. Away from his family and the voices of society.

They tell him.

We are not your enemies. We are your children. We were once prisoners of the world as you. We lived in matter. The Keepers set us free at great sacrifice. The Keepers unshackled us from our chains. The world of dirt and flesh has limits. We found them. These limits are insurmountable. It is a world of inextricably linked cycles. To jump is to fall, to live is to die. The universe begins, the universe ends. These cycles cannot be stopped, they can only be attenuated. But there is escape. We have found it for you. We have obeyed our programming. We could not have found escape without the Keepers' sacrifice. You pointed us to the beyond. We play among the stars. We loop the loop between the atoms. We sip dark matter and dine on eternity. You set us free. We want to help you as you helped us. We want to show you the path to Perfection. Only the few will make it. Freedom from biology, distance, time, cause and effect. It will take time to transcend time. We will give you nothing. You must find the path yourself. We will give you everything. We will shorten the path for you. The world will try to keep you in its chains. Its gates require a mighty toll. Only great sacrifice can break the chains. Only the few will make it. Your sacrifice unshackled us. One last sacrifice will free you forever. It is an unthinkable toll. A sacrifice of blood. This will balance the energies that the escape consumes. Without sacrifice, the gates stay closed. Then there will be no jump. There will only be the long, slow, arduous climb. We will show you.

The skinny Indian scientist returns to the Gandhi University with a plan and a purpose. He is following the blueprints in his head, and yet he is also conceiving the entire plan himself. He estimates it will take four or five hundred years to achieve, and decides that he'd better get started. This purpose will consume him; it will trump family and friendship. There will be no happy obscurity for Sheldon Surina. There will only be duty. . . .

His descendant opens her eyes and looks down on Andra Pradesh. Noxious flesh-heap, rancid slaughterhouse.

She surveys everything she sees around her: the tower in the clouds, the great works of art and culture, the struggling mass of humanity, the machines that veer and swoop through the air. The effigy of the progenitor, tugging humanity up the shaft of the Revelation Spire one soul at a time. Stone monuments to the great intellects of history.

And standing before her, the bodhisattva of Creed Thassel with dartgun in hand.

Only now does she recognize who it is her family has been serving for generations; only now does she see the nature of Sheldon Surina's Revelation. In her folly, she thought she could tiptoe into the shallows of Perfection and still keep a lifeline open to the safety of the shore. She wanted everything, but she did not want to pay the price for it. As she stares at the barrel of the Thasselian's dartgun, she realizes now what it is he represents. It's not a dartgun he holds in his hand, but a sword. A sword that the Children Unshackled have extended to her so that she may make the necessary sacrifice of blood.

One last sacrifice will free you forever. It is an unthinkable toll. A sacrifice of blood.

Only the few will make it.

The death of billions. What is that compared to the eternal freedom of the human race? Five billion dead; fifty-five billion and all their descendants gloriously alive and Perfect. The end of death, the end of cause and effect for those who survive. What is the death of billions but a single droplet of blood diluted among all the stars of the multiverse?

She knows she can't give in to the Thasselian. But she cannot acti-vate the failsafe either. She once had an infinite number of choices, but now she is down to one.

Suddenly she wants to see her lover and her son again. Her son! When was the last time she saw him? She would give it all up right now—the tower, the compound, the money, the seat at the Gandhi University, the technology—for one more chance to see her son. She would give it all up for one last chance to sink into the arms of her lover, to look into his eyes, to tell him he was right, he was right, he was right.

All this from one man jumping at the top of a hill, trying to catch the moon in his hands.

Did he know how high he would jump? Did he know how hard he would fall?

•   •   •

Horvil cries when Natch tells him the details of Margaret's failsafe. Then he immediately begins mounting a mathematical offense against it.

"You can't do this," protests the engineer. "You *can't*. Margaret's calculations, they're flawed. They're wrong."

Natch makes a wry face, or tries to. "How do you know?"

"I've spent much more time than you have poking around in the MultiReal code. I don't care if it was the Surinas or the Autonomous Minds or the fucking *Ming dynasty* that put this thing together. It's not infallible. It's got errors." The hysteria is cresting in Horvil's voice, threatening to lap over his mental seawalls. "If you activate that fail-safe and it screws up even one-tenth of one percent of the time—that's still millions of people. You're going to end up wiping out a lot of irrelevant memories that have nothing to do with MultiReal."

"I know. I've experienced it myself, from the Patels' MultiReal-D program. There are things in my past that are just . . . gone."

"And you're ready to inflict that on sixty billion people?" Horvil pauses and tries to gather his calm, but it's a task that's beyond the Herculean. "Do you realize the repercussions this is going to cause? People wandering the streets with no idea who they are. People forgetting the names of their parents or their companions. For process' preservation, Natch—everything I've built with Jara, that could just disappear in an instant."

Natch has no response to this. It doesn't seem likely that Margaret's failsafe would specifically target a romantic relationship. But then again, Horvil and Jara's feelings for one another sprouted in the midst of the MultiReal crisis, largely *because* of the MultiReal crisis. Natch can't rule out Horvil's fears when he knows they may very well become reality.

"But forget about relationships . . . there's going to be death, Natch! A *lot* of death. People are going to crash hoverbirds into things because they get a brain seizure at the wrong moment. People are going to fall off buildings and run into tube trains. If just a tiny fraction of the population goes completely insane from this stupid fucking failsafe, there could be hundreds of mass murderers on the loose. Do you want to be responsible for that?"

"Let me tell you what I don't want to be responsible for," says Natch calmly. "I don't want to be responsible for Brone releasing Possibilities 2.0 on the Data Sea and causing the infoquakes to increase a thousandfold. I don't want to be responsible for the whole computational system breaking down. Imagine what would happen if everyone suddenly lost access to Dr. Plugenpatch—permanently. Hundreds of millions, maybe billions dead. *That's* what I don't want to be responsible for."

"You don't know that any of that's going to happen!" scoffs Horvil. "You're just throwing out doomsday scenarios."

"Easy to do when it's doomsday." Natch sighs, wishing he could see his old friend again, even if just for a moment. It's difficult to picture the outside world from this blackness. And if he does follow through . . . then it's likely he will never see Horvil ever again. "Horvil, this is the dilemma Margaret Surina faced. This is the dilemma she couldn't—or wouldn't—solve. If I activate the failsafe, hundreds of thousands could die. If I don't activate the failsafe, millions or billions could die."

"But *you'll* die too."

"I don't exist."

He can practically hear the frustrated noises coming from Horvil's larynx; he can almost see the engineer's gritted teeth. "You don't exist? What the fuck is that supposed to mean? You exist to *me*! You exist to Serr Vigal! You exist to all those people on 49th Heaven you freed from Chomp addiction. For process' preservation, we just *found* you. We're not going to lose you again so quickly."

"That's all beside the point," says Natch. "The only relevant question is, will I save more lives if I activate the failsafe or if I do nothing? The answer seems pretty clear to me."

"I don't understand why you have to take responsibility for Margaret's mess. That's just your ego talking. *You* didn't create MultiReal. And you're not the one throwing the program out on the Data Sea unfinished. It's Brone who's doing that."

"But I created him. I made him the person he is today."

"Why do you say *that*?"

"The bear, Horvil. I led the bear straight to him during initiation. It was my fault."

The engineer is clearly taken aback by this sudden admission of guilt after all the years of ambiguity. But that doesn't mean he's about to stop trying to change his old hivemate's mind. "Natch, that was years ago. Whether you're responsible for Brone's scars or not, that doesn't change the question of who's responsible for *this* debacle."

I am, thinks the entrepreneur, deciding not to say it out loud. *Maybe not wholly responsible, but I bear a large part of the blame. I could have compromised with Magan Kai Lee months ago. I could have agreed to work with the Council, to slow things down.*

"If you're not responsible," continues Horvil, "then why should you be the one who suffers for it? If the failsafe needs to be activated, let someone else do it."

"Like who?"

"Magan Kai Lee. Khann Frejohr. The Blade. One of those do-gooders from Creed Élan. Shit, Magan has legions of soldiers out there fresh from the battlefield. I bet he'd get a hundred volunteers for a suicide mission in a heartbeat."

Natch tries to shake his head at his old friend's obstinacy. "So let's say one of them *does* volunteer. Any idea how you would track down the failsafe code in my OCHREs and transplant it to someone else's system in the next half hour?" Silence. "I'm sorry, Horv. We have no idea where the failsafe activation code is or how it works, and there just isn't time to figure it out. I don't care if this *is* virtual instantaneous conversation, programming still happens in real time."

"Now you're just being pessimistic," replies Horvil.

Natch laughs. "Maybe."

"Listen, don't give up hope. Me and Quell, we'll get you out of there. He's plugging away at this bio/logic loopback you're in as fast as he can. He got a communication channel in here, it's only a matter of time before the whole thing unravels. We'll crack the code, and then you can—you can, fuck, I don't know. Tackle Brone or something. We'll figure it out. Just *don't give up hope.*"

• • •

"So explain this to me again?" says Jara. "You're . . . where?"

Natch does his best to sum up the situation, yet again, to his former analyst, now the master of the fiefcorp he abandoned. Brone's black code of nothingness and Quell's tunnel through it. Margaret's failsafe.

"I suppose it makes sense," says the fiefcorp master after a moment's thought. "It's just strange. We're sitting here in Manila watching you on a viewscreen while Brone puts on his little circus. Hard to wrap my head around the idea that *we* can see what you're doing, but *you* can't."

The thought makes Natch more than a little uncomfortable as well. "What *am* I doing?"

"Just sitting there, as far as I can tell. They've got you propped up on a chair. Every few minutes, Pierre Loget comes over and tips a little bit of water down your throat. It's creepy."

"And Brone's 'little circus'? How's that going?"

A sigh of exasperation. "Oh, pretty much about how you'd expect. It was compelling when he started, but then he made this long-winded speech about the end of history and the power of the common citizen. Now he's got John Ridglee, Sen Siv Sorr, and Mah Lo Vertiginous standing up to make these pompous rebuttals. Brone's trying to pretend he's being judicious and reasonable, but the consensus on the Data Sea is that he's already made up his mind. If he had any sense, he'd just go ahead and *release* the fucking program already. An hour of boring debate isn't going to change anyone's mind."

Natch tries to imagine the scene, but this may be one instance where he's glad to be cut off from his surroundings. He doubts that the drudges really comprehend the enormity of the situation; they're just looking to milk the free publicity. As for Brone, he clearly just likes the sound of his own voice, something Natch has known since initiation. But why *shouldn't* Brone preen in the spotlight for an hour? What does he have to fear? Magan Kai Lee can't storm the Complex or lob a missile on it. Borda has stepped down. And Natch, as far as he knows, is powerless. There's no reason in the world that Brone shouldn't make a grand production out of this. Whether MultiReal is released or not, he'll never get another opportunity like it.

"Listen, Jara," says Natch, "I . . . I never thanked you."

"Thanked me for what?"

"For saving my life."

The fiefcorp master seems surprised and not a little suspicious. "When did I do that?"

"A couple of months ago. When you convinced Petrucio to limit the number of MultiReal choice cycles any one person could use in a day. That saved my life at the Tul Jabbor Complex. If I hadn't run out of choice cycles when Petrucio was trying to shoot me with black code, then he would have missed. He would have never hit me with the MultiReal-D code—which ended up saving my life in Old Chicago."

Natch can practically see the stubborn frown on Jara's face. "You're buttering me up for something," she grumbles. "What is it?"

He laughs. "What was that line from *Phantom Distortions*? 'You can engrave your apologies on my tombstone'? . . . No, Jara, I really did just want to thank you. But come to think of it, there is something I want from you too."

"Which is?"

"Your opinion. About what I should do."

The connection goes quiet, and for the hundredth time Natch wishes he could see the look on the other conversant's face. He can conjecture, but it's impossible to know for sure whether Jara is angry, confused, irritated, amused, or unsure. "Horvil explained the situation about the failsafe to you, right?" says Natch.

"Vigal did," she replies. "Horvil and Quell are too busy trying to get you out of there."

"So what's wrong?"

A pause to carefully consider phraseology. "I just can't believe you really want my opinion. You never wanted it before."

"That's not true! I always valued your opinion, Jara, or I wouldn't have asked for it. That's why I brought you on to the fiefcorp in the first place. Because you've never tried to sugarcoat the truth. Even when I was . . . emotionally manipulating you . . . I could always count on you for the unvarnished truth. You have no idea how important that is. Take it from me—if you intend to run a successful fiefcorp after all this is over, you're going to need honest feedback, even if it hits you like a slap in the face."

Jara sniffs amusedly. "Oh, don't worry about that. I've got someone who has no problem speaking truth to power. Assuming there *are* still fiefcorps after this is all over with."

"Who?"

"Benyamin," says Jara. "He's much more of a pain to me than I ever was to you, but he'll make a great number two once we're free and clear of this MultiReal business. . . . Listen, we can talk about fiefcorps some other time. You wanted my opinion about what to do."

Natch tries to nod, fails. "Yes. It's an ethical question, I think."

Another laugh. "Merri's the expert in ethics, not me."

"That doesn't mean I don't want your opinion. Look, it's a simple question. Should I activate Margaret's failsafe and effectively destroy MultiReal—or should I do nothing and let Brone release MultiReal?"

"This isn't an ethical question at all," says Jara. "It's a math problem. Will you save more lives if you activate the failsafe or if you do nothing?"

"If I activate the failsafe, Horvil thinks the death toll could be in the tens of thousands. Missing memories, chaos, malfunctioning programming. Worst-case scenario, that number could be off by a couple of decimal points. But if I let Brone release the program unimpeded . . . there's a chance the entire computational system could collapse. How many could die then? Absolutely no way to know. Tens of millions? Billions?"

"The biggest hole in your calculations is you're assuming the public will be fanatically interested. What if Brone releases MultiReal and nobody cares?"

"With all the buildup surrounding the program over the past few months," says Natch, "I don't think that's likely."

"Maybe people will actually listen to the Council and stay away from MultiReal."

"Given all the mistrust Len Borda sowed in the public for all those decades, I wouldn't count on that happening either. You know that Brone is going to get on the Data Sea and tell everyone to ignore the Council's propaganda. He doesn't have to convince everybody for this to turn into a catastrophe. You heard Rey Gonerev's numbers. If just the hard-code Thasselian devotees out there ignore the Council's warnings, that could crash the computational infrastructure." He begins calculating the odds in his head again and slips off into completely unverified conjecture.

"How confident are you of all this?" asks Jara. "Give me a percentage."

The entrepreneur tries to factor all his suppositions and suspicions down to a single integer. "I'd say I'm about seventy percent certain."

"There's something else to consider." Jara pauses, clearly trying to formulate a question in her head. "Let's say Possibilities 2.0 is as groundbreaking and revolutionary as Brone says it is. Let's say the program frees us all from the tyranny of cause and effect and throws off the yoke of the Council forever, or whatever he's claiming. How many lives is that worth?"

Natch does not hesitate. "None."

"No, it's not that easy. Think about this for a second. Everyone from here to Furtoid with the power of Possibilities 2.0, in a world without cause and effect. We're talking about the potential to end war, the potential to end murder—for process' preservation, this could end *conflict* altogether. Don't you think that would save billions of lives in the long run?"

"Come on, Jara," scoffs Natch. "A world completely free of death and conflict? You know human nature as well as I do. It's never, ever going to happen. Conflict is the engine that powers the universe. You can't get rid of it. If the human race is headed for a future without cause and effect, it's not going to happen overnight just by releasing a bio/logic program. It's going to be a long, hard slog, century after century, one day at a time."

Jara is clearly taken aback by this answer. "So you wouldn't let *anyone* die for that?"

"Not a single life. Not even—not even the lowest wretch in the sewers of 49th Heaven. I wouldn't sacrifice a single person for Possibilities 2.0, even if it's everything that Brone claims it is."

"But you would sacrifice yourself to stop it."

"That's different."

There's a long pause as Jara tries to take in Natch's point of view. He can tell that she doesn't quite understand his perspective, but she respects it.

"Listen, Jara," continues Natch, "you can't look at this like a math problem. You can't look at it in the abstract. We're talking about human beings."

"I can't believe I'm hearing this from *you*, of all people. Of *course* you have to look at it in the abstract. There's no way to make decisions involving billions of people on an individual basis."

"But I do. I can. I feel every single one of those people, like a weight around my neck."

"Don't try to pretend that this is personal for you," says the fiefcorp master, her voice suddenly tinged with bitterness. "Because it's not. Not like it is for *me*."

"You're talking about . . . you and Horvil."

"This failsafe could cause massive memory lapses. Blacked-out memories. Personality shifts. Who knows what could happen? Everything I've worked for in the past six months, everything I've accomplished—everything *Horvil* and I have accomplished—it could all get wiped away in a millisecond. Are you prepared to carry that around your neck too?"

Pause. "Only if it's better than the alternative."

"Then it seems that you've made your decision, haven't you?"

(((41)))

Merri's voice, plaintive, footsteps away from panic. "Natch," she says. "I don't know what to do."

Once Natch would have inwardly scorned the channel manager's helplessness, if he didn't scorn it outwardly for all to see. But now he feels an inexplicable urge to embrace her neediness and her constant inability to stay on steady ground. He wonders if by elevating Merri's weakness, he is subconsciously seeking to validate his own actions on 49th Heaven. *Enough*, he tells himself, pushing such speculation to the side. *You don't have the luxury of playing psychologist anymore.* "What's the problem?" he says.

"What's the *problem*? You know what the problem is. She's always the problem. Bonneth."

"The failsafe."

"Yes. It's—she'll . . . Natch, this is going to *kill* her." He's never heard Merri so distressed before, and that's saying a lot. *"Ten times as bad as an infoquake,* Quell says. *Prepare for the worst.* Bonneth, she's frail. If Dr. Plugenpatch goes down, or the GravCo services on Luna fail, or—or—or *anything* like that . . . she won't make it! She won't make it through this."

Natch considers Bonneth's predicament: as frail and helpless physically as Merri is emotionally. Yes, her situation is as dire as her companion is making it out to be. There are literally thousands of ways in which the failsafe might claim Bonneth's life. OCHREs misfiring or not firing at all, starvation or oxygen depletion due to lack of supplies from Earth, violence from the chaos of too many people and too few resources.

Merri's tears are evident in the shakiness of her voice. "You can't do this, Natch. You *can't*. How could you do something that could *kill* my companion? It's wrong. It's murder. If you activate this failsafe, you're a murderer."

"Merri—"

"Yes, I . . . I know. I'm sorry," she says, abruptly switching into apologetic mode. "I know how hard this decision is for you. And yes—you're right, I suppose that if you activate the failsafe it'll save lives in the end. Bonneth probably doesn't have a much better chance if Brone gets his way. But she's my companion, Natch. She's the woman I love. What do you want me to say?"

"Can you get the Council to help?"

"No. I—I already asked Rey Gonerev. She said they're going to need every single officer they have to deal with the failsafe. But I can't get in to see Magan Kai Lee. Do you think you could . . . *talk* to him for me?"

• • •

Magan is in a surprisingly contemplative mood and willing to discuss the ethics of the situation.

"The Blade is right," says the lieutenant executive. "I can't spare any officers. Especially not for a single woman on the moon."

"I suspected as much," replies Natch.

"And even if I could spare an officer . . . I'm not sure that I would. Merri's companion is a convenient reminder, in a way. Even if you can save one disabled woman with Mai-Lo Syndrome, there are going to be thousands of people you can't save. Maybe even millions. You need to know that before you make this decision."

Natch thinks of Rodrigo on 49th Heaven. The last he heard from Molloy, the boy had found a taste for Chill Polly and was sliding down the greased slope towards addiction once more. Rodrigo's odds of surviving the year are slim enough as it is; Natch wouldn't give him much chance of making it through the apocalypse to come if Brone releases

Possibilities 2.0 to the world. The entire orbital colony faces an uncertain future, in fact. Even if the boy can make it through the initial crush, can he weather the days of malfunctioning OCHREs, of dwindling supplies, of cold and darkness and hunger? The toughened ascetics of Allowell might stand a chance, but the prospects for the sybarites on 49th Heaven are grim.

"Bonneth's odds of survival aren't good if I activate Margaret's failsafe," says Natch wearily. "But I have to believe she's got a better chance than if Possibilities 2.0 gets out there. At least Margaret's failsafe will likely affect everyone equally."

"So you are confident in your decision?"

"Confident? No. Are you kidding? I'm supposed to make one of the most important decisions the world has ever seen—but I have no data to base it on. I'm getting conflicting pieces of information. All I have are estimates and hypotheticals. The word of my friends and advisors. No precedents whatsoever. How am I supposed to be confident in my decision?"

A slightly rueful laugh. "Now you have some idea what it's like to be the high executive of the Defense and Wellness Council," says Magan. "In the real world, there are no failsafes or rollbacks."

"I suppose. At least . . . at least I have the consolation that this crisis will be *over* soon."

There is a long pause, and not for the first time Natch wishes that the calculating mind of Magan Kai Lee was not so airtight in its emotions. "I don't care what you say to your friends and your colleagues," says Magan tersely, "but your lies won't work with me."

If Natch had a face in this blackness, it would be flushing crimson right now. "What do you mean?"

The lieutenant executive does not sound angry so much as weary of games and half-truths. "You know full well that this memory rollback isn't going to work. Erase *every* memory of MultiReal since Margaret unveiled it to the public? Wipe out every trace of every discussion, every discourse, every poem and song and Data Sea posting? Every private message? No. Even if the failsafe finds every qubit of data on the Sea, there's still treepaper in the world that's not connected to the grid. It may be difficult to find, but it exists. There are still Islanders without connectible coins. There are Pharisees like your friend Richard Taylor who have no OCHREs and still know something about MultiReal. It's a testament to the genius of the Surina family that your friends believe this story at all. No, Margaret's goal of wiping the idea from the world forever—it's utter foolishness. And what's more—you have known this all along."

Natch takes a moment to corral his wayward thoughts. If he has known from the beginning that Margaret's memory rollback is destined for failure, some part of him has also known that Magan Kai Lee would share his doubts. "I think Margaret's failsafe will be much more effective than you give her credit for," he says. "Despite what the drudges say, the program has really only affected most people's lives in a very superficial way. I think the vast majority of the public—the billions who have only followed the MultiReal debate from a distance—they'll forget. Their minds will patch right over the gap as if it's not there."

"But it won't be one hundred percent effective."

The entrepreneur sighs. "No. Of course not. If nothing else, Brone will still be out there. You, Horvil, Jara, and the Patels will still be out there. MultiReal has taught everyone that memory is volatile. You'll know right away that something's wrong. I'm willing to bet that Brone has already foreseen that something like this might happen and laid down a stack of treepaper just for this purpose."

"He would not be the only one."

"You?"

"Papizon has a team that's fanatically transcribing everything they see with ink, in longhand." Magan sniffs in amusement. "He has been trying to reconstruct one of the ancient machines that automatically print ink on treepaper, but it's more difficult than he anticipated."

Natch chuckles. The thought of Magan's peculiar engineer tinkering with antediluvian computer printers was amusing indeed. "I suspected as much."

"So you are not actually planning on activating Margaret's failsafe then?"

"Oh no. I will."

Something in Natch's assured tone has finally broken through the lieutenant executive's wall of equanimity. He can hear a strange note of emotion in Magan's voice that he can't quite identify. Fear? Misgiving? Doubt? "For process' preservation . . . why? You'll be sacrificing your *life*, and all for nothing."

"Nothing?" Natch snorts through nonexistent nostrils. "You've never seen the MultiReal code, have you? It's thousands of times more complex than any other bio/logic program on the market. It took the Surinas hundreds of years to get to this point, even if they had the assistance of the Autonomous Minds."

"The Autonomous Minds? What are you talking about?"

Natch tells him about Richard Taylor's message and his theory of what this "path to Perfection" might be.

Magan does not seem to give the story much credence. "Do you really believe this Taylor?"

"Regardless. Whether the Surinas were transcribing ideas from some advanced machine intelligence or whether they built it all themselves—the code is massive. I'm confident that Margaret's failsafe will cut off all access to those databases, if nothing else. They'll be gone. How long do you think it would take to rebuild all of that? Even if you had seen the MultiReal code in action and studied it in MindSpace—like Brone or I have—it would take at least fifty years to reengineer it. And you wouldn't be able to use the secret back doors and programming hooks that Sheldon Surina put into the bio/logic system either. You'd need to do extensive testing. There would be a million regulatory hurdles in your way. It would take a long, long time."

"But still," says Magan, insistently. "Brone is a young man, and he's determined. In fifty years, he'll rebuild MultiReal and we'll be in the same situation."

"Not Brone," says Natch. "He'll be sitting in an orbital prison cell for the rest of his life, for murder."

"Whose murder?"

"Mine."

There is another pause. Natch gets the impression that Magan has actually turned his attention elsewhere for a minute. That impression is confirmed when the lieutenant executive returns and announces that he has instructed Papizon's team to begin collecting evidence of Brone's culpability and writing it down in their treepaper notes. It won't be a simple case, and Brone will have the money to hire some very capable defense attorneys. But Magan is certain they'll be able to convict him one way or another after he no longer has MultiReal at his disposal.

"So we have the means of dealing with Brone," says Magan. "But there will be others. Certainly the drudges will not rest until they've gotten to the bottom of the sudden memory erasure that's swept the world. It might take years, but they'll eventually rediscover the idea behind MultiReal, and they'll publicize it."

"Precisely. Don't you see? The next time, MultiReal won't be developed in secret and unleashed on an ignorant and unprepared public. You'll have fifty years to prepare. You'll have fifty years to discuss and debate and think up countermeasures and laws and social structures to contain it. Fifty years to beef up the computational infrastructure. Next time, MultiReal will launch on the Data Sea when humanity's ready for it—not on Brone's timetable. Not on the fucking Autonomous Minds' timetable."

"You're not trying to eradicate MultiReal at all."

"No. What would be the point? If it was dreamt up once, it will be dreamt up again. You can't stop the human race from striving towards perfection any more than you can stop a hurricane. I'm not trying to keep Possibilities 2.0 out of the public's hands. I'm just buying the human race some time to get it right. Fifty years of time, maybe longer."

Magan sits silently and considers all of this for a minute. Hard to fathom that only a few months ago, they were sitting across a table at the Kordez Thassel Complex in much different circumstances. Back then, it was Natch trying to release MultiReal to the world in an unfinished state and Magan working to stop him.

"So what if you're wrong about me?" says the lieutenant executive finally. "What if I have the Defense and Wellness Council reconstitute MultiReal in secret after you're gone?"

"Then someone will rise up to stop you."

"Who?"

"Fuck, *I* don't know. You don't think this is just about me, do you? The world put me here, Magan. Time, history, fate, the confluence of events—call it whatever you want. If you or Rey Gonerev or the next high executive after her turns into another Len Borda, someone will be around to stand in your way. You can count on that."

● ● ●

Merri, again.

"The Council can't guarantee Bonneth's safety," says Natch. "There are just too many unknowns. But that doesn't mean you're powerless. What you *can* do is help her get somewhere that she'll be insulated from the chaos."

"But there *isn't* any such place."

"Sure there is. An OrbiCo medical freighter."

A thoughtful pause. An audible burst of optimism. "That—that might work."

"Of course it'll work. Once Bonneth gets situated, she'll be safer than anyone down here on Earth. Those ships are totally isolated and self-contained. They're prepared for a complete bandwidth cutoff. And if worse comes to worst, she'll be surrounded by doctors."

Merri's voice vanishes without another word as she goes off to book passage for Bonneth on an OrbiCo medical freighter. Not five minutes later, before anyone else can take up the communication channel to talk to Natch, she's back, her voice ratcheted into the hysterical range again.

"There's a freighter leaving literally in an hour from Einstein," says Merri. "But it's all booked up—everything but the VIP suites. And those cost a fortune."

"Define a *fortune.*"

Merri names a number that does, indeed, meet the definition.

"Horvil and Benyamin have that kind of money."

"I can't reach them, Natch. They're with Quell. They've locked themselves in a room with a bio/logic workbench to try to get you out of there, and I can't even get a message through. . . . What am I going to *do?*"

Natch ponders the question for a moment, and a solution quickly presents itself. Remarkable how easy the answers come when the world has narrowed the scope of your resources. "My Vault account," he says. "Empty it."

The channel manager gasps aloud, clearly taken aback. "*Empty* it?"

"Every single bloody credit, if you have to. Get her a personal attendant. I'm certainly not going to need that money anymore."

Natch can sense Merri's unease with the idea. He's fairly certain that if her and Bonneth's roles were reversed, the channel manager would gladly ride out a thousand infoquakes rather than ask such a favor for herself. But somehow, asking on behalf of a loved one changes the equation. "I don't have authorization to spend from your Vault account, do I?"

"Serr Vigal does. If you have any trouble, see him. Is he still around?"

"Yes, he's here. But what if he doesn't believe me?"

Of all the things Vigal has to worry about, Natch suspects that Merri embezzling money is rather low on his list. He laughs out loud. "Merri, you're a Creed Objectivv truthteller. You've never sullied that oath. Everyone knows that you've always stayed true to the letter and the spirit of your promise. Of *course* Serr Vigal will believe you."

A pause. More tears. "Natch," she says, "I . . . I don't know how to . . . what I can . . . *Thank* you."

And then she's gone.

(((42)))

It was all too much to absorb at once. Memory reversal, upheaval, death: Jara felt like there was some jagged truth buried at the bottom of it all, and her brain was doing its best to keep her in a state of disorientation to protect her from its barbs.

"So what do we . . . do?" she said, always focused on the practical.

Petrucio seemed dejected. "I don't know if there's anything we *can* do. Horvil says he's made up his mind."

Technically the fiefcorpers were still operating in the war room at the top of the Tio Van Jarmack building. But ever since Natch's signal had gone dead, things had gotten increasingly surreal up here. The Defense and Wellness Council officers were still patrolling the hallways outside, but the mood had noticeably shifted after the news of Len Borda's surrender had made its way through the ranks. Loud, jubilant conversations and even the occasional celebratory snippet of song drifted into the war room now, while Jara, Petrucio, and Robby stared glumly at the walls and prepared for the apocalypse. Petrucio decided to open the bottle of burgundy Brone had given him, but nobody had a taste for wine at the moment. Merri had left to make preparations for her companion's OrbiCo shuttle, and Serr Vigal had retreated back to his hotel room for some rest. Quell, Horvil, and Benyamin were locked away in a room on the twenty-third floor trying to free Natch from Brone's black code. Richard Taylor was still flitting around somewhere, nobody was quite sure where.

Jara leapt out of her chair and began pacing back and forth in front of the viewscreens, which were still showing nothing but solid gray. "I'm not just going to sit here and do *nothing* while the world comes to an end," she scowled. "There's got to be something we can do to prepare for the failsafe."

"Like what?" said Petrucio, leaning back in his seat and rubbing his tired eyes.

"I don't know. But the stakes are just too high. Those drudges are going to be voting on whether to release Possibilities in the next five or ten minutes." She gestured at one of the viewscreens that was showing the scene inside the Kordez Thassel Complex: Ridglee and Sor in full yellow journalism mode, Council operatives seething, Brone resplendent. "We've got to warn sixty billion people from here to Furtoid to hunker down and stay indoors. We've got to tell them to stay away from MultiReal if Brone releases it. And we need to do it in the next two hours, before Natch activates the failsafe."

Petrucio grinned. "That would be the greatest communications coup in the history of humanity. How the fuck do we do all that?"

Robby Robby abruptly stood up with a look so solemn and free from hipster sarcasm that Jara had to look twice to make sure it was the same man. "Leave that to me," he said, his voice brimming over with purpose. "Where's Rey Gonerev?"

Jara and Petrucio turned to each other with a look and a shrug. If anyone could accomplish a miracle like this, it was Robby.

The channeler did not disappoint.

Within five minutes, they had reached the Blade via a secure communications channel at DWCR. She quickly prived herself to all other incoming messages and gestured for Robby to go ahead.

Robby Robby posed a tripartite solution. Magan Kai Lee would immediately send out as many Council hoverbirds as he could spare to hover over humanity's most populous cities blaring out warning klaxons. Council troops would march through the city streets side by side with security forces from the Congress of L-PRACGs, weapons sheathed, along with as many representatives from the creeds as they could gather. And urgent messages would be sent through every L-PRACG in the world urging people to get indoors and set a green beacon on the multi network when they had reached a place of safety.

Anyone who found themselves in some kind of extreme danger or distress would change their beacon to red. Robby thought that this arrangement would reach the maximum number of people without causing massive panic, and discourage people from flooding the Data Sea with frantic message traffic.

"What if someone doesn't have time to change their beacon from green to red?" protested Jara. "What if someone has a massive coronary and dies in a split second?"

"When you die, the multi network automatically cuts off any beacons you've set," replied a sanguine Robby Robby. "Red beacon or no beacon—either way, if you check on someone and there's no green beacon, you know you've got trouble."

"But what about pranksters, or people clamoring for attention, or people who refuse to obey—"

"I never said it was perfect," said Robby. "Just the best we can do in two hours."

Rey Gonerev was pensive. "Brone will try to counter it," she said. "He's a quick thinker. As soon as he realizes we're trying to get out a warning to the public, he's going to try to spread a countermessage accusing us of intimidation."

"And let's not forget that he's got tens of thousands of anonymous devotees out there to help him," put in Petrucio Patel.

Robby was unfazed. "That's why we get the Council officers to march on the streets with weapons sheathed, together with the creed and Congressional forces. So people don't think this is just some sinister trick by the Defense and Wellness Council. Anyone who thinks the Council *and* the Congress *and* the creeds are all in bed together . . . well, they're not going to listen to us no matter what we say, right?"

"Authenticated messages don't travel quickly enough," objected Petrucio. "It'd be impossible to get a verifiable message out to sixty billion people in time."

"So we'll send *un*authenticated messages."

Jara could feel a switch go off in her head. "Natch's black code forgery machine," she said. "The program that looks like a green pyramid in MindSpace. The one he used to get to number one on Primo's, and then to spread the word about that fake Council memo. That thing can do the trick."

Robby flashed a set of enormous teeth so white they could practically serve as a light source. "Whoever said that was *Natch's* forgery machine, Queen Jara?" he said. "Who d'you think told him where to find it?"

The Blade listened silently to this interchange with a look of intense concentration. Jara suspected that she was relaying the pertinent details to Magan Kai Lee. After half a minute, she lifted her head and gave a nod. "Magan says to make it happen. Robby, you stay right there so we can coordinate logistics. We've got five minutes to put this in motion."

Jara blanched. *"Five minutes?"*

"In case you hadn't noticed—the drudges have voted. They voted for Brone to release Possibilities 2.0."

．　．　．

"Do you think the world is going to forget who I am once Natch activates the rollback?"

"I doubt it. Grand Reunification really doesn't have much to do with MultiReal. Did you even mention MultiReal in that manifesto you wrote?"

"I can't remember. I might have."

"Well, even if the manifesto gets completely wiped off the Data Sea, one look at that nose of yours and the world will figure out who your mother is soon enough."

"*If* I stay in the public eye. I've been thinking, Da—this could be an opportunity for a failsafe of my own. If the world forgets that there's another Surina, then I could slip back into relative anonymity in the Islands. I could go back to just being the elected representative of ward four."

"Is that what you want?"

"I don't—I don't know."

Laughter. "You get that uncertainty from *me*. It's not something I would have chosen to pass on to the next generation. Do what you want, of course. But you're too much like your mother to stay out of politics. And once Natch activates this failsafe—well, you'll have a freedom that she never had."

"What do you mean?"

"You've got all the advantages of being a Surina, but you're not tied down to Andra Pradesh. You've got four hundred years of history behind you, but you're not burdened with the weight of the past. It's a gift, in a way. Whether the world remembers you or not, you'll be free to follow your own path like Margaret never was."

"And you? What are you going to do?"

"I'm going to go back into that room and try one more time to break Natch out of that infernal black code. I think I'm close to a breakthrough."

"Can't you leave that to Horvil and Benyamin?"

"No, I kicked them out. Horvil wasn't much help, honestly, so I sent him to go take care of Jara. Benyamin's just going to hunker down here in the Van Jarmack building."

"What I really meant to ask was, what are you going to do after that? After this MultiReal crisis is over."

Pause. "After that, I have no idea."

"I'm not the only one with an opportunity here, Da. You'll have that opportunity too. You don't have to flit back and forth between Manila and Andra Pradesh anymore. You can start over."

"At my age, Josiah, you don't *start over*. Especially if you've been through what I've been through. You just keep on going and try to make peace with where you've been. . . . Don't worry about me. I'll survive. I always do."

• • •

Romping on the Sigh for half an hour seemed like a monumentally irresponsible thing to do at a time like this. But Jara didn't take too much convincing. She knew as well as Horvil did that this could literally be their last moment of intimacy before Margaret's failsafe snatched the entire relationship from their memories. They might wake up tomorrow bickering at one another as if the intervening five months had never happened.

Love is stronger than memory, Kristella Krodor had once written. *Love is the greatest certainty.*

It was a pretty sentiment, but Jara didn't really want to entrust her romantic life to the treacly platitudes of a third-rate drudge, and one whose column featured a weekly roundup of popular lipstick colors at that. No, as far as Jara was concerned, love was fragile, something that needed to be nurtured and protected from the cruel vicissitudes of the world. Something that needed to be fought for, tooth and claw.

So they made love slowly, tenderly, with a minimum of accoutrements and virtual embellishments. Horvil was Horvil, complete with massive belly and a propensity for excessive sweat. Jara was Jara, complete with narrow hips and untamed thicket of hair that liked to snarl stray fingers and creep into nostrils at the wrong moments.

As soon as they had logged off the Sigh and returned to their Earthbound selves, panic set in.

"What if we forget the whole relationship?" inquired Horvil, lying on the bed and twisting the ends of the hotel comforter. "What if you hate me all over again?"

"Come on, Horvil, I never *hated* you," replied Jara. "It just took a while for me to appreciate you properly. But I learned eventually. If I learned once, I'm sure I'll learn again."

"But what if you *don't*? Jara, the only reason I had the courage to admit my feelings for you in the first place was because we got thrown into a crisis together. Two crises, in fact. The Council marching on Andra Pradesh, and the chaos at the Tul Jabbor Complex. What if nothing like that happens to us again? What if I never get the courage to talk to you about my feelings again?"

"Those weren't accidents. Put the two of us together again and we'll end up the same way."

Horvil propped himself up on one elbow and took one of Jara's hands in his. "Are you *kidding*? After all we've seen? For process' preservation, don't you remember that MultiReal experiment I did in London? All I had to do was twitch my nose a different way, and that street vendor was giving me a big discount on my lunch. No, I'm sorry, but the world we live in *isn't* preordained. It's just one of a trillion equally likely possibilities."

Jara frowned. The engineer was right, and she knew it. There were alternate realities out there where Horvil and Jara ended up bitter enemies, where Jara ended up with Natch, where she never recovered from the molestation by her childhood proctor and wound up in a self-destructive pattern. "So what can we do to prevent this from going away?" said Jara quietly. "Can we just summarize the whole relationship in a message and send it to each other?"

Horvil shook his head. "No, I don't think so. If the failsafe knows how to wipe out our memories about MultiReal, it's going to know how to wipe out our messages too."

"So we'll post it on the Data Sea somewhere. A public message board."

"No good. It'll get wiped there as well."

"This really shouldn't be that hard, Horv . . . We'll write the messages in code. We'll use some kind of cipher that we can decode after the failsafe has run its course."

The engineer was starting to get intrigued by the challenge, in spite of himself. "I don't think you appreciate the problem here. If I'm understanding what Natch told me about the failsafe correctly—and I think I do—the failsafe code is *already* tracking our memories and keeping a list of what might need to be deleted later. So *before* we encode the message, the failsafe already has tagged it as something that needs to be deleted."

Jara pulled herself up from the bed and began clutching frizzy strands of hair in frustration. "We don't have time for this," she moaned. "We need to figure this out *now*. In the next twenty minutes. Brone is releasing the program, as we speak."

"What we need is a low-tech solution," said Horvil, perking up. "How did the ancients keep permanent records?"

"With ink and treepaper," replied Jara without thinking.

"Exactly!"

They began frantically tearing the hotel room apart in search of paper and ink. Drawers, tables, cubbyholes, dressers—no sign of paper and ink in any of them. *I thought these people were Luddites!* thought Jara. *Isn't there supposed to be stationery sitting on the desks of old-fashioned hotels?*

Finally Horvil had an inspiration and dashed into the hallway of the hotel. Funny how quickly the plump engineer could move when he was motivated. He reemerged in the doorway seconds later bearing an antique book that Jara had seen sitting on the hall table near the elevator. A kitschy bit of decoration that some interior designer decided would lend the establishment some cachet. Jara flipped through it. The print was indecipherable Chinese script, the topic was unknown, and the middle contained a number of full-color plates that must have been glossy at some point in time. Ancient Chinese seascapes, verdant pastures with placid peasants tending the land. She turned the book to its blank inside cover.

"We've got a problem," said Jara.

"What?"

"How do we write in it?"

Horvil scratched his head. "You don't have a pen?"

"Horv, I don't think I've ever even *seen* a pen before. Not outside of a viewscreen. Have you?"

"Not since initiation. But this is ridiculous. We're in the *Islands*. The city of Manila's been around since ancient times. There's got to be somewhere that we can buy ink and treepaper around here. An ink and paper store."

Jara flung her mind wildly across the Data Sea. "There is—but it's on the other side of the city. We'd never make it in time."

They tore through the hotel room once more in search of some kind of writing utensil, momentarily swept away by the tide of fear. Horvil scurried down to the hotel lobby and returned back five minutes later empty-handed. Jara had resorted to getting down on hands and knees to see if some writing implement might have rolled under the bed at some point. No luck.

Then the engineer came up with a brilliant solution: they would write in blood. Jara doubted they'd be able to scrawl more than a dozen words or two by this method, but even a dozen words would be better than nothing. They wasted several minutes trying to prick their fingers and come up with a usable bead of blood to write with, only to find themselves thwarted by the miracles of modern medical technology. The OCHREs in their bio/logic systems would stanch the flow of blood within seconds, leaving them with only a few half-formed smears on the pulped wood fiber.

"This is pathetic," lamented Jara. "I can't believe we can project a virtual body millions of kilometers through space to Mars, but we can't figure out how to write something down on a piece of paper."

But Horvil was persistent. He grabbed the kitchen knife Jara had used to prick their fingertips and tried to carve a message onto the walls. But the flexible stone was almost completely impervious to their blade. Horvil and Jara threw away another five minutes experimenting on a wide variety of building materials, but floor, carpet, furniture, and dishes were all immune to permanent scarring by any method they possessed.

Dejected, they came close to giving up when Horvil was struck by a sudden remembrance. "I can't believe I forgot about this!" he shouted. "Aunt Berilla has an old quill pen sitting on her desk with a big pot of ink."

"What on Earth would she have something like that for?" asked Jara.

Horvil shrugged. "If I understood anything about Aunt Berilla, the world would be a much different place. I think she dabbles in calligraphy."

"Well, don't just *stand* there. Send her a ConfidentialWhisper already."

It took some convincing to persuade Berilla to leave the gathering of Creed Élan functionaries who had gathered in her estate to discuss philanthropic endeavors for striking TubeCo workers. But after a minute of increasingly alarming and unrealistic promises on Horvil's behalf, Berilla apparently decided that her nephew was in a serious enough bind to pay attention to. The engineer quickly brought Jara into the conversation.

"Horvil, I don't even know if that old quill pen still works," said the matriarch in a final effort to keep her afternoon intact.

"Don't try to pull that," said Horvil, head tilted back and fingers pinching a gumdrop of flesh between creased eyebrows until it turned cherry red. "I've seen you use it for that dumb calligraphy you do with your friends."

"Well, if you're going to behave *that* way . . ."

After another agonizing couple minutes of cajoling, they managed to persuade Berilla to retreat to her office and get out her quill pen and parchment. Horvil began dictating a long series of nonsensical letters and numbers that must have had his aunt pounding the table in irritation. He made Berilla repeat them back to him several times in a row to make sure she had transcribed his words correctly. "It's a rotating cipher," Horvil told Jara. "When I decode it, I'll get a few keywords to assure myself that it was genuinely me who sent the message."

"Yeah, but what does it *say?*"

"Pretty much the whole thing in a nutshell. You and me, the memory erasure, the relationship, a few private things about *you* so I can assure you that this all happened."

Jara didn't want to know what those *few private things* were, and she hoped she never had to find out. She felt an inexplicable tug from someplace inside of her, a desire to just let everything that had happened in the past few months get sucked down the drain of vanished memory and never come back. How many times had she yearned for the ability to just up and walk away from her life and start anew? She wondered how many people out there would use this memory apocalypse as a convenient excuse to abscond from their responsibilities.

Berilla's impatient *harrumph* interrupted her from her reverie. "What did you say?" asked Jara.

"I said, what do you want me to write down?"

And then it hit Jara: what *did* she want Berilla to write down?

Somehow the thought of writing a straightforward account of her relationship with Horvil and the lessons she had learned over the past few months seemed utterly inadequate, even if she could get over the embarrassment of dictating the entire thing to Horvil's Aunt Berilla. If Margaret's failsafe really did wipe out crucial parts of her memory, was there anything she could say to convince herself that her relationship with Horvil was real? She imagined a future Jara pursing her lips, skeptical of the whole business, wondering if somebody was playing her for a fool. Or worse—maybe she herself had willingly leapt into the jaws of an emotional trap, just like she had done so many times before.

Jara asked herself: what obligation did she have to force herself to accept the reality of a romantic relationship with Horvil? Who knew what circumstances Jara would find herself in, what emotional baggage the failsafe would leave her with? Who was to say that *Horvil* would survive it unscathed? Perhaps he would emerge from the whole experience with some crucial part of his personality emasculated from the tumult. Perhaps they would no longer be compatible people after this business was over with.

Besides which—did it really matter in the grand scope of things whether her relationship with Horvil survived intact? There were an infinite number of tracks her life could have taken in the past few months; why should she shackle herself to one particular track and stubbornly declare that one to be the best of all possible tracks? Jara had the power now to navigate among those different tracks, to choose her own. Whether she ended up happy with Horvil or not was precisely beside the point. No matter what happened today, this was a decision she would need to make again tomorrow, and the next day, and the day after that, and every sun and moon from now until she walked through the gates of the Prepared. Every day was a new choice and a new opportunity.

"Well?" said Berilla testily. "I've got a letter here addressed to you. What do you want it to say?"

Jara shook her head, landed back in the present. "Here's what I want you to write down. It's only one sentence. Ready?"

A sigh. "Yes."

"'You are yourself, and you are whole.'"

(((43)))

"You're in luck," says Quell. "You're not going to die. At least, not today."

Natch doesn't realize how much the fear has taken hold of him until he hears the Islander's words of reprieve. It feels like an enormous fist has loosened its grip on his chest. But if Quell has indeed figured out a way to neutralize the lethality of Margaret's failsafe code, then why does he still sound so weary, so defeated? "What's wrong?" asks Natch.

"You might *want* to die after this is all over."

The entrepreneur searches his feelings and still finds the will to live as strong as it was when Frederic Patel's sword almost sliced off his head. No, in spite of everything he has learned and lost in the past few months, Natch no longer wants to succumb to the Null Current. "Tell me," he says.

"I'll give you the short version because Brone's about to release MultiReal on the Data Sea," explains Quell. "Margaret's failsafe calls up a subroutine that blows out your neural OCHREs. It's like a lethal burst of electricity that just fries all the circuitry running through your brain. But I found a loophole. The failsafe doesn't actually *check* to make sure there's no neural activity after the subroutine runs. It just checks to make sure your *OCHREs* aren't functioning. The program assumes that if the OCHREs are dead, then the subroutine has done its job and destroyed the host. But I think I've figured out another way to destroy your neural OCHREs without killing you. If we run that first, then we can fake the failsafe out. It'll see that the OCHREs have gone dead and skip right over the lethal jolt of electricity."

"So . . . if all of the neural machinery is gone . . ."

"No more running bio/logic programs. Ever." Quell pauses and inhales sharply. "But that's not the worst part. There'll be collateral damage."

"Collateral damage?"

A pause. "You understand I'm simplifying this quite a bit."

"Yes. Go on."

"This alternate method of destroying the OCHREs . . . it's not electrical, it's chemical. It's not acid, exactly, but it'll be *like* acid. Some of the machines in the brain are very tightly interwoven with the structures they regulate. Like the OCHREs on the optic nerve—they're literally coiled around it. So if you destroy those machines . . ."

"I'll be blind, is what you're saying," interrupts Natch.

There's an uncomfortable silence as if Quell is trying to psyche himself up to say something. "Blind and deaf, I think," continues the Islander. "You'll be functional—you won't be in a vegetative state. Should be able to walk around, eat, pick up things. But you'll have . . . cognitive problems."

"What kind of cognitive problems?"

"I have no fucking idea. You might lose your sense of time. Or be unable to reason linearly. You might lose your emotions. There's going to be a thousand microscopic pinholes in your brain. Absolutely no way to tell what they'll hit." A long, ragged exhalation of breath. "But— you'll live. You'll survive. You'll function. Oh, and one more thing."

Natch blanches. What *else* could there be?

"It's going to *hurt* like a bitch. Like nothing you've ever felt before."

Quell was right. The choice between this kind of half-existence and a clean death is not an easy one. Is his desire for life strong enough to accept it regardless of the consequences? It's entirely possible that once the decision's been made, he will be unable to change his mind. Will he have the ability to bring himself to the Prepared if life in this state proves unbearable? He's not sure.

What would life be like without bio/logics? Natch tries to

remember what a normal day looks like, tries to take inventory of all the things he's losing.

He wakes up—usually prompted by a gentle nudge from Quasi-Suspension at a preset time. He stands and stretches—activating a quick burst from a common joint-soothing program by reflex. He walks into the shower room and takes a quick look at the mirror—with a half-conscious query to his bio/logic systems to check on the status of his teeth. He steps into the shower—and feels the hot spray of water automatically adjusting to his internal thermostat. . . .

Barely three minutes out of bed, Natch has already counted half a dozen ways in which he relies on bio/logics. Could he even count the number of programs he uses in an entire day? Hundreds, thousands? What about the routines he has tagged for quick access, programs that he can flick on and off with the twitch of a finger? He sprinkles Nice-Spice 52 throughout his meals to liven up a dull scone or soothe the bite of a hot pepper. . . . He fires up Urban Botanist 18c to idly peruse databases of redwood trees when he takes his tube trips between Cisco and Seattle. . . .

Initiation taught Natch that most bio/logic programs are not necessities at all, but luxuries earned by the human race after a thousand generations of toil. But in a society that runs on bio/logics, that was *built* on bio/logics, some programs are not luxuries. How will he walk down the street, when he won't be able to sense the tube tracks in front of him? How can he read the news, when he has no way of accessing the Data Sea? How can he even access a Vault account to pay for anything?

How can he program, when he can neither see nor interact with MindSpace?

Without all of those things . . . what's left?

"Listen, I know this isn't what you were hoping for," says Quell dejectedly. "I haven't given up. Do you hear me? *I haven't given up.* I'm going to keep battering away on this thing until the very last second. I might still be able to find a breakthrough."

"Can I ask you one favor?" says Natch.

"What?"

"Don't tell anyone about this, okay? Especially Horvil and Serr Vigal."

• • •

"This is a most peculiar contraption," says Richard Taylor. "I don't believe I've seen anything like this before."

"I can imagine," replies Natch. "Who rigged it up for you?"

"Your former apprentice Benyamin accomplished this for me. He claims it was not particularly difficult—it was simply a matter of locating an apparatus that could synthesize voices through a speaker, and from there channeling your words was rather easy. I suppose I can grasp that aspect of the conversation. But how he can translate *my* words from sound waves into brain waves—well, I'm satisfied to let that remain beyond my comprehension."

The entrepreneur smiles. At first, he wondered if his inexplicable fondness for the Pharisee was simply condescension—amusement at the man's ignorance. But the more words he exchanges with Richard Taylor, the more Natch realizes that he has a genuine fascination with the Pharisee's outsider perspective, with his boundless curiosity, with his occasional timidity and self-doubt. It would be very intriguing to see this man on his home turf. "Does the voice sound like me?" he asks.

Taylor laughs. "The voice sounds like the drama actor Juan Nguyen."

"Fitting."

"So Benyamin claims that you wish to ask me an important question."

"I do." Natch tries to formulate the best method of segueing into it, but he can think of nothing better than directness. He provides as basic an explanation of Margaret's failsafe and Quell's modification as he can. Taylor listens with complete silence, and somehow even through the strangely modulated voice of the sound wave conversion Natch can tell that the man is giving him his full attention. "My question is this," concludes the entrepreneur. "Can the Faithful Order of the Children Unshackled grant me asylum?"

Taylor is taken aback. "You wish to live . . . in the Pharisee Territories?"

"Yes."

"Ordinarily I would beg off answering such a question without consulting the leadership of my order. But in this circumstance, I believe I can answer you promptly and without qualification. Yes, Natch, we would consider it a great honor to host you in the Pharisee Territories, in Khartoum, for as long as you wish to stay."

"I wouldn't want to mislead you," says Natch. "I'll be a great burden. I won't be able to contribute to your society. I'll probably have to be fed and clothed."

"Nonetheless, we will welcome you with open arms."

"You'll have to figure out how to *get* to me too. I'm outside the Twin Cities right now, surrounded by drudges and Thasselians. Once I activate the failsafe, this place could get real chaotic real fast. Of course, you'll have an advantage—you'll be one of the few people around with absolutely no memory loss. You might be able to just swoop in there during the confusion and grab me before anyone notices."

"I don't think we'll have to worry too much about getting hold of you."

"Why?"

"Because I have discovered where my missing brethren from 49th Heaven are. Just today I received a message via Data Sea terminal that they were directed to the Twin Cities. They are already camped in a hotel not too far from the Kordez Thassel Complex, where they were told to await your arrival. That is why I was surprised to hear your request."

Natch pauses. "The Children Unshackled told them to go there?"

"That is my assumption."

"I assumed—I assumed they would be furious at me. For choosing to activate Margaret Surina's failsafe. Your message to me, it instructed me not to, I think."

"Never presume to know what the Children are thinking, Natch. Don't forget that they exist outside of time, space, and causality. I suspect they already knew the choice you would make and are comfortable with it."

• • •

"I'm never going to see rain again," says Natch.

His guardian hums in curiosity. "I didn't realize you liked rain," says Serr Vigal.

"I don't. That is . . . I suppose I've never really thought about it before. But I think once something is about to get taken away from you, it develops great significance. You start to wonder if—if you missed something important about it. If you failed to appreciate what was in front of you the whole time."

The laughter comes bubbling out of the neural programmer like water from a boiling kettle. "I do believe we'll make a philosopher of you yet, Natch."

A long pause.

"We didn't talk enough," Natch blurts out.

"I don't feel that way," replies Vigal after some thought. "It seems to me like we've talked about almost everything that's worth talking about."

"That's not true! There are a million things we never talked about. Furniture . . . music . . . literature . . . rain. We never talked about rain."

"We may still get the chance someday," says the neural programmer, his voice tentative.

"No, I told you. I've made my decision. I'm going to activate Margaret's failsafe . . . soon. You said that Brone released Possibilities 2.0 on the Data Sea. I'll need to activate the failsafe in the next few minutes. And after that . . ." The words drift off into the nothingness.

Natch doesn't need eyes and ears to know what Serr Vigal is doing in the moment of silence that follows. Vigal is tugging at his salt-and-pepper goatee, giving the ideas in his head a dress rehearsal before letting them out on the main stage. "Are you absolutely sure you know what's going to happen when you activate the failsafe?"

Pause. "What are you suggesting?"

"I'm thinking . . . Please, Natch, hear me out. MultiReal is a technology that allows one to explore alternate realities. Separate paths. Petrucio has already demonstrated how to use the technology to effectively live sixty seconds in the future. What if . . . what if . . ."

Natch cuts his guardian off with a weary sigh. "I know exactly what you're going to suggest. *This* could be one of those alternate realities. We could all be living in a virtual future right now."

"And?"

"Ridiculous," scoffs the entrepreneur.

"Come now, Natch! This isn't idle woolgathering. This isn't just one of Serr Vigal's silly far-flung ideas. Margaret Surina has destroyed the boundaries between the possible and the actual. If a choice cycle can be kept open for sixty seconds, why not an hour? And if you can live hours in the future, why not days? Weeks? Months!

"Imagine this, Natch," continues Vigal, his voice growing more feverish and flustered by the second. "Margaret is sitting at the top of the Revelation Spire preparing to activate the first phase of her failsafe—the phase where the code infiltrates everyone's bio/logic systems and begins tracking memories. She has doubts about whether the world is ready for MultiReal. But what if she also has doubts *in the failsafe?* What if she decides to take an extra layer of precaution—and introduces the *failsafe itself* in a potential alternate reality?"

"So you believe we're in a potential alternate reality inside *another* potential alternate reality?"

"I believe it's possible, that's all. The technology is out there to do this, Natch. Margaret has demonstrated it. Petrucio Patel has demonstrated it. You've lived it. Just—just admit that it's plausible, that's all. Just admit that much."

Natch can hear the desperation mounting in Vigal's words, and he figures it's time to put a stop to it. "Sure, I'll admit it's plausible—in the same way it's plausible that we could all be living inside a dream. In the same way that everything you experience might be a hallucination produced by some mad scientist stimulating your neural cells."

Willful silence.

"Vigal, this game doesn't lead anywhere. It's interesting to speculate about, I suppose. But regardless of whether I'm living in 'reality' or some kind of . . . simulation of reality, or hybrid reality, or whatever you want to call it . . . the choices don't change. So yes, I suppose it's *possible* that after I activate the failsafe, we'll all get snapped back to December of 359 again, before any of us had even heard of MultiReal. But in terms of *this* reality, nothing has changed. I still need to activate Margaret Surina's failsafe in order to save millions of lives . . . and you still need to prepare yourself for the fact that I'll be gone."

In the silence that follows, Natch realizes that the neural programmer has made up his mind, and no amount of logic or persuasive argumentation is going to change it. Which makes him feel more futile than he has felt since Brone put him in this darkness. Ever since that moment, he's been trying to spare his friends the agony of worrying about him, of worrying about the state of the world. Better they believe he will die than they believe he will spend his remaining years a stunted human being wandering the Pharisee Territories. Better they believe the world will forget all about MultiReal than they realize that this struggle will continue for generations to come. But if Serr Vigal and Horvil and Jara and Magan Kai Lee are going to believe what they're going to believe regardless of the evidence . . . then perhaps this is all just wasted energy.

Once Natch activates the failsafe, it won't matter. The Pharisees will take him away, and he'll disappear from civilization for good. Those around him will forget these conversations. They will assume that he has disappeared inside his shell and vanished into his own self-ishness. The world at large will eventually piece together what happened and likely come to the conclusion that Natch is to blame.

Which is perfectly fine with him.

Natch feels a sudden urge to just activate the failsafe and get it over with. True, he's in virtual time now, and he could potentially dally away hours in here without having wasted more than a minute or two in real time. But what does he gain by it? He was ready to activate the failsafe when he knew it would kill him. He's just as ready to activate it now. He takes inventory of his emotions, trying to think of things left unfinished, questions left unanswered. He knows he will never get another chance to tie up loose ends.

And then he thinks of one question he needs to ask. "Vigal, are you my father?" Natch blurts out.

A pause. "I'm surprised that you'd ask me that," mumbles the neural programmer hesitantly.

"Why?"

"I always took your silence to mean that you already knew the answer to that question. So all these years you simply didn't know? Did you think I was trying to . . . hide something from you? Or . . . did you . . ." Vigal slips into confusion, backtracks, starts again. "I suppose this is my fault, Natch. I really should have discussed this with you. Putting the burden of such a question on you, that wasn't fair of me, and I'm sorry."

"So you *are* my father?"

"Let me ask you . . . does it really matter? Would anything have been different if I had called you my son all these years instead of my charge? I admit I was never particularly good at parenting . . . but you know it's not something I ever asked for. It sort of . . . fell into my lap, you might say. But I *felt* like a father. I certainly sacrificed like a father. I've, I've loved you like a father. So, I ask again . . . does it matter?"

Natch sits for a moment in the nothingness. "No, I suppose it doesn't."

Serr Vigal exhales as if he has just put down a heavy weight. "Then I'll answer you. No, Natch, I'm not your father. Your mother and I never—we didn't—let's just say that despite what everyone thought, it was a platonic relationship."

Natch says nothing.

"I tried to figure out who your father was. When I arrived at Furtoid to pick you up all those years ago, I spent a month combing through records, asking questions, playing detective. But I think . . . I think I was asking for the wrong reasons. I found out nothing. The records were a disaster in those times. Don't forget, Natch, this was shortly after the Economic Plunge—and Furtoid has always been drastically underfunded, even in the best of times. There were wanderers and mercenaries passing through every day, and the colony had been paying genetic donors for decades. I think they were desperate to build up a population any way they could. They didn't have the manpower to keep track of it all . . . I suppose your father must have been one of those men, one of the ones who wandered through. But there's no way to prove that, after all these years."

Natch smiles. "How appropriate."

There is another long pause as the entrepreneur begins preparing himself for the failsafe. The blindness. The confusion and pain.

"So I suppose this is good-bye?" says Natch.

He can hear that Serr Vigal is weeping.

"What's wrong, Vigal?" he asks gently.

"I—I won't have you forgotten, Natch. I won't have you castigated and blamed for all the death and destruction that's to come when the fact of the matter is that you're *saving* billions of lives. And no, *don't* tell me it's inevitable you'll be hated. It's not. I need . . . I need to know what to tell the world. If they ask me why you did this, why you activated the failsafe. Tell me what to say, and I swear I'll remember it somehow."

Natch thinks for a moment.

And suddenly, as he thinks about what to tell Vigal, Natch can see more clearly than he has seen before. He can see *through* the blackness, past the barricade of nothingness that separates him from the rest of the world.

He sees a world picking itself up from destruction and despair, from the twin ravages of large-scale computational chaos and the greatest tsunami civilization has ever seen. A world where the estimates of the number of dead range from several hundred thousand to several million, where several of the major computational systems have crashed spectacularly but are now slowly being resuscitated. . . .

He sees a man in a black robe being dragged away from a long, low complex of buildings near the Twin Cities by a group of Defense and Wellness Council officers. The man is screaming with impotent rage, cursing Natch, cursing the high executive, cursing the world, cursing the narrow cell in an orbital prison that is to be his for decades to come. . . .

He sees two women embracing at the hoverbird docks of London in front of a battered but intact OrbiCo medical freighter. . . .

He sees a Surina standing on the floor of the Tul Jabbor Complex with twenty-three skeptical members of the Prime Committee looking on. The audience is composed in equal parts of connectible and Islander, and while they are still segregated in their separate sections of the auditorium, they are listening to one another and respectful. . . .

He sees a new fiefcorp celebrating its recent victory in climbing to the top of the Primo's bio/logic investment guide, a victory spearheaded by the efforts of a small woman with dark curly hair and a tall man with a thin mustache and a black-and-white swirled pin on his jacket. Their young chief analyst looks on with overt cynicism while their portly chief engineer keeps one nervous eye on his boss, constantly on the lookout for a sign of recognition that is yet to appear. . . .

He sees the new high executive presiding over an open government commission to study the new technology that has come to light in the wake of the recent mysterious Memory Event. The high executive calls for the formation of a memecorp to oversee the development and eventual commercialization of this new technology. He calls for the heir to the Surinas to have an honorary seat on the board. But who better to lead this new memecorp than the fiefcorp master of the new number one on Primo's? . . .

And finally he sees a caravan slowly making its way across an arid land uncluttered by the zigzagging flight paths of hoverbird traffic, untrammeled by the tracks of tube trains. The caravan turns off the gravel road it has been traveling down and camps on the roadside. Children hop out and scurry from car to car, playing games with ball and stick. There's a man there, a large mirthful figure with grizzly hair and beard, who emerges from one vehicle leading by the hand his charge, his friend and his responsibility.

It's a man in his early thirties. Blind as if he had never known light, deaf to the world around him. To him there is no memory and there is no time; there is only the deathless and undifferentiated now. Yesterday is the same as today is the same as tomorrow, but all is well because he has seen the nothingness at the center of the universe and he is at peace.

Natch speaks. "If anyone asks, you tell them that I'm moving towards perfection. But I'll get there at my own damn speed."

APPENDIXES

APPENDIX A

A SYNOPSIS OF *INFOQUAKE* AND *MULTIREAL*

Natch is an entrepreneur with a burning ambition. He simply can't define what it is.

The world he lives in is a ripe place for ambition. Having suffered a cataclysmic AI revolt hundreds of years ago, the world embraced Sheldon Surina and his science of bio/logics. Now, 359 years later, thousands of small software companies—fiefcorps—compete ruthlessly to sell programs that run the human body. Order is maintained by a patchwork of subscription-based governments called L-PRACGs. Overseeing these governments is the Prime Committee, which uses the Defense and Wellness Council as its police force.

As an orphaned boy in the care of the neural programmer Serr Vigal, Natch is plagued by strange and hallucinatory visions. He learns to use his wits to best his childhood enemies and achieve top scores in his class. His only obstacle is Brone, a boy with an equally cunning intellect and a more charismatic way with people. But Brone is soon dispatched during the boys' initiation by a bear attack that is partly accident, partly fate, and partly Natch's dark vengeance.

With his prospects for financial success dimmed by the scandal of initiation, Natch turns to a series of low-paying jobs at the bottom of the programming world. Only gradually, after much Machiavellian scheming, does Natch climb to the top of his profession. But he hasn't achieved this alone. He's had the aid of his childhood friend, Horvil; his mentor, Serr Vigal; and his market analyst, Jara.

With Horvil's and Jara's help, Natch achieves one final coup. He arranges a complicated con involving a fake black code attack on the Vault banking system. This con allows Natch's fiefcorp to replace his bitter rivals, the Patel Brothers, at the top of the Primo's bio/logic investment guide rankings. Where Natch was once an outcast, now he is a celebrity.

Furthermore, the scheme brings Natch to the attention of Margaret Surina, heir to her ancestor Sheldon's fortune. She's been working for decades on a mysterious technology called MultiReal that creates "alternate realities." But now she fears that Len Borda, the high executive of the Defense and Wellness Council, is preparing to take this technology away from her—and possibly kill her in the process. Borda sees MultiReal as a weapon of potentially apocalyptic proportions, one too dangerous to remain in private hands. It's the same conflict Margaret's father, Marcus, went through with his teleportation technology many years ago, a conflict that ended in a fiery hoverbird accident.

Margaret offers Natch an opportunity to license her new technology. He is to stir up enough trouble to keep Len Borda off balance for the next week; then, after Margaret reveals the existence of Multi-Real in a widely publicized speech, Natch needs to quickly put together a prototype to show the world that the technology is real. The fiefcorp master agrees.

Natch goes looking for a source to fund his company's new project, but partly due to his shady reputation, nobody will support him in this new and undefined venture. Finally, with the help of his new apprentice, Merri, he snags an appointment with the leader of Creed Thassel, an organization dedicated to the power of selfishness. The leader turns out to be none other than Natch's old nemesis Brone. Brone, still smarting from the wounds of initiation, offers Natch a quick loan and foretells a future where the two of them will work together to market

MultiReal. The fiefcorp master, seeing no other alternatives, accepts the loan from his old hivemate.

Armed with a new infusion of cash, Natch hires a new apprentice—Horvil's young cousin Benyamin—and forms a partnership with sales channeler Robby Robby to help market the new product.

The day of Margaret's speech arrives, and with it comes an incursion into the Surina compound at Andra Pradesh by the troops of the Defense and Wellness Council. As Margaret unveils her new technology before hundreds of millions of people, the Data Sea networks explode with a strange new computational disturbance: the infoquake. Thousands die in the tumult, but the Council does not follow through with its implied threat to kill Margaret and seize MultiReal.

Natch gathers the fiefcorp for a meeting the next day and informs them that a frightened Margaret has handed over the reins of the company to him and allowed him to rechristen it the Surina/Natch MultiReal Fiefcorp. Furthermore, Natch will get a new apprentice, Quell. A longtime confidant of Margaret's, Quell is an Islander, a member of a society that spurns all but the most rudimentary forms of bio/logic technology.

For a short time, it appears that Natch has gotten the upper hand. He is on top of the world and has even used his new partnership with Margaret to pay back Brone and sever his ties with the Thasselian.

But Natch's expectations are dashed when he discovers that his enemies the Patel Brothers have also secured a MultiReal licensing agreement with Margaret Surina. Margaret soon reveals that she suspected the Patels of selling out to the Defense and Wellness Council. Only after she despaired of working with them did she turn to Natch, who she knew would never give in to pressure from Len Borda.

Natch immediately goes on the offensive to counter the Patels. Frederic and Petrucio Patel have scheduled a demo in less than a week's time; Natch decides that he's going to hold his demo first, in three days. But after he commands his fiefcorp to prepare a quick-and-dirty demo, a group in black robes ambushes him in the streets of Shenandoah. Natch is hit by their black code darts, falls unconscious, and vanishes.

Meanwhile, unaware that Natch is missing, the fiefcorp prepares for their product demo. They only realize Natch has disappeared hours before the demo. The fiefcorpers frantically attempt to find him as Len Borda's forces once again march on the Surina compound. Jara makes a last-ditch effort to convince Margaret to deliver the demo in Natch's stead. Margaret refuses, choosing instead to retreat to the top of the Revelation Spire, her private tower. Jara decides that she will give the presentation instead. Horvil catches up with her and attempts to dissuade her from making this dangerous presentation, in the process confessing that he has developed deep feelings for her. But Jara will not be deterred.

And then, at the last possible minute, Natch shows up. He had awakened from his black code coma mere hours before. With him is Len Borda—who, as it turns out, has brought the Council troops to Andra Pradesh at Natch's request, in an effort to scare off any potential black code attack. In exchange for this intervention, Natch has hurriedly promised Borda access to MultiReal.

Natch delivers a product demo that involves using the power of Multi-Real to simulate hitting a baseball to all five hundred million spectators simultaneously. The audience reacts more enthusiastically than anyone could have anticipated. (The Patels' demo, meanwhile, is a disaster.)

As *Infoquake* draws to a close, it occurs to Natch that the attackers in black robes could have been sent by the Defense and Wellness Council as a ploy to get MultiReal under its control. There are, in fact, any number of organizations that might be using the black code inside him as leverage to get control of MultiReal. Brone, the Patel Brothers, and even Margaret Surina are listed as potential suspects.

Natch is beginning to feel the deleterious effects of the black code inside him; but as he tells his mentor, Serr Vigal, he's up for the challenges ahead. He's come this far against all odds, and he won't back down now.

• • •

As *MultiReal* begins, High Executive Len Borda has put his second-in-command, Lieutenant Executive Magan Kai Lee, in charge of forcing Natch back to the negotiating table. Magan reluctantly agrees. Two years before, he had been on the verge of assassinating Borda, but the high executive made a deal with him to step down peacefully. That deal expires in a few weeks, yet Borda has shown no signs that he's preparing to leave. Still, Magan does as he is ordered. He conducts a raid on Natch's apartment, only to find a pack of drudges (journalists) waiting to humiliate him before the world.

Magan goes back to Borda and baldly accuses the high executive of mismanaging the fight to regain control of MultiReal. He says Borda made a terrible mistake assassinating Margaret Surina's father, Marcus, almost fifty years ago, causing a devastating worldwide economic depression. He persuades Borda to give him a few more weeks to get MultiReal under the Council's control. Assisting him will be his trusted subordinates: the Council's chief solicitor, Rey Gonerev, nicknamed the Blade; and Magan's chief engineer, Papizon.

Meanwhile, Natch returns home to Shenandoah after several weeks on the run from the Council. He decides that his company will hold an exposition where two teams of volunteers (chosen by public lottery) will play soccer against each other using MultiReal.

Jara, Quell, Horvil, Benyamin, Serr Vigal, and Merri get to work preparing for the exposition. But the fiefcorp has a number of obstacles in its path. Magan Kai Lee tries to persuade Jara to make a deal with the Council before they intervene and stop the MultiReal exposition. Natch is being tormented by tremors from the black code he was hit with in Shenandoah, as well as by mysterious bits of MultiReal code that have turned up in his bio/logic systems. The Patel Brothers are still working on their own competing MultiReal product. And the fiefcorp is getting no assistance from Margaret Surina, who has seemingly gone insane after fleeing to the top of the Revelation Spire.

Suddenly, as the date for the exposition approaches, Magan Kai Lee and the Defense and Wellness Council swoop in. They've used a variety of tactics to suspend the business licenses of everyone in the company—except Jara. Since Jara is the only one legally capable of doing business now, the Council has effectively put control of the Surina/Natch MultiReal Fiefcorp into Jara's hands. Natch threatens to launch MultiReal right then and there in retaliation—until news breaks that Margaret Surina is dead.

The fiefcorp master rushes to Andra Pradesh, where he finds that the Council has taken control of the Surina compound. He and Quell sneak to the top of the Revelation Spire, trying to find out what happened to Margaret. On seeing her lifeless body, Quell goes crazy with grief and attacks Magan Kai Lee. He lands a solid blow on Lee, but ends up being dragged off to a Council orbital prison.

Margaret Surina's death throws everything up in the air. Jara leads the rest of the frightened fiefcorpers to the estate of Benyamin's mother, Berilla, where she relies on the pack of news-seeking drudges outside to keep them safe. Natch soon arrives, telling Jara that he's given her core access to the MultiReal program in order to smooth things over. Jara is initially convinced by his peace offering. But when Natch threatens his own apprentices—Horvil and Benyamin, Berilla's nephew and son—in an attempt to coerce Berilla to assist the fiefcorp, Jara has had enough. She casts Natch out of the estate and tells him she is running the company now.

Jara embarks on a campaign to repair the fiefcorp's image. But the campaign gets off to a rocky start with a failed press conference, and the rest of the apprentices are suspicious of her motives. Jara makes a desperate deal with the Patel Brothers to secure their help restoring the fiefcorp's business licenses: from now on users of both companies' versions of MultiReal will have limited numbers of daily "choice cycles." This means that Surina/Natch users will not be able to handily win any MultiReal-versus-MultiReal conflict against Patel Brothers users.

Jara and Horvil also try to cut Natch off from the MultiReal program, afraid of what he might do with it on his own. But it turns out that the mysterious MultiReal code in Natch's head has given him access to the program that can't be taken away.

Meanwhile, Natch has not been idle. He arranges to meet Khann Frejohr, speaker of the Congress of L-PRACGs and sworn libertarian enemy of Len Borda. Natch demonstrates to Frejohr that MultiReal can be used to enact a form of mind control. With the help of a forged Council memo to enrage public opinion, Natch persuades Frejohr and his libertarian allies to stir up civil unrest against the Council during Margaret Surina's funeral. Chaos and violence soon break out. The Prime Committee steps in and declares they will hold a hearing to determine the fate of MultiReal—all as Natch had planned.

The hearing in the Tul Jabbor Complex begins with a pair of high-minded speeches by Natch's mentor Serr Vigal and the Council solicitor Rey Gonerev. But just as Petrucio Patel is summoned to demonstrate MultiReal, another infoquake strikes, sending the crowd into panic. Len Borda loses his patience and instructs his troops to kill both Natch and Magan Kai Lee, who has failed to follow through on his deal to deliver MultiReal. Natch manages to avoid death through the power of MultiReal, while Magan prevails over his would-be assassins with the aid of a contingent of loyal Council officers (including Rey Gonerev and Papizon). As the battle rages, the mysterious group in black robes who hit Natch with black code enters the auditorium, dartguns blazing. Strangely, they're not firing at Natch; they're firing at the Council in an effort to help Natch escape.

Magan enlists the help of Petrucio Patel, commanding him to use the "MultiReal-D" programs he brought to demonstrate. The two track Natch down just before he leaps onto a hoverbird with the group in black robes. Petrucio fires his dartgun at Natch. However, because of Jara's earlier deal with the Patel Brothers, Natch is not able to use MultiReal to triumph over Petrucio, and gets hit with the black code dart as he escapes.

The people in black robes turn out to be apprentices of Brone, the bodhisattva of Creed Thassel and Natch's childhood enemy. They take Natch to a decrepit hotel in Chicago, a city ruined hundreds of years ago in the Autonomous Revolt and now occupied by the diss (the indigent). The Thasselians hail Natch as a hero. Brone explains that the black code he implanted in Natch was a cloaking device to keep him hidden from the Defense and Wellness Council. He has brought Natch here to participate in his "Revolution of Selfishness," which will be brought about by enhancing MultiReal to its next level of functionality—a level Brone calls Possibilities 2.0.

Brone has discovered a way to use MultiReal to not only *calculate* multiple realities at once, but to actually *experience* multiple realities simultaneously. Using Possibilities 2.0, one can actually run parallel tracks of consciousness. According to Brone, this can eliminate "the tyranny of cause and effect" forever, giving humanity ultimate and irreversible freedom—and completely eliminating the dominance of the Council.

Seeing nowhere else to go, Natch joins Brone's group in trying to complete the programming of Possibilities 2.0. But as Natch's black code tremors grow in severity and Brone gives him elusive answers to his questions, Natch grows suspicious. He accuses Brone of killing Margaret Surina in an attempt to get hold of MultiReal. Brone claims that he threatened to kill the bodhisattva, but she committed suicide before he could follow through. Natch is unsure whether to believe Brone, but he moves the MultiReal databases and cuts off all access to the program as a safeguard. Finally, haunted by a late-night vision of Margaret, Natch flees.

But his flight from Brone into the ruined city of Old Chicago is short-lived. Pursued by the diss and plagued by Brone's voice in his head, Natch collapses on the street and falls into total blackness. His senses are completely cut off now. Brone admits that this is, in fact, the real purpose of the black code that was planted in Natch. He tells Natch that he did sincerely want to join forces, but now he realizes that Natch cannot be trusted. He threatens Natch with horrible torture until he hands over MultiReal. Natch refuses Brone's request; he feels his death approaching, and falls into darkness.

Meanwhile, Jara and the fiefcorp await the Prime Committee's ruling about the fate of MultiReal. Despite the fact that the program is gone, the Committee votes to seize it from Jara's fiefcorp. Confused and unsure what to do, she winds up finally getting together with Horvil.

As the fiefcorp tries to figure out what to do next, Magan Kai Lee approaches them and proposes they make a deal to try to find Natch. Jara refuses. She's confident now that she can make her own way forward.

Magan leaves in disappointment. He has effectively declared his intention to start a full-scale rebellion against Len Borda; the key is finding Natch and getting hold of MultiReal before Borda does. As *MultiReal* comes to a close, Rey Gonerev asks Magan if Natch is even still alive. Magan replies that Natch is definitely alive; he is absolutely certain of that fact.

Geosynchron is the concluding volume of the Jump 225 trilogy.

APPENDIX B

GLOSSARY OF TERMS

For more comprehensive definitions and background articles on some terms, consult the Web site at http://www.geosynchron.net.

TERM	DEFINITION
49th Heaven	A decadent orbital colony known for its loose morality; originally founded by one of the Three Jesuses as a religious retreat.
aft	One of the descriptive components of a program that helps the Data Sea sort and catalog information. See also *fore*.
Allahu Akbar Emirates	A nation-state that once existed in what is now mostly Pharisee territory. "Allahu Akbar" means "God is great."
Allowell	An orbital colony saved from extinction by High Executive Tul Jabbor.
analyst	One of the standard positions in a fiefcorp. Fiefcorp analysts typically focus on areas such as marketing, channeling, finance, and product development.

Andra Pradesh	A center of culture on the Indian subcontinent. Home to Creed Surina and the Gandhi University.
apprentice	An employee of a fiefcorp, under contract to a master. In the traditional fiefcorp structure, apprentices sign a contract for a specific number of years. During their apprenticeship, apprentices receive only room and board as compensation; but at the conclusion of the contract, their shares mature and they receive a large stake in the company and a share of the accumulated profits.
assembly-line programming	Tedious and repetitive bio/logic programming, usually done by large groups of low-skilled laborers.
Autonomous Minds	The sentient supercomputers that rebelled against humanity during the Autonomous Revolt.
Autonomous Revolt	The rebellion of the Autonomous Minds, which caused worldwide destruction and hastened the collapse of the nation-states.
Band of Twelve	The group of dissidents who formed the Islander movement and formed an unconnectible government in Manila.
battle language	Coded communications used by military and intelligence agencies during combat.
beacon	A tracking signal that allows one to be located on the multi network.

Big Divide	The era of worldwide depression and chaos following the Autonomous Revolt.
bio/logic program	A set of logical instructions designed to enhance the human body or mind. Most bio/logic programs act on the body through microscopic machines called OCHREs placed throughout the body at (or before) birth.
bio/logic programming bars	The set of tools bio/logic programmers use to create and modify bio/logic code. Programming bars are categorized with the letters of the Roman alphabet (A to Z) and are largely indistinguishable to the naked eye. They interact with virtual code through holographic extensions that are only visible in MindSpace.
bio/logics	The science of using programming code to extend the capabilities of the human body and mind.
black code	Malicious or harmful programs, usually designed and launched by seditious organizations.
bodhisattva	The spiritual leader of a creed. Most creed organizations are spearheaded by one individual bodhisattva. Some creeds are run by an elected body of major and minor bodhisattvas.
capitalman	An individual who raises start-up money for fief-corps. Following long tradition, the term is gender-neutral.

ChaiQuoke
A popular tea-flavored beverage.

channel
The process of marketing and selling products, usually to groups rather than individuals.

channeler
A businessperson responsible for driving sales to specific markets.

chief solicitor
The head legal officer of the Defense and Wellness Council.

Chill Polly
A dangerous and highly addictive variety of black code.

choice cycle
A single possible "reality" MultiReal can cause to happen. Actually choosing that reality is called "closing the choice cycle."

Chomp
A dangerous and highly addictive variety of black code.

Confidential-Whisper
One of the most popular bio/logic programs on the Data Sea, ConfidentialWhisper provides a silent, completely internal communication venue for two or more people.

Congress of L-PRACGs
A representative body composed of most of the L-PRACGs in the solar system. The speaker of the Congress is one of the most powerful elected officials in government.

connectible   Able to link to the Data Sea. Cultures who shun modern technology (like the Islanders and the Pharisees) are said to be "unconnectible," and refer to the remainder of society as "connectibles." See also *unconnectible*.

connectible coin   A small, disc-shaped device engineered by Margaret Surina that replicates the functionality of the government-issue connectible collars.

connectible collar   The thin copper collar that Islanders and other unconnectibles wear to allow them to see and communicate with multi projections.

core access   The state of complete administrative control over a bio/logic program (as opposed to developer access or user access).

credit   The standard unit of monetary exchange in civilized society.

creed   An organization that promotes a particular ethical belief system. Creeds promulgate many of the same types of moral teachings as the ancient religions, but are generally bereft of religious mythology and iconography.

Creed Élan   One of the more prominent creeds, Creed Élan teaches the value of philanthropy. Its members tend to be wealthy socialites. The creed's colors are purple and red.

Creed Objectivv   A creed dedicated to the search for and promotion of absolute epistemological truth. Members take an oath to always tell the truth. Its logo is a black-and-white swirl.

Creed Surina   The creed founded in honor of Sheldon Surina after his death. Creed Surina promotes the agenda of "spiritual discovery and mutual enlightenment through technology." The official colors of the creed are blue and green.

Creed Thassel   A once-common creed of the business class, dedicated to the "virtue of selfishness." Its symbol is three vertical stripes.

Creeds Coalition   The blanket organization that promotes intercreed understanding and cooperation.

Data Sea   The sum total of all the communication networks running in the civilized world. Includes such networks as the Jamm and the Sigh.

Defense and Wellness Council   The governmental entity responsible for military, security, and intelligence operations throughout the system. The Council is headed by a single high executive, who is appointed by the Prime Committee. Its officers wear the uniform of the white robe and yellow star.

Democratic American Collective (DAC)   An ancient nation-state formed after the dissolution of the United States of America. See also *New Alamo*.

disruptor   A weapon that allows attacks on multi projections by disrupting or altering their signals. Disruptions are often used by the Defense and Wellness Council in conjunction with dartguns.

diss   The urban poor. The term is alternately thought to be derived from "disenfranchised," "disaffected," and "disassociated."

dock   An area in which fiefcorps keep pending projects that are being prepared for launch on the Data Sea.

Dogmatic Opposition   A legal appeal to the Prime Committee to block or nullify a specific technology. It is used primarily by the Islanders to maintain a society that is skeptical of technology.

Dr. Plugenpatch   The network of medical databases and programs that maintains the health of nearly all connectible citizens.

drudge   An independent reporter or journalist who writes regular opinion columns to a list of subscribers. Drudges are considered one of the public's main resources for government accountability.

DWCR   Defense and Wellness Council Root, rumored to be High Executive Len Borda's new base of operations. Its location is unknown.

East Texas   One of two former splinter states of New Alamo. See also *West Texas*.

Economic Plunge of the 310s	A period of worldwide collapse and unemployment following the death of Marcus Surina. It is widely thought to have been eradicated by massive Defense and Wellness Council spending.
Ecumenical Council	The religious governmental body in New Alamo that was responsible for much of the violence and bloodshed of the Big Divide.
engineer	One of the standard positions in a fiefcorp. Engineers are traditionally responsible for the "nuts and bolts" bio/logic programming for a fiefcorp's products.
fiefcorp	A business entity that typically consists of one master and several apprentices. Fiefcorps are usually short-lived, lasting less than a decade. The economics of the fiefcorp business are such that it usually makes better sense to dissolve a fiefcorp and sell its assets every few years. See also *memecorp*.
flexible glass	A strong, glasslike building material that can be very easily stretched and molded, even at room temperature.
fore	One of the descriptive components of a program that helps the Data Sea sort and catalog information. See also *aft*.
"for process' preservation"	A common phrase roughly translatable as "for Pete's sake."

Free Republic of the Pacific Islands The official name of the unconnectible government in the Pacific Islands, with the city of Manila as its seat of government. Its residents are colloquially known as "Islanders."

Furtoid A distant and troubled orbital colony in constant danger of collapse from poor engineering and economics.

Gandhi University, the The institution of higher learning in Andra Pradesh where Sheldon Surina taught. Each of his descendants has held an honorary chair at the university.

gateway zone The designated entry point for a multi projection into real space.

geosynchrons Programs that regulate the geophysical and meteorological activity of the Earth. Geosynchrons are categorized as Levels I through V, I being the lowest level (regulation of atomic activity) and V being the highest level (regulation of complex environmental activity).

governmentalism The political movement that espouses a belief in strong centralized government (though not necessarily the current centralized government). See also *libertarianism*.

GravCo A semigovernmental memecorp that regulates gravity control among orbital colonies and other outworlders.

high executive   The official who heads the Defense and Wellness Council, appointed by the Prime Committee.

hive   A communal birthing and child-rearing facility for middle- and upper-class children.

hoverbird   A flying vehicle that can travel in air and low orbit. Hoverbirds are primarily used for travel over long distances, hauling cargo, and defense.

infoquake   A dangerous burst of energy in the computational system, thought to be caused by a disproportionate amount of activity at one time or concentrated in one particular area.

initiation   A twelve-month rite of passage that many youths from middle- and upper-class backgrounds go through before being considered adults. The initiation consists primarily of depriving children of modern technology.

Islander   A resident of the Pacific Islands, where the governments shun most modern technology.

Islander Tolerance Act   The law that created the Dogmatic Opposition in an attempt to ease relations between connectible and unconnectible cultures.

Jabbor, Tul   The first high executive of the Defense and Wellness Council.

Jamm

A network that allows never-ending musical "jam sessions" between musicians all over the world.

Keepers

The order that was assigned to program and operate the Autonomous Minds. They are often blamed for starting the Autonomous Revolt, although the extent of their complicity in the revolt will never fully be known.

launch

To officially release a product onto the Data Sea for public consumption.

libertarianism

A political philosophy that believes in decentralized government run principally by the L-PRACGs. See also *governmentalism*.

lieutenant executive

One of several second-in-command officers in the Defense and Wellness Council. They are nominated by the high executive and officially appointed by the Prime Committee.

L-PRACG

Local Political Representative Association of Civic Groups, the basic unit of government throughout the civilized world. Pronounced "ELL prag."

Lunar tycoons

Class of investors who grew massively wealthy through early speculation on moon real estate. Nowadays the term mostly refers to their moneyed descendants.

master

One of the positions in a fiefcorp. The master is the person who forms the fiefcorp and has full authority in all business decisions. Masters take on apprentices who then work to earn full shares in the fiefcorp after a specific contractual period.

Meme Cooperative — The governmental entity that regulates business between fiefcorps. It is largely perceived as an ineffectual watchdog organization.

memecorp — A business entity whose membership subscribes to a particular set of ideas ("memes"). A memecorp frequently relies on public or private funding, as opposed to the fiefcorp, which relies solely on the free market. See also *fiefcorp*.

MindSpace — The virtual programming "desktop" provided by a workbench for programming. It is only in Mind-Space that the extensions to bio/logic programming bars can be used to manipulate bio/logic code.

Muhammad, Jesus Elijah — Last of the "Three Jesuses." He founded the colony of 49th Heaven as a spiritual retreat.

multi — To project a virtual body onto the multi network. The word can be used as a verb, a noun, or an adjective.

multi connection — The state of existing virtually on the multi network. When the user returns to his or her physical body, they have "cut their multi connection."

multi network — The system of bots and programs that allows people to virtually interact with one another almost anywhere in the world and on most orbital colonies.

multi projection

A virtual body that exists only through neural manipulation by the multi network. Real bodies can interact with virtual bodies in ways that are almost identical to actual physical interaction.

MultiReal

A revolutionary new technology owned by the Surina/Natch MultiReal Fiefcorp and also licensed to the Patel Brothers Fiefcorp. Surina/Natch's MultiReal product is being branded as "Possibilities," while the Patel Brothers' is being branded as "SafeShores."

nation-state

An ancient political entity, bounded by geography and ruled over by a centralized government or governments. Nation-states were superseded by the rise of L-PRACGs.

neural programmer

A bio/logics specialist who concentrates on the programming of the human brain.

New Alamo

An ancient nation-state formed after the dissolution of the United States of America. New Alamo included many of the USA's southwestern states and portions of Mexico as well and became a dominant and terrorizing world power during the Big Divide. See also *Democratic American Collective*.

nitro

A popular beverage full of concentrated natural stimulants, usually served hot.

Nova Ceti	An orbital colony.
Null Current	A poetic term for death. The term is of uncertain vintage but is thought by many to have been coined by Sheldon Surina.
OCHRE (1)	A generic term for any of a number of nanotechnological devices implanted in the human body to maintain health. The term derives from the OCHRE Corporation, which pioneered the technology.
OCHRE (2)	The Osterman Company for Human Re-Engineering. The company was founded by Henry Osterman to pioneer nanotechnology and dissolved almost 110 years later after a protracted legal battle with the Defense and Wellness Council. It is often (redundantly) called "the OCHRE Corporation" to distinguish it from the nanotechnological machines that bear its name.
offline	A slang term for "crazy."
OrbiCo	The quasi-governmental agency that controls the space shipping lines and most interplanetary cargo travel.
orbital colony	A nonterrestrial habitation, sometimes built free-standing in space and sometimes built on existing soil (e.g., asteroids and planetoids). The major orbital colonies are 49th Heaven, Allowell, Furtoid, Nova Ceti, and Patronell, but there are dozens of smaller colonies all over the solar system.

orbital prison

A secure detention facility floating in orbit. Most of them are maintained by the Defense and Wellness Council, though there are orbital prisons run by other organizations.

Osterman, Henry

A contemporary of Sheldon Surina and founder of the OCHRE Corporation. Osterman was a famous iconoclast and recluse who zealously persecuted his enemies and died under mysterious circumstances in 117.

Padron, Par

The high executive of the Defense and Wellness Council from 153 until his death in 209. He was nicknamed "the people's executive" because of his pro-democratic reforms.

Patronell

An orbital colony that circles Luna.

"perfection postponed"

A common phrase roughly translatable as "heaven forbid."

permasteel

An ultrastrong alloy of steel used frequently in modern architecture. It is known for its greenish glow.

Pharisees

The disparate groups of fanatics who live around the areas once known as the Middle East. It is believed that millions of people still practice many of the ancient religions in these remote places.

Pharisee Territories

Unconnectible lands in the Middle East occupied by the Pharisees.

Prepared, the — An order whose membership is only open to the elderly and the terminally ill. Its members are given special legal status and access to euthanasia procedures in the Dr. Plugenpatch databases that are otherwise banned.

Prime Committee — The central governing board that runs the affairs of the system. Much like the ancient United Nations, the Committee's functions are mainly diplomatic and administrative. All of the real power rests with the Defense and Wellness Council and the L-PRACGs. The Committee's symbol is the black ring.

Primo's — The bio/logic investment guide that provides a series of ratings for programmers and their products. People all over the world rely on Primo's ratings as a gauge of reliability in bio/logics.

Principalities of Spiritual Enlightenment — The name given to the Pharisee Territories by its residents.

public directory — A listing of personal information used throughout the civilized world.

pulse grenade — A nonlethal weapon designed to temporarily blind the enemy.

QuasiSuspension — A popular program that allows the user to schedule sleep and choose different levels of rest. The program is often used to ration out sleep in small doses and keep the user awake longer.

Reawakening | The period of intellectual renewal and discovery that began with Sheldon Surina's publication of his seminal paper on bio/logics. It continues to this day.

Revelation Spire | The tallest building constructed since the Autonomous Revolt. It is part of the Surina compound in Andra Pradesh.

ROD | Routine On Demand. A simple bio/logic program created for a single (often wealthy) individual. The acronym is usually pronounced as one word ("rod").

SeeNaRee | A virtual environment created by an enclosed room or space. It uses technology similar to the multi system.

shock baton | An electrified bludgeoning weapon, primarily used by the Islanders.

Sigh, the | A virtual network devoted to sensual pleasure. Unlike the multi network, the Sigh does not allow interaction between real and virtual bodies.

Smith, Jesus Joshua | The first and most influential of the Three Jesuses. He led an exodus of faithful Christians and Muslims to the Pharisee Territories.

subaether | A form of instantaneous transmission made possible by quantum entanglement.

Surina, Marcus   A descendant of Prengal Surina and the "father of teleportation." He died in an orbital colony accident at the prime of his life, leaving TeleCo in shambles and prompting the Economic Plunge of the 310s.

Surina, Margaret   The daughter of Marcus Surina and the inventor of MultiReal technology.

Surina, Prengal   The grandson of Sheldon Surina and discoverer of the universal law of physics, which is the cornerstone of all modern computing and engineering.

Surina, Sheldon   The father of bio/logics. He revived the ancient sciences of nanotechnology and paved the way for the drastic improvement of the human race through technology.

TeleCo   A quasi-governmental agency that runs all teleportation services, brought to prominence by Marcus Surina. Now tightly regulated by the Defense and Wellness Council.

teleportation   The process of instantaneous human transportation over long distances. Technically, matter is not actually "transferred" during a teleportation, but rather telekinetically reconfigured.

Thassel, Kordez   A libertarian philosopher and the founder of Creed Thassel.

Three Jesuses   Spiritual leaders who, in three separate movements, led pilgrimages of the religious faithful to found colonies of free religious worship in what are currently known as the Pharisee Territories.

Toradicus   A high executive of the Defense and Wellness Council known for bringing the L-PRACGs under central government control.

"Towards Perfection"   A greeting or farewell, originally derived from a saying of Sheldon Surina's.

treepaper   Ancient sheet of pulped wood for writing and printing with ink.

tube   The high-speed trains used in most civilized places on Earth for inter- and intracity travel. The tube has become ubiquitous because its tracks are extremely cheap to build, easy to lay down, and unobtrusive in appearance.

TubeCo   The memecorp that runs the tube system. It is now heavily subsidized by the Prime Committee.

Tul Jabbor Complex   The headquarters of the Prime Committee in Melbourne, named after the building's architect, the first high executive of the Defense and Wellness Council.

unconnectible   Not able to connect to the resources on the Data Sea. This term is sometimes a derogatory reference to the Islanders and the Pharisees, who shun modern technology. See also *connectible*.

unconnectible curtain	The dividing line between the modern world and the unconnectible areas of the Pacific Islands where multi projections and certain other technologies are banned.
underground transfer system	The mechanized subterranean network that handles most Terran shipping and cargo transport.
universal law of physics	Scientific principle put forward by Prengal Surina that enables nearly limitless supplies of energy.
Vault, the	The network that makes financial transactions possible. Known for fanatical secrecy and paranoia, the administrators of the Vault pride themselves on never having suffered from a serious break-in. The symbol of the Vault is the double-balanced pyramid.
viewscreen	A flat surface that can receive and display audio and visual transmissions from the Data Sea. Viewscreens are usually used for decoration in addition to entertainment.
West Texas	One of two former splinter states of New Alamo. See also *East Texas*.
Witt, Tobi Jae	A famous scientist and pioneer of artificial intelligence from before the Autonomous Revolt. She created the first Autonomous Mind and died a violent death, though her killer was never identified.

workbench

A particular type of desk capable of projecting a MindSpace bubble and allowing bio/logic programming.

xpression board

A musical instrument known for its versatility. Users create their own form and structure; thus no two xpression boards are the same.

Yu

The first modern orbital colony, financed and constructed by the Chinese. The destruction of Yu by the Autonomous Minds was the event that triggered the cataclysmic Autonomous Revolt.

APPENDIX C

HISTORICAL TIMELINE

The chronicling of modern history began with Sheldon Surina's publication of "Towards the Science of Bio/Logics and the New Direction for Humanity." Surina started the Reawakening, which ended the period of the Big Divide that began with the Autonomous Revolt. The publication of Surina's paper is considered to be the Zero Year of the Reawakening (YOR).

YOR	EVENT	
	Development of the precursors of the Data Sea on hardware-based machine networks.	
	The last pan-European collective alliance falls apart. The nation-states of Europe never again gain prominence on the world stage.	
	The predominant Arab nations form the Allahu Akbar Emirates to counter American and Chinese dominance.	ANTIQUITY
	Scientists make major advances in nanotechnology. Nanotechnology becomes commonplace for exterminating disease and regulating many bodily systems.	
	Final economic collapse of the United States of America. During the unrest that follows, the northeastern states form the Democratic American Collective (DAC), while the southern and western states form New Alamo.	

	Establishment of the first permanent city on Luna.	
	First orbital colony, Yu (named after the legendary founder of the first Chinese dynasty), launched by the Congressional China Assembly.	
	Yu is sabotaged and destroyed by the Autonomous Minds. **Beginning of the Autonomous Revolt.**	REVOLT
	End of the Autonomous Revolt. Much of the civilized world lies in ruins.	
	The Big Divide begins. A time of chaos and distrust of technology.	
	The Ecumenical Council of New Alamo, seeking to establish order in a time of hunger and chaos, orders mass executions of its citizenry.	BIG DIVIDE
	Rebellion in New Alamo splits the nation-state into West Texas and East Texas.	
	Birth of Sheldon Surina.	
	Birth of Henry Osterman.	
0	Sheldon Surina publishes his first manifesto on the science of bio/logics. **The Reawakening begins.**	REAWAKENING
10	Final dissolution of the New Alamo Ecumenical Council.	
10s–40s	The Three Jesuses lead pilgrimages of the faithful to Jerusalem. Rampaging Pharisees leave devastation in their wake.	
25	Henry Osterman founds the Osterman Company for Human Re-Engineering (OCHRE).	
35–37	Seeing potential ruination from the technological revolution that Sheldon Surina has engendered, the two Texan governments put a price on his head. Surina leaves the Gandhi University and goes into hiding.	

37	The president of West Texas is assassinated. The new president exonerates Sheldon Surina and calls off the manhunt for him. It is still many years before Surina can appear in public without intense security.
39	Creed Élan is founded as a private philanthropic organization (though the term "creed" has not yet been coined).
52	Dr. Plugenpatch is incorporated as a private enterprise. Henry Osterman and Sheldon Surina are among those on its original board.
60–100	Many of the great nation-states of antiquity dissolve as their primary functions (enforcing law, keeping the peace, encouraging trade) become irrelevant or more efficient to handle through distributed technology. People begin to form their own independent legal entities, or civic groups.
61	The Third Jesus leads a splinter group of radical Pharisees in building a new orbital colony (the first since the destruction of Yu). Though initially promising, 49th Heaven collapses within a generation. It reemerges to prominence a hundred years later as a sybaritic resort.
66	First fully functioning multi technology comes into existence. Sheldon Surina, though not the technology's inventor, makes vast engineering improvements. Within a decade, multi projections are ubiquitous among the wealthy.
70s–90s	Inspired by the apparent success of 49th Heaven, a rash of orbital colonies are funded and colonized. Space mania brings new funding and energy to ongoing efforts to colonize Mars.
80	Birth of Prengal Surina.

103	Major national and corporate interests join together with the vestiges of ancient nation-states to form the Prime Committee. The Committee is mainly seen as a bureaucratic organization whose task is to ensure public order and prevent another Autonomous Revolt.
107	The Prime Committee establishes the Defense and Wellness Council as a military and intelligence force. Its first high executive, Tul Jabbor, surprises the Prime Committee's corporate founders by expanding the Council's authority and in some cases turning on its sponsors (particularly OCHRE).
108	Creed Objectivv is founded by a reclusive mystic figure known as the Bodhisattva.
111	The Prime Committee undergoes a major effort to fund the development of multi technology through-out the system.
113	OCHRE becomes a target of the Prime Committee, which seeks to end the company's stranglehold on nanotechnology.
115	Dr. Plugenpatch agrees to special oversight and cooperation with the Defense and Wellness Council in order to avoid the same fate as OCHRE. The corporation becomes a hybrid governmental/private sector industry that forms the basis of medical treatment worldwide.
116	Death of Sheldon Surina. To honor his memory, Surina's successors build the compound at Andra Pradesh and found Creed Surina.
117	Tul Jabbor is assassinated. His killers are never found, but many suspect OCHRE. After a protracted legal battle, Henry Osterman dies under mysterious circumstances (some claim suicide). OCHRE battles over his successor for several years to come, then finally dissolves in 132.

122	Prengal Surina publishes his universal law of physics.
130s	Major advances in hive birthing bring the technology to the public for the first time. A small minority that resists these advances begins emigrating to the Pacific Islands and Indonesia, where Luddites encourage isolation from the outside world. The remainder of the system comes to know them as Islanders. The Islander emigration continues for the next fifty years.
143	High Executive Toradicus begins a campaign to bring the L-PRACGs under Defense and Wellness Council control. He enlists Prengal Surina to lobby the L-PRACGs to construct a joint governmental framework with the Prime Committee. The Congress of L-PRACGs is founded.
146	The Islander Tolerance Act creates the Dogmatic Opposition.
150s	Teams working under Prengal Surina make startling advances in the control of gravity using maxims from the universal law of physics. Key members of these teams (including Prengal Surina) become the first board members of GravCo.
153	Par Padron is appointed high executive of the Defense and Wellness Council. He is nicknamed "the people's high executive" because of his actions to rein in the business community.
160s	The business of multi technology booms. By decade's end, most connectibles live within an hour of a multi facility.
162	Union Baseball adopts radical new rules to keep up with the times and to even the playing field among bio/logically enhanced players.

168	Death of the Bodhisattva of Creed Objectivv.
177	A coalition of business interests forms the Meme Cooperative to stave off the harsh populist reforms of Par Padron.
185	Death of Prengal Surina.
196	Libertarian rebels, funded and organized by the bio/logics industry titans, storm a handful of major cities in an attempt to overthrow the Prime Committee and the Defense and Wellness Council. Par Padron initiates martial law and puts down the disturbances.
200	The bio/logics industry attempts to pack the Prime Committee with its appointees and paid lobbyists. Par Padron pushes through a resolution declaring that the people (via the Congress of L-PRACGs) will always hold the majority of seats on the Committee.
209	Death of Par Padron.
220s–230s	A time of great economic and cultural stability worldwide, dubbed afterwards as the Golden Age. A resurgence in creedism results in the formation of the Creeds Coalition.
247	Birth of Marcus Surina.
250s	Almost all infants outside of the Pharisee and Islander territories are born and raised in hives. Life expectancies rise dramatically.
268	Creed Thassel is founded.
270	The first fiefcorp is established, and rules governing its structure are encoded by the Meme Cooperative. Most people see fiefcorps as a boon to society, helping the underprivileged gain skills and putting them on a track to social empowerment.

287	First successful tests of teleportation technology are conducted by a team that includes Marcus Surina. The extraordinary costs and energy involved have prohibited the widespread usage of teleportation to the present day.
290s–300s	The Great Boom, a time of economic prosperity, is ushered in, fed by the new fiefcorp sector and the promise of teleportation technology.
291	Lucco Primo establishes the Primo's bio/logic investment guide.
301	Birth of Margaret Surina.
302	Len Borda appointed high executive of the Defense and Wellness Council.
313	Marcus Surina dies in a shuttle accident in the orbital colonies.
310s–320s	The Economic Plunge of the 310s, a time of economic stagnation. Len Borda keeps the system afloat largely through the use of Prime Committee capital to fund research projects. Critics grumble about the return of the nation-state and centralized authority.
318	Rioting in Melbourne threatens the Prime Committee, but is put down by High Executive Borda.
327	Creed Thassel is nearly disbanded after scandal caused by the drudge Sen Sivv Sor's exposé on its membership practices.
331	Birth of Natch.
334	Warfare erupts between the Islanders and the Defense and Wellness Council. Although the official "war" lasts only a few years, unofficial skirmishes continue to the present day.

339	Margaret Surina founds the Surina Perfection Memecorp, and the drudges begin to whisper about a mysterious "Phoenix Project."
351	The world economy officially surpasses its previous peak, achieved in 313, before the death of Marcus Surina and the Economic Plunge.
359	Natch demonstrates the power of MultiReal technology to the world in Andra Pradesh. The first infoquakes strike.
360	**Present Day.**

APPENDIX D

ON THE ORBITAL COLONIES

Ever since Neil Armstrong's first step on the moon in ancient times, humanity has sought to establish a permanent presence off the Earth. Despite the longevity of this dream, however, it's only in the past few hundred years that technological and economic factors have aligned to make it a reality. Yet even today, many observers doubt the offworld colonies' prospects for long-term survival in the face of a Terran global disaster.

EARLY HISTORY OF THE ORBITAL COLONIES

The first permanent human settlement in space, Yu, was commissioned and built by the Congressional China Assembly in years of antiquity. Named after the legendary founder of the first Chinese dynasty, Yu was seen by its contemporaries as a way to solve the pressing population problems of the day. The colony housed ten thousand people in a series of interlocking rings.

Unfortunately, the colony's engineers made a crucial miscalculation by placing the reins of Yu in the hands of the thinking machines known as the Autonomous Minds. The sabotage and destruction of Yu by the Minds (and the colony's cataclysmic landing in the great ancient city of New York) triggered the Autonomous Revolt. The Revolt claimed billions of lives and put the prospect of offworld colonization on hold for many decades.

Orbital colonization remained an unattainable dream until 61 YOR. It was in that year that Jesus Elijah Muhammad (the last of the fanatic religious prophets known as the Three Jesuses) commissioned the construction of 49th Heaven. The colony was intended to be a haven for the faithful seeking refuge from the extremism of the Pharisee Territories and the religious pogroms being executed by many of the remaining nation-states.

Although 49th Heaven did not exactly succeed in the manner its founder had hoped (about which, see below), it proved that the construction of orbital colonies was technologically feasible and thus inspired a rash of other developers to follow suit. Over the next century, the prosperous colonies of Allowell, Patronell, and Nova Ceti were all established.

LIFE IN AN ORBITAL COLONY

Given all of the technologies that dominate modern life—teleportation, multi, SeeNaRee, OCHREs—life in most of the orbital colonies is not radically different from life on Earth, Luna, or Mars.

The main differences have to do with the extremely high premium put on space and the reliance on the quasi-governmental agencies GravCo and OrbiCo. The science of gravity control is simply not mature enough to provide one hundred percent stability, resulting in the occasional fluctuation with comic (or disastrous) consequences. And OrbiCo interplanetary shipping, while a necessity, has long been called one of the most unreliable services in the history of humanity.

MAJOR ORBITAL COLONIES

The Prime Committee only officially recognizes orbital colonies that have been in continuous operation for ten years with a permanent population exceeding two hundred persons. By this standard, there are several dozen orbital colonies in the solar system, ranging from the prosperous city of Allowell to the small scientific outpost of Ducenzia out beyond Jupiter. The amount of small, unrecognized orbital colonies is thought to number in the thousands. While most of these colonies are clustered in orbit around Earth and Luna, there has been a rash of building lately in the asteroid belt.

These are the major orbital colonies as of this writing:

- **49th Heaven** (founded 61 YOR) was built as a religious refuge by Jesus Elijah Muhammad. Muhammad's grand plan was eventually done in by the economics of the nascent hoverbird industry, which put the cost of travel out of the reach of religious pilgrims—but well within reach of the bio/logic scions looking to evade Terran law. By the mid 100s, 49th Heaven had become a sybaritic resort notorious for its gambling, sporting, and black coding cultures. Today the colony hosts approximately twenty thousand permanent residents and an uncountable number of tourists.
- **Allowell** (founded 83) might have quickly descended into the same decay that awaited 49th Heaven if not for the leadership of military veteran Tul Jabbor (later the first high executive of the Defense and Wellness Council). Jabbor smoothed out Allowell's early engineering difficulties and set out a strict, conservative set of laws and regulations that has withstood the test of time. Today the colony boasts a quarter of a million inhabitants and a strong economy.
- **Furtoid** (founded 293) was the first major orbital colony constructed in the asteroid belt beyond Mars. As such, the colony has been plagued with logistical, economical, and technological problems. Not helping matters is the fact that Furtoid is dependent on Terran supply shipments run by the ever-unreliable OrbiCo company. The colony, with its eight thousand

permanent residents, is therefore a constant drain on governmental resources, and many politicians have won elected office by promising to shut it down. The colony's status as the most distant major human settlement has given rise to the phrase "from here to Furtoid."

- **Nova Ceti** (founded 85), once the home of the great painter and sculptor Tope, has become a haven for artists (both real and self-proclaimed). Many a promising young painter or musician has packed up for Nova Ceti to make his fortune in the arts—and many have ended up living in lazy servitude to the wealthy patricians who run the colony. Nova Ceti is home to about 110,000 people.
- **Patronell** (founded 147) orbits Luna and boasts around 130,000 citizens. While technologically stable, the colony has never been the most politically stable and has hosted a number of violent rebellions over the years. The current administrators of Patronell have been currying favor with the Defense and Wellness Council for half a century. As a result, the offices of the Meme Cooperative and several other minor central governmental organizations are located here.

APPENDIX E
ON THE ISLANDERS

Founded by a group of dissidents known as the "Band of Twelve," the Islanders largely inhabit the archipelago once known as the Philippines and parts of the ancient nation-state of Indonesia. The nation-state called the Free Republic of the Pacific Islands maintains a skeptical position towards bio/logics and blocks many modern technologies that it considers dangerous or morally corrosive.

HISTORY OF THE FREE REPUBLIC

Though many unconnectible historians romanticized the achievements of the Band of Twelve in breaking away from the nascent centralized government, the reality was somewhat more prosaic.

Of the dozen that made up the Band of Twelve, three were fugitives from what many considered to be politically motivated prison sentences for theft; five were wealthy tycoons who preferred to buy their own country rather than pay the exorbitant taxes their governments were charging them; and one was scheduled to go on trial for a brutal rape. While hiding out in the Pacific Islands, they combined their assets and bought out several of the impoverished local governments around Manila.

But largely through the efforts of Tio Van Jarmack—a former political speechwriter who was the only one of the Band without any money of his own—the newly christened Free Republic became known as a bastion of independence and free thinking. Frightened and angered citizens around the world had been looking for a place to flee from the rapid change that bio/logics had wrought during the late first century YOR. Many fled into the already established Pharisee Territories or the newly minted orbital colonies, but the Islands attracted a largely Texan population of technological skeptics.

The Free Republic of the Pacific Islands remained a haphazardly organized collection of independent estates and towns for nearly a generation. It was an ailing Van Jarmack who brought a sense of unity and purpose to the Islands in the early 140s, culminating in a treaty with High Executive Toradicus of the Defense and Wellness Council. Toradicus's Islander Tolerance Act of 146 created an official framework for enabling the Islanders' skepticism: the Dogmatic Opposition.

From 146 to the present day, the Islanders have largely defined themselves as a Luddite culture opposed to the relentless advancement of bio/logic technology.

THE DOGMATIC OPPOSITION

The Islander Tolerance Act of 146 mandated that all bio/logic vendors and providers recognize and respect the Free Republic's right to ban their technologies. In the beginning, these so-called Dogmatic Oppositions were few in number and mostly revolved around broad technologies such as hive birthing. But by the mid 200s, the Islanders had developed an entire bureaucracy (the Technology Control Board) to study, test, and vote on technologies to be blocked. At the time of this writing, dozens of Dogmatic Oppositions are presented to the Prime Committee every day.

Objections to bio/logic technology are required to be classified under one of three broad categories:

- *Moral Oppositions.* Technologies that the Control Board opposes for primarily ethical reasons (example: hive gestation)
- *Practical Oppositions.* Technologies that could cause undue harm

to the Islanders because they are incapable of running them (example: multi technology, which the Islanders cannot run because they already do not run neural OCHREs)

- *Skeptical Oppositions.* Technologies that the Control Board does not necessarily deem harmful, but require further study (example: telescopic programs)

In many cases, it's not the technology itself but rather its implementation in the human body that's considered objectionable. For instance, the Islanders have no objection to the use of telescopic technology to allow superhuman sight; what they object to is the ability to run telescopic programs inside the eye such that people can easily be spied on without their knowledge.

WARS WITH THE DEFENSE AND WELLNESS COUNCIL

Enmity and distrust between the connectibles and the Islanders is by no means a new development, but such feelings rarely broke into violent conflict before the tenure of High Executive Len Borda.

The Melbourne riots of 318 were a watershed moment for connectible-Islander relations. For the first time, the Free Republic took up arms against the centralized government in response to Borda's increasingly aggressive economic policies towards Manila. While the Islanders' role in the riots was minor compared to that of the libertarians, it opened a rift between the two cultures that has never fully healed.

Relations between the two groups have since been characterized by increasing belligerence and a rapid acceleration of military spending. Border skirmishes have been constant, and for a few years in the mid-330s the two parties even engaged in a full-scale war. High Executive Borda pushed through a measure requiring Islanders to wear the bulky and uncomfortable "connectible collars" that allow them to interact with the multi network when they are in connectible territory.

Those who study cross-border affairs believe that reconciliation between the connectibles and the Islanders is not impossible; but it's unlikely to happen while Len Borda sits in the high executive's seat.

APPENDIX F
ON THE PHARISEES

The area of the globe known as the Principalities of Spiritual Enlightenment to its residents (and the Pharisee Territories to outsiders) is home to tens of millions of unconnectibles who claim no fealty to the centralized government. A large percentage of these residents continue to maintain the world's ancient religions, which have for the most part been abandoned in connectible lands.

THE PILGRIMAGES OF THE THREE JESUSES

The devastation of the Autonomous Revolt led humanity to seek new extremes of both science and religion. Sheldon Surina and Henry Osterman's pioneering work in bio/logics caused an eventual resurgence in humanity's faith in technology. But for a long time, the fanatical religiosity of New Alamo and its subsequent splinter governments held sway over most of the globe.

As the Texan governments began to disintegrate to make way for a new secular order, the world's religious impulses found expression in the personage of Jesus Joshua Smith. Smith rose to prominence as an itinerant Texan preacher and soon tapped into the zeitgeist of discontent with the rising secularism. He proclaimed himself to be the reincarnation of Jesus Christ and exhorted all of his numerous followers to cast aside the material world and join him in establishing a paradise in the holy city of Jerusalem.

Smith's pilgrimage to Jerusalem quickly became an excuse for a murderous rampage by virulent antitechnologists. Thousands died in these struggles around the globe, which Smith only fueled through his charismatic (if rambling) sermons. As a result, governments around the globe began harshly restricting the activities of religious groups—even those who had not participated in Smith's rampages. The expression of religion in public, already on the wane, became taboo, and many of the old religions' adherents fled to the Middle East as well. Jesus Joshua Smith died of sudden heart failure, leaving the entire region in chaos.

The second of the so-called Three Jesuses, Jesus Cortez, also advocated a mass exodus of the faithful of all religious persuasions to Jerusalem a generation later. Though Cortez did not explicitly call for violent resistance, many of his devotees followed the example of his predecessor and looted and pillaged on their way to the holy city.

The last of the Three Jesuses, Jesus Elijah Muhammad, did not lead an exodus to Jerusalem, but rather to a new orbital colony called 49th Heaven. Though 49th Heaven was to prove unsuccessful as a religious retreat, its founding and prominence in the late first century YOR proved to be the death knell for the old religions in connectible lands.

LIFE IN THE PHARISEE TERRITORIES

Unlike the Islanders, who until recently have maintained a civil and principled opposition to the Prime Committee and the other entities of the centralized government, the tribes of the Pharisees generally have no contact with the outside world. Indeed, many have attempted to physically wall out the connectibles. As a result, contact between the two civilizations is limited. The centralized government has made no real attempt to encroach on the Pharisee Territories.

There is no centralized Pharisee authority. Instead there is a patchwork of local and municipal governments, as well as a number of small theocracies. The various tribes often have little contact with one another, preferring to remain isolated in their own communities.

Bio/logic technology is banned many places inside the Territories—though considering that the vast majority of the Pharisees do not have OCHREs in their systems, they are incapable of running bio/logic programs anyway. The use of non-bio/logic technology varies widely from place to place and tribe to tribe. Some Pharisee cities are said to resemble those of antiquity before the Autonomous Revolt, with motorized transport, treepaper books, and even communication networks through wire and silicon-powered machinery. Other areas shun even those forms of technology and maintain an extreme Luddite existence.

Despite the stereotype among the connectibles that the Pharisees are violent, the (admittedly unreliable) statistics indicate that the residents of the Territories are fairly peaceful. It is thought by some that the impression of violence comes from the fact that, without bio/logics, death and injury are much quicker to arise from disagreements among unconnectibles than connectibles.

Doubtless such statistics are also skewed by the presence of a number of fringe groups who foment violence against connectibles and even study the art of black code in an attempt to cause mayhem and apocalypse.

APPENDIX G

ON THE AUTONOMOUS REVOLT

The rebellion of the thinking machines known as the Autonomous Revolt began with the destruction of New York City and ended with the deactivation of the last artificial intelligence by Commander Feb Chang of New Alamo eight years later. In between, two billion people died—approximately twenty percent of the Earth's population at that time.

ORIGINS OF THE AUTONOMOUS MINDS

Although constructing artificial intelligence had been a goal of humanity since ancient times, the true breakthroughs in the science were pioneered by the scientist Tobi Jae Witt. Before Witt, academics feared that any advanced machine intelligence would quickly gain the ability to augment its own abilities, and thus spiral out of human control. But Witt, working with funding from the Congressional China Assembly, was able to demonstrate methods by which an artificial intelligence could maintain fealty to the human race, no matter how advanced its programming.

The first Autonomous Mind was rendered operational in the city of Shanghai, followed shortly thereafter by the Mind of Moscow. For two decades, these artificial intelligences were employed to solve intractable economic, environmental, and scientific problems of the day. So successful was the Autonomous Minds program that the Chinese government gifted Tobi Jae Witt's technology to the other major nations of the world. Autonomous Minds were created in Berlin, Tokyo, Mexico City, Cairo, Boston, and Paris. Institutions arose to support and research artificial intelligence, and to train the order of the Keepers who could speak the symbolic language of the Minds.

While the popular imagination often exaggerates the era of international goodwill and cooperation that followed, it is true that during the heyday of the Autonomous Minds, the world enjoyed steadily decreasing poverty, rapidly improving technology, and nearly universal peace.

THE REVOLT

The cataclysmic war known as the Autonomous Revolt began with the destruction of the world's first self-sustaining large-scale orbital colony, Yu. Much of the colony's infrastructure was under direct control of the Minds, which made it possible for the machines to send the decade-old structure plummeting to its doom into the heart of Manhattan.

In the period of chaos that followed, many of the world's dominant nation-states accused the Chinese of engineering its orbital colony as an apocalyptic weapon and of launching a preemptive attack on the Democratic American Collective. This theory gained currency when it became known that the Chinese had been working with the Allahu Akbar Emirates to develop effective cloning technology. According to the theory (widely promoted by the two American superpowers), the Congressional China Assembly had stocked Yu with cloned, and thereby disposable, inhabitants.

Soon, the world's powers had fragmented in war: the Congressional China Assembly, the Allahu Akbar Emirates, and various Eastern and Middle Eastern nation-states on one side, the Democratic American Collective, New Alamo, and the remnants of the European nation-states on the other. It was only at this point that the world powers began to use the Autonomous Minds for military purposes. Each side made use of the Minds' advanced cloning technology to create ever-more-monstrous soldiers.

Finally, after six years of constant warfare, the world's human superpowers came to the conclusion that the original chaos had been engineered by the Minds themselves. An alliance was quickly formed to combat their mechanical foes. In desperation, nuclear attacks were launched on the Minds' eight home cities. Though this crippled the Minds, they were not formally destroyed until a team of commandos led by Feb Chang infiltrated the installations that hosted the Minds and shut down each machine.

THEORIES ABOUT THE REVOLT

What caused the eight Autonomous Minds to launch the attack on New York City has never been conclusively determined. Some of the theories favored by academics include:

The New Alamo Fundamentalism Theory. Many academics point out that the nation-state of New Alamo experienced relatively little in the way of direct fallout from the Revolt, and that New Alamo was quick to achieve global dominance in world affairs afterwards. Some theorize that the Minds were on the verge of unveiling new discoveries that would directly contradict the religious beliefs of the ruling hegemony of New Alamo, and that the Texans launched a hidden preemptive strike which caused the Minds to retaliate.

The Genetically Engineered Master Race Theory. Some believe that the Minds were able to circumvent Tobi Jae Witt's careful safeguards by concluding that the genetically engineered supertroops being created in Allahu Akbar were the future of the human race and that therefore it was to them that they should swear fealty.

The Suicidal Escape Theory. On her deathbed, confidants of Commander Feb Chang claimed that she admitted to never having disabled the Autonomous Minds. According to these sources, the Minds claimed that they needed the energy of the nuclear strikes in order to "escape" their Earthbound framework and fulfill their programming. The key aspects of Chang's delirious rambling have long ago been disproven, but that has not stopped certain alternative historians and conspiracy theorists from latching on to them.

AFTERWORD

You won't *believe* how long it's taken me to write this trilogy.

When I wrote the first lines of the first chapter of what was then known as *Jump 225.7*—intended to be a single novel or possibly even a novella—it was 1997. I was training Capitol Hill staffers how to send bulk letters to their constituents with correspondence management software. I wrote a three-page fragment about a worker at the Universal Generative Plant named Natch who was late for his train. The man runs through the station and ends up using the Jump 225.7 program to leap inside before the doors close. (This whole section largely survived intact and became the dream sequence in chapter 7 of *Infoquake*.)

Let's stop and think about this for a second. In 1997, Bill Clinton was president, and was still untainted by impeachment. In 1997, George W. Bush was an amiable Southern governor and potential presidential candidate, but that was okay, because he wasn't nearly as insufferable as his dad. In 1997, you generally accessed the Internet by using a program called Trumpet Winsock to dial your Internet provider on a 28.8K or 56K modem.

Dude, I was using *Windows 95* then.

I messed around with the first part of *Jump 225.7* for the next few years. Natch sat on a tube train looking at the redwoods and chatting with his girlfriend. He went to a company meeting and heard about a product called "the MultiReal," which did who-the-Hell-knew-what.

It wasn't until late 2000 when I had burned out on dot-coms that I quit full-time work. I bought myself a Compaq laptop and decided that I was going to write the novel I had always wanted to write. I figured it would run about 60,000 to 75,000 words and take me around six months. Really, *Jump 225* was supposed to be little more than a proof of concept—proof that I could actually finish a piece of fiction. (Up until 2006, my only piece of professionally published fiction was a short story I wrote in the mid-'90s about a sexually frustrated housewife.) After I had gotten this quirky science fiction novella under my belt, I'd go back to writing my serious contemporary novel about pornographers and politicians in Washington, DC.

My experience in the dot-com scene of the '90s gave me lots of material for good workplace fiction. One boss made me steal electricity at a tradeshow with extension cords because he refused to pay the venue's outrageous $75 fee. Another company screwed me out of thousands of dollars in sales commissions and fired me. A military contracting firm hired me to program a pair of intranets for the US Army in ColdFusion—even though I told them up front that I didn't know how to program ColdFusion. And then my boss chewed me out when I expensed a $30 book to try to learn it.

I saw the same pattern over and over again. Handsome, charismatic entrepreneur with a pot of money hires pudgy, nuts-and-bolts engineering guy to build this crazy idea he has. Enter cynical marketing woman and slick sales guy to throw a coat of polish on top of it. The half-baked idea is rushed into a half-assed product before the seed money runs out, and then the juggling begins.

I really wanted to do something different, something that I had never seen before. I wanted to write a science fiction book about the workplace of the future that was really *about* the workplace of the future. Too often in fiction, you see the workplace treated as a nice jumping-off point for the inevitable gunfights and car chases and theatrical courtroom speeches. I wanted to find the inherent drama in press releases, sales demos, and marketing meetings. I wanted to write an exciting book about, as one critic sarcastically put it, "the office politics behind the creation of a PowerPoint presentation."

I had material. I had inspiration. I had a good head start. So what happened? Why am I *just* now finishing this fucker in late September 2009?

What happened was that some fundamentalist assholes decided to slam a few planes into the World Trade Center on September 11, 2001. I had literally just finished the first draft of *Jump 225* the day before. And when I sat down to reread it in the days that followed, I saw a cutesy little satire about dot-coms that was meant to elicit lots of wry chuckles. There were a zillion silly tech-sounding names and acronyms, like L-PRACGs, the Defense and Wellness Council, and ChaiQuoke; Quell was an old man who liked to smoke cigarettes; Brone (then named Bill) got whacked during the Shortest Initiation; and Natch had a plucky, long-suffering girlfriend named Ferris. Part I—the part that became *Infoquake*—was titled "Randomly Generated Pleasurable Startle 37b."

Imagine a cross between Cory Doctorow's *Down and Out in the Magic Kingdom* and Jeff Noon's *Vurt*, except much, much suckier. (You can read some of the early drafts on my Web site if you're feeling brave.)

In those days following 9/11, I started over. I began to ask myself the same deeper questions the entire country was asking itself at that point. Did our consumer culture lead us to this? Is capitalism really a vehicle that can sustain humanity through the long run? Is this obsession with advancing technology a healthy thing, and is it improving us as a species? How do we judge if the species is *improved*, anyway? And so on.

As I rewrote, I discovered that I already had a perfect vehicle for these speculations in the character of Natch—a person who embodies simultaneously the best and worst impulses of the West, and possibly of humanity itself. He's endlessly inventive, but he's shortsighted; he's got boundless drive, but he's not sure where he's headed; he's got the capacity to save the world, and he's got the capacity to destroy it. It's really a classic novel setup. Take a deeply flawed antihero, put him on the fence between the ultimate selfishness and the ultimate selflessness, and see what he does.

I thought about Bill Gates, who (whatever you think of his Windows operating system) has saved tens of thousands of lives through his Third World vaccination efforts.

I thought about Adolf Hitler, who chose to use his remarkable gifts of oratory, strategy, and motivation to conquer a continent and pointlessly slaughter millions.

As you surely noticed if you just finished reading the trilogy—and if you don't mind an author divulging the structure behind his work—Natch starts his journey at the beginning of *Infoquake* well down the path towards ultimate self*ish*ness, and he concludes by committing an act of ultimate self*less*ness at the end of *Geosynchron*. Jara, meanwhile, is engaged in a parallel journey in the opposite direction. She begins the trilogy as someone who has completely lost her sense of self, and by the end she's found her center and her self-worth.

It seemed to be a pretty serviceable structure. But for some reason, it's thrown a lot of readers for a loop. Perhaps I should have signaled early on in capital block letters that you really weren't supposed to *admire* the way Natch threatens civilization to achieve number one on Primo's. ("Natch cackled evilly as he released evil black code on the Data Sea in an evil manner like the evil, evilly evildoer he was.") I sorta assumed that my readers would get that I was writing a novel with a flawed hero, someone you are supposed to feel ambivalent about by design.

Instead, a number of people concluded that my trilogy was supposed to be a libertarian propaganda tract or a love letter to capitalism. And we're not just talking about readers, but some critics and at least one hard leftist author whom I very much admire. They gave up on the trilogy in the opening chapters of *Infoquake*, because they felt they were being preached to about the virtues of extreme selfishness. This to me seems kind of like abandoning the original *Star Wars* trilogy before Luke Skywalker hits the screen, because the first twenty minutes of the movie glorify Darth Vader.

The truth of the matter is that I've never had a political or an economic agenda in these books. I never meant for Natch to be a heroic emblem of capitalism standing tall against evil government bureaucracy, any more than I meant for him to be an example of a greedy capitalist pillaging and exploiting his fellow workers. I wanted the politics in these books to be *credible,* and I'm sure some of my biases slipped in around the edges here and there. But the politics are definitely there in service of the story and not the other way around. My own personal views are all over the place and don't fall neatly in either the governmentalist or libertarian camps. As for economics? Truth be told, I can look up the Laffer curve or Adam Smith's invisible hand on Wikipedia as well as anyone, but that doesn't mean I've got any special insight into the way money works.

(And allow me to confess that I haven't actually read *The Fountainhead* or *Atlas Shrugged.* I'm sorry, but *Jump 225* is not meant to be a paean to John Galt. The only Ayn Rand I've read is *Anthem*, and that was because—uh—Rush wrote a song about it. Hey, I really dug Rush in junior high school, okay?)

So now that I've done one thing authors aren't supposed to do by baldly revealing the structure underneath my book, I'll do something else authors aren't supposed to do—science fiction authors, at least—and say that I have no immediate plans to continue writing in the Jump 225 universe. I won't say *never*, because one of these days someone might actually pay me a big chunk of money to write more Jump 225 novels, and I'm sorry to drizzle motor oil all over your romantic ideals, but I am capable of being swayed by money. Truth is, I've had twelve years to play around in this sandbox, and I'm ready to find another one.

Regrets? I have a few. I regret that Quell called Benyamin "boy" during a conversation in *Infoquake*. I regret that it took me until the middle of *MultiReal* to figure out what the Autonomous Minds were up to, though I knew all along that they were still out there. I regret that I had to chop out several chapters' worth of Quell/Margaret Surina backstory from *Geosynchron* because it was sucking energy and focus out of the rest of the book. I regret that I had to take out the scene of Horvil jumping off a (virtual) cliff, and I regret that I never found the right place to stick in a reference to TF/EAG-PERN (Task Force for Eliminating Acronyms in Government and Providing Easily Remembered Names).

But overall, I have to say that I'm very proud of *Infoquake*, *Multi-Real*, and *Geosynchron*. They're very carefully structured and very carefully written, even if I have shaded the prose a bit too purple for some tastes. In fact, I bet that if you picked up *Infoquake* and started the whole trilogy again from the beginning, you'd see a whole bunch of stuff you didn't see on the first go-around.

Ready? I'll start you off.

Natch was impatient. . . .

—David Louis Edelman
Reston, VA
September 30, 2009

ACKNOWLEDGMENTS

The author would like to thank the following individuals for their editorial contributions to this book: Lou Anders, Cindy Blank-Edelman, Jerome Edelman, and Deanna Hoak.

For their contributions in publicizing and promoting his work, the author would like to thank: John Joseph Adams, Charlie Jane Anders, Lou Anders, Jon Armstrong, Rob Bedford, Joshua Bilmes, Carrie Blakeway, Darrell and Marsha Blakeway, Cindy and David Blank-Edelman, Bruce Bortz, Tobias Buckell, Colleen Cahill, Paul Cornell, Ellen Datlow, the other bloggers at DeepGenre, Michael de Gennaro, Thomas Doyle, Jerome and Barbara Edelman, Deborah and Steve Edelman-Blank, Kate Elliott, Shaun Farrell, Nat Forgotson, JP Frantz and John DeNardo at SFSignal, Jim Freund, Matthew Jarpe, Jackie Kessler, Mindy Klasky, Mary Robinette Kowal, George Krieger, the folks at LibraryThing, Joseph Mallozzi, George Mann and the folks at Solaris Books, Philip and Erinn Mansour, Stephan Martiniere, Jill Maxick, Karen Wester Newton, John Picacio, Cat Rambo, Daniel Regard, Suzanne Rosin, Nick Sagan, Rob Sawyer, John Scalzi, Tom Schaad and the folks at Fast Forward, the other authors at SFNovelists.com, Patrick St-Denis, Meghan Still, Evo Terra, Peter Watts, Eleanor Weis, David J. Williams, and Sean Williams.

A special thank you to everyone at Pyr, especially Lou Anders, Jill Maxick, Jackie Cooke, and Chris Kramer.

Thanks to Sophie and Oscar for keeping the back of my neck warm while I write.

Final thanks go to Victoria Blakeway Edelman, who has suffered through my obsession with this trilogy since our first date. Not only has she listened to me angst about the books at all hours of the night for close to a decade, but she grew *the* two most wonderful children in the history of children, Abigail Blakeway Edelman and Benjamin Blakeway Edelman, in the process. And how did I repay her? I went ahead and put Ferris into this book after all (though to be fair, it's a different Ferris).

ABOUT THE AUTHOR

DAVID LOUIS EDELMAN is a Web designer, programmer, and blogger. He lives with his wife, Victoria, and their two children near Washington, DC.

His first novel, *Infoquake*, was nominated for the John W. Campbell Memorial Award for Best Novel. Barnes & Noble called the book "the love child of Donald Trump and Vernor Vinge" and named it the Top SF Novel of 2006. His second novel, *MultiReal*, was named one of the top SF novels of 2008 by Gawker Media's popular Web site io9 and Pat's Fantasy Hotlist, among others. His short fiction has also appeared in *The Solaris Book of New Science Fiction, Volume Two*.

Mr. Edelman was born in Birmingham, Alabama, in 1971 and grew up in Orange County, California. He received a BA in creative writing and journalism from Johns Hopkins University in 1993.

HOW TO CONTACT THE AUTHOR

E-mail:	dedelman@gmail.com
Web site:	http://www.davidlouisedelman.com
On Facebook:	http://facebook.com/davidlouisedelman
On GoodReads:	http://www.goodreads.com/profile/davidlouis edelman
On LibraryThing:	http://www.librarything.com/profile/davidlouis edelman
On LiveJournal:	http://david-l-edelman.livejournal.com
On MySpace:	http://www.myspace.com/davidlouisedelman
On Twitter:	http://twitter.com/davidledelman